To

DEADLY
CONVICTION

Thanks for reading
the earlier version.
This one's even more
deadly.

Peter McPhie

Peter

PUBLISHER: Peter McPhie
CONTACT: www.petermcphie.com

COVER IMAGE CREDIT: Paul Jay Howarth
COVER DESIGN: Alex McPhie

Deadly Conviction/ Peter McPhie -- 1st ed.
ISBN 978-0-9952877-0-9 (paperback)
ISBN 978-0-9952877-1-6 (e-book)

VISIT www.petermcphie.com

Dedication

To my parents, Ross and Betty, who gave me much
love. They also gave me five siblings, which is a good
start in the close observation of character, particularly
when you're at the end of the list.
And to my wife, Helga, for her love and endurance.
And to our children, Alex, Will, and Emma,
the lights of our lives.

PART ONE
1961

CHAPTER ONE

A cold October rain had fallen on and off all day in Philadelphia, and now, 10:25 p.m., it resumed its tedious beating.

Pino Macky hurried up the elegant front steps of the Hotel Continental then stopped under the awning while he took a final drag. Pino was thirty-three, short and slight, and plain of face. He didn't stand out in even a small crowd, which, in his line of work, was an asset.

Not that Pino actually worked. He had been raised by a father who didn't believe in work and had instilled that ethic firmly in his son. Pino never strayed from that teaching and so his hands were soft and supple. Pino took very good care of his hands.

For Pino was a master pickpocket. His hands could do what others only dreamed of - the bump, the buzz, the two-fingered lift, the palm dip, the thumb hitch - all to perfection. To him a mark was as easy as an open candy jar.

But as talented as he was, he felt he wasn't getting along in life as fast as he should. He had always thought big, but looking at it squarely, big didn't appear likely to actually materialize anytime soon.

He needed to find some big-dollar action, but not do something stupid like he did in Buffalo, trying to reach beyond his talent. There he tripped an alarm and camera sensor at a jewelry wholesaler when a night beat cop was only a block away. And now he was a wanted man. If he were ever caught anywhere for anything, he would be returned by authorities to Buffalo and go to prison. And he never wanted to do time again; he wouldn't survive another vicious beating.

With satisfaction he noted the expensive cars parked nose to tail all down the street, the rain lightly drumming the roofs, shiny under the streetlights. The marks would be lush and ripe tonight.

He tossed his cigarette and entered the hotel, crossed the chandeliered lobby and followed the long marble corridors to the Starlight Room, the hotel's glitzy ballroom.

There were no watchful doormen. The room was low-lit, dusky. But he could see it was a full house, four hundred of Philadelphia's business elite in well-cut suits and stylish gowns. The bar staff was preoccupied in filling endless wine glasses, the servers circulating silver platters of smoked salmon. The small orchestra produced a big sound, backing a soulful black singer who caressed the lyrics of Etta James' new song, '…at last…my love has come along…and life is like a song…' The dance floor was crowded with fifty couples swaying in close embrace.

Pino wore a tailored black suit like everyone else, so he blended. He was unremarkable, uninteresting. If any incident should occur, he wanted very much to be unremembered.

He scanned the crowd as he walked. He was a shrewd observer, careful to note the silent communications of the face, the eyes, the hands, reading attention level and mood. Now, with hours of food and drink behind, most were far less than alert.

Near him a white-haired man and his wife were distressed by a sniping argument between a young couple they were with, the young wife protesting something, her finger raised to her husband.

Pino made his move. An imperceptible nudge, faster than a blink, and the white-haired man's slim wallet slipped invisibly into Pino's jacket. Pino peered back and saw him taking refuge from the dispute in his wine.

Pino deftly removed the bills by feel as he moved on. He would discard the wallet later.

About thirty feet away in a black dress stood a tall, statuesque blond, eyes bright, a diamond choker on her slim neck. She was deeply attracted to the man she was with, giving him a delicious smile, smoothly insinuating her body forward. And the man was focused on her, his back to Pino. A lucrative opportunity.

Watching her, Pino moved to within six feet of the man, casually standing behind him. The band finished the song and the ambient sound quietened. He caught the man's voice clearly. "I will need some time. Not long. Then you will entertain him, Camilla."

The voice had a rich tone. It was distinctive, memorable. It was familiar.

A warning bell began to clang. Pino moved a few steps away and looked back. Camilla put a sensuous finger to the man's lips, and in mock avoidance, he turned his head for several moments in Pino's direction.

A pang of fear drove through Pino. He turned away instantly, perhaps a little too fast. His heart raced. The man's eyes, his face, his bearing, had struck a disturbing chord.

Pino looked elsewhere as if making casual observation, then looked back. The man and Camilla had been eclipsed in the crowd.

It was unlikely, he reasoned, that he had seen anyone he knew. Or more to the point, anyone who knew him. He was in Philadelphia precisely because it offered him anonymity. It was probably one of those tricks of memory that had happened before, particularly when he was working and overanxious.

But still, an uneasiness was building, and a curiosity. He wanted another look.

He spotted them. The man presented a rear profile. He was shorter than Camilla by several inches. But his wide shoulders and the cut of his suit indicated clear upper-body power.

Camilla was leaning back against one of the room's heavy columns, facing the man, holding a glass of champagne in an outstretched arm as if she were handing it to someone who wasn't there. She was looking into the man's eyes, her posture heavily seductive. She seemed oblivious to everything else. Pino thought the glass would simply drop from her hand at any moment.

He threaded his way closer, this time more from the couple's front. The man was regarding her attentively, listening to her speak. Yet at the same time he appeared oddly reserved. Pino didn't recognize him, but somehow he was instantly familiar. He studied him more closely. His hair was full and black except for dashes of grey that suggested he was about forty. The eyes were penetrating, the face angular and hard, not handsome in a conventional sense. It communicated intelligence, or more precisely, shrewdness, calculation. He had a tightly clipped moustache. He projected immense composure, like a man used to wielding unquestioned authority.

Pino returned to the eyes, a bold, predatory quality. They would inspire nervousness in people, he thought, and obedience. They would also attract certain types of women the way diamonds attract light.

Then it struck him - tall blondes! Suddenly it all fit.

Like taking a blow to the stomach, he shuddered, struggling between comprehension and disbelief. The memory had come to him clearly. There was no mistake. He had witnessed a terrible magic.

He moved away and steadied himself and made a quick re-examination. The man had taken considerable measures to avoid recognition. Skilled plastic surgery had made the nose finer. The moustache had been grown. The hair used to be chestnut but was now black with dashes of grey, adding false years. Pino had almost been fooled. Only his keenness had caught the resemblance, had found the lie. And even then, only the voice had told him for sure.

It was simply astounding. Cavaco, the most dangerous man Pino had ever known, here in the flesh, circulating freely.

He recalled from the newspapers back then that there was no good picture of Cavaco on police record. And even if there were, it would be useless today. Regardless, police files were closed; no one was looking for him. Because five years ago, Cavaco had died.

Pino only knew what he had read - a police dragnet, a high speed chase in mountain roads, the car smashing through a guardrail and plummeting, a fireball incinerating the occupants.

Pino shifted nervously as Cavaco put his mouth to Camilla's ear. She looked enchanted, not moving at all. Then he smiled into her eyes. She handed him her champagne glass, opened her purse, and withdrew something very small. Concealing it coyly in her hand, she passed it to him. A room key? Pino worried a moment.

Unhurried, Cavaco walked from her through the throng that had gathered nearer to the band stage. Pino was relieved. It was clear that he was not intending to exit. So not a room key. He appeared to be going to the bar. Pino was soon unable to see him.

Pino assured himself that he hadn't been discovered. Even if Cavaco had seen him, surely he hadn't remembered him. Pino had not been that much to him. And Camilla and he had acted naturally, neither showing the least hint of agitation. No one could dissemble that well.

How long had Cavaco been in Philadelphia? In his new identity he had obviously established himself very well. He was freer now than he had ever been in New York State. No one had anything on him. No one knew who he was.

Camilla glanced expectantly in the direction Cavaco had gone. She still had her glass. Cavaco would come back to her, but eventually they would leave.

Pino could hear opportunity knocking. When they left, Pino would follow, guardedly. He would soon discover who Cavaco was now. And he would turn that knowledge into money. Big money.

CHAPTER TWO

In the corner of the ballroom farthest from the exit, tall drapes partitioned a narrow alcove which contained a bank of wall-mounted phones. A slit appeared between the drapery panels at eye level. Cavaco peered through and spotted the plain, black-suited man in the crowd. He recalled that his name was Pino Macky.

He had met Pino many years earlier in Rochester and explained to him that there were more enriching applications for his nimble fingers than children's magic shows. Soon Pino was lifting keys from the pockets of store managers, warehouse employees, even security personnel.

And now tonight - an unhappy coincidence of time and place. Being recognized had been an ever-present threat. But as the years had passed, the intensity of that threat had diminished. He had thought it was all behind him. And now tonight.

Camilla was exceptionally good, habitually wary. No one credited her, and so her astuteness was all the more valuable. She was another set of eyes for him, and she missed nothing. She had told him of this man who showed too much curiosity, well beyond the usual admiring looks she attracted - her only shortcoming.

Cavaco had managed a look in his direction, had seen the surprise, the puzzlement. And the fear. And from that moment, through Camilla, Cavaco knew all of Pino's movements.

Cavaco had to ensure that Pino said nothing before he was silenced – cleanly, without implication. There was always such a measure of chance in these things.

Through the slit he could see Pino watching Camilla at a safe distance. The parameters were holding. He let the drapery panel close, lifted one of the phones and dialled the number of the Hotel Continental. "Room 308, please."

Lorne Nix answered, "308", the room number, meaning all was well. An answer of "hello" would have meant it was unsafe to talk.

"It's me," Cavaco said. Then softly, emphatically, "I've been made." He paused, knowing the staggering impact his words would have. He continued, his voice a calm whisper. "He's in the Starlight Room. Early thirties, black hair, black suit, plain face, slight build, five-seven. There must be no mistakes."

Nix's voice was taut. "Yes."

"I'll send him to you," Cavaco whispered. A pause, and then again, "No mistakes."

Pino saw Camilla begin to walk slowly, gracefully, somewhat in his direction. She looked casually about her into distances, sometimes lingering a moment, looking about. But she continued to shorten the distance between them and Pino felt increasing unease. Why was she not waiting?

He moved himself out of her apparent line of direction. She seemed to be looking at something as she walked. Pino looked in that direction, too, but saw nothing in particular. He looked back to her. She seemed absorbed.

She passed near but continued on about ten feet then slowed and stopped. Her back was to Pino. She paused, and then, with deliberate slowness, turned around, her eyes lighting directly onto his. She held her gaze as steady as a laser, fixing him. Then began an inexplicable smile.

Pino's mind raced, but the scene played to him in slow motion. He glanced in the direction he had last seen Cavaco. The sickening realization flooded him - he had been suckered, no longer the clever predator but the prey. His eyes darted about the room in search of Cavaco. He was certain he had not left.

He threw Camilla a look as he turned toward the exit. She seemed suddenly surprised, disappointed. Which was what he hoped. She made a move toward him.

He made straight for the room's exit. He rushed along the corridors and through the hotel lobby. He straight-armed one of the wide front doors and bounded down the wet steps, glancing behind. No one followed. He looked around; there were no taxis.

He hit the sidewalk in a half sprint. A light rain continued. He ran a half block, glancing back to the Hotel. He made a quick left into a narrow lane, empty and dark, bordered by tall brick buildings.

In a shadowed stretch of sidewalk across the street from the hotel's entrance, Lorne Nix walked quickly. He was in his early thirties, tall and solid. He was at an angle to the end of the lane which Pino had entered and so was now unable to see him. But he could hear the echoing of his footfalls.

Pino reached the end of the lane and stopped, breathing hard. He looked back. Nothing. He grimaced from the exertion; too many cigarettes. The lane here was intersected by a mature-treed street, stately old houses with deep yards. If he were chased, they would offer concealment.

He crossed the street to the sidewalk. He wanted to get to Edward Street, three blocks over, where he knew taxis parked. He threw another backward glance and walked briskly.

A lone car approached from behind. Pino left the sidewalk and melted into the shadows. Without slowing, it passed noisily on the rain-wet street.

He trotted and walked. The dark back yards might offer escape, but most were fenced. Once in, he could become trapped.

A block ahead, a black sedan turned onto the street in Pino's direction. It travelled only a quarter of the block, then slowed and pulled to the side. Wary, Pino crossed to the opposite side, his eyes fixed on the car.

The driver's door opened; the engine was still running. Nix stepped out and began to walk across the street, appearing to be going to one of the houses. Nix held his collar close against the light rain. Halfway across the street, Nix looked back to the car. He called out, not loudly. "What? But it's raining!" Then he threw up his hands in apparent exasperation. "I'll get it. It's in the trunk."

Pino was relieved. The man was just dropping something off. Pino took a long look back as he hurried on, still in the direction of Nix's car.

Nix opened the trunk lid. Pino could not see him now.

When Pino was sixty feet away, Nix backed away from the trunk, coming into Pino's view, carrying a cardboard shoe box. Without closing the trunk, Nix started to cross the street in Pino's direction. Nix suddenly looked up at Pino as if startled.

Pino glanced to the car. There was no one inside! Nix was closing the distance, looking directly at Pino, balancing the box in his left hand, his right hand hidden inside it.

Pino began to run. Nix pointed the box and fired two quick shots from the silenced pistol inside, the second shot catching Pino. He clutched his side and staggered, falling to the gutter on his back. Nix walked to him and drew the box up close to Pino's chest. Pino's eyes were wide with horror. "No!" he struggled.

The loud guttural sound of a souped-up car roared to life from down the street. Nix looked. The headlights of an older Chrysler flicked on, several older teenage boys and two girls boisterously piling in, the windows down.

Nix looked coldly into Pino's eyes and fired. He pocketed the gun, and holding the shoe box under his arm, he grabbed Pino by the feet. He began to drag him across the street towards the open trunk, Pino's head scraping and bumping along the asphalt.

The Chrysler burst backwards out of the driveway, lurching to a stop in the street. The driver threw it into gear and gunned the engine. The tires screeched. Quickly into second gear, the car picked up speed coming in Nix's direction. Nix hurried his dragging, looking at the Chrysler angrily.

But it was too late. Its headlights now picked up the entire scene.

Nix was almost to the trunk. The Chrysler braked to a screeching sideways stop not eighty feet away. The teenagers gawked through the open windows. Nix heard a kid say, "Take a picture with the instamatic."

Nix hesitated, then dropped Pino's feet. A picture is harder to beat than an eye witness. He was certain Pino was dead anyway. He jumped into his car. Its engine roared and he fish-tailed away from the curb, tires squealing, the still-open trunk lid wagging in the air.

———————

A police car was parked sideways where Pino lay, its lights flashing, its doors open, its radio crackling. Two very young officers were beside Pino, one kneeling over him. The other glanced to the unmarked police car just pulling up.

A young detective, Paul Locke, leaped out of the passenger door.

The police officer who was kneeling got up and spoke. "He's not dead, Sir. Came to once. Didn't say anything. Kids got a good look at the car. Description's been broadcast."

Teenage boys know their cars. Two of them gave a perfect description: a 1960 Ford Thunderbird, raven black. A very popular model, however, so there would be hundreds in Philadelphia of exactly that model and color.

One of the girls had memorized the out of state Illinois licence plate. But that too would soon prove unhelpful. The plate turned out to be stolen.

The car was, in fact, four miles away, already being fitted by Nix with replacement plates in a lo cked private garage which had untraceable ownership. It would remain there until it was safe to move and clear through a certain car wholesaler in New Jersey.

The wail of an ambulance siren carried, growing ever nearer. Locke knelt over Pino whose eyes were closed. He held Pino's hand. He was clearly dying, blood rippling too quickly from the gaping hole in his chest, oozing too from mouth and side.

Locke said, "His name?"

The officer who had a wallet open in his hand said, "Pino Macky."

Locke leaned low and spoke gently, "Pino. Who shot you?"

Pino didn't respond. Locke squeezed the hand and turned to the officer. "What do we know?"

"Last known - Buffalo. New York State licence. An outstanding warrant for arrest."

Pino sensed he had fallen headlong into a turbulent black pool. He struggled, sinking rapidly, unable to breathe. He fought to stop the descent, to swim upwards, but his strength was ebbing.

Locke spoke again, his voice soothing. "Pino. Hang on. Help's coming. Speak to me. Who shot you?"

Pino was intensely cold. But he heard a voice under the water. Like a strong arm it pulled him up through the dark pool and he blinked, surfacing on his back on the pavement of the street. Straining, he held his eyes open for a moment, registering the blurred image of a man kneeling beside him. He closed his eyes again.

Locke spoke again. "Pino. Who shot you?"

Pino stirred and Locke saw a flicker. He bent lower. Pino's eyes opened and closed slowly. Then opened. His eyes saw Locke. Concentration came over his face. He gurgled and coughed a small red spray. Then came sounds, rasps, almost inaudible.

Locke lowered his ear to Pino's mouth, feeling the small struggled puffs of air, touching the hot moistness of his blood. He whispered. "Tell me, Pino."

The two young officers watched in earnest from several yards away, glancing to each other. They heard only indistinct sounds. It was evident Pino was struggling to formulate words. But the officers could hear none, if, indeed, any words were being whispered at all.

A long minute passed, Locke not moving a muscle. The young officers looked at one another.

With the effort, Pino now felt himself slipping. The voice was covered by the water and he was sinking, ever faster into the blackness.

A gasp of air escaped from Pino, a final shudder. Then air slowly releasing. Pino's eyes were still.

Locke didn't move. He still looked at Pino. Then, with a gentle hand, he closed the eyes. He raised his head and stared at nothing, concentrating, not getting off his knees.

He finally turned his eyes to the officers, but only for a moment. He looked back to Pino but did not seem to see him. After a moment he said quietly, "He's dead."

CHAPTER THREE

Paul Locke's son, Andrew, looked out the window and watched the autumn wind play among the rows of empty corn stalks in the field just beyond the school grounds. He was in the second grade, his small desk in the row by the windows, opposite in the room to where a kindly Miss Coulter stood speaking. "Never eat soggy wheat. North, East, South, West." She tapped her rubber-tipped pointer on the large wall map to accentuate each word.

Andrew's eyes tracked a biplane silently plowing through the sky, soon swallowed in a cluster of bulky clouds. He continued to watch, waiting for it to reappear, but it did not. He guessed it had turned south out of his view.

People described clouds as being like cotton balls, he thought. But these were not like that. They were knotted, more like - wool! Yes. The clouds were like woolly sheep grazing across the sky.

Then his face dimmed and he shifted in his chair. He remembered he didn't like sheep anymore. Shepherds were abiding in the fields, watching their flocks by night. He had been a shepherd once, last year in the Christmas play, presented to the parents in the auditorium. He was on the stage with two other shepherds. On cue the tin-foil star was lowered into view from the ceiling. He stepped forward to the front of the stage and raised his arms to the heavens to deliver his line. Just then the left side of his beard fell off, dangling from shreds of the still-fastened right side. He opened his mouth to speak but ripples of laughter washed over him and he forgot the words. He stood silently, his eyes searching the laughing faces for his father.

"Andrew Locke."

The words seemed distant and vague, and came to him as if from somewhere in the sky. He looked around and his face coloured. The class was looking at him and tittering. He looked at Miss Coulter.

"You're a dreamer, Andrew Locke." She said this gently, almost to herself, without a hint of criticism. But fresh giggling erupted from the students. She stung inwardly. She cast her eyes quickly over the class.

"Who can tell me what time it is, please?"

All of the children focused on the big wall clock. She well knew that only Andrew was capable of correctly telling time, a skill which raised his esteem among the children.

"Ten minutes past three," he offered.

"Very good, Andrew. And class, that means..."

They chorused loudly, "Time for dismissal!"

———————

Andrew shuffled alone through the yellow and rust leaves that had freshly blown and were now gathered in the long, winding, gravel laneway leading to his small country home. Surrounding it were hundreds of acres of farm fields and forests, properties owned by the neighboring farmers. The nearest house was over half a mile.

He thought about the picture in the library book in the knapsack strapped on his back. He would make a bird-feeder exactly like that. Miss Coulter said the almanac predicted a long winter, so the winter-birds were going to need help.

He climbed the back steps slowly and took the key from his pocket. It was attached by a string to one of his belt loops. That had been his idea. That way no one could ever take his key and make a wax impression.

He was glad that he was able to come directly home after school this week and not go to the sitter's. His father was home days because he was working nights. But he would be asleep upstairs in the bedroom, and so the door would be locked. He turned the key until he heard the bolt slide free. He pushed the door open.

Standing in the mud-room he closed the door behind him. He un-slung his knapsack and hung it on a wall hook. On another hook was his cowboy gun-belt with a silver pistol in the holster. He lifted the gun-belt off the hook and strapped it onto his waist.

He swaggered into the kitchen, which gave directly off the mud-room. The house was dead quiet. He walked toward the fridge then stopped suddenly and froze.

He spun and his revolver leaped into his hand. He pointed it straight at the wall and his eyes narrowed. "So there's two of you," he said in his best drawl. Then a small smile appeared. "Well there's two of me, too. Behind those rocks over there. It's my dad. Perhaps you've heard of him - Paul Locke, the Detective."

Andrew nodded slowly, letting the point sink in. "That's right. Best shot in the territory. Now just lay them revolvers on the ground and back away. Rrreeeaaal slow."

With flair, he holstered his gun. He took a glass from the cupboard and opened the fridge. He poured himself a glass of milk.

He stood in the middle of the kitchen and took a slow sip. A narrow shaft of sunlight reached from between the kitchen curtains to the floor. His father had called them sunbeams. He had seen light do this in the cathedral in Philadelphia at his mother's funeral. Sunbeams had stretched from the highest stain-glassed windows down to the shiny marble aisle. He wondered if angels really did slide down those sunbeams as his father said.

He took another sip.

Then he heard the sound, very faint at first. Then again, the pitch higher. The back door. The yaw of the hinges, slowly becoming louder. Someone was opening the door and trying to be very quiet about it.

He stood perfectly still, straining to listen, staring toward the mudroom, the glass tight in his grip. His heart quickened. No one except he and his father ever came in by that door. His father would have given it a hearty push. But all he heard was a creeping slowness.

A slightly different pitch, ever so gentle. Someone was now in the mud room and was very carefully closing the door. Anyone entering by that door had to pass through the kitchen. Andrew found that he couldn't move, his legs numb and unconnected. Although he opened his mouth to call out, his throat was tight and no sound came.

Then he saw them.

His eyes widened in terror. He dropped the glass.

———•——

Upstairs in the half-light of the curtained bedroom, Paul Locke had given up trying to sleep. He had worked on the investigation through the night and all morning, getting home only hours ago. Although he was fatigued, sleep had been impossible, his mind agitated, the events of the night threading restlessly. Had he made the right decision?

Paul reached over and stubbed another cigarette into the full ashtray on the night-table. He had heard Andrew downstairs in the kitchen, heard the fridge door thud close. He swung himself slowly out of bed. He drew back a curtain and put on his pants and a shirt.

And now he heard a glass smash downstairs in the kitchen. He listened for a moment expecting to hear Andrew comment. But strangely, he heard nothing. He descended the stairs.

He reached the hallway leading to the kitchen and called out, "Andrew." His tone clearly demanded an answer, but none came.

As he approached the doorway, he saw Andrew standing in the centre of the kitchen, his terrified eyes looking directly into Paul's. Over a broken glass? Just as the incongruity presented itself, Paul entered the kitchen and saw them. Two burly gunmen, each holding a silenced .45 calibre revolver in black-gloved hands.

Paul knew instantly they were professional killers - calm, imperturbable. There was no surprise in their faces, their eyes steady, unresponsive, cold. They had expected to confront him. They had taken no precaution to conceal their identity, had no fear of his seeing their faces. There was only one conclusion - they would be killing him.

Somewhere he had made a mistake.

Andrew's legs unfroze and he stumbled to Paul. He grabbed his father around the waist. As much as he wanted to, he couldn't seem to cry.

Neither of the gunmen took their eyes from Paul. One spoke flatly. "Anyone else here?"

Paul shook his head.

"Anyone expected?"

"No."

The gunman assessed Paul for a further moment and decided he could accept the answers. He nodded to the other who went to the window and made an all-clear sign. The first gunman stepped to the phone and severed its cord with a quick knife stroke.

The back door opened and closed. Cavaco appeared, dressed in a full length black coat, his head and face concealed in the frightening black cloth hood of an executioner. His dark eyes looked out from the two holes in the hood.

Cavaco walked close to Paul, his dark eyes carefully examining, deeply curious. The eyes then passed to Andrew, lingered for a moment, then returned to Paul.

Paul said quietly, "Have them put the guns away. Please."

"No, Mr. Locke. I'm a cautious man. I won't be vulnerable." He peered intently at Paul. "Don't risk your son. I don't hesitate to do the unthinkable."

Paul said nothing, his only movement an unconscious firming of his hold on Andrew's shoulder.

Cavaco walked down the hall and paused at the closed French doors to the living room. He pushed one of them open. He signalled that he wanted Paul to come.

Paul kneeled and released Andrew's hold. "Andrew, you must stay here."

Cavaco and Paul stood alone in the living room. The French doors were closed. A grandfather clock gave a resonant "tick-tock, tick-tock." Cavaco looked about the room, his eyes lighting momentarily on a droll family portrait taken at the County Fair - Paul, and Andrew age five, each in homespun, each smoking a corncob pipe. Seated between them was Andrew's young mother, a radiant beauty with long dark hair, in flowing period dress, smiling to the camera.

Cavaco, remaining hooded, studied Paul. "I was vulnerable last night. I may be still."

Paul said nothing. A moment passed.

Cavaco continued. "I've learned a lot about you in the past twelve hours. You have a high reputation, an exceptional investigator." A pause, and the eyes again searched Paul's. "You know why I'm here, don't you, Mr. Locke?"

Paul said nothing.

"An unfortunate incident last night. I was alarmed to learn that Pino Macky was not yet dead when you arrived. Those two rookie officers were puzzled....and talkative. They believed Macky whispered something to you. You seemed...struck by some realization, some insight. But you said nothing. I have, of course, inside sources, as I think you speculated might be the case."

He paused, breathing quietly under the hood. "I was relieved to learn that your report said nothing about Macky talking. But then it occurred to me that your report might be purposely incomplete. It didn't say you attempted to have Macky speak. It didn't say that Macky said nothing, which I understand is good police practice. It was open-ended, odd given the significance. A simple oversight? That would be unlikely in you."

He walked slowly and brought his leather-gloved hands together for a moment, fingers pressing the covered lips. "I understand from a lawyer friend of mine that a statement made by a dying man can be admitted in evidence in Court. An exception to the hearsay rule. The reason, I suppose, in the eyes of the Court, dying men don't tell lies." He looked directly at Paul. "Their words can hang a man."

He tapped his finger tips together. "Naturally you scoured Macky's record for anything that would say he had associates who might be unhappy with him. You saw he had connection with Buffalo, and naturally looked for links there. Reasonable enough. But... you went one step further. You requested some detail, without explaining why, on a file on a Salvatore Cavaco. To the best of my knowledge there is no known record connecting Pino Macky to Cavaco apart from the geographical coincidence - they both worked in Buffalo at one time. Why would you do that? And why would you not explain to colleagues why you did that? A shot in the dark? Grasping at straws?"

Cavaco looked towards the window considering something. "No connection to the ballroom was made until this morning when that stolen wallet on Macky was traced back to its owner. The spotlight is now on the people who were in that ballroom. That narrows the range of possible suspects much too much. That made my decision."

He breathed a sigh of resignation. "I have pieced together all I can. From there I go on instinct. I know you are an exceptional man. I tried to imagine how you would act in these circumstances. You are capable of a higher plan, withholding information from your colleagues, telling no one what you know, waiting for the evidence to come in. Make a connection that only you could make. Then strike! That's what I surmise. And that makes you very dangerous, Mr. Locke. At the very least you're a loose end, and I can't suffer that."

He studied Paul carefully. "Pino Macky told you, didn't he?"

Paul said nothing. Cavaco smiled under the hood, assured of himself. In the kitchen, Andrew glanced at the gunmen. They seemed as big as bears. Their faces were lumpen as if they had no facial muscles, and their eyes were dull. They stared back at him, their guns still drawn.

Andrew saw his father appear in the hallway alone. Paul held out his arms to Andrew. Andrew ran to him. The gunmen followed.

Paul led Andrew into the living room where they were alone with the hooded man. Andrew buried his face tearfully in his father's waist. The gunmen remained in the hallway, outside the French doors.

Paul looked at Cavaco and spoke softly. "You know his mother has passed?" Paul looked steadily at Cavaco's eyes for several long seconds, Cavaco looking coldly back.

Paul knelt down and wrapped his arms around Andrew, closely hugging him. Andrew whispered. "What are they going to do, Dad?" He could feel his father trembling as he hugged him back. But he knew it was not fear, for his father feared no one and no thing. It was the trembling he had felt when they had hugged at his mother's funeral.

Paul was bursting inside, fighting to keep from breaking. What to say now? And forever. He wanted to tell Andrew so much. It came down to simple words. Maintaining the illusion that their words were indeed private, he whispered. "You are a fine... fine son. I'm...so well pleased. I love you... Andrew. So much. Know that. I will always be with you."

He stroked Andrew's small head.

Andrew began to sob. "Dad. No. What are they going to do?"

Paul knew he could not keep himself together for much longer. He hugged Andrew one last time. Andrew looked up to his father, and now broke into full sobs, squeezing his father tightly, never taking his eyes from his father's. "No, Dad. No. Don't let them."

Paul forcibly released Andrew's hug. He stood, holding Andrew at arm's length by the shoulders. Paul locked his eyes on Andrew's and spoke as firmly and calmly as he could. "You must go to your room with the man. Someone will come for you later. Do as I say, Andrew. Now... son. Now."

Andrew stood still, tears streaming. He looked profoundly at his father. Then he looked into Cavaco's eyes, holding the man's level gaze. Then he looked back to his father.

Paul led Andrew to the hall. He held him close one more time. Then he released Andrew's hand, and held him firmly at arm's length. "Do as I say, son." Andrew could see in the intensity of his father's eyes and face that he must do what he was told, that he, too, must be strong.

The gunmen were so large and the hall so narrow. One led Andrew by the arm, but Andrew stopped at the bottom of the staircase, gripping the bannister. He turned and looked back to his father. His father nodded to him, and smiled. "Go, son."

The gunman led Andrew up into his bedroom, then left, closing the door. The gunman tightly wrapped a cord around the outside handle of Andrew's door, tying it securely to the handle of the closed door across the hall. The gunman tested the hold, then clumped quickly downstairs.

Andrew tugged but could not open his door. He put his ear to it, crying silently, listening to the voices in the living room, low and muffled. He knew when it was his father who spoke. Often, when his mother was alive, he would lie awake in bed at night and listen to his father and mother in their bedroom, the door closed, their voices muffled, his father's deep tones intersecting with his mother's light ones, her soft laugh. Often these sounds were the last things he was conscious of before drifting warmly off to sleep.

He heard the back door of the house. He ran to a window. His father was being led across the lawn by the gunmen, a black sack covering his head, tied close at the neck. His hands were tied behind his back.

There were two cars. The gunmen positioned his father behind the trunk of one. A gunman opened the trunk lid then guided his father into the trunk.

An uncontrollable anger seized Andrew. He screamed through the closed window. "No! No! Don't do that!"

The gunmen paused and looked up. Paul Locke curled himself into position. One of the gunmen slammed the trunk lid shut. Andrew shook violently.

Then he remembered the rope under his bed. His father had shown him how to do it. If there were a fire downstairs in the night and passage down to the front door was blocked, tie one end to the bed leg, open the window, throw the rope out and climb down the wall backwards.

Andrew tied the rope to the bed leg, opened the window on the other side of the room, and tossed out the rope. He ran back to the first window and saw the gunmen entering their car. The hooded man stood behind his own car, the one with his father in the trunk. The gunmen's car began to drive away.

Andrew grabbed the rope, stepped out through the window, and pro-pelled himself down the wall. He let go at four feet off the ground.

He burst around the corner of the house. The gunmen's car was at the end of the long gravel driveway, just turning left out onto the road. Cavaco's car was just starting to move slowly away from the house, Cavaco still hooded. Andrew caught up to it and leaped at the driver's window, pounding it with his pistol, screaming, "Stop! Stop! You can't take my Dad!"

The car braked and the door thrust violently open, slamming Andrew's whole body hard, flinging him to the gravel, his pistol flying into the long grass. Cavaco jumped out and grabbed Andrew with both hands, smashing an angry fist across his face. Andrew fell.

But he quickly got up. Cavaco swung hard again, twice, his fist-ed-hand hammering Andrew's face and head. He collapsed. He felt a spinning and confusion.

He was vaguely aware only of a car crunching gravel, the sound moving away. His mind fought to collect its pieces. The car was slowing at the end of the long lane. He tried to get to his feet, but staggered.

"Dad," he called, but his voice was oddly weak. He wobbled and fell to his knees.

"Dad."

Turning right, the car burst onto the empty country road and surged powerfully. Andrew watched as it quickly climbed and crested the ridge, and then, reaching the other side, it dropped completely from sight.

PART TWO
1971

CHAPTER FOUR

The Stanton Reformatory for Boys was without architectural pretense, an old, red brick, two story cube of a building. It embodied its simple, no nonsense motto: 'Structure and Discipline'.

At his desk in his corner office, psychologist Dr. Phillip Shaw closed the thick file on Andrew Locke. He eased back in the chair, thumbing the pages of the report absently. He had been through Andrew's report twice that week. And, as before, he was struck by the anomalies Andrew presented.

After his father had been taken, never to be seen again, Andrew had been sent to live with his only relative, an unwell grandfather, a depressed alcoholic. In retrospect, thought Shaw, it was easy to see by anyone with sense that Andrew and his grandpa had been like two drowning swimmers, alone in an overpowering current.

Andrew's crimes were all thefts. There was never an act of violence, never vandalism, never fraud. He had never been caught in the act. But when confronted by the police, he never shrank from owning up, always took it on the chin.

At fifteen he masterminded a large theft from a major electronics store. Not long after, he was informed on. No one came forward to offer bail, and with nowhere else to go, he lingered in secure custody awaiting sentence. The Judge saw before him 'a young man gone wild,' his behavior a 'cry for help.' The Judge noted that Grandpa had clearly lost any control over Andrew. That was not surprising, he remarked, as Grandpa had long ago lost control even over himself.

Andrew was sentenced to two and a half years. He had entered the reformatory at 15 years 8 months. That was two years ago exactly. Andrew was now 17 years 8 months. And he wanted out. Badly.

He applied for early release when he still had eight months to go, being the six months remaining on his original sentence plus a further two months for an assault that happened only a few months ago. He wanted to go to twelfth grade out in the community. And school started in one month.

Normally such a request would be promptly rejected. It wouldn't get by psychologist Shaw who guided the Reformatory Board in such decisions.

Shaw had arranged for a private interview with Andrew because he was intrigued. Andrew had scored 145 on the Wechsler Adult Intelligence Scale putting him in the highest few percentiles of the general adult population. And he had completed three years of high school in the two years here. That showed diligence enough. But remarkably, he scored an average above 90% on standardized State-wide tests in all subjects.

Clearly he was bright. Clearly he was motivated. But who was he? Shaw needed to get a real feel for this young man. And as intrigued as he was, he knew this Andrew Locke would have to be truly exceptional in many ways before Shaw would even begin to consider early release.

There was a knock at the door. Shaw called out. "Come in."

Andrew Locke looked older than his 17 years 8 months, due in part to his tall, obviously muscular build, and in part to a mature, confident look.

He appeared relaxed. He smiled. "Thank you for seeing me, Sir." His words seemed genuine to Shaw.

"Take a seat," Shaw smiled back. Shaw recalled the words of one of the senior staff. 'I think Andrew's in every phys ed program we offer. He's tough, but respectful. Well-liked by the staff.'

"I want to just jump in to some of the things on my mind," Shaw said. "I like to get to the goods right away. You know?"

Andrew nodded, "Yes. Anything, Sir."

Shaw said, "I see you got an additional two months for a fight you were in only four months ago. You put two others in hospital. That's a big problem in an application for early release. A very big problem. There is a concern you have an anger management issue. A tendency to violence." Shaw overstated it for effect, to see how Andrew would handle the accusation.

Andrew said slowly, calmly, not raising his voice. "I have no tendency to violence, Sir. Only protecting myself. Nothing more. One guy had his arm around my throat while the other one held a screwdriver to my face. At that moment I wasn't too concerned about the two months. The correctional officer only saw the damage I did. So I was nailed."

"You didn't try explaining it, defending yourself. Either here or in Court."

"No disrespect, Sir, but it's not a schoolyard in here. You don't say, 'He started it.' You don't say anything. Here or in court. You just take your lumps."

"You're saying this was strictly self-defense?"

"Strictly. I have never started a fight in here. Or anywhere for that matter."

He speaks with a calm maturity, Shaw thought. This kid is a surprise, presents well.

Shaw glanced at his notes. "You were in fights in the first month you were here."

"They weren't fights, actually. They were beatings. I was skinny and vulnerable then."

"What were they for?"

"Just making sure I knew who was who."

"That was the first time."

"Yes. The second time was just a reminder in case I didn't get the first message."

"You didn't report them. You didn't pin anybody."

"No. But I needed medical attention. That's why you have a report."

"There was another more serious incident. You had only been here four months. It was to do with an exam." Shaw flipped through some pages and stopped to quickly read something.

"I had been here actually five months, Sir," Andrew said, "Not that it makes a difference, I suppose."

"Oh... Yes. Quite right. Five months. Okay so... tell me about it."

"It was a 50 question multiple-choice exam. As a special... incentive we were told that those who passed would get a month's pass to the cinema room. Everyone wanted those passes. The teacher was away. There was a substitute. Not a very watchful one. May have had a hearing problem, too. Right away Big Graz and two others pulled cheat sheets from their pockets. Full answer sheets."

Shaw nodded.

"The answer sheets were passed around to everyone. Except, when it was handed to me, I didn't take it. Big Graz was watching me. He wanted *everyone* in on it. His eyes just...iced over, glaring. Later he and two others asked me if I thought I was better than they were."

"And you took a beating."

"That was the worst one."

Shaw knew Big Graz, older than Andrew and an intimidating hulk who was now in federal penitentiary for violent assaults. He thought of Andrew, then a 'skinny and vulnerable' kid, refusing to cooperate with Graz. The pressure to conform would have been enormous in those early months. But he had not bent.

Andrew said, "I decided then that I had to bulk up, train hard, or I wasn't going to make it in here. I hit the gym big-time."

"It looks like it."

"Added 45 pounds and 2 inches of height."

"Let me guess... 6' 1" ...190."

"You could work in the circus."

Shaw burst into a laugh. "I'll keep that in mind. And you found boxing."

Andrew nodded. "Better to do your fighting in the ring where there are rules, where everyone can see you're not afraid to fight, that you can handle yourself."

"You appear to excel at it. You've won the last five matches. Now the reigning champion in here."

"Well...at least no one is pulling my chain anymore."

Pleasant, well-spoken, thought Shaw. But although relaxed, Shaw sensed an intensity about him. That intensity both impressed and disturbed Shaw. It could be harnessed for good, or for bad, and either way was a powerful force.

"Let me change topics. Life with your grandfather. Not easy."

"No. Grandpa's only child was my mother. When she died, I guess he just began to fall apart."

"But he got custody of you after your father was gone. He was able to convince a Court that he was capable of caring for you, raising you."

"He put his best foot forward. He meant well, I know that."

Shaw had read that Andrew's father's money had been used to pay for his mother's battle with cancer. What little was left, a Court had given to Grandpa to provide for Andrew's food and clothing. But it seemed most of it found its way to Grandpa's purchase of drink.

"Your Grandpa became an alcoholic?"

"Yes."

"Tell me a bit about daily life with Grandpa."

"Where to start? Most days I would come home from school and grandpa would be asleep, snoring on the couch. A half empty bottle of bourbon would be on the counter. No diner anywhere in sight. I was hungry a lot. At school I never wanted anyone to see what my lunches looked like."

Andrew's hand absently brushed the arm of his sweater. "My clothes were always secondhand. Always a size too large so I would grow into them." Andrew laughed a moment. "I had so few clothes I would wear them out before I grew into them anyway." He became serious again. "But the worst was they smelled. I found out the hard way. 'Don't sit near Andrew or your nose will burn off.' I began to wash my own clothes when I was nine. Didn't tell anybody. Not even grandpa. It would make him feel bad."

"You were taking care of grandpa's feelings?"

A small wince and Andrew paused, "He...was all I had."

"What about recreational activities, playing games with you? Things like that?"

"He was always tired. Didn't like to go outside much. Wasn't interested in doing games or anything. Once he gave me a kit for a model ship when I was eight. It had about a two hundred pieces, complex, meant for older kids, and I had never done one. I was excited. I spread all the pieces on the cement floor in the basement, not sure where to start. Grandpa was looking at all the pieces, just staring at them. 'We can do it, Grandpa,' I said. He gave me a big grin. 'You get it started,' he said. 'Just get a start on it. I'll be back in a few minutes.' He went upstairs. I heard the clink as the bottle touched the glass." Andrew stopped talking and looked out the window, as if he heard that familiar clink all over again.

Shaw said, "And he didn't return."

Andrew shook his head. "I think life sort of had too many pieces in it for Grandpa."

Shaw nodded. "Yes. But the social workers, they checked up on things. Their reports showed a positive home life."

"Grandpa always knew when they were coming. Put on a good front."

"But you were questioned, too."

"I had heard stories of foster homes that scared me. At least Grandpa never scared me. So I put on a good front, too."

"You don't hold anything against your grandpa?"

"No. By the way, he passed away last year."

"I think you're letting Grandpa off too easily."

Andrew reflected a few moments. "He was broken. I would often hear him whimpering in his bedroom. He just couldn't beat it. It has taken some time for me to sort that out. I have more sympathy for him now."

"Your school marks didn't suffer."

"School seemed to come easily. Something to focus on. There wasn't much else."

"You express yourself well, Andrew. Do you read a lot?"

"Yes."

"What other adult influences were there in your life?"

"I had some good teachers. I looked up to them. A couple of the other kids' dads were good to me, too. Got me onto baseball teams for a couple of summers. I was 10 and 11."

Andrew became more animated. "And there was a friend of my father, Mr. Lawrence. He was with the FBI. He always came just before Christmas. He brought me gifts and the biggest box of chocolates I had ever seen. I think he even gave Grandpa some money. He would stay for hours. He asked me what I liked to play with and I told him airplanes. For the next several Christmases, Mr. Lawrence brought me model airplanes."

Shaw saw glimpses of a young boy's enthusiasm. Andrew continued. "Not those plastic ones, but very detailed, wooden kits. And we built every one of them together. He stayed for hours and hours. Complicated kits. Wooden biplanes with fat elastics and wind-up propellers. We would go out into the park and see if it could fly a full circuit." Andrew laughed, "Usually it just crashed into the fencing."

Andrew became more serious. "One day I'm getting my pilot's licence. And get a biplane. Maybe a Tiger Moth. Or a Pitt. Open cockpit. Goggles. How much freer could you feel?"

Shaw smiled. "Do you still have contact with him? Lawrence?"

"No. I haven't heard from him since I was twelve. I'm sure he got very busy."

"At thirteen your behavior turned delinquent. Then criminal. An unpredictable, 180 degree turn. No one saw it coming."

"No one was really looking. I wanted to belong. Kids from good families had so much ...security. They didn't know a thing about what my life was like. I found that the ones who really did came from broken homes. We had a bond. We knew what it was like to go home at night. We were kicking back at life."

"Shoplifting."

Andrew nodded. "I didn't have things other kids had. But I'm certainly not defending my actions. They were wrong."

"I read something you wrote for a probation officer, that what you call your 'life circumstances' began with the abduction of your father. Do you feel that your criminal actions were something inevitable? That you couldn't control your behavior. That you couldn't make proper choices." Shaw wanted to be provocative.

"We don't all have the same opportunities. Bad choices are a lot harder to resist for some people than others."

"But these were criminal choices."

"Yes. Started with little stuff. Things gradually got...bigger. I wasn't looking too far ahead. Sometimes things move along for whatever reason. Little steps. The slippery slope thing. I was acting out, by choice. I understand that. Perfectly. But I've made new choices."

That intensity was clearly there, Shaw observed. Intensity, but not defiance.

He had gravitated to bad characters, had gone down a bad road. The question remained, was that road really behind him? Or would he follow it again if circumstances arranged themselves?

Shaw said, "I understand it's your hope to one day pursue a career in law enforcement. That's not something that you've kept to yourself in the ...lions' den in here."

Andrew smiled. "It is indeed that, an education in basic human nature. *Very* basic."

Shaw smiled broadly.

Andrew continued. "I hope that some of the guys who don't have a problem with me, who see that if I want to become a policeman, that all cops can't be bad."

"Do you think your career choice arises directly from your father's career?"

"My father…was following an honorable calling. I see myself following in his footsteps."

"How much does it bother you not to know what happened to your father? Why he was taken?" Shaw wanted to get at the emotive level of the issue for Andrew, not just its content. Would it engage angry, unresolved feelings? Were they buried, long suppressed? Where had he put them? Or had they been sorted through and released?

Andrew showed hesitation. He had been leaning slightly forward during the conversation to this point, quite relaxed. Now he leaned back, easing into the chair, an audible exhalation, as if he would have to consider this carefully. He drew more into himself.

"If my dad had been killed in a car accident, or if like my mother, he had died of cancer, you know, something a kid could understand and even accept, well, that's one thing. I could accept that life just isn't fair. Plain and simple. But…nobody knows why my dad was taken. Nobody knows who did it. Nobody knows what happened to him. Like all other kids who've lost parents, I feel loss and pain. But I live with something else too, a riddle, that gnaws at me. I take what happened… *personally*. That I would lose my dad, and be basically orphaned by someone's decision, I take *personally*. I just know my Dad wasn't at fault, didn't deserve to be killed. There is someone evil who's responsible. And that someone also knew I would be just…fallout. I take that personally."

"Do you desire to *punish* serious criminals, to seek revenge …"

"I'm not a raving…avenger, if that's the word. My life went off the rails because of the act of someone who is evil. I feel it intensely. It's part of my makeup. But I'm not, you know, blinded by rage or something. I can live with it. None of us is perfect. But I'm not crazy."

Shaw said, "You seem philosophical about it, what's happened to you. Almost unique in my experience."

"Can you change what's already happened? No. But you can stop looking back. Consider what you have, what you can do, what you can be. And go for it. Take no prisoners."

"Take no prisoners?"

"It's just an expression."

"Sure. Okay. It all sounds good. Rational. Inspirational. But realistic? We're not machines. We're emotional creatures. We're tied to our past."

"I've read biographies of people who've gone through hell on earth in one way or another. And they are stronger for it. Better for it. For reasons that might not fit with your... predictions. I mean no offense by that, Sir. But they are stronger. And better. And I intend to be one of them."

Shaw looked at Andrew a long moment. Then his eyes dropped to his notes, and he slowly considered his next question. But then he set the notes down, his eyes lifting to Andrew again, and he sat back. He looked at Andrew, studying him, but said nothing. Andrew held the gaze, and for long, wordless moments, each took the measure of the other.

Then Andrew spoke slowly and quietly. "It's quite simple, Sir. In all that has happened to me, in all the major screw ups I've made, in the struggle with my emotions, one thing now shines through to me clear and strong. To make something of myself. And to honor my father, do him proud. It gives me direction and strength. It's what I hold onto every day."

CHAPTER FIVE

Andrew had been riding the Greyhound an hour and the heat in the bus was stifling. Everyone was flushed. The driver had apologized for the breakdown in the air conditioning. The heat wave was in its third day and he said the compressor had finally just given up the ghost.

But to Andrew, none of that mattered. It felt like the best hour of his life, an hour that had taken him from the hell of the Reformatory where he had lived an eternity.

For the hundredth time his mind revisited the scene of the Board hearing held only last week. He wore a suit, hair neatly trimmed. Psychologist Shaw sat at a table with some others whose reports had been introduced and questions fielded. The chairman had spoken. "Andrew Locke. You have said you are determined to put your past behind you. I sincerely hope so. The Board is prepared to grant you an early release. We base it largely on the extremely persuasive recommendations of Dr. Shaw. He believes you have achieved mature insight into your behaviors and are now exceptionally well-motivated. As long as you follow your conditions strictly, you will never have to return here. But, I caution you, do not breach any of your conditions in any way. One misstep and you will be back here."

Andrew had been so grateful. "Yes, Sir. I understand. I respect your faith in me. I will not disappoint you."

The chairman had looked hard at Andrew. "Or yourself."

Even though it was now twilight, Andrew's eyes drank in the passing scenery as if he had been blind until now. The simplest things were so impressive - a farm tractor silently turning in a distant field, golden hay bales stacked, a snaking stone fence, an old, arched cement bridge spanning a brooding river.

He studied the people around him, bored faces, fanning with

magazines, most having given up trying to read but not looking out at the world. He wondered about their lives. Did they appreciate the gloriousness of their freedom? He would never give that up again - that was an absolute. He would never do a stupid thing again.

He put his baseball cap on and reflected. He saw his future stretching before him in a straight line. He would achieve excellent marks in twelveth grade and secure entrance to a good college. He would do a four-year degree, probably in criminology. That would serve him well in applying eventually to a good position with the FBI or another law enforcement agency. Maybe even the Philadelphia P.D. He looked out the window. Dad would have been proud. And Mom, too.

But to have that opportunity, he would have to tow the line. Every day. Never deviate. Never give anyone any reason to think his wayward past wasn't past.

He grabbed his pack. It held all he had in the world - some clothes, a couple of books, some family pictures. He opened a pouch and lifted out a picture.

He was seven in the picture. He remembered the day. They had walked the woods looking for signs of rabbit and deer. They had found fox scat. They had done a stint of target practice with cross bows. The picture was of him and his Dad, each holding his own crossbow in a mock serious pose on their front lawn. They stood on either side of a hay bale on which was draped a large, colorful bull's eye target, two arrows firmly dead center, side by side, one from each.

He felt the beginning creep of the familiar sadness - his longtime, stealthy enemy.

Stay positive. Stay resolute.

His other enemy was the nightmares - waking in a cold sweat, shaking, disoriented. They happened frequently. He had never told anyone about those, certainly not the psychologists. That would only open up speculation about emotional instability. That could kill his chances of ever getting into law enforcement. It was going to be hard enough as it was.

He looked at the picture again. That's what he had to do, he knew. Hit the bull's eye again. Life's bull's eye. Again and again. Be focused. Be steady. Know the wind that can push your arrow off the mark.

The heat in the bus made trickles of sweat on his forehead. He placed the picture back in a pouch. He opened another pouch and felt around inside. Although he was parched, he had been saving his water for as long as he could stand it because he had a three mile walk once he got into Denton. He stretched open the pouch and looked in. His water bottle wasn't there! He suddenly recalled, and cursed himself. He had set the bottle down on the bench while waiting for the bus.

It would be another twenty minutes before they arrived at Denton, a town of about 10,000, his new home for a year. It would be dark when he arrived. He would get a drink at the terminal before doing the three mile walk to the supervision house he was to report to. Check in by 11:00 p.m.

Shortly the bus pulled into a dark, empty parking lot in the center of town and halted with a shush of air brakes. Andrew glanced all around for a terminal. There was no terminal. There was no building at all, just an unlit parking lot.

Three passengers got up and walked to the front of the bus. Andrew waited for them to exit then asked the driver if he knew if there was a convenience store nearby.

"Which way you going?" the driver asked.

"West, out Sherbrooke St."

"There's nothing out that way. You'll have to go north up to Lake St. I know there's something there."

His throat as dry as sawdust, he walked three blocks north imagining desert explorers. A block further he finally saw a neon sign, '**Joey's**'. He hurried towards the door. The lights seemed awfully dim inside. He pulled on the handle but the door wouldn't open. He put his face to the glass and scanned and saw no one inside. But he could see the coolers' lights and rows of dazzling cold drinks inside. He tugged at the door again.

Then he saw the sign. 'Closed for funeral.' He thought, how can every employee have to go to a funeral? Are they all related? Was there a massacre?

The pavement gave off heat like a furnace. His thirst was extreme. He turned and walked the four blocks back to Sherbrooke St., back to where he had started, berating himself for his unbelievable stupidity in forgetting the water bottle.

Three miles to walk in this suffocating heat. He wiped his sweating forehead, his tongue like sandpaper. He wished he hadn't seen those cold drinks in the cooler. Even desert explorers were spared that hardship. It was hardly a level playing field.

Two full blocks ahead he saw more neon, louder than 'Joey's'. This was 'STACEY'S'.

He hurried the two blocks, but then halted. It wasn't a convenience store but a tavern. A 'Cold Beer' sign flashed, a picture of a shimmering glass of beer beckoning, condensation running down its outside.

Someone was talking in the phone booth a few steps outside the tavern door.

Andrew considered his dilemma. He was on strict probationary terms and underage. Couldn't be in a drinking establishment. Or was it, couldn't be drinking *alcohol* in a drinking establishment?

He certainly had no intention of drinking a beer. But the tavern would have water, in the washroom. Then he would be out of there. The whole thing would take thirty seconds.

He drew his baseball cap lower and entered the tavern. A murky half-light, a long dark bar, heavy dark wooden tables, dark wooden captains' chairs, wide-planked dark flooring. Everything dark so you wouldn't notice how cruddy it really was in there. The smell of spilled beer wafted in the air. Three Dog Night was declaring, "Mama told me not to come... That ain't the way to have fun..."

There were maybe twenty people at the tables. Andrew spotted the washroom sign and made a beeline. The two urinals reeked of urine and the single toilet stank of recent puke. There were two wash basins. The handle of one spun aimlessly without producing water. The water from the other ran yellow-brown and smelled of a foul gas. Andrew decided he couldn't drink it. He would ask for a glass of water from the bar. It would only take a second.

The lone bartender had an ill-natured look. And he was busy doing two jobs at once. Andrew hesitated, worrying the bartender wouldn't appreciate a request for a water at this moment. But he was *so* thirsty.

A waitress wearing a low cut T-shirt with 'STACEY'S' emblazoned across an ample bosom arrived at the counter and shoved an empty tray at the bartender. "Four drafts," she half shouted, seeming put out, casting her eyes back to a table where several men were leering at her and laughing.

When she was loaded up and away again, the bartender grabbed up a large keg and struggled it into position to hook it up and replace the old. Andrew tugged at his cap and strolled to the bar. He leaned nonchalantly and tried to sound older. "Can I get a glass of water?"

The bartender cursed as his hand worked at a stubborn hosing attachment. There was shouting and Andrew heard a glass break somewhere behind him and saw the bartender's eyes zero in on the trouble. The bartender grimaced. His eyes still watching the commotion, his hand cranking at the attachment, he said impatiently, "And what else? A glass of draft?"

Andrew didn't want to raise the bartender's hackles. Just go with the flow. He had no intention of drinking it. "Ya, sure," he blurted. "Ya, thanks."

The bartender kept wrenching at the hosing piece. Andrew dug into his wallet. He had seen beer was $1.75. He slid $2.00 across the counter without looking at the bartender.

Another waitress wearing the same low cut 'STACEY'S' T-shirt suddenly appeared beside Andrew and smacked an empty tray on the counter. The bartender looked up at her with concern.

"Three singles and a pitcher," she barked, really ruffled, an annoyed set to her flushed face. She wiped a trickle of sweat from her hair line. "And keep an eye on table seven. I've never seen them before. They're getting real rowdy. And pinching me more than I'm gonna take."

The bartender nodded and watched table seven anxiously as he worked a glass at a draft spout. He slid the single draft to Andrew and quickly turned and swiped up three clean glasses and an empty pitcher from a counter. He began to pour more draft, but his eyes were on table seven again.

"How about the water?" Andrew ventured.

The bartender had clearly forgotten the water. With the commotion, he was even more impatient now. "Go have a seat. One of the ladies will bring you the water. Give us a minute."

Andrew took his beer and sat in the furthest rear corner. He looked at the bartender and the waitresses, working like they were putting out a fire. When would he get the water? Or would the bartender forget again? He looked at the beer, tortured.

And that's when things erupted.

CHAPTER SIX

They looked like bikers - tattoos, long unkempt hair, a few with scraggly beards, muscle shirts showing thick arms. Five of them at table seven. Three more at the next table.

There was one girl at each table. Tough, battle-hardened girls.

The one at table seven began to bang her empty beer glass in a sudden tantrum. "Aren't you gonna do anything about her?" she bellowed to a muscled biker across the table who wore a red bandana. "You know fucking well she did it," she said, pointing to the girl at the other table who, along with three bikers seated there, was watching these proceedings. "I mean it! You gonna do something?"

Red Bandana's face was flushed and he looked ready to break someone's neck. He stared at the girl at his table who stared back and leaned closer. "Well?" she provoked, her eyes blazing. "You gonna fucking do something?"

Red Bandana got up and walked to the other table. His jaw muscles squeezed and his hands made fists causing muscles up his arms to ripple. He pointed at the other girl. "I want you the fuck out of here. *Now!*"

The three bikers at that table had a different idea for their paramour. The clear leader of that table, a muscular guy in a black muscle shirt, said, "Why doesn't your little girlfriend get the hell out of here instead? Or stop pointing fingers. Or I'll fucking break them."

"Fuck you," said Red Bandana.

"Fuck *you*," said Black Muscle Shirt, tipping his beer glass in exaggerated slowness for another swig.

"Fuck *you*, I said," said Red Bandana, glaring.

"I said fuck *you*. You fuckin' deaf? Or fuckin' stupid?" said Black Muscle Shirt.

And then it happened. So many chairs moving all at once, so many people lunging, and so many fists flying. He had seen fights break out before, of course, at the Reformatory. But these guys were all…adults.

All of the customers quickly melted to the door and were gone. None wanted to be collateral damage or even have to give evidence if anything went down here. But Andrew was deep in a dark rear corner, blocked in by the action.

Red Bandana and Black Shirt were the real combatants and really locked horns. The others were less enthusiastic and their scuffles almost immediately broke up. Instead, they gathered around Red and Black, both good fighters from Andrew's trained eye. Both moved quickly for guys who had been drinking. Both landed mostly body blows.

The fight moved quickly across the floor towards the door. Red and Black were now locked in an embrace, twisting and turning. Red slipped on a beer-slick on the wood floor and fell, taking Black down with him. They rolled and grunted.

The outside door threw open and a young policeman stepped in.

Andrew panicked. Somebody must have called, maybe from the phone booth out front because the bartender hadn't made a move. Andrew suddenly felt claustrophobic. Shit! Had he broken the terms of his early release not twenty-four hours into it? He had no water to back up his now probably useless story.

The policeman was only mid-twenties, a boyish face. Andrew sized up people quickly, a skill honed in incarceration. He saw no toughness in the officer's demeanor, no steadiness, no firmness of conviction. Nerves plainly showed as he took in the scene before him, two tough looking guys landing body punches, and a circle of six other goons egging them on. He was daunted. He needed backup and quickly. He reached his hand to the mini radio on his shoulder.

What the officer didn't know, and what every biker there did, was that both Red and Black had outstanding warrants for arrest in another city. And a long rap sheet for assaults. If they were taken into custody, they would face lengthy incarceration. That's why they were doing their drinking here, not there.

Red and Black suddenly noticed the policeman and stopped their swinging. A biker who moved behind the officer glanced to Black and showed a beer bottle. Black nodded. Just as the officer flicked the button on the radio, the biker raised the bottle and smashed it on the back of his head. The bottle shattered. The officer's eyelids dropped and he teetered, then toppled, full length forward, his forehead slamming with a crack as it bounced off the edge of a thick-slabbed table top, the floor thudding with the sudden reception.

He was out cold. Or possibly worse. He hadn't been in the tavern fifteen seconds.

Andrew was stunned. The guy didn't have a chance.

Red and Black, still breathing hard, looked down at the policeman, a mutual problem to be solved. The six other bikers stood around him, their expressions defiant.

Black looked at the bartender. "You didn't see anything. Right?"

"No. I was in the back when it all happened."

"Go and check your inventory."

The bartender didn't hesitate, ducking into a back room. The waitresses had earlier vanished at the first sign of trouble.

The officer let out a low, painful moan. Maybe he was coming to. The bikers all looked down at him. Two of them, one from each rival table, were positioned at his head. They had all been drinking, but these two were closer to drunk. Angry drunk.

One said, "You didn't hit him hard enough, Roddy."

"We gotta square this thing up," the other one said. "We're all together on this thing, right?" He looked for approval from Red and Black.

The first one said, "How about we make this fuckin' pig's memory real fuzzy. So he don't remember who he fuckin' seen here."

The other said, "Ya. How about we each give him a good fucking boot in the fucking head?"

They each looked to their respective leader, grinning with the clever boldness of their plan. There was no sign of disapproval from either Red or Black. The other bikers were nodding. Putting this pig down had served to bond the two factions again.

Andrew's insides were tightening. And a fury was building, a deep, deep fury. Power surged in his body. His head cleared of all extraneous thought.

"Stand back," the first biker slurred, a boasting in his tone. "Give me some fuckin' kickin' room." He took a step back.

Andrew could see the helpless young officer motionless on the floor.

And the biker's heavy boots.

Like a steel spring unloading, Andrew charged. The surprise and force of his tackle carried the kicker hard into a solid wall. The kicker's head bounced like a ball off the wall and he crumpled and fell unconscious to the floor.

Andrew spun just in time to duck the swing of a biker who clearly hadn't expected to miss, not from behind. The biker hadn't kept anything back, leaving himself fully exposed. Andrew threw a straight right so hard, planting it in the stomach so perfectly, the biker's eyes bulged and he dropped immediately to his knees, puking.

The others were stunned. Their momentary lapse let Andrew get to an open area away from tight spaces, away from where he could be cornered or jumped from behind, where his footwork might give him some edge.

Two bikers came quickly, scowling, flexing arms. Andrew felt the mix of fear and adrenaline surge. But he also saw their wariness. They wondered, what the fuck is this guy's problem? He looks even fucking underage, too. But still, he laid Tony out with one fucking punch.

Andrew knew his timing would be better than theirs. But still, they were brutes. He had to work their bodies, not their heads, or his bare hands wouldn't last many rounds. And he couldn't allow himself to be grabbed and held or he was finished.

He faked a jab and a loose swing concealing his real hitting speed. He assessed their reaction time, saw their favored hand. And he kept moving according to his training, lightly bobbing and weaving. His eyes never left theirs, recording every flicker, reading every move a nano second before it happened.

The bigger one made the first move, throwing a roundhouse swing, which told Andrew everything he needed to know. He ducked it and unloaded a solid left into the floating rib area. Although Andrew was right handed, he had worked to develop serious power in his left. He heard a crunch and the expected gasp. Then a feint with his left to the same spot. The guy's defensive reaction was as predictable as the sunrise. Andrew planted a stiff jab directly on the now unprotected nose. As the guy belatedly raised his dominant hand instinctively in protection of his face, Andrew drove his right, tearing into the guy's stomach. The air was taken away and he fell to his knees.

Andrew blocked three wild throws from the anxious second guy. He quickly found which fakes the second guy would buy, then penetrated with a right, left, right, delivered in such a flurry, the second guy could only manage one weak blow to Andrew, glancing off his cheek.

A pained expression on the second's face and Andrew stepped it up. Hit. Block. Fake. Then into the bread basket. Once. Twice. Then to his nose. Which Andrew flattened, blood spurting like a geyser, the guy staggering backwards falling over a chair.

From the time he had tackled the kicker, less than a minute had passed. And four bikers were down or crawling. Andrew registered that the officer had stopped moaning. Was he dead? Andrew now had to stay disciplined, stay focused, stay smart, because now his own life might depend on it. Red and Black were coming.

They wanted to bring this fucking fiasco to a rapid conclusion. Red put out his hand to stop Black. "I'll handle this." Red felt he had under-performed in his earlier fight with Black and wanted to regain his place of deserved respect. And this kid had gotten seriously under his skin.

He wasted no time. He threw two quick punches which Andrew narrowly avoided. A third glanced off Andrew's arm. Andrew responded with two good body blows. But Red's expression didn't change one iota.

Red's movements were faster, more obviously practiced. Andrew's footing gave out momentarily, something wet on the floor. He caught a sliding punch to his stomach and a stiff jab to his forehead. He backed up quickly, bobbing, fighting the shakes off. Andrew was just shy of eighteen, Red ten years his senior. Andrew felt more pain and power in that hit than he had ever felt.

He feinted quickly with the left, drove a right to the solar plexus, two stiff jabs to the bread basket. But it was almost as if Red had allowed them, to prove something. Again his expression didn't change, except for a small smile that now crept on his lips.

Okay, all the meat goes to the head, Andrew thought. Only fakes to the body. He hoped his hands would hold up to the beating he would have to deliver.

Red surprised Andrew and connected a stomach shot that staggered Andrew. He backed off, needed to recoup, get his breath. He dug deeper into himself, into his emotional power. He had to keep believing in himself. He was better than this guy. He would somehow outsmart him. But he was willing to take punishment, accepted he would take punishment. Because this guy was not going to go down easily.

Andrew feinted high with his right, brought his left low looking like a stomach shot. Red took the feint and blocked, anticipated the low left and blocked. But it wasn't a low left. It was now an uppercut left. It connected with Red's jaw. Red's head jerked. Andrew worked the advantage, throwing a quick series of punches, all to the head, only a couple of which actually landed, but with little real force because Red was quick.

Andrew had committed to the head. Red could see that Andrew threw only fakes to the body because real body hits to Red just wasted Andrew's precious energy and exposed Andrew in turn. That was Andrew's plan. Make Red see that, to firmly believe that, to commit Red to a single expectation, a single defensive strategy. And then Andrew would deviate once. For one split second. Would it work?

The liver punch is delivered with a left hook. If done well, it is devastating and can paralyze a boxer. But it is hard to do well because you have to be in close, risky in itself. Andrew hoped that by setting predictable parameters, Red wouldn't commit to a body block. He would hesitate his block, anticipating a head shot. And it would be all Andrew needed.

He worked his feet faster, sped the movement of his head, locked his eyes on Red's, faked to Red's body twice and drove a punch to Red's head, which Red expected and blocked. But in a lightning move, Andrew stepped in, shifting his weight as he did, throwing the left hook with the commitment of a pile driver.

Red didn't commit to a block. The hook drove unimpeded into Red's side. His face contorted, the smile vanishing into a pained grimace. He staggered back, his hands lowering a fraction, his legs suddenly heavy. He was suffering.

Andrew landed a stiff right jab, then that left hook again. Red now blocked as Andrew guessed he would, permitting Andrew a locomotive straight right. Red wobbled, staggered, his eyes unfocused.

Black saw it all. "I'll deal with him. Back off." Red did, with gratitude, leaning full forward onto a side table. Redemption could wait another day.

Black got in close, his eyes those of a cold killer, a no holds barred, calculating killer. And Black was furious. Not only had Andrew hurt several of these guys, but he had seen and heard more than he should have. "You're going down," Black uttered. "And you'll be staying down."

Andrew knew not to let those eyes unnerve him. They were part of Black's arsenal, but Andrew would blank them out. They were irrelevant. Only fists mattered.

And Black's fists were concern enough. Andrew knew Black was the best here. And he was rested, while Andrew was tired, his breathing fast, craving oxygen.

A quick exchange from both sides, neither penetrating the other's defenses. Andrew backed off, sucking air. Black pressed, robust, moving the fight across the floor, throwing a flurry of punches with speed, landing two body blows. Andrew registered that Black's right was a powerhouse.

Black pressed unrelenting, wanting to get this over quickly. He again let loose rapid fire, catching Andrew twice, one on the cheek, one in the ribs. Andrew felt more pain than he had ever felt before.

He had to slow Black's momentum or he would be overrun. Even throw feints to slow him, then lunge into the best onslaught he could muster. He bobbed, he weaved, letting Black get in fractionally closer, making him fractionally less defensive minded, waiting for a moment when Black's balance wasn't solid.

Andrew unloaded everything into a sudden straight right to Black's nose. Black's head jerked fast. Andrew's right fist glanced off the side of the head. But he felt sudden pain in the hand. He worked the left, delivered one to Black's jaw, then backed off.

Black seemed unperturbed. He slipped through Andrew's defense, landing a solid left into Andrew's rib cage. Andrew felt intense pain, but nothing had cracked. Andrew circled more quickly. He needed to break Black's timing to make an opening. He needed this to end soon. But with Black, ending would take more than putting him down. He would have to put him out. Or Andrew would take a serious beating here. Or worse.

Andrew ducked a lightening, long-reached straight. At the same moment, he knew Black would be less balanced. Andrew stepped in and drove a left uppercut. Black mistimed his block. Andrew caught Black square on the chin for the second time. Black's head flew back. But he stood his ground, shaking his head.

Andrew decided to risk a straight right to the face. He was exhausted.

He needed to make this stop. He saw Black's patience eroding after that last hit. And that would make Black less smart, more impulsive, accessible, vulnerable. Andrew kept moving, waiting for the moment.

Black pressed. Andrew dug for energy to make himself light, to support rapid foot movement. He blocked everything to his head, but took painful blows to this body. But he sensed a careless moment.

He countered, a blur of feints, more than Black could track. Then Andrew unloaded it. A straight right into Black's nose. Square contact.

An explosion of pain in Andrew's hand. Shit! He had broken it!

Black staggered from the crushing blow, reaching for his nose. He backed up three steps, his head down, shaking it from side to side. His face was flushed, his eyes watering heavily. Then his eyes focused on Andrew. And they were hate.

He drew a switchblade from his pocket. The long blade snapped open, gleaming even in the room's half-light. He lunged, slashing at Andrew.

Andrew jumped behind a table. His right hand was almost limp. He grabbed up one of the wooden chairs with his left, his right forearm offering only balance. He held it in front like a lion tamer, legs forward.

Andrew saw only one clear hope. Work Black until he was two or three feet in front of the stout pillar that went from floor to ceiling. Andrew would then rush him, crush him into the pillar.

Black worked the knife in his right hand. Andrew feinted the chair to Black's left, once, then twice, always maneuvering him. Then a determined lunge to Black's right so he moved left to line up with the pillar. Black jerked back and left but sensed the pillar.

But not quite fast enough. Two legs hit Black in the chest and the crosspiece pinned Black's right arm against the pillar. Andrew threw all his weight against the chair. Black shrieked, his right arm getting crushed. But still he gripped the knife.

Andrew released pressure a fraction for a split second then slammed the chair with all his might. Black screamed. The knife fell from his hand. He dropped to his knees in pain, holding the crushed right arm.

Andrew dropped the chair, scooped up the switchblade and jumped back. His chest was heaving. The officer moaned, then came a painful whimpering rising in pitch. Andrew stepped to him, not taking his eyes from the others in the room, holding the knife forth.

The tavern door flew open and three policemen ran into the room, guns drawn. Immediately they took in their downed colleague on the floor and Andrew brandishing a switchblade.

"Drop it! Now!" the lead officer shouted, pointing his gun at Andrew as the other two officers flanked him into the room, their guns swiveling from one biker to another around the room. The lead officer was shaking with rage, his friend and colleague lying there, moaning so desperately. "Everyone on the floor! Face down! Now! Now!"

No one hesitated to obey. All were quickly handcuffed and arrested. Including Andrew.

CHAPTER SEVEN

In a bleak, windowless interview room at the police station, the two waitresses sat silently and alone in chairs against the wall, still wearing their loud '**STACEY'S**' tops. Although at the tavern they presented toughness of mold, they had something of the deer-in-the-headlights look as they waited here.

Police Chief Hennessy entered the room, his head down reading notes. He was mid-fifties, a hard exterior, but everyone knew he had a soft streak as wide as a door and cared about his 'boys' like a father. He wore a deeply worried expression. Still reading, he closed the door behind him. Then he looked up, giving the girls a quick once over.

He spoke slowly for emphasis. "Now...I've got a badly hurt officer. A fine young man. I want to know as much as you know about what happened tonight. Give me your names, please."

"I'm Jennifer. She's Jill." Jennifer spoke in bursts, like a machine gun. Last names could wait.

"Who made the calls?"

"Jill did," Jennifer said. Jill nodded agreement.

Okay, thought Hennessy, Jennifer's the talker. "Okay, Jennifer, tell me what happened?"

Jennifer spoke in rapid fire. "Jill and I were the only ones on tonight. Being a Tuesday night. So it's almost ten. There were maybe twenty customers. Including the eight biker types. They were seated at two tables. Getting real rowdy."

"Jennifer," Hennessy said, putting up his hand, "This isn't a race to the end kind of thing. Can you just...slow it down."

"Oh, sorry, when I'm nervous..."

"I understand," Hennessy said slowly, to give example. "Go on."

"Well, all of a sudden, a fight broke out. Amongst themselves. Fists flying. People getting knocked over. The other customers right away ran out the front door. Jill and I went out through the supply room door. It's a door that opens to the alley. I told Jill to phone you guys from the phone booth."

"What about the bartender?"

"Sam... I guess he...I don't know."

"Slow it down. Then what?"

"I went back into the supply room. I stayed out of sight. But you can see a bit into the parlor. So the officer walked in from the front entrance. And then...one of the bikers smashed him across the back of the head with a beer bottle."

The Chief's body stiffened. "Did you see which biker?"

"No. I was stunned." She stopped talking, seemed suddenly at a loss for words, her fingers moving in agitation. A tear rolled from one eye. The veneer was melting. And now she spoke more slowly.

"He fell...just straight down...like a tree. His head kinda...smacked off the tabletop and then hit the floor. It was really awful. I didn't know if he was dead. He didn't have a chance."

The Chief absently scuffed his foot on the floor, an overload of nervous energy. "Go on."

"Jill was still outside. I told her the officer had been knocked out and to phone again." Jill nodded.

"I ran back to the supply room. I got a better view this time between the cases of empties. Right away I heard one of the bikers, I couldn't see which one, say they should.... kick the officer in the head. Like a few times. So he wouldn't remember anything about what he saw." She sniffled and brought her hand to her nose. "It was terrible."

Chief Hennessy's face was as still as a block of wood. "Are you sure they said they were going to kick the officer? Kick him in the head?"

"Yes, I am."

"Could you see the officer?"

"Yes. He was on the floor. He wasn't moving." She looked down, tears coming. Jill put her hand on Jennifer's arm.

The girls could hear the Chief swallowing several times.

"The next thing, the young guy came out of nowhere at one of the bikers who was beside the officer. They crashed into the wall. It knocked out the biker. Right away another biker took a big swing at the young guy from behind, but he ducked or something and hit this other biker in the stomach so hard the biker puked."

Hennessy hands were clenching into fists, opening, closing.

"Then, like two other bikers went after him and they fought and he put them both down. He's like a...I don't know...a boxing machine."

Chief Hennessy listened in growing awe, not speaking a word.

"Then one of the leaders, he has a red bandana, he fought with the young guy. There was a lot of punches. I was so scared. The young guy, I could tell he was hurting. I could see it in his face. But then he must have really whacked the biker because he kinda really staggered and backed off. And that's when the guy with the black muscle shirt fought him. But then he drew a switchblade."

"Who drew a switchblade?"

"The guy with the black muscle shirt. Oh, please God, no. I didn't even want to look when that happened. But, thank God, the young guy did it. Nearly took the guy's arm off with one of our chairs. Grabbed the knife. And that's when three of you guys came in."

⎯⎯⎯ • ⎯⎯⎯

Thirty minutes later, Andrew was brought up from a holding cell and placed in an interview room. He was handcuffed. His right hand was swollen and discolored. Ugly red welts showed on his forehead and cheeks. An officer stood in the corner of the room.

Chief Hennessy walked in carrying a file. He observed Andrew for a moment. To the officer he said, "Did it check out?" The officer nodded.

"Okay, Rick, I'll take it from here." The officer left the room.

Hennessy took Andrew's hands and with care took the cuffs off.

"Andrew Locke?"

"Yes, Sir."

"Just released from the Reformatory today."

"Yes, Sir. But I can explain."

"On very strict conditions. You're already late for reporting in. You're about three years too young to be in a tavern. And the bartender said you ordered a beer."

"Yes, but..."

"And fighting. And now you're arrested."

Hennessy had had his bit of fun. He had built up so much tension in the last hour. And the night was long from over with eight bikers in his cells.

Hennessy smiled a warm smile. "Relax, Andrew. I know your whole story. A waitress saw it all. Rick even confirmed that **Joey's** has been closed all day. Odd sort of thing isn't it?"

"Yes, Sir."

"The bartender...when I told him I wasn't interested in whether you were underage or not, that I wasn't going to lay charges against STACEY'S, he finally said you had really asked only for a glass of water. But he sold you a beer. Made you wait for the water."

Hennessy looked at Andrew for a long moment. "And, Andrew, I thank God he did. Or you wouldn't have been there. And one of my boys, a young father, might have died tonight."

Hennessy now pulled a chair up and sat close to Andrew. "You put a lot on the line...your early release...and a whole lot more. Like possibly your life. Why?"

Andrew was holding his swollen right hand in his left, to relieve pressure. He looked at his hand. "I just...reacted."

"I don't know many people who would do what you did. There were eight bikers in there."

Andrew nodded. "I got to meet most of them."

Hennessy smiled a moment, then asked seriously, "Why, Andrew?"

"The officer was ...hit from behind by cowards. Helpless. I didn't think my life was on the line."

Hennessy took a slow, deep breath, nodding. "Andrew, I checked you out. Your father was a cop. I read what happened there. I'm very sorry. He... would have been very proud of you."

Andrew's eyes lowered. He gave a slight nod.

"Listen, Andrew, all charges against you are completely dropped. You're completely in the clear. As for the Reformatory, don't worry. I'm going to smooth any wrinkles there. How's the hand?"

Andrew looked at it, purpled and misshapen. "Broken."

Hennessy put his hand on Andrew's shoulder for several moments. Then he got up and opened the door and yelled, "Rick, get somebody to take this young man to the hospital. Right now, please."

Hennessy walked back to Andrew. "I want to thank you... for the life of Tim Bondar. The word from the hospital is that it was a close call, but he's going to be okay. We are all deeply indebted. I'm going to see that something is done for you, starting with supper at my house when you get settled in. I know where to find you."

An officer in uniform appeared at the door, holding car keys.

Hennessy held out his hand to Andrew. "Thank you," he said.

The night was finally over. Andrew could now relax, allow himself to take the measure of his body, feel all of his pain.

He smiled and shook with his left.

The account of what happened made Andrew an instant hero in the community. The story made it into even the big papers. Learning he was without family or support, the locals took up a donation to assist him with his future college expenses.

And then came a single, anonymous donation. $15,000. Enough to pay for two full years of college by itself.

Andrew long wondered who it was. And why they would do that for him. When he eventually learned, he found it was not for reasons anyone might expect, but for chilling, unimaginable reasons, shattering his world once again.

PART THREE
1981

CHAPTER EIGHT

Alone in his ample office on the top floor of the FBI building in Philadelphia, Wesley Lawrence stirred a morning coffee and pondered his soon to arrive visitor.

As the special agent in charge, the SAC, of the Philadelphia field office, Lawrence directed more than fifty agents and a hundred support staff. He was forty-seven, but looked older, lines imprinting a weary face, all of his hair grey. A once stocky build had long ago lost definition. He was well-liked by his agents and staff, and more important, was well-respected as a leader and a diligent investigator. They had long ago accepted, however, that he was a very private person, often withdrawn. He didn't socialize except on a rare occasion when he would go with colleagues to a nearby bar for a quick beer. He didn't accept dinner invitations, and he didn't have people over. He didn't talk wives or girlfriends; they knew he had neither, and had never been married. He lived alone. They didn't suggest in any way that maybe he would enjoy himself more if he broadened his social life. No, he was a standup guy, knew life as well or better than they, and, well, each to his own.

Lawrence was waiting for Senator Bloom, who had early this morning requested a highly confidential meeting. Lawrence knew that only yesterday Bloom had buried his wife of many years. So the timing of the request was odd. Surely there was some connection.

There was a rap at the door and Lawrence's assistant, agent Cummings, ushered Senator Bloom in and made introductions.

Bloom was about sixty-five, white-haired, and distinguished-looking. But today he was haggard, shrunken, anxiety etched on his drawn face.

Lawrence said, "I was very sorry to hear about your wife."

Bloom nodded slowly. "Thank you," he said quietly.

Bloom and Cummings each took a seat in the leather armchairs.

Lawrence sat behind his desk.

Bloom's gaze went to the window and held a few moments, abstracted, a hollowness in his face. Lawrence noticed Bloom's hands trembled lightly.

Bloom's eyes came back to Lawrence. He spoke quietly, slowly, and in reverence. "Anna was my wife of forty years. My special love. My rock. Life holds little for me now."

He looked to Cummings a moment then back to Lawrence. He focused his attention. "Anna knew nothing of what I am about to tell you. She would never have believed it." His hands trembled more, causing the fingers to involuntarily tap the arm of the chair. "I could never have done this while she was alive. I was afraid for her. Not many knew she had such a weak heart."

Bloom paused and breathed deeply. "I don't say this with any exaggeration. I am in the grip of a killer. I have never met him. He calls himself 'The Watcher'. He has been extorting large sums from me for eight years. He keeps himself unknowable."

Lawrence said, "He has something on you?"

"Yes. My crimes...my...shameful crimes. Very large sums deposited to secret offshore accounts so I would make sure certain corporations got very lucrative government contracts. Other monies I took over the years to use my influence to block charges of tax evasion against many wealthy individuals. Other very generous and very illegal campaign checks in return for large favors."

Lawrence said, "Those details can wait for the moment. You came here because of the extortion."

Bloom nodded. "Yes. That's what's urgent for me. I became a senator ten years ago. Eight years ago I received an extortion threat from The Watcher. He wanted twelve large payments a year. If I didn't pay, certain information about me would be made public. In politics, you get threats. But this was different. He had very detailed, accurate, provable information against me."

Bloom spoke slowly. "I would be ruined. I would go to jail. Or The Watcher would cause me to ...disappear, as I will explain. But worst of all...I feared the revelations would kill Anna."

His tone spoke shame. "The money I had to pay to The Watcher over the years was far less than the money I took in from my crimes. So

I carried on. Changed nothing. Said nothing."

Bloom looked firmly at Lawrence. "But that's behind me now." Bloom leaned forward, a determination showing. "The Watcher is a killer. But it's time for me to do the right thing, to make amends. Even if it means giving up everything. Everything."

Bloom became suddenly more emotional, swallowing, holding back a tear. "Anna deserved... so much better in me."

Lawrence said, "It's alright. Take your time."

After a few moments, Bloom composed himself. He reached into his suit pocket and withdrew an envelope. "At the time The Watcher made the threat to me, I got a visit from a friend of mine, Tasker. He had been told to see me. He was already a victim. Tasker said 'just do what you're told. It's safer than the alternative.' Tasker had been extorted for years. I asked what he meant, 'safer than the alternative.' He said that over the years he knew of three men who were being extorted by The Watcher and had disappeared without explanation, never to be found. Tasker showed me three letters, one letter for each of the three men, one in Boston, one in New York, one in Washington. In each case The Watcher had sent a letter to all those he was extorting explaining that the named man had failed in his arrangements with The Watcher and so the man had to disappear, to be made an example of. A warning was always included in the letter - never go to the police, never get behind on payments. But here's what was exceptional and convinced me of my serious peril - the date on the envelope in each case showed that the letter was processed through the post office the day *before* the disappearance of each of the men. The Watcher wanted it to be seen by his victims that he was without question responsible for the disappearance, and bold enough to say so."

Bloom set the envelope and letter on Lawrence's desk. "I got this yesterday, regular mail. I found it when I got home...after Anna was buried."

Lawrence picked it up and examined the envelope.

Bloom said, "You can see the sender identifies itself as **'Extract Enterprises'**, a private joke. You will find their address is nonexistent. They purport to be a mining company. The letter begins with the usual solicitation of investment monies for their supposed ventures. A lot of boilerplate, intended to disguise the real content of the letter. Anyone looking at it wouldn't twig to it. But look at page two, about the middle. That's where they are speaking directly to me and the other victims."

Lawrence took out the letter and glanced down the first page. He turned with care to page two. He read until he found sentences that appeared to be unconnected to the context. He read aloud. 'Theodore Tasker in Philadelphia declined to honor his payment obligations under our arrangement. He made only empty promises. He tested my patience. Note the envelope's date, and watch the news.'

Lawrence examined the postal marking. "It's stamped Monday, in Trenton. Today is Friday."

Lawrence slid page two of the letter across the desk to Cummings.

Bloom said, "Mailed Monday. Tasker was home Monday night. He called me about Anna. When I got the letter yesterday, Thursday, I phoned Tasker. I had to leave a message. He didn't call back. I'm certain he's disappeared."

Lawrence said to Cummings, "Check out Tasker, please." Cummings hastened out the door.

Bloom said, "I checked into reports on those three missing men, all unsolved disappearances. This is the first one in Philadelphia. How many others live under this man's threat?"

Lawrence asked, "Did Tasker go to police to your knowledge?"

"I don't know. I thought you might know...so I gather not."

Lawrence said, "Did you know anything about Tasker's financial circumstances?"

"He's had a couple of bad years. Fell into depression. Drinking heavily. We weren't talking often. It appears from the letter he wasn't paying. I'm certain you're going to learn that he has disappeared, probably Tuesday. And he won't ever be found."

Lawrence lifted the envelope, looking again at the post mark. "Mailed Monday. That would be bold..."

My next payment is due in four days. I'm prepared to be your bait."

Lawrence considered Bloom a moment. "How are payments made?"

"Cash, divided into four separate envelopes and mailed as instructed."

Cummings came back into the room and nodded to Lawrence and said, "Philadelphia P.D. put out a bulletin. Tasker's reported missing. Last seen Tuesday morning."

Lawrence tapped a finger on the table. He sat back and looked at

Bloom. "Have you told anyone you were coming here?"

Bloom shook his head. "No one."

———

Lawrence reviewed FBI reports and found they verified Bloom's information in all respects. The three disappearances remained unsolved, no suspects generated, and no bodies ever found. And now Tasker, a fourth disappearance.

The next afternoon Lawrence and Cummings strode a corridor in the Bureau offices as Cummings filled Lawrence in. "The team's assembled. Half are our people. Half are Philadelphia P.D."

They entered 'the war room' where thirty men and women were seated in rows of chairs, talking among themselves, a few in police uniform.

Lawrence walked to the podium and spoke. "You've been briefed on what we know of The Watcher. And it is brief indeed. But we know he has a large extortion operation and has caused the disappearance of at least four men. We have a shot at learning much more now. Senator Bloom has offered us this unique opportunity. He will continue his normal routines unchanged. No one on the outside is to suspect anything. He will have our close protection at all times. He will mail his payment, $20,000, as he was instructed. The bills are marked. Some of you are assigned to surveillance, others to protection, others to tail teams at the post office. We will follow the money. And we will find this Watcher."

CHAPTER NINE

Although Lorne Nix was now fifty-four, he still carried his tall athletic frame as he did when he was twenty-five. He stood at the wall of window in the living room of his 30th floor penthouse contemplating the Delaware River, an inky band winding by Philadelphia as the twinkling lights of the skyline hardened in brightness against the darkening sky.

Nix was an attorney, specializing in corporate work with a decidedly international flavor. He had an office in downtown Philadelphia, but no secretary. He had but one client, a conglomerate of corporations registered in several tax havens - Panama, Barbados, the Caymans, Switzerland. The real ownership of those corporations was untraceable, identity shielded in secrecy through trusts. The real business of the corporations was unknowable.

At the moment he was considering how best to launder the $125,000 in cash which couriers had collected for The Watcher that week. There was no question it had to be laundered. You can't make a deposit of cash like that without the authorities quickly knocking on your door. Nor can you buy land, or stocks, or even an expensive car, with cash. And in any case, as a precaution, all cash received by The Watcher was always laundered because the bills might be marked as part of a police investigation. Better in that case the bills show up in Panama where no one is looking than in your local bank account.

Getting large amounts of cash out of the U.S. to your foreign bank account without detection was always a problem. You could, of course, fill a suitcase with the cash and fly to the Caymans and deposit it there.

In the current instance, Nix decided to use the 'Panama Dry Cleaners', The Watcher's private courier system. The cash would be delivered to a certain individual in Panama City. No bank official there knew, or asked, where the cash originated. It would be deposited to a series of accounts held in the name of legitimate Swiss companies. From those accounts, portions would flow out into accounts held in other safe havens, principally Barbados and the Caymans.

Nix poured himself an ounce of smoky, peaty, 16 year Lagavulin single malt and walked into his teak appointed study. He hit the rewind button on the voice activated, reel to reel tape recorder on the credenza. The reels spun for fifteen seconds which told him there were several messages. These came via four short wave radios which faced the recorder, each radio set to a different frequency. Nix hit the play button and settled into a deep leather sofa.

The Watcher had a network of informants within many major police departments, the Philadelphia and New York offices of the FBI, some government departments, and some private industry. The money offered was so good, the anonymity so secure, recruiting informants was never difficult.

An informant always first encoded the message. He never had to pass a plain text written message to anyone. Instead, he radioed the coded message to the 'radio house', the location of which was unknown to informants. From the informant's point of view, it meant he never had to meet anyone and risk being seen. From The Watcher's point of view, it meant the informant didn't know anyone in The Watcher's organization.

At the radio house, the coded message was transcribed to plain English then radioed to Nix in short snippets using the four different frequencies. This evaded eavesdroppers. The radio house also telephoned the message to an anonymous number in an empty office in Atlanta where an answering machine recorded it. This allowed Nix to phone in from anywhere at any time and get the latest informant or cell message.

The messages Nix got today quickly drained the color from his face. Informants in both the Philadelphia P.D. and the Philadelphia FBI field office had made reports. Piecing them together, Nix learned that Senator Bloom had gone to the FBI informing them he was being extorted by an unknown - The Watcher, and that the disappearances of four men were now linked to The Watcher. Further, Bloom was now under FBI and Philadelphia P.D. protection. Bloom's payment would be made using marked bills and the mailed envelopes would be tracked by a special team. Concealed cameras had been installed at the Trenton

Post Office. Two plainclothes tailing teams would be at the post office around the clock.

Nix sat absorbing the shock. This was momentous and would become a fundamental test of The Watcher's resources and resolve. Because if this information ever got out to the public, it could put The Watcher's extortion operations in serious jeopardy.

He picked up the phone and dialed Salvatore Cavaco.

———•———

Salvatore Cavaco was now fifty-four, too, but looked younger with his smooth olive complexion. Tonight, as usual, he was immaculately dressed. To women, he was magnetic.

On paper, Cavaco had emigrated from Argentina in 1958. On paper, he was Alfred Armano. Of all the people in the world only Nix knew he was actually Salvatore Cavaco, born and raised in Buffalo, New York.

Cavaco, too, was looking at the Delaware River from time to time that evening. His sprawling 8,000 square foot Georgian estate house abutted the river for a sweeping 2,000 feet. That long frontage and twelve acres of treed estate grounds ensured him spacious privacy. From his luxurious games room, he looked out past the hundred yards of softly lighted grounds to the river, where his 75 foot Benedetti yacht, 'Miss Nomer', was docked. Its glittering lights defined its shapely lines, and from its interior cabins a soft glow emanated. One of the house staff was preparing the master cabin for later.

Cavaco's tall, blonde, Finnish-model girlfriend leaned over the exquisite purple felt of the billiard table, her tanned silky arms carefully positioning the cue. "Is this going to work?" she asked with noticeable Finnish accent, her clear blue eyes surveying the balls, then flashing to him in question. She was his latest acquisition, and new to pool. He liked the blond against the purple.

"See for yourself. You'll learn faster. Pool is like life," he mused aloud, "a game of angles, best learned by playing." Facile games' room philosophy, of course. But then again, he wasn't in conversation with Aristotle. "You've got the curves", he said. "Now acquire the angles." His smile showed strong, perfect teeth.

"Oh, Alfred," she laughed and leaned forward, concentrating on the balls, the long blonde hair splaying out across a foot of rich purple felt.

He didn't know, was it her Finnish background or what, but she always wanted to make love on the yacht, not in the house. Maybe it was the motion of the water. Perhaps the novelty.

Nix and Cavaco had known each other before Nix went to law school. It was Cavaco, in fact, who saw the benefit of having a lawyer confidant and so financed Nix through law school.

Nix and Cavaco were the only two people who knew The Watcher was not one man but two – Nix and Cavaco. For they had over many years carefully constructed an organization while wrapping themselves in secrecy, insulating themselves at the top of the pyramid. Several layers separated them from those who carried out the nasty day to day business.

The Watcher's people were very well paid, and in clean cash. None knew the identity of The Watcher; all knew it was better that they not. None had criminal records. None knew real names of the others. The less they knew about each other, the less harm they could be to each other. They respected this and did not break the bond.

Many of The Watcher's operations were entirely legitimate, funded from money which was originally dirty, then laundered and invested in assets in the U.S. These were managed by reputable, certified public accountant firms.

But many of its operations were criminal - acquiring insider trader information, confidential government reports, confidential police information, all through bribery or threat. And some were extreme - extortion, brutal intimidation, even cold murder. It was the knowledge that The Watcher would carry out that final act that compelled obedience and silence from most who came to be within his grasp.

The telephone in the games' room was ringing. Cavaco went to the table in the corner and picked it up.

It was Nix, who quickly said, "It's imperative we speak."

"Come right over," Cavaco replied. It would take Nix fifteen minutes.

A clack of balls and a plunk. "Yay! I got two balls in. In a... line? Is that the way you say it?"

"It'll do," Cavaco said curtly. His mind was racing over recent jobs, speculating on what may have gone wrong.

"Is something wrong, Alfred? Is someone coming over?"

He had been away. Tonight was to be theirs. Even when her face was wrinkled in distress and disappointment, it was sublime.

"Nothing's wrong. An urgent business matter. It may take a while. You'll have to entertain yourself on Miss Nomer."

"But I thought we…" She stopped herself. She had learned never to question him when it came to matters of business. She didn't know what he did exactly, but whatever it was, it was his first priority. And it was highly successful.

She walked to him, taller than he, lightly stroking the cue, her generous lips making a small pout. "I shall be lonely, Alfred."

"Yes you will. But you'll live through it. And I'll make it up to you."

Her eyes brightened, her disappointment dissipating like soap bubbles in a wind. "Oh?" she said. "A diamond, perhaps?"

Cavaco smiled. She was unflinchingly greedy. But, of course, that was why she was here. And who was he to disparage unmitigated greed.

———————

When Nix told Cavaco that Senator Bloom had gone to the FBI and told them everything, Cavaco looked at Nix in amazement, then in angry comprehension. Bloom had been told *never* to do that. He had been told of the deadly consequences of ever doing that. Perhaps, Cavaco thought, Bloom's wife's death had something to do with it. Perhaps grief had caused him to lose his better judgment.

Cavaco said, "Bloom thinks he's safe. Or he doesn't care. When did this happen?"

"Yesterday morning. They're tracking his payment."

"Of course. They might show occasional glimpses of ingenuity, but really, we have nothing to worry about. They don't know who we are, who they're looking for, or even where to begin. They're nowhere."

Nix pressed, "The real worry for us is if it gets out that Bloom went to the police. It could inspire other brave souls to do the same. Jeopardize our receivables."

Cavaco mused, "Yes, it would be bad press. The police will keep it quiet for now, not show their hand, see if they can cleverly follow the money. But the long term concern is that it will get out. When the police realize they've hit the wall, they may put it out to the public, try to entice more of our customers to come forward, give the police more information to work with."

Cavaco paced slowly and gently rubbed his hands together, a habit Nix had long observed when Cavaco was concentrating. "The real trouble isn't that Bloom has gone to the police," Cavaco said. "The real trouble is that he's gone to the police and remains *alive*. That would be bad press. But if he's gone to the police and *dies while in police protection*, that's excellent press! Our receivables arrive like a Swiss train."

"Bloom's going to be under serious protection. It would be a difficult hit."

"Yes, but worth doing whatever it takes to make happen. And what choice do we really have? It will reinforce our resolve to our customers. Their memories get short. They need a stunning reminder of what's best for them. What better way than seeing one in their position getting rubbed out while under police protection."

"We'll need very good information."

"Sure. The informants will need extra incentive. Put out extra good money."

"Meanwhile, we can't let the police think we know the payment's being tracked."

"No. So we can't let it sit in Trenton. If we stop moving the money, they would know we know it's being watched."

"I'll keep it moving. Won't use our usual routes or couriers."

A wide smile now broke on Cavaco's face. He seemed to relish the prospect of this highly dangerous undertaking. "We want to know everything the police and FBI know at every step," he said eagerly. "*Everything* that goes on in Philly P.D. and the Philly FBI office. Every fly that's killed with a paper clip. Put out extra big money."

At a corner cabinet he opened a tall door. "Let's celebrate. Scotch?"

Nix nodded and walked to the window. He looked to the river and scanned the lines of Miss Nomer. A white light turned off in the master cabin. In its place, a soft purple light turned on.

Nix said, "How's what's her name, Miss Helsinki, or whatever she was?"

"Still tall, blonde, greedy, and not asking questions."

Cavaco walked to Nix and handed him a glass. Cavaco said, "You need to get a girl again. Some brains, but never of a really curious mind. And always selfish and greedy. Those are their deepest virtues."

He raised his glass. "And now, to the end of Bloom."

CHAPTER TEN

A ndrew Locke listened carefully to the engine note. The roaring gurgle of the biplane's Lycoming was music. He opened up the throttle and the peppy little Pitt began to race across the grass, at speed the tail coming up and the grass blurring. He pulled back on the joystick and the wheels lifted gently.

From as far back as he could remember, he had been fascinated by planes, magically held aloft by nothing apparent to the eye. After his father was gone, his fascination only increased.

The desire to fly stayed strong. Through college he spent all of his spare money on flying lessons, and in his final year he obtained his pilot's license. When he had been accepted into the FBI three years ago, and was training in Quantico, Virginia, he joined the Quantico Marine air-base flying club. There he rented and flew Cessnas and Pipers, stoking his love of flying.

When he graduated as an agent and got his first transfer to the FBI field office in Minneapolis two and a half years ago, he had quickly taken out a bank loan and bought the used Pitt, an open cockpit, aerobatic biplane. A two seater, two separate cockpits, one behind the other. To Andrew the Pitt was not a separate thing of simple metal and wire, but was a creature, a living extension of himself.

Today, a day off work, he was flying. And a fine day it was at two thousand feet, the mid-June sun warm, the sky clear but for wisps of cirrocumulus powdering the blue.

And more enjoyable still, his wife Madeleine was with him, seated directly in front of him, wearing a leather flying helmet and goggles. She leaned over to watch a patch of forest slide by below. He loved when she came along. It was the first time in a long time she said she was ready to come again.

He had met Madeleine in his sophomore year at college. Before that he had been plodding methodically forward, pushing the painful past out of his life, the task made all the more difficult because nothing was big enough to make life new.

Then came Madeleine. It was as if science had overlooked a dimension until then. Everything changed. Life began again, more wonderful than he had ever known. He found himself always looking forward, never back, looking always to her She was a beautifully nurturing person, a trait that had drawn him to her like a magnet.

And soon the nightmares that had been his steady companion for thirteen years became far less frequent. He would wake up in the morning fresh, aware only of happiness derived from his knowing her.

He had married her, Emily Madeleine Nelson, six years ago when they were both only twenty-one, still in college. Andrew felt like the luckiest man in the world. And a year later, Chris came along, now age five, the light of their lives.

They were cruising at 140 mph, the bawling of the engine largely muffled by the audio headsets built into the leather helmets which allowed pilot and passenger to communicate, if you yelled.

Andrew gained altitude to three thousand feet. Then he said into the microphone, "I'm expecting a little turbulence."

He heard Madeleine's "okay".

Andrew waited a few moments then executed a perfect snap roll - a quick, complete rotation of the Pitt, upside down, then right side up. He heard Madeleine's voice over the headset, lightly sarcastic. "Yeah, right."

Now he put the plane through a barrel roll - flying a horizontal cork screw, slowly turning upside down and continuing to roll until it righted again, one complete turn.

"Okay, okay." She was laughing. "Enough with the turbulence already."

"How's that indigestion?"

A long pause. "Hey, it's actually gone. Just what the doctor ordered."

After thirty minutes, he knew she had had enough. He began a gentle bank to follow the railway track that would lead them back to the airfield. Andrew eased off the throttle and pushed the joystick slightly forward. They gently descended, now feeling their speed as the Pitt flew low over the faint rises and contours of the hills on approach to the runway.

———•—

Andrew and Madeleine walked into the airfield's tiny terminal building, Madeleine still brushing her long, thick, chestnut hair newly released from the leather helmet.

A voice called out, "Hey, Andrew."

It was a fellow agent, Sidney. He came up to them.

Andrew said, "Hi Sid. This is my wife Madeleine."

Sid couldn't take his eyes off Madeleine, knocked out by her stunning good looks. "Very pleased to meet you, Madeleine." Looking to Andrew he gushed, "Where did you meet such a beautiful woman?"

Andrew said, "Oh, at some grungy bar."

Madeleine laughed and gave Andrew a playful slap on the arm.

Andrew laughed, continuing, "I was drunk. She picked me up. That's as much as I can remember that night."

Madeleine slapped him on the shoulder harder, laughing. "Stop it."

"Actually, we were students together at the University of Pennsylvania. I saw her playing squash one day. I did more stunts than I do in that plane to get to meet her."

Sid said to Madeleine, still admiring her, "Still play squash?"

Madeleine smiled. "No. I wasn't very good. But," nodding toward Andrew, "it paid off."

Sid said, "Andrew's talked about your son. Do you work as well?"

"I'm an educational diagnostician with the school board." Sid looked vague. Madeleine continued. "I administer tests to children who show difficulty in learning. I interpret those results and make recommendations to the teachers on the most effective learning strategies."

Andrew said, "She absolutely loves working with those children."

Sid suddenly glanced to his watch. "Hey, sorry, I've got to be somewhere else quick. It's been a real pleasure meeting you, Madeleine." As Sid left, he gave Andrew a secret, exaggerated thumbs up.

———•—

Perhaps it was Sid asking how they had met, but as Andrew and Madeleine drove along the quiet country road away from the airport, she found herself remembering the first time she ever went to Andrew's tiny apartment at college. While he was making them a coffee, she had with infinite curiosity poked her head into his bedroom. She had seen a framed picture on a dresser, a wedding portrait, presumably his mother and father, a handsome couple full of dreams of life together.

She had thought it a bit strange for a young guy to have such a picture when he was away at college. So she asked him. He told her he didn't have any other home. Both parents were gone. He carefully explained all of it.

It broke her heart. She couldn't stop crying even though he gently soothed her. They had held each other for a very long time that day.

Madeleine's roommate in college was heavy into abnormal psychology, saw everybody through that particular prism, and in 2rd year already spoke like a seasoned therapist. When Madeleine was first telling her about Andrew ('bright, handsome, loving, humorous, fun, fun, fun'), her roommate launched into a grave lecture. "Most people suffer from a feeling of poor connectedness to their parents when they were a child. Certainly Andrew must have had that to a very significant degree. It's highly probable that he has suppressed huge anxieties, immense when you think about it, and that's a worry because those early anxieties exert a radical shaping influence on one's development. So…"

Madeleine hadn't signed up for the lecture. "Blah, blah, blah. Listening to you feels like writhing in quick sand. If he's got problems, and who doesn't, they're not jumping out anywhere that I've noticed. But if they do, well, I'm just the answer, someone of high spirits, someone who can just *turn them around*." She twirled her finger to display the ease with which just such a thing could be done.

And his past, as sad and tragic as it was, had quickly seemed to her to be just that - the past. Because Andrew was just so wonderful, full of life and enjoyment with her. And it never came up.

Maybe it was mulling those thoughts of early loss to Andrew that now triggered the sudden sadness from her own recent loss. Would she ever get over it? She felt helpless in its grasp.

Andrew said, "How much longer 'til we pick up Chris?"

She was looking out the window. "An hour and ten minutes." She hadn't even had to look at her watch.

"Think we could stretch it to two hours?"

"Why?"

"I want to take you to a romantic place in a remote wood and make passionate love to you." He glanced to her brightly. "I brought some wine and a blanket."

Normally she would make a spirited response. But she stayed quiet, looking out the window. He wondered if she just wasn't in the mood. Then he registered how sad she was.

He knew right away. He reached over and took her hand and kissed it. He continued to hold it. The baby. Stillborn. A terrible blow. She was sometimes still very frail and he found her often retreating into herself.

She turned to look at him, then quietly said, "She would have been six months old this week. Eagerly crawling to me...." Tears formed. "Sometimes it really catches me…"

Andrew squeezed her hand. "I know, Madeleine. I know."

He thought about Madeleine's capacity for caring, like a deep well, and the very dark days after they lost the baby. There had been nothing he could do to alleviate her suffering. He had felt utterly helpless.

The loss of the baby had made her more protective of the family. She had spoken more often of her anxiety about the danger of Andrew's work. Andrew loved his work, loved the guys, but his having been shot twice in two years, although minor wounds and incurred through sheer bad luck, played on her mind always.

They drove on awhile without conversation, Madeleine watching the forests and fields, lost in her thoughts and feelings.

He hated to see her sad. "Hey, how about we pick Chris up early and go to that pet shop you were talking about. The one with the hamsters. He'd love that."

She turned to him. "And get one? I thought you weren't that keen on getting a pet?"

"Well, I was thinking, you know, it would be good. Teach him responsibility, having to care for something. As long as you agree it would be *his* job, and not yours."

"Ya, I know."

"Hey, I've got an idea. We could name it 'job'.

Madeleine laughed lightly.

Andrew continued, "You know, as a kind of constant reminder."

Madeleine laughed again. "Andrew, you're crazy sometimes."

Andrew laughed, too. And crazy he was, but for the next five miles he saw a little smile on her face. And he worshiped that smile.

That afternoon they took Chris to the pet store. Andrew said to Chris, with what seemed unbridled enthusiasm, "Let's name it either 'job', or 'chore'. Pick one. For example, you could say to your friends, 'I really love my 'job'."

Chris looked like a spell had turned him to stone. Not even his eyes moved.

Madeleine intervened, laughing. "Why don't we brainstorm for a name later?

Chris suddenly unpetrified and wanted to name it 'brainstorm'. And it stuck.

That evening, an hour after Chris was asleep, Andrew was in the living room, studying a parts' manual for his Pitt. He was absorbed, comparing diagrams and specifications.

He was aware that Madeleine had come down the stairs into the living room but he hadn't looked up from the book. After a short time, he sensed she hadn't taken a seat anywhere. And hadn't said anything. He looked up.

He was struck by her beauty. She stood poised against the french doors, the black silk nightgown clinging, her long, full chestnut hair combed out and flowing over the front of her shoulders. Her lips and eyes were lightly made up, and her eyes were fixed on Andrew. She didn't say a word. She didn't move a muscle.

He gently set the book down on the lamp table. He got up and walked to her, not taking his eyes from hers. He gently kissed her lips. He lifted her and carried her upstairs.

CHAPTER ELEVEN

In the theater room at the FBI offices, Lawrence and his assistant, Cummings, watched a surveillance tape on a large screen. There was no audio. Senator Bloom was depositing four envelopes into a mail slot at a Philadelphia post office.

Cummings said, "Each envelope's $5,000. They're all addressed to a PO box in Trenton. The box is registered to a fictitious company."

The film cut to a heavy, middle-aged man inserting a key into a tiny, silver, post office box door in a wall of tiny, silver doors. "Trenton," Cummings said. The man opened the door and withdrew the four envelopes. "This guy's been identified. There's nothing on him."

Lawrence said, "A courier. Won't know anything useful. But keep a tail on him."

The man inserted the four envelopes into a larger envelope which was already addressed and stamped. He put it into a mail slot. Cummings said, "The envelope went to Newark. Another PO box. Presumably a shake off."

The film cut to a smartly-dressed woman in her thirties in the Newark post office, glancing around as she withdrew the large envelope from the box and inserted it into an even larger envelope. "This time to Valley Forge. Funny, uh? Tiny post office. An easy tail."

Lawrence countered, "But also easier to know if it's being tailed. It would make sense, wouldn't it, that The Watcher might have eyes and ears in those post offices and has already figured what we're doing."

Cummings said, "But if he knows, the natural thing to do would be to leave the envelopes there untouched."

"But that would tell us he knows." Lawrence pondered. "If he does know, why is he keeping it moving?"

Cummings said, "The downside for him, we see more of his couriers.

More links. He's exposing himself more in doing that."

Lawrence was quiet a few moments. "But he's confident that's of little or no consequence to him. Listen, I think if he didn't know the money was being watched, he would have collected it by now. I think he's decided to keep us believing he doesn't know anything, that he's still cleaning the route. But I don't like it. He may be playing us for time."

Cummings bristled. "You're thinking he may make a play for Bloom?"

"Possibly. Those letters he does, flexes his muscles to his victims. He may be assessing Bloom's routines right now. Calculating the best opportunity for a hit."

Cummings nodded. "He's bold enough to try it."

Lawrence's finger played along his lip. "We can't risk Bloom being exposed any longer. I want him underground, into a safe house. He's to let on he's come down with the flu or something. The Watcher may make a move, show his hand, give us something to work with."

CHAPTER TWELVE

Lawrence's father and mother and his sister, Marilyn, lived in a modest house in Coatesville, an hour west of Philadelphia. When Lawrence visited, he always first went to Marilyn's separate entrance at the back of the house. She was his kid sister, forty-one, six years younger than Lawrence.

He gave a tap at the door, then opened it an inch. "Can I come in?"

"Please please do." Her voice was light, like a feather on your skin. Her smile was always there, her beautiful eyes radiant. But there was also another impression which always caused Lawrence to catch himself. Her body seemed always a little frailer, the wheelchair always a little bigger. He leaned forward and they gave each other a long hug.

"It's so good to see you, Wes. You look so terrific."

"So do you. The prettiest sister anyone ever had."

She smiled, taking the compliment with grace.

Marilyn had been married only four years when she was diagnosed with multiple sclerosis. Paralysis progressed quickly and when she was only thirty-two she was in a wheelchair. Stresses in her marriage resulted in a consensual divorce a year later. There were no children. She moved back home.

She and their parents had moved here from the home near Buffalo, the home Lawrence had grown up in, to be closer to Lawrence in Philadelphia. Their father was not a keen driver, especially in the direction of bustling Philadelphia, so the visits were one way only, which suited Lawrence in any case.

Lawrence took the handles of the wheelchair and pushed her along the hall and up a shallow ramp to a small open elevator connecting to the main floor of the house.

She said, "Have you now got things the way you want at the cottage?"

"Getting there. Still working on the new dock."

"I can't wait to spend some time there. That day is coming, right?"

"I'll finally get some holidays later in the summer. And then we're on."

In fact, there was no new dock. Lawrence hadn't told her what he was really building was a wheelchair ramp into the cottage and a long boardwalk down to a wonderful new deck at the lake's edge for her. She would be knocked out when she saw it.

They gained the main floor where the smell of mother's roast beef dinner made Lawrence salivate.

"Oh, Wes," his mother's arms reached, hands in oven mitts, eyes tearing when she saw him. Father was very proud of his son and shook hands and clapped him on the back.

His parents respected that Lawrence could say very little about his work, so his father always just said how good he felt about the work that Lawrence must be doing and the weight of responsibility that must be on his shoulders. Lawrence would only give a small nod.

Dinner conversations were largely recollections about the good times they had had as a family, childhood years, teenage years, the years before Lawrence got into policing. Many of the colorful incidents became a regular staple and took on a new life of their own, to the point where actual recollection and creative recollection blended into one happy reminiscence. And what did it really matter anyway? They were a family having fun, sharing love around a table.

After the meal, after the coffee, after Lawrence had looked at his watch twice, his mother would say, "Well, Wes, we know you have to get going. We miss you. But you're a man with a lot of responsibility."

After the hugs with mom and dad, Lawrence would always take a few minutes alone with Marilyn. She would look at him with unabashed admiration. She never wanted him to go.

Always her last words to Lawrence were the same. "You don't know how proud mom and dad are of you."

And the words would again stab him in the heart.

They would all go outside to the front, final hugs all around. Lawrence would get into the car. Father would step around behind the wheelchair, his hands on the handles. Lawrence would smile and wave goodbye from the car. They would give a round of waves back. As he drove away, he would toot the horn.

And always he would think at that moment - if they only knew. Knew what he had done, who he really was. Often he could not hold off the pain and guilt that again freshly clawed his insides. If they only knew how their three lives dangled on a thread...all his doing. But there was nothing he could do about it. Nothing.

CHAPTER THIRTEEN

From informants in the Philadelphia FBI office and the Philadelphia P.D., Nix learned that Bloom had been moved to a safe house. But its location was so confidential, none of the informants knew its address. To have them probe deeper could put them at too much risk.

Cavaco had accepted that, confident he could learn of its location through indirect means. He had told Nix to have the informants merely provide the names of two agents who were detailed to do shifts at the safe-house. "Even an agent on safe-house duty gets to go home after a shift."

The Watcher's surveillance cell watched the homes of two agents for two days. Late the second afternoon, one of the agents kissed his wife good-bye at the front door, got into his Honda Civic, and drove himself to the FBI office. He did not know he was being followed.

There he met up with another agent, and together, dressed in plain-clothes, they were driven from the office by a third agent. Unknown to them, they were followed into an old residential neighborhood in Cedar Park in West Philadelphia to a stately, two-story, yellow brick house set well back on a large, treed lot. They were dropped off to begin their 7 p.m. to 7 a.m. shift.

The following night a black Camero drove in that neighborhood passing slowly by the yellow brick house. All the windows of the home were curtained. Outside lights lit up parts of the spacious grounds.

Nix was driving, Cavaco in the passenger seat. Both studied the safe house as they passed. Nix said, "Bloom's calls are forwarded here so he can maintain the appearance he's still at home. The phone is answered here by a Philadelphia policewoman posing as a housekeeper. The phone is tapped. All calls are recorded and traced. Two heavily armed SWAT team members are inside around the clock. Bloom never comes out. A next to impossible hit."

"Next to impossible. Not impossible. There was a phone booth at that last side street."

Nix looked to Cavaco, who said, "Tell me what do you think of this."

———•———

Two mornings later, Nix, wearing a dark suit and carrying a black leather briefcase - quintessentially lawyer - walked through the front door of a squat, professional office building. He didn't take the elevator. It was always too slow for him. Taking two steps at a time, he climbed the three flights of stairs to the top floor. He strode a length of corridor stopping at a stout oak door which proclaimed, 'Lorne Nix, Attorney-at-law.'

He unlocked the door and entered the outer office. It contained a reception/secretarial desk and two waiting chairs, although there had never been a receptionist or secretary or even clients. He locked the door behind him and pressed four keys on a number pad on the wall just above the baseboard. He walked past the desk, across thickly luxurious carpet to another door, unlocked it, and entered an inner office.

Again, he locked the door behind him. Again, there was excessively plush carpet, and on two walls hung heavy Persian carpets, all suited to muffle sound. There was a large desk with a phone, a wall of recessed shelving filled with legal textbooks, and a deep leather swivel chair. Set near the window was another table, massive mahogany, on which sat a radio transmitter, a microphone, and two reel to reel tape recorders. And on one of the walls were the stuffed heads of two real tigers, teeth exposed in an open, snarling mouth, eyes piercing.

He glanced at his watch, 9:50 a.m., then looked out the window. Dark clouds were building. The weather report called for light rain all afternoon and evening, a helpful backdrop to tonight's doings, he thought.

He took off his suit jacket and threw it over the chair. He sat at the table. He switched on the transmitter and turned the frequency dial. From his briefcase he withdrew a thin, 3 ring black binder displaying several colored tabs.

He opened the binder and flipped to the blue tab. His finger ran down a list of hotel names. He glanced again at his watch. 9:55.

———•———

In an upscale, high rise condominium several miles from Nix's office, Allan Kell sat at a table by a window with the drapes drawn. He was in his mid-twenties, clean cut, good looking. He glanced at his watch. 9:57 a.m.

A small ham radio sat on the table. He raised its antenna and switched it on. He located a particular frequency, then opened a thin, 3 ring binder with several colored tabs, identical to Nix's.

At precisely 10:00 a.m. Nix's voice came over the radio. "Group three. Frequency K. Group three. Frequency K."

Kell quickly changed the frequency to K, a coded reference to a specific frequency. Sometimes, during a long message, the frequency was changed three or four times for enhanced security. Fifteen seconds later, Nix spoke. "Blue Martha. Blue Martha."

Kell's finger opened the blue tab. On the left side of the page was a column of twenty women's names in alphabetical order. Opposite each name, in a column on the right, was the name of a hotel and the city in which it was located. Kell drew his finger quickly down to M. 'Martha' was the Hotel Clarendon, Philadelphia.

Nix said, "Blue Martha. 18 dash 115. 18 dash 115. 18 dash 115."

Beside 'Hotel Clarendon', Kell jotted '6pm, rm 511'. The room number was always given backwards.

Nix said, "End transmission."

Two years earlier, Kell had been offered big money for small jobs, such as delivering a parcel to a bus station locker without asking questions. He felt he had been hand-selected, and he was honored. He was paid well because he was clean - meaning he had no criminal record, had never been fingerprinted, was unknown to the police, was not on anyone's radar. Clean.

And smart, fit, and single. Those were the hiring criteria. All prerequisites.

Soon Kell was paid bigger money for bigger tasks, such as driving a car stashed with dirty cash across a border. Then one day he came home to find a short wave radio transmitter/receiver in his apartment. He had made the big time. He was an enforcement cell member, one of the elite employed by The Watcher for more daring tasks, with pay commensurate to risk. Very handsome pay. No quibble on that score. More than he could ever make doing anything else.

Next to the money, Kell liked the anonymity. Cell members didn't know each other's real names. You just chose a name, first names only, whatever you wanted. He decided on Zeus - exotic, godly, maybe a little over the top. It seemed the other guys had little imagination, happy to be called, for example, 'Steve'. Steve was short; there was that going for it. And it was generic.

Kell came to respect how precise, how thorough, the planning was for the assignments. Things always went like clockwork, tickety-boo. No cell member ever got hurt. No cell member ever got arrested. But if you ever were, and nobody had ever been, you were promised the best defense attorneys money could buy. All without cost to you. And so long as you kept quiet, wads of money would be yours. But if you weren't quiet, you soon would be, and on a permanent basis. There was no doubting that. Kell had been on enough assignments to know that The Watcher's reach was long and unerring.

At 5:55 p.m., Kell walked the last block to the Hotel Clarendon. He checked automatically for any sign of a setup, any car that might be an unmarked police car, any man or woman too stationary or too observant. The police were usually better than that, of course, but not always. Kell knew he always ran a risk. That's why the money was so good. Higher risk, higher return.

He entered the hotel alert to anything and everything and, as per policy, took the stairs, not the elevator. Fewer eyes. Nobody ever took the stairs but rambunctious kids.

He knocked the customary signal on the door of room 511. The door was opened by Leader, not only his name but also his function. Sitting close around a table were the others of the cell: Steve, Franks, and Smithy. Kell didn't actually know any of them, never saw any of them ever except on a job.

Kell took a chair. There was no talk among them, no smiles or ges- tures of familiarity or even connection. They were focused solely on the information to be obtained for this job.

Leader set an 8" x 11" glossy picture on the table. It depicted a stately old home on a large residential lot, and captured the dimensions of house and lot. "That's a safe house. Inside is Senator Bloom."

Leader set down a second glossy. "That's Bloom. We're terminating him. He's guarded by two FBI SWAT and a policewoman."

Kell could feel new tension in the room. Franks and Smithy glanced around, catching the eyes of the others. There were small nervous movements, a chair pushed back, hands pressed together. This was not the cell's first kill, but it was their first time up against SWAT members.

Leader looked around to each member. "I know what you're feeling. Naturally we're expecting collateral damage. But all on their side. It's a good plan. And payment's double."

He leaned forward and put his finger on the house picture. "Now here's exactly how we're going to do it."

CHAPTER FOURTEEN

It was raining lightly and very dark just before 10 p.m. when a black Lincoln slowed and pulled to the curb. Steve was driving, Leader beside him. Kell, Franks, and Smithy were in the back. Leader glanced down a side street and saw the payphone booth thirty feet away.

All was quiet but the lazy sweeping of the windshield wipers as Leader peered down the block to the safe house. The street was empty, no walkers to consider. The safe house was not visible from the payphone itself. After a few moments, Leader looked at those in the back and nodded. "Okay. Let's do it."

Steve killed the engine. Kell, Franks, and Smithy, wearing black trench coats, left the car, one at a time, thirty seconds apart. Kell and Franks walked on the sidewalk on opposite sides of the street. Smithy hustled around the block to approach the house from the other end.

Two minutes later Leader saw Smithy's flashlight go on and off twice. So the perimeter of the property was clear.

Leader got out of the car and walked to the phone booth.

In the safe house, the two FBI agents were in the living room reading the newspaper and eating Chinese. They wore vests and large-caliber revolvers. Two M-16 automatic rifles were racked nearby. On the second floor in a bedroom, Bloom read work papers at a desk.

The cell knew that The Watcher had not been able to determine which bedroom the senator used. Were it known, it would be child's play. So this was plan B.

Kell crouched in a shadowed length of brick wall. To his left about six feet, and to his right about six feet, were curtained-shut first floor windows. Up the brick wall to the second storey were two windows again, one to Kell's left, one to his right. Kell studied those windows. Both were curtained and dark.

In the payphone booth, Leader switched on a two-way radio and quietly said, "Clear?"

At the house, Kell whispered, "Clear."

Leader now dialed the payphone. He held the radio close to the speaker.

Inside the house, a phone rang downstairs and upstairs. The two SWAT agents continued to read and eat, taking no obvious notice. A uniformed policewoman passed through the living room and quickly climbed the stairs.

Kell could hear the phone ringing softly in his radio. He watched the two second floor windows and waited.

Cavaco had speculated that the forwarded calls would be taken by Bloom on the second floor where he would have privacy. The problem was, in which room was the phone? The telephone company kept records of phones and locations. They did not know it was a safe house; nobody was to know that, of course. So they were helpful in answering an enquiry from the apparent owner of the house who was helpless in matters of phones, and who wanted to put in another phone upstairs 'for Grandma'. The company patiently explained there was already one phone on the second floor. Did the caller wish a second phone installed on the second floor? The caller appeared directionally challenged and could only understand the conversation if told which street side the room with the current phone was. Cavaco soon had what he needed.

The policewoman reached the second floor and entered a small den and snapped on a light. A ringing phone sat on a desk, recording equipment hooked underneath. She hit a button on a recorder, then picked up the phone. "Hello."

Kell heard the 'Hello' over the radio. A moment before, he had seen a sliver of light appear at the edge of the curtain on the window above him and to the right.

At the payphone, Leader said, "Is Harold in? I'm a friend from college days. Gerry Walker." There was a pause. Kell could hear it all. Leader continued, "I've been away. Just heard the dreadful news about his wife. I was hoping to pass on my condolences."

The policewoman said. "Okay. I'll get him for you." She put down the phone and exited the room.

Franks and Smithy were fifty yards away and fifty yards from each other, watchful of any hostile movement. Kell waved to them and they sprinted over into the shadows. Kell moved to his right, directly under that second floor window.

Bloom entered the den and picked up the phone. "Hello, Gerry?"

Leader, muffling his voice said, "Harold? Is that you. I can't hear you?"

Franks and Smithy hoisted Kell to their shoulders and braced him with their arms. He was eight feet directly below the window. Kell's outstretched left hand rested against the wall. Through the radio they could hear Bloom faintly say, "Gerry? You're not clear."

In his right hand, Kell held a brick sized metal object, an explosive device with a two second delay. He lowered his right arm and with a strong thrust pitched the object at the window. The window smashed. Kell hit the ground. The three scrambled from the wall.

A grand explosion followed, the window and frame and adjoining brick blasting outward.

In the living room, the two agents dived grabbing for their rifles.

As Smithy and Franks ran, each produced a short, Uzi submachine gun from under their trench coat. They and Kell were almost across the treed side of the property as the Lincoln approached. Smithy and Franks each dropped behind a different stout elm to cover the Lincoln.

One of the agents burst from a side door. Smithy already had his gun trained on it and squeezed the trigger for a full two seconds, riddling the agent who slumped forward in the doorway.

Franks was covering the second floor. He saw a window smash and the policewoman jabbed a rifle out firing wildly at Smithy. Frank's angle and firepower completely surprised her. He emptied half a magazine, dancing her like a rag doll back into the room.

The Lincoln slowed to a roll grabbing up Kell and sped on another half block out of firing angle from the house. Shots from the second agent began from a ground floor window. Franks and Smithy fired bursts simultaneously from their two divergent angles. The agent retreated into the room. Continuing to fire, Franks and Smithy in four precious seconds sprinted the half block to the Lincoln, jumped in, and it sped away.

Lawrence was on the highway when he heard the news on the radio. "Senator Bloom has been killed tonight along with an FBI agent and a Philadelphia policewoman in a downtown home. Another agent has been rushed to hospital with life threatening injuries. Details are sketchy, but it is believed Bloom was being sequestered by the police for reasons at present unknown. Neighbors reported that an explosion, like a bomb blast, occurred at 10:10, followed by about a minute of intermittent, automatic gunfire. There have been no arrests and there is no word on who is responsible. We will provide updates as we learn more."

Lawrence felt his body shaking. He pulled off the highway and parked. He got out and stood by the car.

The Watcher knew. Found the house. Knew the set up, everything. Our information isn't secure.

A feeling of sickness hit him like a wave. His legs weakened and he leaned heavily against the car. He thought he would wretch. He ripped at his collar button, snapping it off. He gulped at the air.

Senator Bloom killed. An FBI agent killed. A policewoman killed. A bold, arrogant assault. Who was The Watcher? He hoped, actually hoped, he **didn't** know. Because what had made him experience the sudden, gripping nausea was the overwhelming fear that he did. And that he was utterly to blame.

CHAPTER FIFTEEN

'Surveillance' comes from the French, meaning 'to watch from above'. And that's what Andrew Locke was doing, flying an FBI Cessna surveillance plane north of Grand Forks, North Dakota. The FBI field office in Minneapolis was responsible for three states: Minnesota, North Dakota, and South Dakota, a very large territory for a medium size office.

For the past four months Andrew had flown surveillance on suspected drug making and dealing operations. In many situations it is impossible to conduct ground surveillance without being discovered, whereas Andrew was far less noticeable at three or four thousand feet. He could make close observations through stabilized binoculars and get to locations quickly. The plane's cameras also produced photographs unobtainable any other way.

This afternoon he was on his way to a suspected lab in a rural property where high fences blocked ground-level view. But no warrant was necessary to fly over it and take a few pictures.

The radio in the Cessna crackled. "Andrew, do you read me?"

"Roger that".

"We have an emergency. We need you on the ground."

That didn't sound good. The only reason they would ever need him on the ground was that he was SWAT trained and a sniper. Because he had been shot twice since becoming an agent, the Bureau thought he should be put on other assignments indefinitely. As he was a trained pilot, the best option was obvious. Madeleine had been overjoyed. She had become dreadfully fearful of Andrew being directly in harm's way again. She never wanted him in another firefight. Now, as far as she and he knew, he wasn't to be so assigned.

"What's up?" Andrew asked.

"A standoff. Three kids, 18 or 19 years old, pulled a robbery on a bank in Devils Lake this morning. The local police have them holed up at a house in a remote area near Starkweather, about thirty miles north, but they're thin on men and experience. The kids have a couple of rifles. They're taking shots from the house. Police can't get within 300 yards."

When he heard that, Andrew knew it was his sniper skills they wanted.

"Andrew, the whole SWAT team is on a domestic gone real bad in Minneapolis. Could be easily until tonight before they can get to Starkweather. We need you to help contain this. Your gear and rifle are being flown to the Devils Lake airport."

"Roger", Andrew said, "I'll be there in forty-five."

———————

A veteran state trooper met Andrew at the airport. As Andrew changed into full SWAT dress, the trooper said, "The kids have been taking potshots at our fellas. Sheriff thinks they may be on drugs. Acting real stupid."

The trooper dropped Andrew five hundred yards from the isolated, red, insulbrick-sided house. Andrew moved out from cover, flattened himself on the ground and studied the landscape. It was mostly barren, a few spindly trees in a wide, low-rolling grassland, two lines of old, gray, split rail fencing going off in different directions. Grazing pasture in better times. But no decent cover anywhere as you got closer.

Two black and whites were parked in a field about three hundred yards from the house, just off the long, narrow lane leading to the house. A policeman and a policewoman crouched behind one of the cars. The Sheriff squatted behind the other. An unmarked cruiser had driven wide over the grassland to cover another side, also out three hundred yards from the house. Two troopers kneeled low behind the unmarked car.

As Andrew crawled zig zag pattern for two hundred yards, a shot rang out. He stopped, head down. Waited. Saw nothing. Heard nothing more. He carried on to the Sheriff.

About forty-five and slim, the Sheriff was talking with forced calm into a radio phone. "Look, Bernie, you got carried away. You didn't mean to take it this far. We know that. And it will go a lot better for you if you just come out peaceful and we can all go home. You don't want to get into a firefight with us."

Bernie retorted, "We've got the same firepower as you." The radio phone's receiver was on maximum volume. Andrew was able to hear everything clearly. The voice was young, squeaky, and Andrew figured, fueled on something unnatural.

"That may be, Bernie," said the Sheriff. "But we're trained in how to shoot them."

"You can't shoot nothing but the breeze. At Dunkin' Donuts." A chorus of high-energy cackling from the kids could be heard. Then Bernie hung up.

The Sheriff gave a look of despair. He turned and saw Andrew, saw the sniper rifle. "Glad you're here. We've been here two hours. With them taking the odd wild shot. My nerves are getting jangled. I've never done this before. Nervous as hell how this thing's gonna end. They're just kids."

"I understand."

The Sheriff said, "What do you think?"

"You're deployed well, a good 'L' formation, no crossfire issues. What about to the south, if they make a run for it?"

"Yeah. I'm worried about that. Sooner or later they might try it. I've got to make them understand they're gonna get themselves killed."

Andrew had never killed anyone. And he didn't want to ever have to. But if he did, he sure didn't want it to be some scared kid.

Andrew viewed the house through his binoculars for thirty seconds. He set them down and picked up his sniper rifle, a Remington 700 with a Leupold scope. He peered through the scope for thirty seconds. Then he picked up the binoculars again and took another look.

Andrew said, "I have an idea. You might say I had a light bulb moment."

"What is it?"

"Well... I see a light bulb."

"Ya, so?"

"The living room window is open."

"Ya, that's where they were shooting out of."

"In the living room, a bare lightbulb, dangling from a cord. About five feet down from the ceiling."

"Ya, so?".

"The kids think they have a chance in some kind of shoot out or break out. They don't, of course. I want to make them see that."

"How you gonna do that?"

"Tell them I'm going to shoot that tiny light bulb. So think what I can do if they ever poke their big heads out to point a gun at us again."

"Okay, good. Worth a try."

The Sheriff grabbed the radio phone and waited for the connection. "A *light bulb* moment," he said to himself, half chuckling, heartened at Andrew's company. "You might even say, it's worth a *shot*."

Andrew smiled. "Okay. We're even with the funny stuff."

The phone was answered. "Ya, whadya want now?" As much as he tried not to, Bernie's nerves were showing.

"Hey, Bernie, listen," said the Sheriff. "Like I said before, I don't want anyone getting hurt here. And like I said, we can shoot a lot better than you can. I want you to look at the light bulb there in that living room. See that tiny light bulb?"

"Ya."

"Well, I have an FBI trained sniper here You can't even see him. He's almost three hundred yards from you. Like three football fields. But he's going to shoot it."

The Sheriff put his hand over the phone and said to Andrew. "One shot?"

Andrew nodded.

"One shot, Bernie. Light bulb gone. Now, think about your head. Bigger than a light bulb. Big as a balloon. You try poking your head out to shoot at us again, you'll already be dead before you can even aim. You think about that tiny light bulb. Do you get me?"

No answer.

"Bernie, you watch that tiny bulb. Then think about your head. Do you get me?

Still no answer.

The Sheriff looked at Andrew and shrugged his shoulders. "Well, I'm hanging up now, Bernie. Keep your heads down in there."

Still no answer. He hung up and nodded to Andrew. "Okay. The show's all yours."

In the military, a sniper hits the enemy in the torso. In the FBI, the sniper must shoot a head shot because a hostage-taker may be holding a gun to a hostage, so you get only one shot and it must totally disable. So the FBI shooting benchmarks are extremely exacting. A trained FBI sniper can hit a business card at 200 yards. At 100 yards, the best graduates can put five rounds into a dime. Andrew had been the top graduate in his sniper class.

But Andrew was nervous. He hadn't been to the practice range in over four months because of the change of assignments, and confidence and accuracy drain quickly without regular, rigorous practice. And a light bulb is only a dot at 300 yards, even in high powered optics.

He had already assessed the weather conditions: about 75 degrees, faint breeze southerly, humidity not an issue. Overall, good shooting conditions.

And he had already begun relaxation exercises. Breath in, hold it for seven seconds, exhale for seven seconds. He repeated the sequence. Repeat. Repeat.

He moved out from behind the car and crawled twenty yards until he found the ground he wanted. He positioned the rifle in front, resting it on the bipod. He lay out his full length. FBI gunsmiths fit the rifle to the individual. This rifle had been made for Andrew and was accurate in the extreme – at least when he had been practicing.

He eased the stock into his shoulder, then tugged it snug. It wasn't true of all rifles, but with his rifle, the first shot, known as the cold shot, was absolutely dead on. Then, as each successive round was fired and the barrel got hotter, he knew the bullets would hit lower and lower. But he desperately wanted the cold shot to do its work.

He continued the breathing exercise as he adjusted his legs to best stabilize himself, digging his right foot back against earth. He looked through the scope and acquired the target. The light bulb's glass looked odd in the optics. And it was bobbing up and down - he wasn't relaxed enough. He felt tension in his left shoulder. He had to be still. He did the breathing sequence twice more. Then a slow release until he was empty. His heart was calmed to a gentle fifty beats a minute.

He eased the trigger until there was no more play. One more breath in, hold, exhale, empty the lungs. The bulb was as still as a picture.

He pulled the trigger.

The recoil punched his shoulder and the explosion carried out across the wide open landscape.

Then dead silence for several moments. Until, "Did you get it? Did you get it?" The Sheriff was calling out from twenty yards behind.

Andrew couldn't find the light bulb in the scope. Dangling from a cord, it would be moving if hit. After a moment it slipped into view, and slowly stopped its gentle swaying. A single, minute shard protruded from the empty socket.

"Got it," Andrew called back.

"Damn," said the Sheriff, his voice cracking with the tension.

They watched the house. Two minutes passed.

The front door opened. Three stringy kids came out in single file, heads down, hands up over their heads. They walked a hundred feet, then stopped and gaped towards the black and whites, eyes searching, waiting for somebody to tell them what to do next.

CHAPTER SIXTEEN

Madeleine paced the livingroom, half watching Chris play with Brainstorm while her mind was really elsewhere. Andrew was very late getting home and no one from the office had called her back. She was fretting as she looked out the window.

The phone rang. She answered it. "Oh, hi. Thanks for calling back." She listened for thirty seconds and her face darkened. Her voice quavered as if she couldn't quite control it. "Oh, I see. Okay, thanks again." She hung up.

"Is Dad coming home soon?"

She walked to the window and stood looking out. Whereas before she fretted, now she seemed tormented. But she spoke evenly and quietly. "He should be here soon. I would like you to go upstairs and finish that project you were working on. Take Brainstorm. I want to talk to Dad."

She resumed looking out the window and paced again more slowly. Soon she sat on the sofa and waited. Then she began to cry lightly.

After an hour, she saw the lights of the car turn into the driveway. She heard the car door shut. Shortly the front door opened. She heard Andrew in the hallway. Then he came into the living room.

He could see she had been crying. He already knew she knew what had happened today.

She said, "You got shot at." There was a roller coaster of concern and upset in her voice.

"I had to go to a standoff. It all went well."

She stood up, protesting, "Andrew, it didn't go well. I was told they *shot* at you."

He could see new tears forming.

"They just took some pot shots. Not specifically at me."

"Pot shots can kill, too! Went well? Just because they didn't hit you this time?" She was getting wound up. "You weren't supposed to be assigned to any SWAT work. Nobody could shoot at you anymore!"

"The SWAT guys were all tied up in a takedown in Minneapolis."

She was now blustery and teary. "They said you would not have to be doing that anymore. They realized you get shot too much. The very last time you were out you got shot. *Again*."

"In the finger."

"Oh well, that's fine of course. Luckily these cold killers only aim at your finger. Very considerate of them."

He went to her and held her. "Maddy, you worry too much."

She began to cry more. "Worry too much?" she sniffled. "You get *shot* too much! You *attract* bullets! *Two* years in the FBI. Get shot *two* different times. Think of a *twenty-five-year* career. Do the math!"

Andrew held her. "Maddy, Maddy."

She burst into fulsome crying. She struggled through her sobbing. "One day... you might not...be coming home."

"Maddy, Maddy." He hugged her tightly.

"You have...Christopher to think about. I worry...so much about you. I can't help it...these days." She was sniffling heavily. "I don't want to ever be without you. Or Chris...to ever be without his Dad. You're everything to him."

"Hey, now, hey, I'm always going to come home."

"Ya, sure," she grabbed a tissue from the table. She was sniffling. "Sure you are, Superman."

CHAPTER SEVENTEEN

The next day when Andrew arrived home from work, he called out with excitement from the hallway. "Madeleine!"

She came from the kitchen. "What is it?"

He was waving an envelope. "I've got fabulous news! When I got back today, my SAC took me into his office and told me I'm being reassigned. He handed me this sealed letter. It was couriered, private and confidential. We're going home, Maddy!"

Her eyes were wide. "Philadelphia?"

"Yes! And it's just surveillance and flying."

Madeleine grabbed him, tears springing. "Oh, Andrew."

Madeleine's younger sister, Nadine, was in college in Philadelphia and they were close. And her parents were retired and living in Hershey, just two hours away.

"This is a very special assignment. Super classified."

"What's that mean?"

"It means I'm going underground. Not even other agents are to know about this, not where we're going, not what I'm doing. We can't tell friends anything except that I've been transferred east. I'm told we should be able to let them know things in a few months."

They sat on the sofa. "No one is to know I'm in Philadelphia except one person, the SAC in Philadelphia, Wesley Lawrence. Madeleine, he's the guy I once told you about. He knew my father. He used to bring me presents when I was a kid, model airplanes. We built them together. He's the only one who will know I'm there. I get my assignments from him. I report only to him. I have no contact with other agents. Working solo."

"So you don't go to an office?"

"No. The instructions emphasize the absolute secrecy that must surround this assignment. People we meet in Philadelphia, like neighbors, or anyone else, can't know I work for the FBI. Total secrecy."

"Sounds like an internal problem in the Bureau or something if you can't even meet other agents."

"Possibly. I'll get all the answers when I get there. Another thing, the house is to be rented in your name alone for now. Your maiden name. Same for the phone line."

"Wow. You really are going underground. Can you still be my husband or what?"

He laughed. "That isn't changing. And I won't be in harm's way. No more getting shot at."

She wrapped her arms around his neck and kissed him. "That's the main thing. And let's keep it the main thing. I've got to thank this Mr. Lawrence. What a wild coincidence."

A second confidential letter arrived two days later. Andrew was to report to Lawrence, but to maintain confidentiality, not at his office, not at any office. And not at a hotel room or Lawrence's house, where you would expect privacy. No, the meeting was to be at Lawrence's very remote cottage. And Andrew was to get himself there not by car, but by plane. Fly himself. And not in a Bureau plane, or a rented plane, but in Andrew's own Pitt. And land at a grass airstrip on some farmer's field a mile from the cottage.

To Andrew these arrangements seemed exceedingly strange. This took secrecy to a whole new level. Was there precedent in the Bureau for anything like this? He was only a junior agent, while Wesley Lawrence was a SAC with twenty plus years' experience. Who was Andrew to question? There would be method in the madness. It would be made clear to him.

Still, Andrew thought, what am I doing, a junior agent, in what is clearly a sensitive, probably complex, probably internal investigation. How do I really fit in? What can I bring to the table? How am I the best candidate?

The obvious kept recurring to Andrew - his long ago connection to Lawrence figured in this somehow. The coincidence was just too high. Was Andrew getting favored because he had been shot twice, and Lawrence somehow knew about it, knew Andrew was even in the FBI and pulled some strings? If so, why hadn't he at any time in the past few years ever communicated, just some small acknowledgment of Andrew?

They had not spoken since Andrew was twelve.

Andrew knew more was expected of him by the Bureau than SWAT work and flying. Perhaps, he thought, the Bureau wanted to direct his career into complex investigation work and this assignment would begin a close mentoring. But such a direction had never actually been discussed with him by anyone.

He felt uneasiness at this second letter. He decided not to tell Madeleine about it for now. It might cause her to be uneasy, too. Better he waited to get some answers. She had worried about him long enough, and she seemed to be doing better now about the baby. This could be the new chapter she needed, to let her settle in and be really happy again.

CHAPTER EIGHTEEN

A ndrew was flying the Pitt easterly at two thousand feet in a taut blue sky over Schuylkill County eighty miles north of Philadelphia.

A mile ahead, the tiny tell-tale lake now appeared, right where it should be. He looked north and soon spotted the wind sock he needed to find, lightly waving atop a thirty-foot red pole, the grass airstrip running parallel to a long field planted in crop.

He eased the joystick forward and dropped to five hundred feet. Lawrence had made arrangements with the current farmer and as Andrew dropped further and made a quick pass, he observed that the grass had been cut low on the runway.

But he did not want to land yet. He pulled back on the joy stick and gained altitude, banked sharply, then turned south. In a few moments he spotted Lawrence's green-roofed cottage, a mile south of the airstrip in a clearing of about three acres fronting on the tiny, land-locked lake. No other cottages or buildings were visible for miles. Lawrence had said he owned a hundred and twenty acres. Andrew could see Lawrence's private lane snaking its way a half mile along the length of his very private property in from the public road.

He flew over the cottage, dropping to eight hundred feet, and made a tight circle. The cottage was back about a hundred feet from the lake. At the front, a large open verandah faced the lake and the pristine woods which surrounded the lake. Very private. Lawrence had the lake all to himself.

Turning north, Andrew shortly saw the windsock lifting in the westerly ten knot breeze. He made an easy landing, then set out on the twenty-minute walk along an old tractor path that ended near Lawrence's cottage.

As he approached the cottage he could hear music on a stereo, something classical. Large flower beds beautified the place. A new, cedar, wheelchair ramp accessed a side door. Sono tubes and cedar framing marked the beginnings of a hundred-foot ramp running down to a newly built cedar deck at the water's edge.

Andrew knocked at the door. It opened almost immediately. They looked appraisingly at each other. Then Lawrence, smiling warmly, offered his hand. "Welcome, Andrew."

They went into the cottage which was furnished simply but adequately.

Lawrence asked, "Any trouble finding the place?"

Andrew said, "None at all. Everything just as you said."

"Very good. Can I offer you a drink? A beer?"

"The Pitt doesn't like it when I drink. Anything else would be fine, Sir."

"No need to call me 'Sir'. Please call me Wes." Lawrence got two cokes from the fridge. He said, "So you got a place and you're in?"

"Yes. A cardiologist was setting off to sail around the world. Wanted someone responsible to take care of his house for eight months. He was very taken with Madeleine. It's beautiful, and furnished, so our stuff can stay in storage."

Lawrence poured the cokes into tall glasses. "And your plane? Does it have a home?" He handed Andrew a glass.

"Yes. I got a hangar and flying privileges at an aerodrome just north of the city."

"Good. Good." Lawrence held up his glass towards Andrew. "Here's to working together."

Andrew smiled and raised his glass. "To working together."

Lawrence went to the stereo and turned it off. "Please, take a seat," he said and motioned Andrew into the living room. Its walls and ceiling were pine planked. The view of the lake was magnetic.

Andrew asked, "How long have you had this place...Wes?"

"Three years. Took me a while to find it. Quiet, remote, no phone, no traffic, no nosy neighbors. Only one road in and one road out, and a long and winding road at that."

"I saw you're doing some major work outside, the wheelchair ramping, and access to the lake."

"Yes," Lawrence said. "My sister has M.S. She and my folks live in

Coatesville."

Lawrence took a drink and said, with a note of sadness, "Andrew, you were only twelve when I saw you last."

"Yes," Andrew said, surprised that Lawrence would remember exactly how old Andrew was. "I remember the day well. We made two planes. I see one of them sitting on your bookcase there. A Sopwith Camel."

Lawrence smiled and nodded. "That is so. You insisted I take one home and that I come back in the spring and we fly them together." Lawrence sighed and the smile was then gone. "I'm very sorry, Andrew, that I didn't make it back."

"That's okay, Wes. You had your own busy life. I really appreciated you for your contact those years. You know, other than social workers, you were the only adult person who visited me after my dad was gone."

Lawrence looked genuinely sorry. "I should have visited you more. Done more."

"No, Wes. I'm grateful for the times you did come. You were someone I could look up to. Someone who reached through the mess of my world back then. Gave me …something to aspire to."

Lawrence seemed to want to dismiss the compliment. He said, "I remember you asking me that last time whether there were any leads of any kind in your Dad's case. And I had to say 'no'. Five years had passed since your Dad was taken. I knew you still held out some dim hope for him. But there were no leads. Nothing. You were older and understood more. You were gravely disappointed."

"You knew that at the time?"

"I felt it."

Andrew had never considered what Lawrence might have felt. But that was long ago. "Well, I really appreciated your visits back then. But I knew you had a lot of other obligations."

Lawrence looked at his glass a few moments, as if remembering a sadness. "You're being charitable to me to say that, Andrew. I did get too busy. But I should have visited you. You don't know how much I wish things had been different for you…and for me."

After a moment he looked at Andrew and his face cheered. "But you have turned out to be such a man. You are the spitting image of your father. He would have been proud."

"How well did you know my father?"

"Well enough to know that you were the world to him."

"Did you socialize together?"

"No, but we worked together a lot. I was the liaison man at the FBI field office in Philadelphia. Your Dad was liaison officer for the Philadelphia P.D. We worked on a number of joint task forces together, face to face." Lawrence eyes looked down and his hands moved the glass in a small circle, his voice solemn, honoring a memory. "He was an excellent detective. An excellent man. And, I know, an excellent father."

After a moment, Lawrence said. "But, Andrew, tell me about Madeleine and your son."

"She and Chris are everything to me. Chris is five, and... just great. And Maddy, when I met her, my life did a 180. We're very happy. She was ecstatic to be coming back to Philadelphia."

"I had some idea."

"Her sister is here and they're close. Her parents are only a couple of hours away. We're very grateful to you. She would love to have you over, to meet you, to thank you."

"That's kind of you. Tell Madeleine I'm happy for you both. But, for now, that cannot be arranged. This is a unique assignment. You might even say ...peculiar. You and I, Andrew, are never to be seen together. We cannot be known to talk together. No other agent here must ever know of you. I want you totally insulated. It's just you and me. Nobody but Washington knows you're here."

"Exceptional measures," Andrew said.

"Exceptional problems." Lawrence said. "The assignment is more important than I can explain right now. It's absolutely critical that no one knows you and I have any connection. Success depends on it."

Lawrence set his glass away and leaned forward, his hands clasped together. "Highly confidential information is leaking out of our office, or the office of the Philadelphia P.D., I don't know which. Perhaps it's both. We're being sold out. A drug raid failed. A take down failed. I believe they knew we were coming. And a leak led to the recent assassination of Senator Bloom. We're working on rooting out the informants. But in the meantime, to protect the secrecy of some key investigations, I needed someone working alone with me. Someone not known in my office or in the Philly P.D. Someone capable of independent action. Someone with whom I share select information, information held back from everyone else so no informant knows the whole picture."

"So I'm not at all involved in any internal investigation?"

"That's correct. You will carry out surveillance in high priority out-side work."

That eased Andrew's mind somewhat, but still.... "Why me, Wes? There would be others more qualified. I'm frankly puzzled."

Lawrence smiled. "I would be disappointed in you if you weren't. You fulfill many requirements. No agent here knows you. You know the city. You know this part of the country. You are SWAT trained."

"I didn't think my SWAT skills were being called on."

"Well, that is so. The SWAT skills are just, let's say, a bonus. Also, not many agents are pilots. And not many who are own their own plane, and in particular, a stunt plane. Nobody would ever suspect you're law enforcement."

"How is my flying my Pitt integral to this assignment?"

"It's only one aspect of it. You will do text-book ground surveillance. But I see covert aerial surveillance as possibly making a difference in the success of some of our investigations. Washington agreed. We will be maintaining our conventional aerial surveillance, so no one on the inside suspects anything has changed. But, like all our information, I believe it may become compromised. Moreover, the bad guys are becom-ing aware of our planes. They have their eyes to the sky, too. No one would ever believe you're the law. That's how I sold Washington on *your* particular transfer here, with your Pitt. They thought it was rather... special."

Andrew had to smile. "Probably unique in the annals of Bureau history."

"You and I alone will know certain information. It can't be leaked that way. Which brings me to the final criterion I had." Lawrence stud-ied Andrew a few serious moments. "I needed someone whom I could trust implicitly. Without question. Without fail."

Andrew felt honored. He nodded affirmation. "Yes, of course, Wes."

Lawrence smiled. "Thank you, Andrew."

Lawrence reached for his glass and took a long drink. Then setting it away again, he said, "Now, onto some housekeeping." He clasped his hands together. "As for communication, we never meet face to face any-where except *here*. Our only other contact is by phone. You will never call me at the office from your home phone because all incoming numbers are recorded and can be traced. You will always use a payphone. And you will always just say "It's Harry." Also never call me at home except from a payphone, because, again, there must never be a traceable link between you and me."

Andrew said, "Understood."

"I want you to install a *second* phone in your house with an *unlisted* number, registered in Madeleine's maiden name. An answering machine is to be connected. The phone is never to be answered. And no calls out are ever to be made. One-way communication only. If I need to reach you, I will phone from a payphone and leave a message. Should I ever leave that message, call me at my office, my direct line. Call in on the hour until we connect."

Later, after Lawrence had queried Andrew more precisely on his field work experience, Lawrence gave a generous smile and said, "Andrew, you know, I'm even more impressed with you than I had hoped to be. I feel certain things are going to go well. One more thing, I've decided I can make a small exception to our basic rules, just for one occasion. I would like to see Madeleine and Chris. Not meet them, just see them, from a distance, to see you three together. You must not acknowledge me whatsoever. They must not know we have any connection. I eat at Franky's in the Bella Vista district on Thursday nights. Why don't you take a table near me at 6:00?"

Andrew smiled at the notion. "Thank you, Wes. I would love you to see them. Just *see* them. And I would think between you and me, we could pull off just such a covert action."

Lawrence laughed and slapped Andrew on the back.

CHAPTER NINETEEN

The cardiologist's home they rented was Cape Cod style with large dormers in a mature neighborhood of Chestnut Hill with beautiful, tree-lined streets. The property boasted a deep, tree-studded backyard backing onto a green belt. Madeleine was smitten.

When Andrew got home the sun was pouring through the windows, the stereo cranked high. Madeleine was dancing with a broom in the living room. Diana Ross was singing "Someday...we'll be together."

Madeleine saw Andrew but just eyed him romantically as she kept dancing and mouthing the words, loving the music, pointing her finger to Andrew, "... you you you possess my soul, honey.... and I know you possess my heart..."

They danced out the song clutching each other, with Chris now watching from the hall embarrassed for them. When the song finished, they embraced in a long kiss.

Madeleine turned off the stereo. "How did it all go?"

"Went well."

"Can you tell me a little more?"

"Not really. Only that I'll be flying in the Pitt."

"What?"

"Ya. All part of the covert aspect. It seems the Pitt is what got us here. My distinguishing feature."

Madeleine broke into a wide smile. "Well thank you Pitt!"

"Also, Lawrence wants me to have a *second* phone line. It's to be an unlisted number and have an answering machine. You're to set it up in your maiden name. Cloak and dagger, uh?"

"I feel like I'm living with James Bond." She reached and kissed him. "Oh," she suddenly remembered, excited, "the neighborhood is gathering for a back yard party tonight two doors down, and the people across the road insisted we come along. They said the hostess always invites *all* the neighbors. So we're just to come along. I know you don't want to draw much attention to ourselves but we can't appear antisocial. They insisted and I couldn't say no. It's good to know who your neighbors are. And I *really* want to see inside that house." She started for the kitchen. "And dinner's almost ready."

Andrew called out. "Where is that buckaroo? Time for bucking bronco?"

Chris raced down the hall and into the living room. "Yes!"

Andrew got down on all fours. Chris clambered onto Andrew's back lashing his arms under Andrew's chest and squeezing his legs. Andrew started slowly, a lazy, uninspired bronco.

Chris spurred with his heels, "Come on, horsey. Go!"

Andrew sped the action, heaving up and down, Chris squeezing to stay on.

Madeleine came in. "Where's your lasso?"

Chris managed to raise a hand above his bouncing head and made a twirl.

Andrew laid it on now, snorting and bucking, his hands popping off the floor, his back rearing.

Madeleine was laughing. "You sound like a frantic pig."

Andrew intensified the herky jerky and worked in side to side action too. Chris was mostly airborne with little hope of hanging on.

Madeleine said, "I've got to finish rustling up some grub for you cowboys," and went into the kitchen.

Chris finally bounced off. Andrew rolled over on his back on the carpet and stretched out, breathing hard. "Horsey ...needs a rest." He closed his eyes and lay still, catching his breath.

Chris walked in a big circle a couple of times, then walked over to Andrew. He sat down on Andrew's stomach.

Chris's demeanor had changed. "Dad," his voice carried sorrow, "did your dad play bronco with you?"

Andrew said, "Yes, he did."

"Did your dad love you like you love me?"

Andrew opened his eyes and looked at Chris. "Yes."

"You aren't ever going to leave me, are you?"

Andrew lifted Chris off his stomach and sat up. "No, Chris. I would never leave you. Don't you ever worry about that."

"But your dad left."

"With my dad, it was different. It was like... an accident...he couldn't avoid."

"Mom worries that you'll have an accident...maybe get shot."

Andrew said, "Mom used to. But not anymore. I don't do what I used to. I don't want you worrying about things that aren't going to happen."

Madeleine yelled, "Dinner!"

Andrew rolled Chris over onto the floor and got himself up onto all fours again. "Hey, this horse is getting mighty hungry. Let's make some tracks, pardner."

Chris mounted and gave a kick and off they road into the kitchen.

That evening, as Andrew and Madeleine were getting dressed to go to the neighbor's party, Andrew said, "Okay, so remember about my work, what you're going to say if asked."

Madeleine was putting in her earrings at the mirror. "I know. I know. You work for the government as an analyst. Usually that's enough to make anyone's eyes glaze over and they go away. But if anyone asks more, I just say that you're on a project for the US Department of Commerce, Bureau of Economic Analysis. That way, if one of us accidentally mentions 'Bureau', it's *that* Bureau. And if that doesn't deliver the knock-out punch, I'm to say, 'Well, I don't understand what 'gross domestic product' is. Do you?' And they say, 'No.' And I say, "So, where can I get some good shoes in this town?"

She stood back and assessed the earrings. "Did I pass?"

Andrew didn't look up from tying his shoes. "You're very good, you know."

At the backyard party under the garden lanterns, hostess Gloria, thirty-five, flamboyant, attractive and very shapely, recently divorced from an older, rich neurosurgeon, and now rich herself, and quickly becoming an alcoholic, took a very obvious liking to Andrew.

She stood close to him. "I understand you're the new neighbor. Only two doors over."

Andrew said, "Yes. Just moved. Wonderful neighborhood."

She took a step closer. "We should become friends," giving him a wide, perfect smile, her eyes dancing lightly as she sipped wine and studied his face.

Andrew showed a noncommittal smile and took a sip of wine.

Gloria sipped more. "What is it you do, Andrew?"

"I'm an analyst."

"Ohhhhhh," she said, implying something mysterious and exciting. "And what is it you analyze?" The way she worked her shoulders and hips and lips suggested he should drop whatever it was he usually analyzed and start analyzing her.

"I work for the government. Boring stuff."

"Oh. So you get ...*bored* sometimes? I know I do." She laughed and touched his hair, her blood alcohol level showing. She stepped a little closer and her leg brushed his.

Andrew took a small step back. "It actually has its challenges."

"I understand, yes, I do. I like *challenges* too. If you know what I mean." Her eyes were flashing at him like Christmas decorations.

"Well if Andrew doesn't, I *certainly* do." From nowhere Madeleine suddenly appeared and inserted herself at extremely close quarters to Gloria. "Hi there," she said in Gloria's face. "I'm Madeleine. I'm Andrew's *wife*." Madeleine's eyes flashed like fireworks on the fourth of July.

Andrew exited to the punch table. Madeleine and Gloria stayed locked in a sparring of eyes. Although Madeleine knew she shouldn't, she was just a little too incensed by Gloria's brazen display, and she said, "I'm not worrying about him straying. But something I really detest is a bold attempt at seduction in my presence. I don't want to ever see that again."

Madeleine wasn't going to say anything more. But it was the way Gloria now looked back at her, a defiance, a challenge, that made Madeleine keep going, her hand knotting at her side. And no doubt a large glass of wine played its part. "Or it'll be a lot harder for you to look at all pretty."

At home after the party Andrew said to Madeleine, "So did you and Gloria get off on the right foot after I left?"

"Gloria? Gloria?" Madeleine feigned nonchalant ignorance. "Oh yes, the hostess. Lovely woman."

"Because the last thing I want to do is antagonize anyone around here, or give anyone any special reason to be curious about me."

"No, Gloria and I are on a grand footing. We had a nice chat. I think we really understand each other."

CHAPTER TWENTY

It was Thursday and they were almost at Franky's.

When Andrew had told Madeleine that he wanted to take them to Franky's, she had said, 'Why?', and he had said, 'To celebrate coming home to Philadelphia.'

And she had said, 'Okay, but why Franky's?' And he had said, 'A recommendation in a tourist book. We're playing tourist. The food's supposed to be very good.'

And she had said, 'And why tonight? A Thursday night?"

And he had said, 'Same thing. Tourist book. Says you just can't get a table there on Friday or Saturday.'

When they entered Franky's, Andrew quickly saw where Lawrence was seated. Andrew neatly manipulated the waiter to obtain a table two over from Lawrence. Once seated, Andrew casually surveyed the room taking no extra time in Lawrence's direction. The place was three quarters full. He noticed that Lawrence was already on his main course.

The waiter brought the menus and served water.

Andrew said, "Okay, Maddy, let's order drinks. What would you like?"

Madeleine smiled as she studied the menu.

Andrew said, "I'm going to have a whiskey sour. Something different for a change. How about you, Maddy? Chris, do you want a lemonade?"

"Yes, please."

Andrew looked to Madeleine. She was studying the menu, but lifted her eyes to him and gave him an odd smile.

"Maddy, what would you like to drink?"

"Oh, just deciding." She smiled coyly. She looked back at the menu, but shot little glances to him, still smiling inexplicably. "Maybe some water."

"Water? Don't you want that Bahama Mama colorful thing with the cherry?"

She laughed. "Ohhhh......." stretching it out like an elastic. Then she gave him a Mona Lisa smile.

"Maddy, you're acting a little strange. What's going on?"

She said, "I don't think I should."

He said, "What do you mean? Have a drink. We're having a little celebration outing."

She laughed. "I know. But I shouldn't...be drinking."

"What do you...." He stopped himself. His eyes searched hers. She kept looking at him, her eyes unwavering, and with that smile. He leaned forward, staring at her. He began to smile. "You're not kidding me, are you?"

She laughed lightly and held his gaze.

He said, "You didn't say anything! Really? We're expecting?" His face was now as bright as the moon.

She reached her hand to his. "I wanted to surprise you. On our little...outing."

Andrew hopped in his seat. He slapped his hand on the table. He took both of her hands in his and kissed them. Then he jumped up and walked around to her. She stood up and they hugged and kissed for a whole minute. Everybody around them stopped eating and watched.

Suddenly aware of all the attention, Andrew looked around at everyone, trying not to look at Lawrence. Embarrassed but beaming he blurted in explanation, "She just told me! We're expecting!"

There was a round of enthusiastic clapping. Some even raised beer glasses.

———————

That night at home, Lawrence sat very still in his living room in almost darkness, one small lamp projecting a dim yellow light in one corner. He was alone. As he always was. A deliberate choice.

His mind followed a too familiar path. He had worked hard to be a good cop, a good investigator. He had solved many crimes. Worked harder than anyone. Brought many to justice, more than most. He had put everything into his work. No family. No hobbies. He was respected, admired. Received high praise, high commendations.

He had done everything he could to serve justice.

Except turn himself in.

A silent war raged in him. All of the good work he did, all of the accolades of his superiors, all of the respect of his colleagues, didn't count for anything. For they did not know him, did not know who he really was.

He could perform, and perform well, but a performance was all it was. He was only an exceptionally trained seal balancing a ball on his nose. And he knew he could not balance the ball forever. The mental, the emotional, the physical stresses necessary to do it 24/7 were slowly, but most assuredly, killing him. His capacities were diminishing as rapidly as his years were advancing. He was forty-seven. But he felt much older. And he looked much older. Everyone commented on it, the standard litany: 'You should take more time off. You owe it to yourself. The job will be here when you get back."

He appreciated the sentiments, the concern behind the comments, delivered by tough men who didn't usually talk with sentiment, but who really liked him, admired him, respected him, and tried to say so.

None of which he deserved. None of it.

He had, of course, thought to do the right thing, to make a clean breast of it. To take his punishment - at best, prison for life. Not that he would survive very long in prison anyway. But that didn't matter. He would be happy to face justice. But there was his sister. And his mother and his father.

How do you live with that every waking moment? From the time you're only twenty-one. Knowing you don't deserve it. Don't deserve anyone's respect or admiration. Not one bit of it. Knowing you have betrayed the uniform to the core. And far worse.

You hide. You bury yourself. You immerse in a demanding job, working long hours, building a wonderful shell so others cannot see you. And you try to cease to feel. But you can't. And while you engage the world, it is no more than the trained seal engaging its audience.

Sometimes the shell cracks, the pressure from within too much, and the lava of hot feeling flows and burns. And there is only one way to assuage it. As he had found. You surrender to the white magic.

With a delicate key, he unlocked the small desk drawer. His hand reached blindly to the back of the drawer, past the small handgun. Might he oneday surrender to the handgun?

He withdrew the clear plastic packet of white powder. His hand reached in again and felt, and found, the needle.

CHAPTER TWENTY-ONE

All across the southern United States Dylan Kipling was being hunted. When you kill a federal circuit judge in cold blood and then try to burn his wife alive, the law pulls out all the stops.

Three months had passed since March 21, 1981 when Kipling entered the home of Judge Thomas Barnes in Dallas late at night. He first shot the Judge's wife, Eleanor Barnes, as she ran from him towards the kitchen. He then went upstairs and shot the Judge twice in the head. Badly wounded, Eleanor Barnes had still managed to lock and bolt herself in an oak-doored pantry off the kitchen while Kipling was executing the Judge. When Kipling then turned his attention back to her, he was unable to shoot his way through the pantry door.

But no bother. His plan had always been to set the house on fire after the executions anyway. The five gallons of gas he had brought along would take care of Mrs. Barnes. He thoroughly doused the main floor rooms with something extra for the kitchen.

He hadn't counted on Eleanor Barnes being so stouthearted. Courageously she dragged her body through the blazing inferno and survived the horrifying burns to fifty percent of her body. Three months later she was still in a burn trauma unit undergoing serial skin grafts. But she had been able to nail Kipling's identification perfectly.

For his pains, Kipling was paid $100,000 by a drug lord, 'Chem' Kennedy, whose trial Judge Barnes had been in the middle of hearing at the time. Barnes was the Judge toughest on drugs in that circuit, and as the evidence in the trial mounted steadily against Kennedy, and his lawyers' arguments evaporated under the glare of Judge Barnes, Kennedy had made the extreme decision to bring in Kipling.

A trial without a judge brakes quickly to a stop. The jury was dismissed and Kennedy was remanded in custody to await the start of a whole new trial. A week later, Kennedy escaped, and now he too was being hunted all across the South.

⸻

Through his source, Lorne Nix was advised of the want ad that appeared in The New York Times: 'Seeking parts for vintage stop-watches.' This was the coded way in which a service from the Watcher could be requested. The ad provided a phone number.

Nix radioed the usual instructions to the specialist he used for this particular operation.

The placer of the ad might receive calls from a variety of people offering vintage parts. But it was only when the caller said, 'I have no stopwatch parts, but may have a service you need', that the placer of the ad knew he was talking to someone who could put him in touch with The Watcher. The Watcher's people would vet the placer of the ad to ensure there was no police set up, no rat lurking.

The placer of the ad was always a front man for someone more powerful. In this case it was 'Chem' Kennedy who sought a service. The heat on Kennedy in the south was so intense and so widespread, he had traveled in disguise north to Philadelphia to join Kipling, his unwaveringly loyal gunman. Kipling had already holed up without detection for almost three months.

But Kennedy wanted further security. He wanted to have advance warning if the police ever learned where he was and were preparing a takedown. He had heard The Watcher's inside people could provide that service.

⸻

An investigative request had just come in to Lawrence by teletype from the Dallas field office.

```
Title:
        DYLAN KIPLING;
      · JUDGE THOMAS BARNES (Deceased)
- VICTIM;
ELEANOR BARNES - VICTIM
UNLAWFUL FLIGHT TO AVOID PROSECUTION -
```

MURDER; ATTEMPT MURDER; ARSON
Synopsis:
Request to locate and arrest subject
DYLAN KIPLING
Subject KIPLING is wanted for the
murder of the deceased, the attempted
murder of the second victim, and arson,
all occurring on March 21st, 1981 in
Dallas, TX. According to a confidential
source, KIPLING may have fled to the
Philadelphia area.
PHILADELPHIA at PHILADELPHIA,
PENNSYLVANIA:
Conduct logical fugitive investigation
to locate and arrest subject
        DYLAN KIPLING
ARMED AND VERY DANGEROUS

Lawrence called the Dallas field office and was quickly filled in. A $10,000 reward had been offered by the Dallas office to anyone who supplied information leading directly to the arrest of Kipling. The confidential source was a one-time cell mate of Kipling who had now just been arrested on an armed robbery and would soon be facing a very stiff sentence. He had heard of Kipling's misdoings in Dallas and that the law couldn't find him. He wasn't interested in the $10,000. He wanted some leniency and felt he had a bargaining chip.

He was interviewed by an FBI agent and said that Kipling, in a moment of sentimental forthrightness, once said that he had a place just north of Philadelphia that nobody knew anything about. He had been real smart, careful never to take anybody there, and it wasn't even registered in his name. It was by some water, maybe a pond or something, because Kipling complained about the damned ducks quacking, driving him crazy.

When the agent asked how he knew Kipling was being truthful, the cell mate said, 'It's true. Because Kip later said it wasn't. That it was just bullshit. That he had just had the jailhouse blues. But I knew different. He had dropped his guard in a weak moment. Kip wasn't one who daydreamed about nothing.'

Lawrence had pictures of Kipling placed around Philadelphia and in the outlying areas.

CHAPTER TWENTY-TWO

Andrew spent a week modifying the Pitt for aerial surveillance, then Lawrence called a second meeting. At the cottage they discussed further operational rules and Lawrence touched on some cases he might bring Andrew in on. Lawrence then asked about the Pitt.

"She's all outfitted now," Andrew explained. "Three high resolution cameras under the fuselage, configured like in the plane I flew out of Minneapolis. Each with a different telephoto lens - long, medium, and close shots. They're operated by a remote control unit on the dash. Each camera shoots four pictures a second."

Lawrence nodded with satisfaction. "And what about range?"

"I had a supplementary fuel tank installed. I now have a flying time of two and a half hours, a range of over 300 miles."

Lawrence smiled. "Your enthusiasm for that plane is very obvious."

Andrew laughed. "Yes. Maddy tells me the Pitt is a jealous mistress."

Lawrence suggested they take a break. "I made up some tuna sandwiches. Is that alright?"

"Sounds delicious." Lawrence passed him a sandwich and Andrew sat on the sofa. Lawrence took a chair.

Andrew said, "Wes, did you join the FBI straight out of college?"

"Well, I did two years of college, then joined the Buffalo P.D. in '55. I was twenty-one. I was there only a year. Wasn't happy. I wanted to finish my college degree, which I did, then joined the FBI in '58. In Philadelphia."

"Were you connected to the investigation into my Dad's disappearance?"

"No. Our two most senior investigators were assigned to the investigation and coordinated with Philly P.D."

"But you were acquainted with the facts?"

"I followed the case very closely."

"Wes, in hindsight, do you believe that everything was done that could have been done?"

Andrew was surprised, and uneasy, at how slow Lawrence was to answer, seeming disturbed, his eyes casting out toward the lake, his fingers agitated. Regardless of what Lawrence might now say, Andrew felt the real answer would be far from clear.

Lawrence said, "Washington sent in a specialist team as well, working alongside our team. Followed every lead, however small. Produced nothing."

Andrew pressed. "What were the essentials of the case?"

Lawrence's finger rapped absently on the arm of the chair. He cleared his throat and began slowly. "Your Dad's disappearance was believed linked to the murder of a pickpocket, Pino Macky."

Andrew detected something in Lawrence's voice. Was it reluctance, or just a sadness? Or was it...guilt? But why would that be?

"Macky was shot on a residential street about 11:00 p.m. Some teenagers came upon a tall man dragging Macky towards a parked car with its trunk opened. The man took off in the car, leaving Macky on the street. The car was never traced. As Macky lay dying, your father attended on him. Macky died on the street."

"Macky didn't ID his killer?"

"There was nothing in your Dad's report to that effect. Robbery was not the motive. Macky had a lot of money on him. Your Dad quickly checked Macky's background and found he was on the lam, wanted by Buffalo P.D. Your Dad was looking into anyone who might be motivated to kill Macky. He certainly had enemies; he had ratted out people in prison to gain favor with authorities. Might there have been a price on his head? Nothing was ever substantiated."

Andrew said, "That wouldn't have explained someone taking my dad anyway."

Lawrence looked at Andrew a few moments. "Certainly not." He got up and walked the length of the room. "A wallet was found on Macky belonging to an older man who was in the ballroom at the Continental Hotel that night at a businessmens' gala. The man was located early the next morning. He was certain he had his wallet at 10:30 p.m., only half an hour before Macky was shot. This led naturally to the theory that

Macky had been at the gala, although he was certainly not there as a guest. The organizers and hotel management put together a list of all the guests and hotel staff working that night. And over the next several days, a picture of Macky was shown to all guests and staff. Nobody recalled seeing him, including the man who had lost the wallet. And nobody had left the gala until after Macky was killed."

"How many people at the gala?"

"Four hundred. More than half were men, successful, well to do businessmen. Investigators worked from the assumption that someone in the room was somehow connected to the killing of Macky. Everyone who had been in that ballroom was thoroughly vetted, full background checks were conducted. Turned up nothing in the end."

Lawrence stopped walking and turned to look at Andrew, a sudden sympathy in his face. "But you offered us something. You were a very brave boy. You said that the hooded man who came to your house was shorter than your Dad, his eyes level with your Dad's chin. We believed that made him no taller than about 5'6", certainly much shorter than average anyway. You said he had a low voice. Intense surveillance was conducted for two years on all men who had been at the gala who were shorter than average, whose voices were lower than average. Phones were tapped, hidden microphones, forensic accounting. Nothing connected anyone at the gala to Macky's murder… or to your Dad's abduction. In the end, investigators decided the wallet was not the vital clue they thought it was. It led to the gala but that led nowhere. A red herring. If someone at the gala was behind it, he had an ironclad cover."

Neither spoke for a few moments. Then Andrew said, "I've long wondered why the man who came to our house wore that black hood. What would he care if my Dad knew who he was? He was going to kill my Dad anyway. I used to think he just didn't want *me* to be able to give a description. Then something else occurred to me. Did the two gunmen not know who the hooded man was and he wanted to keep it that way? There were two cars, not one. And the hooded man, with my father in the trunk, drove away in the opposite direction to the one the gunmen took. Perhaps the gunmen didn't even know where the hooded man was going."

Lawrence said nothing, not acknowledging that Andrew had said anything the least bit unusual, which Andrew thought odd. Maybe

Lawrence had been over it all too many times before, although he had not been directly involved in the investigation.

Andrew said, "You know, I still see my father ... and that man. It haunts me. I've lived my life wondering why my father had to die."

Lawrence's eyes went to Andrew, but he didn't say anything; he seemed to be reflecting. After a moment he walked close to the living room window and looked down to the lake, his back to Andrew. It was clear he didn't want to talk about the matter further.

Andrew stayed seated, wondering what effect those memories had on Lawrence. He wouldn't press it now. He would take it up another time when he got to know Lawrence better.

Lawrence was still at the window. Andrew spoke up, a lighter tone. "A totally unrelated matter, Wes. I meant to tell you when I was here last week. Ten years ago, when I was just released from the reformatory, I helped a policeman who was knocked out in a tavern. A college fund was set up for me in appreciation of that. There was an anonymous donor who gave $15,000. It was unbelievable. That alone was two years of college paid."

Lawrence's back stayed turned to Andrew. He said nothing. Andrew said, "I made a lot of inquiries to find out who it was, but I never learned."

Andrew waited, watching, saying nothing more. Lawrence finally half turned and Andrew caught a wary flicker in Lawrence's eyes.

Andrew said calmly, "Was it you, Wes?"

An uneasy hesitation.

Andrew said, "It *was* you, Wes."

Lawrence looked away, seeming embarrassed.

Andrew got up. "Wes, why didn't you ever say? All this time. Why didn't you ever say? You ... you changed my life."

Lawrence was uncomfortable.

"Why did you do that for me, Wes?"

Lawrence's voice was tight. "It was something I felt was right. An opportunity to help." Lawrence gave a brief, awkward half smile. "I would rather you not tell Madeleine. I would rather you not tell anyone for now."

"Wes...I don't understand."

"I... didn't want any attention. And I don't want it now."

Andrew saw Lawrence's discomfort was genuine, not a simple

modesty. "I understand," Andrew said, although he didn't. "I really want to thank you. But just telling Madeleine, would that not be ok?"

Lawrence said, "Not yet, please."

"Of course, Wes. I will respect your wish. For whatever your reason."

Lawrence seemed to force a cheered face. "You know, I haven't even congratulated you on the news of Madeleine's expecting. I'm very happy for you both. She's a lovely woman. And Chris is a wonderful kid." Then, in a more wistful note, "You're very lucky, Andrew."

"Thank you, Wes. I feel I am."

Awkward silence. Andrew said, "You mentioned your sister. Any children there?"

"No."

"And you, Wes, I gather... never married?"

"Never married."

Andrew tried to sound light and casual. "Never that right girl?"

Lawrence smile was short. "Never that right girl."

Andrew sensed he had overstepped. He felt the urge to thank Lawrence again for that the incredible gift, but desisted. Leave well enough alone.

Lawrence walked to the kitchen table and began to gather some loose paper he had earlier spread out - some reports, charts. But he stopped and looked out the kitchen window, his eyes following the breeze as it rippled the lake's surface. "There was, in fact, a girl." After a few moments he looked back down to the papers, his hand sliding a report absently. "She died."

"I'm sorry, Wes... that I brought that up."

Lawrence carried the documents to an accordion file on a table. He began to insert them into pockets. He stopped for a moment and lifted his eyes again to the window, not really seeing outside, seeming about to say something more. But then he looked back to the papers, his eyes focusing, and he concentrated on the task.

CHAPTER TWENTY-THREE

A ndrew was tucking Chris into bed. The bedroom door was open, and across the hall in the master bedroom, Madeleine was changing the sheets, overhearing as Chris asked Andrew questions about what Andrew's Dad was like.

"Well, he loved the outdoors, camping, canoeing. He made me that small crossbow and we'd shoot targets in the woods."

"The crossbow that you use now, did he make that, too?"

"Yes he did. That was his when I was a boy."

"Could he hit a can sitting on top of a post like you can?"

"He sure could."

"Did he sit on the bed and tuck you in at night, too?"

"Yes. And he would make up exciting adventure stories. And I would be the hero."

Chris sat up, eager. "That would be FUN, Dad!"

Madeleine smiled as she spread a sheet on the bed in the master bedroom.

Chris said, "Can you tell me a story your Dad told you?"

A long pause, then she heard Andrew say, "Okay. But I'll make it you and I instead of my dad and I. Okay?"

"Yes, please!"

"Okay, so Chris and his Dad were deep in the woods, dark clouds overhead, all very quiet. They crouched behind a large boulder and looked into a ravine where a mother bear and her cub frolicked in a stream. Chris whispered to his Dad, 'I wonder where the *father* bear is.'"

Madeleine decided the top sheet could wait. She stood close to the hall, out of sight, listening, putting a pillow into a pillowcase.

"Chris's Dad didn't seem to hear. His Dad whispered, 'Let's get closer. I've got the camera.' They crept from boulder to boulder. But

Chris sensed something was wrong. 'The wind, Dad. It shifted.' Chris was very smart. The wind would now carry their human scent directly to the bears. Chris and his Dad ducked and stayed low. Dad then raised himself carefully and held the camera to his eye. Just then, Chris saw it! The angry *father* bear galloping towards them! 'Dad!' Chris screamed."

Madeleine clutched the pillow.

"Chris's Dad saw it. They had no gun. They had only their cross-bows. His Dad stood up and made himself as tall as he could and yelled and smashed the camera on the rocks to make metallic noises. Then he hurled the camera at the bear. But the bear kept coming. Chris's Dad fumbled trying to load his crossbow. The bear was now almost on them. His mouth opened in a snarling ROAR. Chris had been quicker. His bow was loaded. The bear's mouth opened wide as big as a garbage can, huge sharp teeth. Chris aimed and fired. The arrow went right into the bear's mouth. The bear threw his head back high, swinging it back and forth, making painful noises. Then he backed off and scrambled down to the stream. When he got to where the mother and cub were, he coughed up the arrow out of his mouth."

Chris said, "So the bear didn't die?"

"No, he just had a really sore throat for a while."

Chris laughed. Madeleine laughed.

Chris said, "Did your dad tell you that one?"

"One like that."

A few moments passed. "You look sad. Do you miss your Dad?"

Madeleine's face was quiet.

"Sometimes I do."

"And your Mom?"

"Yes."

"Does it hurt?"

A pause. "Sometimes."

"I don't want you ever getting taken away."

"Chris, I don't want you to be even thinking about that. Okay? There's nothing to worry about."

CHAPTER TWENTY-FOUR

A week after Lawrence had wanted-posters of Kipling placed, a likely sighting was phoned in by a woman. Lawrence requested she come in to be interviewed by him personally and privately.

She was middle aged and credible, and told Lawrence she was quite certain she had seen Kipling filling his car at a gas station just north of the city. He was with another man and she gave his detailed description also. They were alone, driving a light green, newer car, the make uncertain. 'Not European or Japanese. American, like a Chevrolet sort of. I'm a lot better with faces.' She didn't get the license.

When Lawrence reviewed the description of the other man with Dallas FBI, they said it fit perfectly with 'Chem' Kennedy.

Lawrence then immediately got another break. Sixteen-year old Randy Taylor hoped to be a policeman one day and always took special interest whenever he saw a wanted-poster. Randy had phoned in. Lawrence requested he attend the office, again privately with Lawrence.

Randy brought along his new girlfriend. He said they were driving about twenty-five miles north of Philadelphia, between Doylestown and New Hope, following behind a light green, 1977 Monte Carlo, two-door hardtop that he had taken an interest in. This had immediately intrigued Lawrence as he had not yet put out a public notice respecting a light green, possibly Chevy product, the information being too vague. Lawrence said, "Hold it. Why was that car of interest to you?"

Randy, showing shyness, hesitated then glanced to his girlfriend who spoke up. "He remarked to me as we were driving behind that car that it was the most beautiful he had ever seen. And I said to him, 'That's odd, why?' And he said, romantically, "Because it's exactly the color of your eyes."

Lawrence noted her eyes were a beautiful, light green. Randy's face was now a ripe crimson. Lawrence said, "Okay, then what?"

The girlfriend said, "I said, 'why don't you pull over. I want to give you a very nice kiss.' He did. And I did."

Lawrence thought, I can see Randy as a policeman. And she could write romances.

Lawrence said, "Okay, but you were following the Monte Carlo."

She said, "No. It got way ahead of us."

Lawrence supposed it was a very long kiss.

She continued, "But then we caught up to it again. I saw it was pulled up at a country convenience store, nearer New Hope, and pointed it out to Randy."

Randy said, "We were only doing about fifteen miles an hour as we passed it. I got a very good look at the guy as he walked from the store to the driver's door. At that moment, I knew I had seen the face somewhere but couldn't remember. It was only later that I put two and two together."

Lawrence said, "Anyone else in the car?"

They both said, "Didn't see anyone."

Lawrence considered the information. If it were Kipling, the fact that he was still around carried a high probability that 'Chem' Kennedy was also still around. That Kennedy had come this far to hide out with his gunman suggested strongly that Kennedy wouldn't go off running on his own. They were probably convinced their hideout was secure and were going to stay hunkered.

Lawrence said, "It's vital neither of you say anything to anybody for now. Can you do that? It could mean saving lives."

They nodded seriously.

Lawrence decided for the time being not to release any of this new information within his office. Not for a few days yet. He wanted to bring Andrew in on it.

CHAPTER TWENTY-FIVE

Andrew had flown most of a day looking for Kipling's light green Monte Carlo possibly parked at a country house in the vicinity of New Hope or Doylestown and near water. He had covered about 80 square miles with no luck.

Now, at the kitchen table at Lawrence's cottage, they finished reviewing a series of high resolution maps detailing the areas he had flown. Andrew began to explain the next day's search area, consulting the maps. He wanted to finish up soon as it was getting on to evening and he still had to fly back to his aerodrome before dark.

Although Andrew was certain Lawrence was taking it all in, he had noticed some level of distraction. Lawrence had often glanced away, not concentrating on the maps. Something appeared to be playing on his mind.

Andrew finally said, "Wes, is there something I'm not explaining clearly, or is something the matter?"

Lawrence looked at Andrew a moment and his face became gloomy. "That girl I mentioned the other day...."

Surprised, Andrew also felt a pang of guilt, sensing he had unearthed a painful memory.

"Yes," Andrew said.

Lawrence walked to the kitchen and looked out the window at the lake. "Why don't you have a seat in the living room, Andrew."

Andrew knew he really had no choice but to hear Lawrence out. He sat on the sofa.

Lawrence turned to face Andrew. His voice was quiet. "I was twenty-one that year, a rookie cop with the Buffalo P.D. Her Dad was a cop on the force. A very tough guy. The kind you wanted to see coming through the door when you called for backup." Lawrence absently rubbed a hand on the counter. "Her Dad was hosting a barbecue at their house for some of the guys from work. I was the new cop, still wet behind the ears, everybody kidding me. She was there. Cute, slight, quiet. I thought shy. We talked a bit. A nice girl. But she stayed mostly out of sight at the barbecue. Her name was Sylvie."

Lawrence began to pace the kitchen area. "Not long after, she just dropped in on me at my place one night. I lived in a big old house that had been converted to four apartments. I had a ground floor apartment. I hadn't spoken to her since the barbecue. She seemed to be very interested in me, and wasn't too shy about showing it. I figured that when her father wasn't around, she came out of herself. She told me her Dad and Mom didn't know she was visiting me. In fact, nobody knew, and she wanted to keep it that way. We talked a lot. Had a couple of drinks. We enjoyed each other's company. Laughed at stupid things. You know how it is. Then some hugging and kissing."

Lawrence walked into the living room to the easy chair and sat. The room dimmed and Andrew was aware of clouds blocking the evening sun. "A few days later she came by again. She said nobody knew she was there. Not even her girlfriends. Otherwise it could get out and her Dad would learn of it. She said he was over-protective. Wouldn't let her go out to do things other girls could, even at her age of eighteen."

Lawrence tapped the leather arm slowly. "I felt uneasy, her Dad being a colleague. But we had a few drinks, some kissing. She told me she thought she loved me. Passion ran away with us." Lawrence stopped tapping. "One thing led to another."

Lawrence paused a few moments. "I didn't see her again for a few days. I had decided that, even though I didn't want it to end, this relationship could not go on if it had to be kept a secret. She came by a few days later. I told her my feelings. She told me she agreed. She said it should end, end now. Before anything happened. She was abrupt, clearly agitated. I didn't understand. I said, 'End? Before anything like what happens? Like your father finding out?' Sylvie was very quiet. She looked away from me. And then she said, 'I am only fifteen.'"

Lawrence got up. His voice became agitated and louder. "The words hit me like a hammer. Fifteen! I was stunned. My *kid sister* was fifteen. I got angry with her. She had deceived me. I yelled at her."

Now Lawrence's voice quieted. "Then my feelings rapidly turned to leg-weakening fear. Here I was, twenty-one, a cop, and I had had intercourse with a very under-aged girl. The act had occurred only once. But there it was. Statutory rape. It could end my career, devastate my parents. Then it struck me. There loomed a *much* worse possibility. We had been drinking heavily leading up to intercourse. To a court, drinking like that would take statutory rape up to forcible rape. Prison time. Me. Twenty-one. And newly a policeman. Very proud parents."

Lawrence looked at Andrew as if to decide how much he should say; Andrew looked a sympathetic hearer. Lawrence continued. "Of course, nothing would happen if she never spoke of it. And we agreed on that. I told her I could never see her again. She left."

Lawrence began to walk the livingroom like a prisoner in a cell. "But I lived in continuous fear. She was so young. If she ever felt compelled to tell someone sometime, a girlfriend maybe, if she just had to tell some-one, it could get out. It was a sword hanging over my head. Her father would push charges all the way. If he didn't kill me first."

Lawrence stopped and looked at the lake. "Weeks went by. I didn't hear from her at all, just as we agreed. Then one night, there was a knock at my door. It was Sylvie. She looked ghastly, washed out."

Lawrence turned and looked at Andrew. "She told me she was preg-nant. Fifteen and pregnant. Everything was going to come out now. She was very scared. And me, head spinning fear. But still, nobody but us knew. One minute she said she wanted to talk to her mother. The next minute...she wanted to harm herself, that would be just so easy and painless. She hadn't slept in two days, hadn't gone to school. I was beside myself, fearing what she might do. She was so unstable. Her mother and father had just gone to Florida for a week. Her older brother was at home. He didn't know anything. I hugged her to calm her down. But I couldn't think straight. I was afraid what would happen if she talked to anyone. I told her there had to be a way out of this, that she could have an abortion. It was so early in the pregnancy. I would make private arrangements. It made sense then, in my young life."

Lawrence wrung his hands. "Can you imagine my fear, Andrew? The whole world for me, my whole life, at twenty-one, was going to tip one way or the other."

Andrew felt tremendous unease at hearing all this. Why was he being told? So obviously hard for Lawrence, so very personal, and Andrew hardly knew him.

Lawrence said, as if remembering the hope in it, "She said 'yes', she would do it. Naturally we couldn't go to a doctor, not at her age without her parents involved, and I couldn't let that happen. And anyway, abortions weren't even legal then. It was criminal then. I told her that I would take care of things. I had heard at the station of a file on a woman who was charged with performing a 'back alley' abortion, but the charge had been dropped before it went far. I looked in the file, found out where the woman lived. I went to see her. She said she would do it."

Looking inconsolably sad, Lawrence glanced to Andrew. Andrew felt he had heard all he should hear. It seemed all too much for Lawrence now.

Andrew said, "It went badly?"

Lawrence nodded. "We do things when we're young, Andrew, that haunt us, that follow us like a beast."

Andrew said, "She died?"

Lawrence nodded again, "I can't forgive myself for what happened. Life has a way of unraveling..." He looked intensely at Andrew. "Andrew, *no one* ever knew what I did."

"Wes, it was a long time ago. You didn't mean harm to her."

Lawrence nodded. "I've never told anybody. Just you."

"I ...understand, Wes." But Andrew really didn't. Why was he the one, the only one?

Lawrence said, "I had to be sure I could trust you. I had to get you to know me, to make you trust *me*."

"Trust you?", Andrew said, thinking it an odd thing for Lawrence to say.

"We have to work closely. It will often be just us two. We have to trust one another. So I wanted you to know."

By the time Andrew left the cottage, both had put on a good face. But both were ill at ease. Andrew could still feel deep, dark currents flowing in Lawrence. Andrew wondered why Lawrence had told him all this. Why he had never told anyone else before. Was his life so without trust, so without a friend, that he had no one to tell?

Andrew couldn't shake a nagging worry that something important was missing. Lawrence had carried this burden far too long. It ran to his core. There was something here and Andrew was quite sure he didn't want to know what.

When he arrived home about 9:00 p.m., his mind was still absorbed, mulling it.

Madeleine heard the door and met him. She was in a light-hearted mood. "Welcome home. But it's getting late." She wrapped her arms around his neck and gave him a kiss. "You suggested this morning that we should... get cuddly later. So... whadya say?"

It was nowhere in his mind. "That's... right."

"Do you have to sound so completely lackluster, Mister fun and games?"

"I was just thinking, if a woman died having an abortion 25 years ago, there would be an autopsy. Especially where the abortion was illegal."

She humphed. "What an opener to getting cuddly, Don Juan. Surely there would be an autopsy either way if she died. And the doc would be charged and his license yanked."

Andrew paused, considering further. "Yes. Particularly if it's *not* a doctor but some woman in a back alley. Could be manslaughter or worse. But here's the thing, if the whole thing was set up by someone else, the criminal investigation's going to search out that someone else. The prime suspect is the guy who got her pregnant."

"Presumably," she said dryly, with obvious indifference. She started for the kitchen. "Hey, by the way, Casanova, you really know how to kill a mood."

Andrew followed her, saying, "And the woman who did the abortion, she's going to want to give up the identity of the guy who set it up. To get a better sentencing deal for herself. Because the cops are going to push especially hard on this one."

Madeleine opened a cupboard and grabbed a bag of cookies. She didn't really want to encourage this conversation, but she said, "And why especially on this one?"

"Because the dead girl's father is a cop." He looked at Madeleine. "And they would have the baby's DNA. A link to identifying the father. If that was in some measure available in 1955. But even if not...there's going to be something." Andrew then mused out loud, "But he said no one knew what he had done. How is it they didn't get him?"

Madeleine bit off a large chunk of a cookie. "I admit this is just fascinating, Andrew. But perhaps it's too much fun. Wanna do something else?"

Andrew looked at her and stopped. She was looking back at him, clearly less than amorous now, chomping with unseemly vigor. And they weren't even hard cookies.

Andrew broke into a laugh. "Hey, Maddy, I'm sorry. I didn't mean to bore you." He took her in his arms and kissed her neck. "Don Juan here, humbly at your service." He nibbled her ear.

She reached for another cookie. "Good." She bit into it and made loud, delectable sounds. "Don't forget the other ear."

CHAPTER TWENTY-SIX

A ndrew was flying the Pitt at 2500 feet and 90 miles an hour, tracing a grid pattern without being obvious, not flying in straight rows. He appeared to be a stunt flyer practicing, every couple of miles making a simple aerobatic maneuver.

Lawrence had expressed his fear of this Kipling search getting leaked. It was impossible to know if the leaks arose in both the FBI office and the Philadelphia P.D. or not. There didn't appear to be any rhyme or reason - sometimes a leak, sometimes not. And the gravity of the information was not the determining factor. There was no observable common factor - one takedown worked perfectly, another was spoiled.

Andrew had been flying an hour and a half and had covered an area of about forty square miles. This was day two. Yesterday he had refueled twice and covered about eighty square miles. The broad parameters were find a house, probably something private, not close by a neighbor, probably cheap looking, with water nearby big enough for ducks, that isn't obviously an active farm, and that has a light green, 1977 Monte Carlo, two-door hardtop parked, hopefully, plainly in sight. Maybe there would even be a sign that said "Kipling is here!"

Andrew was getting punchy. It took a lot of concentration to fly the Pitt, keep track of where you've been, do aerobatics, and carefully survey the ground for hours on end. He pushed his aching shoulders back, twisting his head up and around, back and forth, trying to work out a beginning kink. Then he did a slow barrel roll.

———•———

In the screened-in back porch of a wood sided, older frame home badly in need of painting, Kipling said to 'Chem' Kennedy, "Look at that," pointing to a biplane in the distance. "Some stunt pilot. I've been watching him. Every so often he does some stunt. Maybe he's giving someone a lesson. How to pull stunts."

"Here, Ace," Kennedy called to a thick-bodied, big headed, vicious looking pit bull, and threw two hunks of cooked hamburger patty. Kennedy looked up at the plane and said, "Not my preferred way of flying. Not much in-flight service."

Kipling said without expression, "No movies. Coffee wouldn't stay in your cup."

Kennedy grunted, "Not even in your stomach."

———————

Andrew had seen the older frame house half a mile from any neighbor and an elongated pond nearby surrounded by bull rushes. He had dropped to 1500 feet, had taken close pictures of the house and surroundings, and of the garage, the door of which appeared open to the street. If that were the property, the car was either gone, or the owner wasn't making any attempt at concealment of it.

As Andrew passed, he saw a screened porch and a large lean-to affair at the back. No driveway went to it, but he noted two tracks of brown grass from the driveway to the lean-to, possibly made by frequent crossing by a vehicle. The pictures would better tell. And as he passed, he saw through the binoculars sunlight glinting off something metallic and rounded protruding from the lean to, like a car's front end. The angle of the sun caused glare prohibiting a view or good pictures. But bulky clouds were swiftly moving across the sky in the direction of the house; the sun would shortly be blocked out. He would time another fly past accordingly.

He flew on another ten minutes. The winds at 3,000 feet caused the clouds to scud at a good clip. He gained height to 4,000 feet. Now he put the Pitt into a tight circle, its wings almost vertical, then levelled and flew towards the house. At three miles out, he could see that clouds were now beginning to shadow the area of the house. The glare would be gone.

He eased off the throttle and dropped to 2000 feet. He looked long and hard through the stabilized binoculars. It was definitely a car. And of some light color. And from the photos he had memorized of the front of the '77 Monte Carlo model, this car had definite possibilities.

He lined things up, eased off the throttle more, and began a slow bank, dropping in quickly, leveling low at about 800 feet when he flew by, positioned to get the very best camera angle on the lean to. He held his thumb on the cameras' remote button for five full seconds, the multiple cameras whizzing through twenty pictures each.

He then pulled up sharply into a spiraling, perfect vertical climb, the engine wailing in protest. Just like in the best air shows, he held the vertical until he reached the apex, then seemed to hang in the air. Then a tail slide into a hammerhead stall. Then a kick of the rudder and into a free fall. He could feel the audience hold its breath. He hauled back on the joystick and eased out of the fall, bottoming at a thousand feet, gained another thousand, and headed home.

He had done the formidable stunt for two reasons: first, he had seen a man standing in the shadow of a screened-in porch at the back of house, looking up just as he flew past. Andrew wanted to quash any notion the man might have that the plane was the law. And second, it was a jubilation ride for Andrew, because he got a very good look at that car in that lean-to - a light green Monte Carlo with the right grille markings.

CHAPTER TWENTY-SEVEN

A ndrew called Lawrence from the aerodrome. They arranged to meet at the cottage after Andrew got the pictures developed at a commercial photo shop and did the twenty-five-minute flight.

At 3:30, Andrew touched down at the grass strip. With him he had twenty selected color photographs, some showing the layout of the property itself, others the surrounding properties to 500 yards, all for orientation for the SWAT team. But three of the photos very clearly showed a car of exactly the correct description. And as important, two others caught precise images of the man standing beside the screened porch - about thirty, solidly built, of Kipling's general description. Andrew had no photograph of Kipling. But Lawrence did.

When Andrew got to the cottage, he saw Lawrence's mood had greatly improved from the evening before when he had told Andrew of the girl. With a wide smile he took the envelope of pictures from Andrew and quickly spread them on the kitchen table. They were crisp and clear. "Excellent, Andrew. Absolutely excellent." He studied them all, nodding often, excited.

From a briefcase, he withdrew FBI pictures of Kipling and Chem Kennedy. He held them close to the pictures of the man by the screened porch. Blond hair. Broad forehead. Wide, jutting jaw. Powerful shoulders. There was no question. It was Kipling.

"Eureka!" said Lawrence. "The needle in the haystack. And there's a very good chance Kennedy's there too."

He studied the pictures of the house property itself and the wider surroundings. "Three points of ingress and egress. A more complex takedown operation. I'm going to the office and prepare the logistics and coordinate with Philly P.D. I need to get detailed maps of the area. I can't use your photos, of course. Nobody can know you are involved, or that *anybody* else is involved. Not yet."

"How are you going to explain how you know Kipling is at this location?"

"An anonymous, credible tip. And that because of my concern about leaks, I'm playing my cards close. No one will question my actions. They're my decisions for my reasons. I answer only to Washington."

Lawrence concentrated. "The takedown will be at 5 a.m. I've got a lot of work to do. A dozen of our men to be contacted, jacked up, fully briefed. A similar number from the Philly SWAT team to be coordinated. Roadblocks in every direction. A lot of hot communication. All in complete secrecy." His mood was changing to annoyance. "Damned leaks! It's a lot to keep quiet. Only takes one to let the cat out of the bag. Sometimes I feel I might just as well cable the sons of bitches, tell them we're coming."

He picked up the pictures of Kennedy and Kipling. "Of course, I need to know they're still there tonight. You know the whole set up, Andrew. I want you on the ground there about 9:30, just after dark. Call me at home right away if the Monte Carlo's gone or it appears they're not there. But if someone's there, you stay put until they're settled in for the night. Then you clear out and call me at home to confirm."

⎯⎯⎯⎯•⎯⎯⎯⎯

The night was black with thick cloud cover, but no threat of rain. At 9:45 Andrew positioned himself 250 feet from the rear of the house just by the pond. Through his night vision goggles he could see everything with the clarity you have about twilight. The Monte Carlo was still there. It looked like it hadn't moved an inch.

Andrew was dressed head to toe in black, wearing Kevlar protective gear, and carrying a semiautomatic, Smith and Wessons 459 9 mm pistol, and an M-16 assault rifle, the rifle he had trained on before becoming a sniper. At this close range, his scoped sniper rifle would be a liability. Not that he expected he would need to use any weapon tonight anyway.

The windows of the house were curtained shut. But there were lights on in four rooms, too many if they were just on timers. Kipling had to be there. And maybe 'Chem' Kennedy.

The ground between him and the rear screened porch was level and overgrown with low, wild grasses. There were no trees. No cover.

Andrew noted that the location of the lean-to in relation to the pond, the house, the roads was well chosen. Anything parked in it would be unobservable unless you were already standing in the back yard. And leaving the garage door open to the road as they did would tend to deflect any suspicion that the occupant was hiding anything.

There were no neighbors for a quarter of a mile.

All was quiet. But Lawrence had said to wait until it appeared they were tucked in for the night. Andrew settled in, lying flat. He glanced at his watch. 10:05 p.m.

———————

An hour earlier, in an empty office in Atlanta, a phone had rung. As no one was ever in, the answering machine recorded an urgent message. The caller also radioed the same message which was picked up at Nix's home and his office on the voice activated tape recorders.

It wasn't, however, until 10:40 p.m. that Nix took the message - a joint FBI/Philadelphia P.D. SWAT force was being assembled to conduct a takedown of Kipling, and possibly 'Chem' Kennedy, at 5 a.m.

Nix smiled. It was satisfying when things worked this seamlessly, especially in such an urgent matter. Mr. Kennedy would be eternally grateful, his money very well spent.

Nix jotted a phone number from a file, threw on a light jacket, and grabbed the elevator down to the underground parking where he entered his sleek Porshe 911.

He drove only a minute. Three blocks past a payphone booth, he parked and walked back to the phone. He dialed. He glanced to his watch. 11:14.

After five rings, Kipling's heavy voice said, "Hello?"

"The early bird gets the worm," Nix said.

There were several moments of silence, Kipling stumbling around in his mind trying to remember the code. He finally blurted, "When?"

Nix said, "Five a.m.", and hung up.

Take downs were always very early morning. The early bird gets the worm.

———————

Andrew had noted that two of the four lights had been turned out at

10:50. What appeared to be the bathroom light had been turned on for five minutes, then shut off. What seemed a bedroom light then turned off. Only one light was still on, which Andrew figured was a bedroom. Things were winding down for the night.

But at 11:15, three lights in different rooms came on in quick succession. He heard a muffled shout from inside the house. So someone else was there. 'Chem' Kennedy? Andrew knew from the FBI pictures what to look for - squat build, round, sour face, jet black hair, probably a stubbly beard, and looking older than his 39 years. Andrew's body tensed.

The back door opened slowly with obvious caution and a man's head poked out, quickly looking around and listening. Then he stepped fully outside. Through the goggles, Andrew saw a scowling Kipling, two hundred muscled pounds wearing only jeans squinting into the darkness. Then he went back in.

In the still quiet, Andrew next heard the door at the front of the house, the hinges faintly yawing. Was Kipling checking out the front? But why? And why all of a sudden?

Inside his bedroom, Kennedy was moving quickly, throwing clothes into a suitcase, grabbing up shoes, looking for a wallet. Ace, the pit bull, was moodily watching from the hall.

Kipling closed the front door and came back in. "Darker than the ace of fucking spades out there," he cursed aloud as he quickly came down the hall and turned into his own bedroom. He grabbed up an automatic rifle and jammed in an ammunition clip.

Nerves playing, Kennedy whispered angrily out into the hall. "Well that's fucking great. I want to know *for sure* nobody's watching us. If we're into a firefight, I want to know where it's coming from *before* it fucking comes."

Kipling threw on a heavy shirt then zipped on a loose, bulky coat. He dropped several ammunition clips into its pockets. He picked up a second rifle, then swept a pistol off the dresser top and dropped it into a coat pocket. He crossed into Kennedy's bedroom and leaned one of the rifles in a corner and said, "It's loaded." He threw a spare clip onto the bed.

Kennedy was more controlled now. "I want to be *sure* we're in the clear. Have Ace check it out. I'll grab the other stuff."

Kipling took Ace to the front door, the road side. Ace smelled the growing fear in the air. Before opening the door, Kipling whispered angrily to the dog's ear. "Get him, Ace. *Get* him." Ace fully understood. He began to growl deep in his throat and his body quivered.

Kipling opened the door slowly and whispered again, "*Get* him, Ace." Ace raced out into the front of the property, his eyes searching for quarry. He ranged across the front of the wide property, dashing behind trees and along the ditch. He ran along the road, his head in the air smelling. Kipling could hear the angry growls.

Ace found nothing. Kipling went out the front door and crept around the side of the house to get to the back yard, Ace always staying a few yards ahead.

At the back corner of the house Kipling knelt, holding Ace, pointing into the blackness of the yard and whispered, "Get him, Ace."

Andrew lay flat 250 feet back, his rifle aimed, but he didn't want to give himself away or reveal his position killing a dog. Ace rushed into the weeds, snarling, searching, seeking. He came to within 100 feet of Andrew and stopped. He looked back to Kipling. Half crouching, Kipling moved further out into the yard, peering into the darkness, his rifle pointed.

"Get him, Ace," Kipling encouraged, Ace picking up on Kipling's nerves, gathering more and more intensity in this odd midnight hunt.

Then Ace stopped. His growl intensified, his nose feverishly working the grass. When Andrew had first arrived, he had taken a position at that spot, a hundred feet closer, but had then moved back. Ace snarled as he detected the scent more fully. He sniffed the grass greedily. He lifted his big head, his nose working the air, his eyes probing in Andrew's direction. He stalked forward.

At eighty feet, Ace saw the goggles. His killer eyes widened as he fixed on Andrew. The lips curled, fangs bared. One unbroken, bloodcurdling growl came leaping from deep in his throat.

"Get him, Ace!"

With savage ferocity, Ace raced through the grasses toward Andrew with the promise of flesh tearing death.

Andrew fired, hitting Ace's bounding shoulder. It took the second, piercing his face, to stop him. Ace toppled with the hard punch of it, his hurdling body rolling twice, coming to a convulsing death stop within feet of Andrew.

Kipling fired two wild shots as he ran back toward the house. Andrew yelled, "FBI! Stop! Put down your weapon!" Andrew had never shot at a man. Although a trained sniper, in his two years he had never had to shoot at a man.

"Shit," Andrew said as Kipling slipped into the lean-to. He heard the house's front door hinges. Kennedy, or someone else, was out of the house now too!

Andrew yelled, "Kipling! This is FBI! Put down your weapon and come out!" His heart was racing. He wished he could have said, "You are surrounded!" He had never been alone on a stakeout. Who was ever alone on a stakeout? "Kipling, don't try to mess with me. Hear me?" It wasn't approved FBI text, but Andrew was angry. And afraid.

Andrew saw it was Kennedy. He jumped around a corner and dove into the lean-to from the other side. They were going to try to make a break for it in the car. Andrew thought they must have concluded there was only one agent here, and they had a good chance if they could get the car around to the front.

Andrew heard the Monte Carlo's engine start. Two shots came from behind the lean-to. They weren't well directed because Andrew was lying flat and almost impossible to see. But still, they were shooting at him with every hope to kill.

The Monte Carlo began to move out from the lean-to, Kipling giving cover fire from behind the lean-to while Kennedy swung the car out to make a break for the front. Kipling would then get himself to the front yard by diving back into the house and running through it, shielded from Andrew's fire.

Andrew fired three shots into the rear side of the moving car, hoping they would just give up. The car lurched around continuing its mission, reverse, then forward. Kennedy wasn't surrendering. And Kipling fired two shots back at Andrew.

Andrew thought, if I don't do it now, it will be too late. They will get away, or worse, I could get killed. And that just isn't going to happen.

The car was now turning. Now or never. If they only knew I just don't miss. I have never killed a man.

Oddly, at that moment, he thought of brave Eleanor Barnes in Dallas and that inferno of a kitchen. He took aim. He knew he wouldn't miss.

Three rapid-fire shots through the driver's window. The car rolled to a stop. Kennedy was dead.

Then Andrew shot Kipling, one quick round to the head, because he thought Kipling, being a gunman, might now be wearing chest armor. Andrew fired a second round, to the chest, for good measure. Kipling's body sat slumped, his back against the lean-to.

Andrew made his way forward. When he was close, he saw blood coming from Kipling's chest. No chest armor.

From a payphone outside a darkened country store a mile from Kipling's house, Andrew phoned Lawrence. It was 11:40.

Lawrence could tell that Andrew was rattled, his breathing erratic. Lawrence said, "You're sure they're both dead?"

"Positive."

"They must have been tipped off. Exactly what I feared might happen. A good thing you were there."

"I guess. Wasn't so sure then."

Lawrence knew it was the first time Andrew had killed. Lawrence had never killed. He couldn't be sure what Andrew was feeling, apart from an obvious case of nerves. "You did exactly as you had to do, Andrew. And you did it well."

"What are you going to do about the takedown?"

Lawrence said, "I'll call it off. I'll send a team out to the property to clean things up."

"They'll know you know what happened. That means the secrecy of my assignment is blown."

Lawrence had realized that, and it was a big loss. But it couldn't be helped. Spilled milk. "They'll only know someone is working with me. But your *cover* isn't blown, Andrew. No one is going to learn who you are. You are still very valuable that way. There will be other assignments."

"What are you going to say?"

"That I took steps to countermeasure the serious possibility of a leak. That I brought in some outside help, and the details must remain confidential to me alone."

"There will be a lot of questions..."

"I'll handle it. None of that is your concern. I'm going to keep your cover safe. I need your cover safe. I want you to come to the cottage tomorrow. For now, Andrew, go home and get some sleep."

CHAPTER TWENTY-EIGHT

It was 1:45 a.m. when Andrew got home. He sat in the living room in semi-darkness, his mind hyper alert, waves of anxiety ebbing and flowing.

Tonight he had killed two men. And nobody was to know it was him, except Lawrence. It all seemed surreal. He had been in Philadelphia only two weeks and he had killed two men. Alone. No fellow agent to talk to. Just lock it up and throw away the key.

He heard the bedroom door open and Madeleine's footsteps on the upstairs hall. He had told her that evening that he had a surveillance and that he would be very late getting home.

She came down, wrapping a housecoat over her nightgown, speaking quietly, "Andrew? Are you coming to bed?"

They had shot at him, wanted him dead. He would not have come home.

She came into the room and could see him better now. Something was wrong. She sat beside him on the sofa and looked at him, saw his anxiety. "What is it?"

He looked at her for a few moments. He leaned over and hugged her close. It was not at all like him to be so somber. After a moment she gently pushed him back to see his face, her eyes full of concern. "Andrew, what is it?"

He didn't know if he should tell her. He took her hand, stroked her hand. He knew he had to tell her. "I killed two men tonight."

She clutched at his hands, studying his face in disbelief, her eyes horrified.

He said, "It wasn't supposed to happen. I was just to watch the house."

She kept looking at him, shock on her face. He said, "I had no choice.

They fired on me. They tried to get away."

She covered her mouth with her hands. "You're alright?"

"Yes. The SWAT team was coming later...."

Her eyes dropped and she seemed not to have enough breath to make the words, her voice barely a whisper. "You could have been killed."

He didn't answer.

She began to cry silently.

"I know, Madeleine.... I know."

Her hand went across her womb. "Why were you there?"

"I can't tell you any more about it. I'm sorry."

Her tears increased. "Andrew..."

He held her. "I know...I know."

She shook her head, and sobbing quietly said, "No. You don't..."

He held her, his voice soft. "I know better than most what that would mean, Madeleine. I think about it every day. I love Chris and you and the baby more than anything."

"I'm ...fighting for my family. I feel overwhelmed when I think what could happen. We love you so much. We need you so much."

They held each other for several minutes. Andrew kissed her running wet cheeks.

"I'm going to talk to Lawrence," he murmured. "Things are going to change. I promise."

CHAPTER TWENTY-NINE

When Andrew arrived at the cottage, Lawrence was in a chair on the verandah looking out at the lake. He appeared meditative, a faraway look. Even when Andrew announced himself, Lawrence was slow to respond. He got up and a sadness seemed to take hold. All he said was, "Let's go inside."

In the kitchen Andrew said, "I have never killed anyone before. And I have never come as close to getting killed myself."

Lawrence simply said, "How was Madeleine?"

Andrew was struck at the leap. "She took it very hard."

"But she doesn't know anything more?"

"No, nothing. But it's not easy. I don't think you've got the right person for this assignment. I made a promise to Madeleine..."

Lawrence looked suddenly very tired. He half smiled, "Andrew, Andrew," he said slowly, his voice a mix of respect and compassion, "I've got the only *possible* person for this assignment."

"I'm not so sure. What did Washington say?"

Although Lawrence smiled, the aura of sadness was still there. "They were...very happy. Had our plan not been in place, Kipling and Kennedy would be long gone. It was the perfect justification of my original proposal to them. You will be recognized one day for what you've done. I promise."

"I'm not looking for recognition. I'm looking for a little normalcy. What did your people say about the takedown being called off?"

"There were questions. I told them I brought in outside help to counter a possible leak. It was a kick in the teeth to them. But obviously a leak had occurred. So they couldn't say much."

Up to this point they had been standing in the kitchen. Andrew went and sat in the living room and looked at Lawrence, making it clear he wanted to talk. Lawrence came in to the livingroom and sat down opposite, and waited.

Andrew finally said, "Wes, look, last night was big for me. I want to discuss what I'm doing here. Things don't feel right. This 'peculiar' assignment, to use your word...some things make sense...some things don't."

Lawrence nodded. "Andrew," he said sympathetically, "that's precisely why I asked you to come today. There is, in fact, a little more to it. I'm afraid that last night was really... only a side show."

Andrew felt himself tighten. His killing two men was a side show?

Lawrence looked steadily at Andrew. "That time I told you about Sylvie. It wasn't an abortion. There was no abortion."

Andrew's stomach knotted. Why is he going on about Sylvie? What has she to do with my assignments? After I have just expressed my reluctance to continue with this work. And why had he let me believe there had been an abortion? There was a big, unpleasant hole here. He had been deceived, and he began to feel a burning frustration.

Lawrence pressed on. "I arranged for the abortion through that woman." There was grief in Lawrence's voice. "I had arranged for Sylvie to come to my place that night, and I would take her to the abortionist. Sylvie showed up at my apartment at 8:30, a half hour late. She was greatly agitated. She said her parents would be coming home in three days. She didn't want to go through with the abortion. She wanted to tell her mother everything and get proper help."

Lawrence got up, his face showing strain. "I tried to explain but it was soon obvious we had very different perspectives. She didn't appreciate the outcomes for me if this got out – prison and the end of my career. My parents' shame. Her parents' shame."

Andrew could see Lawrence's anguish, but it didn't moderate Andrew's frustration. Lawrence began to pace. "She began to get in an awful state, angry, then crying, then angry. It got worse. She became hysterical, shrieking like she was in sharp pain, so loud I was afraid other tenants would hear. It scared me, you can imagine, my emotions like a roller coaster. She began yelling at me, 'You took advantage of me that night! I trusted you! Why did you have to do it?' Fear and anger boiled in me, but I tried to calm her. It only made her worse. She told me not to touch her."

Lawrence was absorbed by the agitation of the memory, his hands clenching. "In a sudden move she jumped at me. I was startled, her eyes blazing like she wanted to kill. She screamed, "Why did you do it?" She punched me hard on the nose, a punch with her fist, no mere slap, a sharp, stinging pain. And so quickly I didn't see it coming. That sudden hit...I was already on the edge."

His hand tremored and squeezed. "In a pure reflex action, I hit her. Once. Just once. Square in the face, with my fist. I know there was power in it. I know...it knocked her out. She was small and light. She fell straight back, her body rigid. Her head... struck the edge of the brick hearth. A bone splitting crack..."

He looked at the floor and blinked several times, as if he saw her again. "Her eyes didn't move. Her face... serene. I fell down to her. Her very pretty face. Now just a child's. She wasn't angry with me anymore. She was gone, her young life over. And there was nothing I could do about it. Nothing...I could do about it."

Andrew's insides were trembling. Although he didn't want to know the answer, he asked, "Does anyone know this?"

Lawrence shook his head. "No."

Andrew sucked in breath and got up. He walked to a side window. He turned and looked at Lawrence. "What is the truth here?" he said sharply. "Tell me what's going on. Why I'm hearing all this."

Lawrence said quietly, "It's the only way."

Andrew's voice was loud. "The only way *what*? *Why* did you tell me? This is *way* out of line!"

"It's the only way you might understand."

"Understand *what*? Stop talking in riddles!"

"Understand everything that's gone on in my life since then."

"Why *me*?"

"I need *you* to know this. I need *you*...to know."

An angry surge and Andrew's voice rose. "This whole thing, getting me here, getting me the transfer east, was all a sham. *Right*? You wanted me for some *ulterior* reason. *What is going on here? Tell me!*"

Lawrence shot back with the same angry tone. "Do you think this is *easy* for me? I'm *confessing*, Andrew. I'm not going to get up and run away. You can arrest me if you want. But just listen first. Trust me a bit longer."

"*Trust you?*" Andrew looked at Lawrence with fire. He had been pro-foundly tricked.

Lawrence's eyes pleaded for calm and he motioned to Andrew to sit. Andrew took a deep breath. Yelling was of no help to either. Not taking his eyes from Lawrence's, he sat down.

Lawrence said, "I am very sorry." He paused to let the waters settle, then he sat. "I was so afraid. Please try to understand what I was going through at those moments, Sylvie's body lying there."

Lawrence's body was shaking lightly. "What I then did was so wrong. But please try to understand, I was only twenty-one. All I could think was to protect myself. And to protect myself from one thing, I had to do something else. I was jumpy, couldn't think straight at all. Nobody knew she was with me. Her older brother was at home, but she said she hadn't told him where she was going. It was our secret. I kept telling myself her life was over. I couldn't bring her back. God help me, I hadn't intended that to happen, never in all imagination. An innocent girl."

Lawrence got up and walked, nervous energy building. "I tried to be calm, think practically. Self-preservation, that was now uppermost. My concern was the body. Without it, what's the proof of any crime, of her even being dead? But with it... there would be an autopsy. There was the baby... my blood on my hands. Everything told me to bury her body."

Lawrence's hands clenched. He walked the room. "It was just after dark. Only one other tenant's car was in our parking lot. I moved my car into a near dark corner. I put the shovel in the back seat and opened the trunk. I went back and carried Sylvie out, cradled to my chest. I was setting her in the trunk, my heart pounding like a hammer, when there was a sound, like a scrape of shoe on the unlit road. I thought I saw something move...a shadow. I waited, didn't see anything. Thought it must have been my nerves."

Lawrence's fist worked at his chin. "I knew a woods not far from where I grew up, where I used to hunt squirrels as a kid, well off the old highway ten miles out of Buffalo. Nobody ever went there anymore."

Lawrence's eyes darted as he remembered. "Two shallow ruts left the highway, mostly overgrown. A hundred yards in there was an old gate. I opened it and drove another hundred yards. I carried her into the scrub. I dug a half hour, hard ground. I covered her. I knew it was too shallow. But I began to think this wouldn't be her final resting place. I would wait for a few days until I was more sure of myself and find some place further away, more secure."

"I came out of the scrub, stupidly carrying the shovel. An old man was walking his dog, carrying a flashlight, the beam bobbing as he walked. The dog was loose, a big lab, and it made a happy dash for me before I could get in my car. The man flashed the light towards me. The dog started jumping up, pawing me on the chest, barking. The man hurried over, apologizing. 'Didn't know anyone was along here,' he said. 'It's not like Buster to be aggressive like this,' he said, slapping the dog down."

Lawrence looked at Andrew. "He smelled the blood, of course. On my sweater, where Sylvie's head had rested twice. I figured there might be blood on the ground and into the scrub to the grave. The man looked me over, concerned. I didn't think he saw the blood in the poor light. But he saw the shovel. I felt it was more suspicious to say nothing, so I said, 'I just buried my old dog. He was hit by a truck on the road tonight.' That would explain the blood on my chest if he had noticed. It would also explain my obvious agitation. I said, 'We used to walk in these woods years ago.' He said he was sorry, knew what it meant to lose a dog. He leashed the lab and headed back in the direction of the gate."

Lawrence looked at Andrew a moment, then sat down, his face grim. "I waited a bit to give the man time to be gone. I was sick with fear. I knew that dog would find the body, maybe the next time into those woods. I considered digging Sylvie up again right then, but then what? I couldn't think straight and needed rest. I would go back at first light and remove the body. And this time with a proper plan - a lake, or a river, tied and weighted with rocks. As I was driving out, just past the gate, I saw him still walking. I waved. His flashlight beam rose and held, catching the rear of my car as I passed. I thought of my license plate."

"When I got home, the phone was ringing. At first I thought of not answering it, but then thought it would help my alibi. In an odd way I hoped it would be one of the guys from work. It would help anchor me, settle me down."

Lawrence looked desperately sad and his eyes closed a moment and he took some breaths. "It wasn't. A man said he wanted to talk to me… about a girl's body. That it would be in my best interests to have a talk before anything went wrong. I made like I didn't know what he was talking about. I was shaking like a leaf and my voice wasn't any better.

He said don't play this thing stupid, that the abortionist had learned that I was a cop, she's no fool. She figured it was a set-up, to nail her because the cops were sore she got off the first time. She told all this to a friend of hers, because she was proud of herself, smart to have seen it for what it was. That's why she had lasted as long as she had. But this friend, the guy she had talked to, wasn't convinced. He saw that if it was all real, that if a cop actually wanted an abortion done illegally, the cop was very vulnerable. The guy saw opportunity in it. Because the guy knew another man, Salvatore Cavaco, who would pay to get something like this on a cop, to put a cop securely in his pocket, to get inside police information from time to time. Cavaco learned I wasn't on shift that night at all, that there was no abortion sting underway. He figured things were for real. So he sent a man, the man who was on the phone with me, to the abortionist's place to check things out. When Sylvie and I hadn't shown up as agreed, this man came around to my place, saw lights in my apartment, and wondered what gives. He said, "I saw the hanky panky, you stuffing her in the trunk. I know the woods your girlfriend is in. The man with the dog was very helpful.' Then he said, 'Cavaco wants to meet with you. Tonight.'"

Lawrence looked at Andrew. "Did I have a choice?"

Andrew sat intensely still, watching Lawrence with full concentration, a chilling fear taking hold as Andrew began to realize where this was going.

Lawrence continued. "I met him that night. A deserted country property in darkness. I never actually saw him; there was a stone wall between us. He said, 'You killed her. You buried her body. And you've got to hope the police never find that body, because with the body comes the baby and the belief that you killed her *because* she was pregnant. Not a nice picture. The abortionist would testify it was you who came to her. But I can help you. I have the body. And it's going into a very cold freezer. Nobody will ever know about it if you cooperate with me. The man with the dog isn't going to remember your face, your car, your license. And this won't cost you anything. Except information from time to time. Do we have an understanding?' I said we did. He said that if I ever failed in my obligation, or if he were ever arrested, the girl's body would be produced to the police with a full statement attached. And more, he said, 'I know you have a sister who you are fond of. Same age as the dead girl.

You wouldn't want anything tragic to happen to her either.'"

Andrew asked coldly. "Who was this Cavaco?"

"A very clever man. Had an outfit. Bank robberies, Wells Fargo heists, jewelry store robberies, fencing diamonds. Buffalo, Rochester, other cities in New York State, sometimes into New Jersey and Pennsylvania. Outfoxing us continually for several years. A name well known in law enforcement circles. Even though I was only a rookie at the time, I asked to be assigned to his case. My bosses saw I was eager to learn, had no other commitments. I was involved on a daily basis in his investigation for almost a year. I was in the perfect position to pass information to him through his channels, always keeping him one step ahead of the law. I know he had other informants."

Andrew's face was still. He stopped watching Lawrence. He focused only on putting the pieces together.

Lawrence continued. "Towards the end, Cavaco was striking more and more often. There were upwards of a dozen police in Buffalo working solely on this case. And probably half again that number in Rochester. And the State Police and the FBI had manpower on it. More and more leads were coming forward weekly. The heat was on, the net closing. Then a takedown opportunity. The information was that Cavaco and two others were holed up in a motel in the Catskills. A dragnet was thrown. I leaked information on the impending takedown. But it was as if he didn't get it in time. He fell right into the trap. There was a police chase in the mountains. His car plowed through a guard rail and fell 200 feet into a ravine. There was an explosion, incinerating everyone inside. Only charred remains. I was stunned but utterly relieved. As were the police who were desperate to end it. And so there it was, case closed. My pact with the devil was over. But I had to get out of Buffalo. I needed a new start. I finished college. Then joined the FBI."

Lawrence looked to Andrew knowing how ironic, how fraudulent, it would seem to him that Lawrence went back to law enforcement. "I was desperate to do the right thing, Andrew. What could I do with my life to make up for what I had done? I saw a possibility. Do everything to take down serious crime around me. Devote myself to becoming the best investigator, the most tenacious, hardworking, never stop investigator. Make life sacrifices again and again. Do my penance my own way. Make amends every day. Remember every day, every waking moment, what I had done."

Andrew hit his fist on the sofa. He jumped up and barked, "You put your own skin ahead of everything else! Nothing more complicated than that! Nothing better than that! Nothing noble in that!"

"I used to see life that way, too..."

"I don't want to hear about it! Tell me why I shouldn't turn you in *right now*!"

"Because you need me out for a while longer."

Andrew looked at Lawrence in challenge and said coldly, "And why is that?" But even as he said it, he knew the terrible truth. That Lawrence had the upper hand. He would have the last word. Because he had the answer that Andrew had needed his whole life.

Lawrence said calmly. "Your father knew who Macky's killer was."

Andrew's mind raced. If his father knew Macky's killer, it meant his father knew his own killer. And for Lawrence to know that meant Lawrence knew as well. The man who stood before him knew who had killed his father, and more, had known all along. Andrew could feel his insides crumbling. His voice was suddenly weak. "How did you know who killed my father?"

Lawrence's eyes were calm and steady. "Your father told me."

But Lawrence had never told anyone. And now Andrew knew why. In the floating pieces he found the inescapable conclusion, and he knew why. His voice was almost a whisper. "Salvatore Cavaco didn't die, did he?"

Lawrence shook his head. "No."

It all began to make sense. Andrew felt as if he had been bludgeoned.

CHAPTER THIRTY

L awrence's voice was quiet. "Be patient with me. I, too, have known suffering and immense loneliness in this. Please hear me out."

Andrew could see Lawrence only strangely now. And as an enemy. He disciplined himself, stilled his coursing impulse to strike, because he needed answers now. Answers, not blood. Not yet.

Lawrence spoke with an even tone which begged calm from Andrew. "About noon on the day your father was taken, he called me. He told me he was at a pay phone. Calls from the police station are logged. He wanted the fact of our conversation to remain confidential. He said he had attended a murder scene late the night before - Pino Macky. That when he arrived, Macky was dying quickly. When he asked Macky who had shot him, Macky whispered only 'Cavaco… is alive.'"

Lawrence stopped a moment, remembering, taking a deep breath. "Andrew, I was stupefied. If Macky was to be believed, Cavaco had only staged his death. I was afraid."

"Why had my father wanted his call to remain confidential?"

"Cavaco's case was notorious because of his spectacular successes, his cleverness, and because of his use of informants - corrupt police."

Lawrence nodded, the ready admission he was among them. "He always had ears on the inside. Your father certainly knew this so wanted to hold his cards tight to his chest. Your father ran a rap sheet on Macky that night. He learned that Macky had been operating in Buffalo and Rochester in the early to middle 50's when Cavaco was very active. Your father told me there were sufficient connections in his mind to make him convinced Macky knew Cavaco. He believed that if Cavaco was actually alive and was behind Macky's murder, it meant he was operating in Philadelphia and there was the real risk he would have informants here. Or he would soon have, to monitor the progress of the investigation into

Macky's murder. If we got too close, Cavaco would know and he would vanish once again. We would lose the opportunity."

Lawrence looked at Andrew and paused, seeing in his face and manner Andrew's father again so clearly. "Your father knew that I had been involved in the investigation of Cavaco in Buffalo six years earlier. For that reason and because I was the FBI's liaison man, he wanted to speak to me, confidentially. He proposed a two-part investigation, one conducted by the Philadelphia P.D. as a routine homicide, they being entirely unaware that Cavaco might be alive, the other conducted secretly by the FBI, piggy-backing on police information fed to us by your father. We would identify and snare Cavaco without his being aware we knew he was alive."

Andrew got up, nervous energy overbuilding, and walked to one side of the room, his face firmly set. He turned to Lawrence. "What exactly happened that day?"

Lawrence cast a sensitive look back. "Your father and I agreed to meet at 6:00 that evening at your house."

Andrew said pointedly, "But that put you in a predicament, didn't it? You would be at risk again with Cavaco alive. If he were ever arrested, he would expose your killing of Sylvie."

Lawrence nodded, "Yes."

"Did you tell anyone that day what my father told you?"

Lawrence shook his head. "No."

Andrew leaned aggressively. "And then, conveniently for you, my father was already taken, about two hours before your meeting time."

"Andrew, I didn't know that was going to happen. I would never have wished it to have been that way. Believe me. I arrived at your house and found police cars there. I...turned and left."

"Of course. And told no one what you knew about Cavaco, about what my father told you." Andrew thrust his finger and shouted, "My father *trusted* you!"

He fought to control his outburst. He knew rationally it was better to let Lawrence talk without threat. Lawrence would say more, protect himself less. In a restrained voice he said, "What were you going to do if my father had not been taken?"

"I would have cooperated, done my job. But kept my head down. If Cavaco were found, and he chose to expose me to gain some advantage,

I couldn't do anything about that."

Andrew said angrily. "*If* he were found. *If* you didn't whisper slyly in his ear in the meantime!"

"I would never have done that."

"But that didn't come to pass for you anyway. Because my father was taken. Only you knew Cavaco was alive. You had to make a decision. Say nothing and you were safe, or tell what my father told you and let the chips fall. And, of course, you said absolutely nothing."

Lawrence spoke quietly. "All true. But Andrew, even if I had spoken, it would not have saved your father. It would not have made the least bit of difference. It was already too late. I know it with certainty."

"It would have made a difference *to me!* I would not have had twenty years of not even knowing why my father was taken! I would at least have had some satisfaction in knowing that the law was hunting Cavaco down! Do you have any idea what I lived with?"

Lawrence's eyes lowered and his hands came together, but he didn't speak.

After a few moments Andrew said, more quietly, "How convenient it was for you again, that it wouldn't have made any difference if you had spoken up. Already too late to save my Dad. Easy on your conscience. And you didn't say anything afterward either. All those years."

Lawrence said calmly, "You have every right to be angry, Andrew. It was never my intention to hide all this away, to bury what I knew. Not at all. I wanted to have it both ways - find out on my own who Cavaco was, then, maybe, take him out myself. And silence the threat to me, and to my family."

Andrew watched Lawrence closely with every fibre. All this was leading to something exceptional and Andrew had to let the past go for now, put aside any thoughts of immediate retribution.

Lawrence said, "You are thinking that it all would have been so easy for me back then, that the right path was so obvious. That if I just revealed what your dad told me it would be a simple matter of going out and arresting Cavaco." Now Lawrence's voice rose. "*But no one knew who he actually was. What he looked like. What his name was. Where he lived. What he did. There was no picture of him.*"

Lawrence took a breath. "Cavaco had never been arrested, never photographed by police, never printed. When I was involved in the investigation in Buffalo, there was only one known photograph of him, a high school class picture, taken when he was 14. In Buffalo we relied purely on sightings of those who knew him back then. He had no doubt altered his appearance after he 'died'. What did he look like now? And more, it appears he was *not* at the gala in the Starlight Room that night. Believe me, I watched that investigation like a hawk, knowing precisely what to look for. As the evidence accumulated on every man at that gala, I scrutinized every one."

Andrew was measured, composing himself, "Do you know who he is today?"

"No. I doubt that anyone does."

"Do you know if he is alive today?"

"I... believe he is. But I don't know who he is, where he is, anything. Andrew, I want you to understand what was going through my mind twenty years ago. Speaking up back then would offer little in catching Cavaco. He would learn he was being pursued and he would disappear, probably out of the country. He would never be found, never apprehended. Your father's killing would go unpunished. But I would have much to lose if I had spoken up. Cavaco would learn through his informants it was me. Sylvie's body would be produced. I would go to prison; a contract would be put out on me. But worse, I feared his wrath on my sister, on my parents, at being forced away again."

Andrew said with energy, but control. "Yes, you would go to prison. You would probably die. But I'm not convinced your family would ever be at risk. Arrangements would be made. There are witness protection plans. You lean on the protection of your family to justify your silence."

"No protection plan on earth would shield them from him. He would dig and dig through intimidation or bribery until he got to someone who would tell him something. And he would build on that, finding someone else who would tell him something more. Eventually he would find them."

Andrew said, "Only if he wanted to, and very badly. His killing Macky and my father were acts of self-preservation. Running after your sister and parents expends energy to little purpose."

Lawrence said with deep feeling, his voice strong, "You don't have to believe my fears for my family are justified. You can arrest me now. Put my sister and parents in protection. But Cavaco will find out and vanish and *you will never find him*. I have lived my life for twenty years *against* that playing out. Regardless of what you think of me, I am more valuable to you here, not in some prison. At least not yet. I have not had a future since I was twenty-one. No relationship. No love. No wife. No child. Guilt and shame have made me a living shell of a human being. *You realize I didn't have to tell you anything about this! Expose myself like this! Ever!* I could have let life go on. Or if I was going to get you involved, it would have been much simpler for me just to tell you I had received an anonymous tip, and let you run from there. Without exposing all of myself to you. *Understand?* I am detestable. Yes! I am abhorrent. Yes! But I wanted to come clean with you! I felt I owed it to you! I've told you because I believe with your help, this unique opportunity, we can get the man who killed your father. Put him and his organization beyond hurting anyone again. And then I turn myself in. And my family, though shamed in the end, at least is not at risk of being killed."

Lawrence was agitated as if he might be overcome. He looked at Andrew, appealing, "You're the best hope. So I wanted you to know everything I know. We need each other to see this through."

Andrew sat still, replaying what he was being told, letting himself calm more. Neither spoke for a long minute. Then Andrew asked, without accusation, "Why not seek out another colleague long before me?"

"No other colleague would have enough invested in the capture of Cavaco. Who but you would be motivated enough to bear the risk, to carry this out to a conclusion? Another colleague would be duty bound to turn me in. Or not prepared to risk their career in an unorthodox situation. You have no other duties. Your time is mine. And no one here knows you're here."

Andrew thought for several moments, then asked, "Your plan twenty years ago ..." His voice trailed off, still thinking it through.

"I adopted the position your father did. Keep my cards close to my chest. Protect the information. But in my case, tell no one. Wait for the evidence of the investigation to come in. See if I could make a match, discover who he is. Without him knowing anyone knew he was alive let alone hunting him."

Andrew said, "And when you made an identification of Cavaco, arrest him? Or kill him outright, and avoid him ever revealing your past?"

Lawrence said, "Honestly, I didn't know. I had to first identify him, see exactly what I was dealing with, and then decide. But the practical difficulty presented itself as the case was investigated. For two years it went on. I had access to all of the investigation material. And it was thorough. There didn't appear to me to be any match between anyone who attended the gala and Cavaco." Lawrence looked introspective, looking at a puzzle. *"There was something somewhere that had been over-looked. There had to be."*

Now he had a defeated look. He said quietly, "But there it was. Time passed. My resolve weakened. I threw myself into my work. I received accolades. I was promoted. I... was safe doing nothing."

Andrew saw a glimmer of Lawrence's past, his long struggle. Andrew said, "But something happened."

Lawrence nodded. "I was tormented. I fell into drug use, even heroin. I was living a private hell. Then, one day, I read about you. The tavern fight. Your incredible courage. You reached a hand out to me. The article said you wanted to pursue a career in law enforcement."

Andrew said quietly, "You sent that money."

Lawrence nodded. "I knew you would achieve whatever goals you set. I kept myself aware of your progress. I hatched a vague plan." Lawrence paused and looked at Andrew, weighing something. Then he said, "You know, you don't get into the FBI with blemishes in your past. Rejection was written all over your application. Have you ever wondered about that?"

Andrew was stunned. "Are you saying... you did something?"

"I knew people with influence. I asked them to let me know when your application came in. I went to Washington, to HQ. I made your case. An exception was made."

"What did you tell them?"

"I told them many things. About your father. About the very impressive young man I knew you were. I told them I would ...stake my life on you."

Andrew was quiet. He had ached to be accepted into the FBI. And when acceptance did come, he felt so honored, so unbelievably lucky.

He weighed all he had heard. The point was, for whatever Lawrence's personal reasons, justifiable to Andrew or not, what had been done was done. Or more to the point, what had *not* been done. But that was now in the past. There was only the future, the next step.

Andrew said, "Do you know anything about Cavaco now? Anything new?"

"I have no precise knowledge of anyone who might be Cavaco. My radar was always up for any telltale signs."

Andrew could read something new on Lawrence's face. "We experienced some assignment failures, very random, but we speculated there might be a leak in our office, and possibly in Philly P.D. We have been monitoring things as tightly as we can. Then last month, Senator Bloom, who was sequestered in a safe house, was killed. Bloom was being extorted by someone known as 'The Watcher'. The location and other details of the safe house were leaked. That's the way Cavaco worked."

"You think Cavaco is The Watcher."

Lawrence opened his hands. "Possibly. The Watcher makes men disappear, several over the last years. And they are never found. Not in a dumpster. Not in a river. Nowhere. It was the way he worked even in Buffalo. No body, no crime."

Andrew pondered, "My father was taken away. Not just killed. Never found. And Macky, too, was being dragged to a car trunk…That way Cavaco controls the evidence."

Lawrence nodded, well aware of that connection. He waited a few moments, appreciating how much he was asking Andrew to digest. Then he said, "Something else. Cavaco always jealously guarded his identity. The identity of The Watcher is closely guarded. Bloom described him as 'unknowable.' When I contacted the Boston office in relation to one of the disappearances, I learned that two men had been arrested and questioned regarding a so-called 'Watcher' and were told they had done some small jobs for him, but that no one had any idea who he was. And in the case of Bloom, all The Watcher's couriers who were collecting Bloom's payments at post offices were picked up and interrogated and it was clear they were only small cogs. None knew who was at the top, or who was even directly above them. In a regular organization, something would have surfaced over time. But here it's highly coordinated secrecy."

Andrew reflected. "Cavaco was hooded at my house, in front of his own men."

"Exactly."

Andrew got up and paced. "Is Bloom's investigation getting *anywhere?*"

Lawrence shook his head. "Nowhere. And whoever The Watcher is, he has informants. He's aware of our progress. Every step."

Andrew said, "You want me to pick up where you were twenty years ago. And find Cavaco."

"Where your *father* was twenty years ago. And with the evidence I now know, inside and out. I can narrow your work. And you have an edge. Cavaco knows me, but he doesn't know you."

"And if I find Cavaco, then what?"

"When he's behind bars, I turn myself in. I will be grateful, Andrew. I will have reached the end."

"And what about me? My career?"

"You are acting solely on my direction in complete secrecy to uncover this Watcher in the murder of Senator Bloom. Washington knows you're assisting me in the face of leaks. Your taking out Kipling and Kennedy proved the strategy."

"Yes, but if I find Cavaco, and he's not The Watcher, there will be questions."

"We didn't have this talk tonight. You know nothing about Cavaco. I will explain I kept that from you. But if you find Cavaco, you stumbled upon him in the pursuit of The Watcher. I gave you direction to pursue him without explaining all the background."

"And if I don't find Cavaco?"

Lawrence seemed suddenly weighted. He spoke slowly. "You really mean…. what do you do about me? Now that you know …everything."

Andrew watched Lawrence very carefully. Lawrence folded his hands and said quietly, "I want this man, Andrew. As much as you do. Maybe more. I accept whatever comes to me if I know he is no longer free. But if you don't find him…" a small tremor moved on Lawrence's lips, "my life… everything…it's up to you. I'm now in your hands."

CHAPTER THIRTY-ONE

Cavaco hurled the crystal goblet across the room, shattering it against the stone wall. That was now two. Nix knew there would be more.

He watched Cavaco fill a third goblet with the dark red wine. He and Nix were in 'the cellar' at Cavaco's home, a spacious, subterranean, private room sunk deeper than the basement, a room whose walls and high ceiling were made of rough cut stone, its floor black slate. The chandeliers were dimmed, a bright fire in the open stone hearth supplying the real light, casting shadows on the walls. Dark leather furniture and heavy slabbed tables completed the appearance of a drinking room out of medieval Spain, appealing to Cavaco's sense of heritage. And it was soundproof. He liked to descend here when he was unhappy and wanted to brood and drink. And throw glasses.

"We're going to look ridiculous!" His voice echoed in the cavernous room. The killing of Kennedy and Kipling had greatly disturbed Cavaco, shaking to the core his confidence in their very well paid network of informants. His voice boomed. "If we can't protect people who ask for our services, who pay for our services, then we're going to be out of business! Our one-of-a- kind reputation is based on the *excellence* of our information. *Inside* information. *Timely* information. People pay us *big* because they know they can stake their *lives* on it!" His voice suddenly quieted. "Until now."

Immediately on hearing the news of the killing of Kennedy and Kipling, Nix had sought every scrap of information from all of his sources to find out what the hell had happened. All had reported the same thing: nobody in the FBI or the Philadelphia P.D. had known that Kipling's and Kennedy's hideout had been located. Nobody on either force had been involved in that search. The first indication that their whereabouts were known was Lawrence's surprise announcement that evening of takedown preparations.

Although Nix had clear concerns about what had happened, he didn't share Cavaco's calamitous view exactly. Nix had learned from their sources that the bullets used in the killings had come from only one gun, and that markings on the ground confirmed there was only one gunman. It could hardly be called a police takedown. Nix would be the voice of moderation to Cavaco's rant.

"Our service to Kennedy," Nix began, "was to give advance notice of an impending takedown. And we gave him notice, six hours ahead of time. What happened to him and Kipling after that was outside the terms of our contract. We didn't take his money to protect him from every contingency. A lone gunman operating with only Lawrence's knowledge is not something we can protect against. We're not a personal bodyguard service."

Cavaco looked at his goblet as he turned it by the stem. "Counsellor, counsellor," he intoned quietly now. "Technically correct. Kennedy was not snuffed in a 'takedown', the very word referenced in our arrangement with him." In a mocking tone with theatrical flair, Cavaco continued. "That was the deal, your Honor, the stipulations of the contract, advance notice of any *takedown*. That's what Kennedy paid for. That's what Kennedy got. The fact that somebody with very good aim was sitting on Kennedy's very doorstep long *before* the takedown is sad indeed, but irrelevant to the terms of the contract. May his soul rest in peace. I rest my case."

Cavaco swirled the wine in the goblet and took a deep drink. His voice was full and loud again. "But this isn't a tidy courtroom full of legal niceties. How will it play on the *street*? That's what's important. People will hear Kennedy came to us. And I'll tell you what they're going to say. 'The Watcher says pay the big bucks and you're protected. But Kennedy was stalked and was killed. On The Watcher's *watch*! The Watcher knew squat. Is that what you call irony or what?'" Cavaco drained the wine then flung goblet three with a fury. "We'll be a fucking joke!" He grabbed up another goblet and, gritting, launched it, goblet smithereens noticeably accumulating.

He sank heavily into a deep leather chair. "I don't want it to ever be on anyone's lips that The Watcher failed. I don't want even the perception of failure again. Never another job botched..."

Nix calmly poured himself a Lagavulin and savored its peaty

smokiness. "Rest assured, our inside informant network is not broken. Not in the least. Lawrence explained that he got a solid tip on Kennedy's whereabouts and that, to avoid a possible leak, he went to outside help. Given the Bloom leak, he said he was being precautionary. And he isn't spilling the beans even to his closest colleagues about who he went to."

"Infuriating," Cavaco mumbled, staring at the fire. "Making us look like a joke."

Nix paced slowly as he spoke. "Our concern is whether Lawrence might side-step our informants again, go to outside help again, on some file important to us. If there is some new game on, we want to know the players so we can stay a step ahead."

Cavaco leaned forward to refill his goblet, it being spared for the moment. "Ironic that we've been outplayed by none other than Wesley Lawrence, our friend from so long ago. And he doesn't even know it's us he's playing with."

"Indeed," Nix nodded, and went on, "so how do we beat Lawrence? I learned that on the night Kipling and Kennedy were killed, Lawrence had come to the office at 6:00 and announced the takedown. He stayed at the office until 9:00 directing the preparations and coordinating with Philly P.D. Then he left. According to forensics, Kennedy and Kipling were killed around 11:30. Lawrence returned to the office just after midnight and called the takedown off. There certainly wasn't enough time in the interim for him to have been at the scene itself. So he had to have heard from his mystery help that Kennedy and Kipling had been taken out."

Cavaco was nodding, a faint smile. "By telephone, probably at his home."

"Yes, the simplest. The most likely." Nix reached and tossed a small log onto the fire sending a burst of orange sparks upward.

Cavaco sat up, more animated. "I see where you're going. That's a start. Let's get his telephone records back a month. Check calls that came in that evening and find out who belongs to that number." He leaned back in the deep chair, a glimmer of satisfaction showing. "If we have a matter in future where Lawrence could be involved, we keep his outside help under close watch, too."

Lively shadows now danced on the wall. Cavaco watched them a few moments, but his look then settled, morbid as before. His voice rose,

"Because I don't ever want The Watcher to look ridiculous again." His dark eyes searched the far stone wall. With an angry grunt, he pitched the goblet.

———•+•———

Teresa Clemens, a seasoned, twenty-five-year administrator at AT&T, got the call at home in the evening when she was on her second glass of sherry. It had been some time since she had had a 'special request', as she called them.

It had begun many years ago when a very nice gentleman who said he was a private investigator approached her seeming to know she was in embarrassing financial straits at the time. He had asked if she would do just a small thing for him - divulge the private phone records of a certain man believed to be having an affair. He had explained it was a difficult file because the man was being 'dodgy'. (At the time, Teresa was recently divorced and, coincidentally, had often described her own husband as exactly that – dodgy. And for good reason, she had learned, as he, too, had been having an affair.)

She had at first balked at the shameless insolence of the request. But he had then promised her so much money, her moral clarity became blurry and her trepidation was quieted. Fulfilling special requests had thereafter become an occasional occurrence.

In the current instance, she was asked to provide the details of all calls in the last month in connection with the home phone of a certain Wesley Lawrence, 5 Link St., Philadelphia, who was, the usual explanation, allegedly having an affair. Such detail was to include the phone numbers Lawrence called, their dates and times, including the names and addresses of the registered holders of those numbers, and the phone numbers making calls to Lawrence, including the dates and times, and the names and addresses of the registered holders of those numbers.

Teresa confirmed she could manage that request, reminding the caller that it would be processed 'upon the usual payment being received as per usual'. When she hung up, she was feeling tipsy. She laughed lightly at herself engaging in this mischievous cloak and dagger. But those men deserved it.

She reached for another cigarette, poured a third sherry, and considered with some delight what she might buy with the naughty lucre.

CHAPTER THIRTY-TWO

A ndrew returned to Lawrence's cottage as they agreed. He saw a stack of labelled banker boxes in the living room - a copy of all FBI investigation materials in the case of Macky and his father.

Andrew sat at the kitchen table as Lawrence brought in documents from another room. Lawrence said, "Cavaco was never at any time arrested, printed, or photographed. The only picture we had of him was a high school class picture taken when he was fourteen."

Lawrence laid a glossy picture before Andrew, a class of twenty young adolescents, pimply and awkward. "I cut this out of the yearbook and had it enlarged." Lawrence put his finger on one of the boys - olive complected skin, dark hair, dark eyes, shorter than most. Andrew studied him closely. Even at that age, Cavaco's look conveyed boldness.

Lawrence said, "He must have recognized the danger of having his picture available to authorities. He never posed again." He set down a large newspaper clipping dated 1955, a forensic artist's depiction of Cavaco, age-progressed from 14 to 28, his then age in 1955. "This is what authorities went on. The artist was aided by an anonymous source who knew Cavaco."

A shiver traced down Andrew's spine as he looked at the supposed face of the man who had killed his father. He stared at the eyes, eyes he had seen twenty years before peering out from holes in a black hood.

"In '61, your dad was taken. I waited two years, hoping the investigation would pinpoint a suspect who I alone would know as Cavaco. Of course, it never did. In '63 I went to a private forensic art lab which specialized in children gone missing. I showed them the enlarged high school photo. I told them he was a cousin of mine. I didn't show them the 1955 'portrait'; I didn't want to bias them. I had them do a progression to age 34, Cavaco's age in 1961."

Lawrence placed another age-progressed portrait of Cavaco on the table. Andrew noted immediately the similarities in critical features between the 1955 portrait and that of 1961. Two different artists working from the same early picture had produced amazingly similar results, a convergence that gave credence to both. The cheekbones had taken on more prominence, the face broader and lengthened, the eyebrows filled in, the chin fully formed. The face had grown somewhat downward and outward, the bridge of the nose a little higher, the cranium expanded, eyes narrowed, mouth widened, nose lengthened.

Lawrence said, "Note the eyes. The artist said a person's basic 'look' holds true throughout life, most notably in the eyes." Again Andrew felt a visceral tension as he studied them.

Lawrence went on, "Photographs of 40 of the men at the gala, men somewhat shorter and with lower voices, had been taken, most of them surreptitiously. I had access to the records of the investigation, including those pictures. I made comparisons with that last age-progressed portrait. It was a huge disappointment that not one man's picture really squared in any probability. I recognized that Cavaco would likely have had plastic surgery, made hair color changes, perhaps a mustache, and so forth. I accounted for those possibilities. And assumed he would have tried, if anything, to make himself look older, not younger, given his real age of only 34 at the time. But still nothing."

Lawrence walked over to a cabinet and pulled open a drawer. "Of course, while investigators had been searching almost blindly for a needle in a haystack, I knew that needle would be 34, maybe look a little older, and that he would have an olive complexion, something he couldn't change. I knew his eyes were dark brown, although might have been made blue or green by contacts. And his hair would not be made blonde or red, or even light brown, not with that skin complexion. Probably black, or dark brown, perhaps artificially graying. Those are all things I looked for. But I still came up empty."

Lawrence reflected on his disappointment. "I want you to know everything investigators knew. Everything I knew. I want you to understand what they were facing. What I was facing."

Lawrence reached his hand into the drawer and withdrew a laminated 8x12 color drawing. He studied it a few moments. "A year ago I visited another forensic lab. I gave them the enlarged high school photo, the only hard starting point we have. Cavaco is now 54. Admittedly it's a difficult task to project what someone might look like 40 years later, particularly when the baseline is a 14-year-old. But the science is much better now. Much more reliable growth data allows better predictions of structural changes. And computers are now available to process and analyze that data."

Lawrence set the drawing on the table, a portrait of what Cavaco should look like now. Andrew looked at it with steel cold attention. Cavaco had developed jowls, his lips were thinner, his hairline somewhat receded. His face had grown somewhat longer.

Lawrence said, "The artist has made a set of assumptions on hair color, style, and length favoring a narcissistic view, reflecting choices a man would be likely to make today who is no longer ducking his description."

Andrew picked it up and sat back in the chair, taking a deep breath, burning the image into his mind of the man he vowed he was going to find.

Just north of Philadelphia off 611, Andrew pulled into a quiet motel, the Weeping Willows. He had seen it on his many trips to the aerodrome and decided it would suit. He wanted seclusion for a few days, free of all distractions, free of Madeline asking any questions. He had told her he had to be away on an investigation but would call her every day.

He backed his car up close to his unit's door. From the trunk he toted eleven bulging banker boxes into the unit. Ten contained the investigation materials and reports on the murder of Macky and his father's disappearance. The eleventh held transcripts of interviews of possible suspects and a copy of reel to reel tapes of those interviews.

He rearranged the furniture. The small desk went to the middle of the room. The single twin bed was shoved several feet over up against the wall. He relocated the lamps to give the desk good light. The two-seat couch, he dragged to the left side of the desk to support stacks of files he wanted in arm's reach. A single sofa chair he situated to the right side for the same purpose.

He unpacked the boxes and arranged the materials: interviews and tapes onto a lamp table, the lamp removed; bound summary reports onto the couch; loose documents and photographs categorized and placed in neat stacks behind the desk on the floor; detailed surveillance memos piled up on the sofa chair.

An hour and a half later all the boxes were empty and he stacked them against one wall. From his luggage, he pulled out a coffee maker he had picked up. He knew the two-cup variety offered by the motel just wouldn't cut it. He set two bags of coffee on the little coffee stand.

Then he stood back and surveyed the room. The volume of paper was staggering, thousands and thousands of pages. An initial investigation of 250 men, reduced in short order to about 40, and ultimately a comprehensive drilling down on 15. But much would be repetitive. He knew he could slice through a lot of it, having a critical advantage over those original investigators. He hoped he could sift and screen this mountain of paper enough to make it give up just one telling detail that had been overlooked.

He reached into a file folder and took out the laminated 'portrait' of Cavaco as he should look today. He walked to the television and propped the portrait on top. He sat back down at the desk. He looked around the room one more time. A lot of paper. A very big haystack. He was under no illusions. Lawrence had said the paper gave up nothing. 'I don't think Cavaco was at the gala'. Andrew knew he would battle fatigue and despair. He hoped he would not fail.

He looked at the portrait staring back at him, Cavaco's eyes cold, bold, taunting. Cavaco would keep him resolute.

CHAPTER THIRTY-THREE

'Miss Nomer' was now under full sail under a sun drenched sky. Cavaco was at the helm wearing a rakish seaman's cap working the magnificent teak and brass wheel. Nix stood near, sunglasses glinting as he perused the open water ahead.

A tanned Miss Helsinki in white French bikini appeared with a silver tray bearing colorful drinks. She served one to Cavaco, along with a succulent kiss to his cheek, then, with exquisite poise, served Nix, along with a sparkling teeth smile. She floated away with a ballerina's grace, disappearing down a hatchway.

Nix had just made it to the dock moments before departure. At that point, Cavaco had been preoccupied in getting off and sails up as quickly as possible. Now with 'Miss Nomer' on a long, straight tack, Cavaco could be attentive to what Nix had to report. And he knew Cavaco would not be pleased.

Nix began, "We hoped to discover who Lawrence's secret outside help is. This morning I received his home phone records - calls in, calls out - for the last month. He's not a big talker. Three calls to or from the office – not his secret help there, of course. A few calls out for pizza or Chinese, a few calls to a hardware store and lumberyard. But... there was the one call *in*, right on the money, 11:40 on the night Kennedy and Kipling were killed. It came from a payphone outside a general store a mile from Kipling's house. I'm certain that's how Lawrence knew what had happened because twenty minutes later he appeared at the office and surprised everyone by terminating the takedown operation."

Cavaco was not pleased. Nix could see his tension, his arms pushing needlessly against the wheel. "A payphone! So, after all that, we can't trace who called Lawrence?"

"No."

"We're absolutely no further ahead."

"Well," Nix proffered, "we know he didn't use his home phone to call *to* this other help. At least not in the last month. But he had to be communicating somehow. And not likely from the office."

Nix knew Cavaco was still stinging from the failure of the Kennedy job, how the tables had turned against them. He knew Cavaco wanted to know how it had happened, even if it was a one-off and Lawrence would never go to outside help again. Because Cavaco hated loose ends, unsolved puzzles, particularly when he had been bettered.

Cavaco said, "He must have had meetings away from the office. Maybe still does. Maybe at his house. Let's tail him when he's not at the office. See if he's doing any secret meetings anywhere."

"Yes. Because it's now become imperative we know."

Cavaco looked at Nix. "What do you mean?"

"We just got a new customer - Lorenzo Marza. And the job's within Lawrence's bailiwick. And it's big. And it's difficult. But it's an opportunity to redeem our image. If it goes well for us, it will erase any doubts out there about The Watcher's ability. So we need to know if Lawrence is communicating outside again and with whom."

Cavaco's finger tapped on the wheel, a sign of excitation. He said, "So tell me about this Mr. Marza."

———— · ————

With infinite disdain, Lorenzo Marza considered the cheese sandwich on a dinky paper plate. One thin, dry, plastic cheese slice on stale white. No butter. No lettuce. No mayonnaise. No flavor. He thought of Parmesan tortellini casserole and garlic chicken. And a good Chardonnay. He hurled the sandwich into the prison-orange wastebasket.

Marza was the head of a wide ranging, prosperous, illicit-drug organization. So Marza was rich, very rich. He had everything - the houses you dream about in places you dream about, the fast cars, the faster women, the best restaurants, the usual baubles - everything. Except, at the moment, his freedom.

He was in custody awaiting trial. For three months he had lingered in the dank, dirty, stench of a jail. Three very long months for a man like Marza, a man used to the high life.

Not that he was ever in any physical danger in custody. Or even harassed. His status as an underworld overlord quickly became known. He retained body guards on the inside for the duration. To even look at him the wrong way would cause you to have your body parts rearranged.

But, even as rich as he was, there he was. You don't get bail, even with all your money, when you're charged with a double homicide, especially when one of the victims is a five-year old girl. And when you have serious priors and are not, in any other respect, a sterling citizen.

But he would walk soon. He knew that. Things were underway.

Not that he wasn't guilty. Of course he *was* guilty. He had gunned down on the street, with a rather loud submachine gun, Ted Filion, a guy who needed to be dead, a guy who threatened the smooth running of Marza's smooth operation.

As for the five-year old kid, how was Marza to know some mother and her kid would be walking on the sidewalk that late. And that they would turn the corner just when he was spraying bullets all over the goddam place. The kid should have been at home in bed at 10:00 PM, like good kids are.

What really got to Marza was that he had grabbed the machine gun from his hit man in the first place. Marza never did his own shooting. Why, as the boss, would you ever be the one actually pulling the trigger? But he had become enraged in a moment. Filion had just stood there, defying Marza, brazen, confident, even smiling his twitchy mouth smile, throwing everything back in Marza's face, not cowing to Marza's threats. Marza had felt his mind reeling as if his brain had been instantly submerged in testosterone. And Marza had made a split second decision, if you could call it that, to kill Filion then and there. He had grabbed the Heckler and Koch 9mm machine gun from his man and just let Filion have it. Although not without some initial aiming problems.

Marza wasn't very adept with a machine gun, never having fired one. And so it took a little getting used to to compensate for its kicking recoil as Filion ran away. Filion managed a hundred feet before Marza got the hang of it, before he could get the juddering, jerking barrel to stay in one spot, to get the spray off the bricks and parked cars and train it on the quickly receding Filion. Sure, his aim was still a little wobbly, but he managed quite evidently to sink a couple of bullets into Filion's back. Where the other bullets were flying he didn't know. The kid should have been at home at that hour, not walking on some goddamn dark sidewalk.

Yes, Marza thought, the mistake had been in grabbing that gun in the first place. He really had to learn to control his temper. When he was released, maybe he should take some anger management classes. He wondered who else would be in the classes. Probably just losers. A bunch of losers. Could he take being with them? Not bloody likely. Losers would royally piss him off.

Yes, he was guilty. Not that he had confessed to that, of course, or was ever going to confess. If they wanted his head, they were going to have to prove he was there at the time, and that he was the one who pulled the trigger. They would have to prove every element of the offence. Proof beyond a reasonable doubt.

And he was going to make sure they couldn't. There was a lone witness, a men's clothing wholesaler, Fleming, who had happened to be in one of the parked cars Marza had sprayed. Neither Marza nor his hit man had noticed anybody around. Fleming was probably sitting slouched, and progressed even lower when the bullets were flying. This Fleming had given a pretty accurate description of what went down, later identifying Marza from photos as the killer. It was Fleming who had called the ambulance for the girl. But there wasn't much left of her to save, machine guns packing a pretty wallop.

So what to do about Fleming? The prosecution's case turned on his identification. Take that out and the case would fall like a house of cards. He didn't want Fleming actually rubbed out. That would only serve to put the heat on him forever for another murder. What he needed was Fleming to have a serious case of uncertainty, to actually testify, but now back away from a positive identification of Marza. Killing Fleming would be easy. But pulling off an intimidation of Fleming that would stick, that would hold under the pressure of a prosecutor in a courtroom, that would be difficult. That would require special talent.

The question had occupied Marza for months. The problem was that the police had locked down surveillance on Marza's people so tightly, they couldn't take a piss without being followed and notes taken. Aggressive, around the clock surveillance. Make any move, especially against Fleming, and police would be on it like a cat on a woolen ball. And, to boot, Fleming himself was being provided around the clock personal police protection.

So what to do about Fleming? Marza was the head of his own

successful organization because he could think outside the box. If he couldn't make any move from within his organization, it occurred to him he could go outside it. Not something he had ever had to do.

Marza had put out the question and had been told there was only one outfit that could do it, *guaranteed* - The Watcher. Nobody knew who The Watcher was or where he was. Nobody actually went to the Watcher in a conventional sense. It was a one-way street. If the thing you wanted done was something that interested the Watcher, he came to you.

Marza wasn't going to settle for anything less than guaranteed in his circumstances. Frying in the electric chair was one electrifying experience he could do without. And so an advertisement seeking vintage stopwatch parts had been put in the New York Times.

CHAPTER THIRTY-FOUR

I t was midnight of the fifth long day at the motel. Andrew sipped at a black coffee as he sat on the edge of the bed, his eyes and mind bleary. It was always dangerous to venture close to the bed, let alone sit on its edge. The pillow and soft linens were a siren's call.

He got up and walked to the middle of the room, an act of resistance to the bed. He did a few stretches. He had set goals for himself each day. And tonight he had miles to go before he slept.

The room, once orderly, now appeared in chaos. What had been neat piles of documents were now indiscriminate masses of paper on the floor, like someone had taken a push broom and spread things around to hide every inch of the carpet. No level surface area in the whole room - not on a table, not on a chair, not on a counter - was devoid of paper. Except for the bed. Or at least that part of the bed where the pillow was, plus three feet where he curled the rest of his body. The rest of the bed was a sprawl of documents spilling onto the floor.

And there were the walls. They had been recruited, too. With a gummy adherent he had affixed dozens of large, colored, squiggly charts he had devised. There were even stick figures. But he was no artist. The walls looked a lot like the walls in Chris's kindergarten classroom, less the smiley faces.

At the time of the original investigation, with the help of Hotel management and the gala organizers, a complete list of all guests was reconstructed, numbering some 400 men and women. Although all women were questioned, they were eliminated rapidly. When investigators looked at the 250 men, they were looking for three possibilities: first, the killer of Macky, a man described by the teenagers as white and at least six feet tall; second, the hooded man who had taken his dad, and was shorter, probably five and half feet tall, and had a lower voice; third, any man whose background or current activities even hinted at involvement in criminal enterprise.

Initially every man had to be considered a suspect. Each was backgrounded and screened. Investigators whittled first to eighty, then to forty. Eventually twelve men were elevated to possible suspect status. For two years, phones were tapped, secret cameras took pictures, intense surveillance was conducted. All producing nothing. No charges were ever laid.

Was Cavaco's cover just that good? Or wasn't he there?

Andrew had a leg up on the original investigators. If Cavaco were there, he should be identifiable on the basis of those additional indices that Andrew knew: Olive skin color, dark eyes (although changeable through contacts), dark hair (so not credibly altered to blonde or red with that skin tone), and his age - in his thirties. And, of course, the age-progressed portrait, the one Lawrence had done in 1963. Although Cavaco would have had facial alterations, plastic surgery could only do so much; and Andrew was quite certain Cavaco would not want to look altogether new, like a stitched together Frankenstein.

Andrew was very aware of Lawrence's own conclusion that Cavaco wasn't there, based on Lawrence's own review of the same evidence that Andrew had. But he had to be absolutely convinced himself before he considered next steps.

His first goal in vetting the material was to see if he could identify Cavaco, whom investigators could only refer to as 'the hooded man'. If he could not find Cavaco, he would review the material looking for Macky's killer, testing it against the investigators' conclusion that Macky's killer was also not in the room. If that produced nothing, he would look for anything missed, or an erroneous conclusion made, about men who might, in a wider sense, be connected with crime, and so might have figured somehow into Cavaco's organization.

Andrew had first reviewed the pictures covertly taken of about sixty men. He had compared them, as had Lawrence earlier, with the 1963 portrait. Many fit many of the parameters of height, skin tone, voice, and age, but didn't square well with the portrait. Andrew had decided not to give the portrait as much credence as Lawrence had, although it was still highly useful. He made generous allowances for error, but held the line at skull shape. Plastic surgery didn't go *that* deep.

Of those who had any reasonably possible resemblance, Andrew drilled down, reviewing every scrap of information, cross checking every detail. He considered that Cavaco's documentation would not be a legitimate U.S. birth certificate, of course. He would either have a false U.S. birth certificate, or he would be, apparently, an immigrant, again with false documents.

He traced every piece of evidence on the six acknowledged immigrants who broadly fit the parameters and who had arrived in the U.S. between 1951 and 1961. Two were from Latvia. Andrew decided their skin color was just too light to be the olive complected Cavaco. And anyway, the original investigators, not aware of any skin color criterion, had turned every leaf, even going to Latvia to shake out the evidence that legitimized the immigration documents.

Two more were from India, patently East Indian. Andrew confidently ruled them out.

The final two intrigued him, one immigrant from Panama, one from Lebanon, each a single man, mid-thirties. There were enough broad similarities in the faces to be just possible. But as Andrew had dug further, it was verified in the case of the Panamanian that he had a divorced wife and two children, age 8 and 11, in Panama. Agents had traveled to Panama and interviewed reputable people in that town who confirmed the man's residence for the past ten years. He owned a successful hat making factory, but had always wanted to move to America. His children showed unmistakable facial features of their father.

Andrew was the most optimistic about the Lebanese, based on facial appearance. He had apparently immigrated in 1957, was five and a half feet tall, had a low voice, right skin tones, dark eyes, and, initial reports indicated he was hiding something. An eight-month covert surveillance revealed that the man was doing very well at his recently established middle eastern bakeries, far better than he was declaring in his tax return. Maybe that was the reason for his uneasiness at being investigated. Surveillance in the following seven months determined that all the man did, day and night in an eight by ten storefront, was make pizzas. Or train others to do so, with a view to eventually blitzing the city with take-out pizza locations in every tiny nook and cranny. Knowing what Andrew knew of Cavaco, that pushed a cover way beyond Cavaco's tolerances.

Andrew had broadened his search. There were others who might have sneaked into the U.S. but claimed to be born here, producing false birth certificates. He checked every one. He paid special attention to anyone who had a shallow history in the U.S., anyone who did not have independent confirmation of family or work connections going back ten years. Again he found the investigators spared nothing to verify all documentation through cross checks with living people where there was any possibility that the document might be false.

For days Andrew had reviewed the interrogatories of the investigators, the wiretap transcripts, the background checks. He had read reports, reports, and more reports. He had analyzed the careful logic used in eliminating one suspect after another.

He now eased back in the chair, stretching his arms and back. He was exhausted. He closed a thick report and slid it to the side of the desk. He weakly lifted a fresh report from another box and set it in front of him. He stared at the report's cover a moment. He yawned. He looked at the bed a moment, like a lover.

He got up and stared out of the motel room window for several minutes watching the headlights on the distant highway, like moving white dots on a black canvass. He let the drape drop and walked back to the desk. He poured himself a coffee from the carafe without even looking at the cup.

He sat down. He looked at the cover of the report. He opened the report. He resumed his reading.

CHAPTER THIRTY-FIVE

The Watcher had radioed instructions to the enforcement cell members. Now, at four p.m., Kell quickly climbed the stairwell of the St. Andrew Hotel to get to the cell briefing. He never knew what he would be called on to do. But he had never been disappointed.

He knocked the customary knock and Leader opened the door. All of the other cell members were already seated: Franks, Steve, and Smithy. Kell took a chair, completing a ring of chairs around an oak coffee table. Quick glances were exchanged.

Leader laid an 8" x 11" color picture on the table. They all studied it - a narrow face that spoke of nervousness, an unconvincing smile. "His name's Fleming. He's a key witness in a murder trial which starts in three days. He needs to have a serious memory problem so he can't positively identify our customer. But we're under strict instructions not to hurt him. Terrorize, yes. Intimidate to the core, yes. Hurt, no."

Leader slid another photo onto the table, a picture of a small gravel parking lot and the rear of a brick building with a loading dock. He continued, "He's under police protection. Two officers sit in an unmarked car in the parking lot at Fleming's clothing warehouse. By the time we get there, Fleming will be alone inside, finishing up before closing. But the officers will still be outside."

Leader said to Kell, "You and I will be in police uniform. We'll be riding in the back of a cube van. It was recently acquired and painted and stenciled to conform precisely to the required markings. It will appear to be making a late delivery."

At his warehouse, Fleming glanced out the window to the gravel parking lot. He was a jittery little man. Even after three months of continuous police protection, he still habitually looked out the office window to the police car for reassurance. It was there, of course, as it always was, two policemen in the front seat, the windows down.

The trial was always on his mind. It made him edgy with worry. He was the principal witness, for heaven's sake, in a trial against a criminal gang leader. However, at no time had there been the slightest threat. But perhaps that was only because he had good police protection.

A solid-black cube van with slanted silver lettering declaring it to be *'Phil's Clothiers'* turned into the gravel parking lot. The two policemen turned their heads to follow it in. Phil's Clothiers' vans had made appearances two and three times a week for months now. Another routine delivery. The policemen sat back comfortably in the seat.

The van driver and passenger, Steve and Franks, carefully noted the police showing no concern, one of them turning the page of a magazine, and knew that The Watcher had orchestrated well: routine is the biggest enemy of vigilance.

The van reversed and backed slowly to the raised loading dock, bringing the rear door of the van almost flush to the wall of the warehouse. More out of boredom, the police watched Steve exit the driver's door scanning a clip board. Still reading, he reached around and rubbed his back and made an awkward stretch, giving a slightly pained expression. Franks exited the passenger side and took a last draw on his cigarette.

Steve looked up from the clipboard and called over to Franks, just loudly enough for the police to hear, "Only a small delivery. You get it? My back's really acting up."

Franks nodded, "Ya, no prob", stubbing the cigarette into the gravel with his foot. He walked over and Steve handed off the clipboard. Franks walked to the rear of the cube van, squeezed up through the tight space between the rear of the van and the wall of the warehouse, and pulled on the van's rear door cord, noisily drawing it up.

Franks entered the rear of the van. A moment later he trundled a trolley with a rack of suits out of the van disappearing into the warehouse.

Steve stood in the lot, twisting and rubbing his lower back, watching a crow squawk in a tree. He made a half wave to the police to acknowledge their presence. The one on the driver's side nodded.

Just inside the warehouse, Franks parked the trolley and approached Fleming whom Franks could see standing in his small office, its walls made of glass from the waist up. Fleming watched Franks' approach, Franks reading, frustrated, flipping through pages on his clip board. At the open glass door to the office, Franks said, "Hi. Phil's. Just trying to find your order."

Surprised, Fleming said, "Oh. Wasn't expecting that yet." He glanced at his watch. "You're delivering late today."

Franks said, "Damned order forms are mixed up. Just a second. Let me check the paperwork with my partner."

Fleming said, "We can just check my paperwork. The order will be here."

Franks said, "I better check with him. I'm new." He turned and quickly walked back to the rear of the van.

Outside in the parking lot Steve was still rubbing his back and trying some back bends. He gave it a couple of quick jerks. He saw the policemen smiling at him. Steve called out, "Can't swing a bat anymore without throwing it out. Real temperamental." Their smiles broadened. Policemen know bad backs.

Fleming was shuffling papers at his desk to find the order. Franks approached, pushing the trolley of suits right to the office door. The trolley obscured Leader and Kell, two fully uniformed policemen. They suddenly appeared in the office. Fleming looked up, startled.

Kell slapped duct tape over Fleming's mouth and held his head as Franks held his arms. Leader closed the door, enclosing everyone in the small office. Fleming's eyes were wide with fright.

A brutal jerk and Kell rammed Fleming down to the floor. Leader drew a short machete from inside his jacket. Fleming mumbled terrifically, shrinking against the wall. Leader's eyes on Fleming, he stepped to an upright mannequin. With one terrible blow, he severed the manne-quin's head. It fell into Fleming's lap. He shrieked under the duct tape.

The Leader said, "I'm going to explain some simple facts to you. Beginning with the fact that you do not have, and will never have, police protection."

Five minutes later, Fleming, shaking with uncontrollable fear, peered through the window and watched the cube van pull slowly away from the parking lot. He looked, too, at the patrol car where the policemen continued to sit on guard duty.

CHAPTER THIRTY-SIX

For another two days and most of two nights, Andrew had pored over documents. And now it was midnight again. He always seemed to notice when it came.

Tonight he had been reading three reports conducted very early on when all persons who were at the gala were being questioned. Those reports yielded a monotonous litany: nobody had seen Macky at the gala; nobody had seen anything unusual occur at the gala; nobody had had any money, or jewelry, or other valuable lost or taken at the gala, or at the Hotel at all. Except that wallet, of course.

The whole thing was so frustrating, a complex puzzle with pieces missing, reminding him of Churchill's 'a riddle wrapped in a mystery inside an enigma.'

He was fatigued, in part because of the endless hours of concentration, and in part from the growing recognition that nothing seemed to have been overlooked, that he could shed no new light on any of it, that he had no new insights. That he had failed.

He pushed himself back from the desk and rubbed his aching eyes.

At the end of each day, when he had finally exhausted his ability to sit upright and read, when his eyes were lumps of pain, he had gotten into the routine of lying in bed and listening to the taped interviews of the dozen or so men who had most interested investigators. It usually helped him get to sleep.

He took a tape and put it on the spool and wrapped the free end around the other spool. He hit the play button and went over to the bed. He laid down and put his head on the pillow. He heard the familiar sounds of one of the detectives clearing his throat before an interview actually began. Andrew thought he could hear something unusual in the background - sobbing?

The detective said 'October 13, 1961. 6:20 P.M.'

It was the day his dad had been taken.

The detective continued. 'Interview conducted at the home of Detective Paul Locke. Interview and statement of Andrew Locke, age seven.'

Andrew sat up. He heard the sobbing growing louder as a microphone was brought closer to him, age seven.

He had been unaware that any such tape existed. It had never occurred to him, even though he knew vaguely he had been asked questions at the time.

"Andrew," the detective began, in a gentle voice, as fatherly as he could be, "I understand you can tell time."

Andrew heard his young voice, quiet, breaking with a sob, "Yes, Sir."

Andrew had never heard his child's voice before. There had never been any family recordings.

"What time did you arrive home from school today?"

A delay with more sobbing. "Here's a Kleenex, Andrew. I know this is difficult. You're a brave boy."

The little voice squeaked. "3:45." Andrew heard a nose blowing. A child's.

"And the hooded man, when did he arrive?"

Andrew sniffled, "After five minutes."

"When did the hooded man and the other two men leave the house with your father."

"I don't know, Sir. I ...was worried for my dad." The sobbing intensified again.

"I know, Andrew. I know." The detective's voice was consoling. Although there would be no consolation. "Would it be ten minutes later? Or a lot longer, like half an hour?"

"I don't... know...for sure...maybe fifteen..." His sobbing broke up the words. He struggled to get them out evenly.

"The man with the hood, Andrew, what color was the car he drove?"

"Green."

"What color were his eyes?"

"I don't know."

"Please try, Andrew. Try to see him and remember."

"I can't. I'm sorry...."

Now an uncontrollable weeping. A cry that swelled loud. A pain reaching unfathomable depths. Through it he struggled to say, over and over, with difficult breaths, "Please ...help my ...dad. Please ...help...."

"We're going to do everything, Andrew. Everything." There was a tremble in the detective's voice. He called for water. His voice quavered. "Let's break for a few minutes." Andrew heard the detective sniffling.

There was a click. The recorder had been turned off.

He realized he was shaking. He got off the bed and walked to the front door and opened it. He felt tears coming as memories pushed through. He took a deep breath of the night air.

After a few moments, he heard a click, the interview resuming. He closed the door and sat on the sofa.

The detective spoke. "Are you doing better now?" A long pause. "Here," the detective whispered, "hold my hand." A pause. "Is that better now?" Another pause.

"Andrew, you said the man with the hood, his eyes were only up to your dad's chin. Is that right?"

"Yes."

"How do you know for certain?"

"They were talking close together." Andrew seemed to be catching his breath, still sniffling.

"His voice, do you recall was it high or low?"

"Low... like Mr. Sadler's."

"Who is he?"

"The principal.... at my school."

Andrew recalled a file had referenced that Sadler was interviewed. He was a baritone in the church choir.

"Did the hooded man speak the way you and I do? Or did he have any accent? Do you know what an accent is?"

Andrew's voice had begun to tremble. "When ...you say words.... different because you really speak German...or Spanish."

"That's right. Did he have an accent?"

A growing quaver, "No...he... talked like us."

"Did he ever take the hood off? Did you ever see his face?"

There was no answer. Perhaps he was shaking his head 'no'. Sobbing worked its way back again. The detective asked no more. It was evident Andrew was again overwhelmed. His crying grew louder. And louder.

The words he struggled to say fell out like small puffs of air, unintelligible.

But Andrew knew what he had said all those years ago. He had said it, prayed it, unendingly for months afterward. "Please... help my dad. Please.... help my dad."

The questioning appeared to have ended.

Andrew didn't move. The reels turned faintly for a whole minute. Then the player clicked and stopped. The tape ended.

So strange to hear his voice as a child. Far stranger still to hear those very words, and spoken at that time. He felt his body again shaking, the vivid memory of the struggling, defeated little boy crying in a corner for his dad to come home.

Andrew sat still in the silence of the room, the sound of his desperate cries still in his head. He wished he could go back to be there with him, to hold him, to offer some comfort to a small boy who felt, in the end, he had no one.

He finally got up. He shut off the lights and lay in bed in the darkness. But he could not sleep. "Please ...help... my Dad.'

He remembered things too well now. He was so young then, his innocence ravaged. Fragments floated in and out, stirring him, memories sharp and stabbing. The hooded man standing in the living room talking, his father quiet. His father holding him for the last time, looking at him for the last time - loving, brave, preparing to die.

Cavaco was not going to get away. He would find him - somehow. He would not stop until he did. Nothing, *nothing*, was going to stop him.

Much later, his eyes finally closed.

CHAPTER THIRTY-SEVEN

Madeleine and Chris ate breakfast on the floor in the family room, Madeleine watching the morning news. The anchorwoman announced, "The trial of Lorenzo Marza is in its third day." A picture of Marza flashed on the screen, bull necked, a smug expression. "He's charged with the murders of Ted Filion and of five-year old Samantha King." A picture flashed of a bright-eyed, wide-smiling girl, front tooth missing. Madeleine stopped eating. The anchorwoman continued, a halt in her voice, "She was walking nearby with her mother and was killed instantly by stray bullets. In other news..."

Madeleine hit the 'off' on the remote. She stared at the blank screen a moment as in a trance. She glanced to Chris who had not seen any of it, intent only on his cereal. She reached over and gave him a hug. He giggled at her surprise squeeze, trying to balance his spoon full of cereal. He said, "don't squeeze. I don't want to get cereal on my pajamas." He pointed to his primary-yellow pajamas. "My teacher said yellow is *sunshine*."

Madeleine said, "And *happiness* and *warmth*. You know, when you were little, you couldn't say 'yellow'. You said 'Yeyow. Yeyow.'" She poked him as she said it, Chris squirming.

———————•+•———————

The courtroom was filled to capacity with spectators and the press. The tension in the room was palpable. All eyes were on the witness, Mr. Fleming, whose strain was obvious. He unconsciously traced a nervous finger along the wood trim of the witness box.

The District Attorney was at the edge of outright anger. Fleming was, after all, the key witness for the State. But he was not cooperating. The DA had stood ever closer to Fleming during the questioning, and was now not two feet from him.

Lorenzo Marza looked on calmly, coldly, his eyes never wavering from Fleming.

The DA leaned close to Fleming. "Mr. Fleming, I'll ask you again. Please look at the accused." Fleming glanced to Marza momentarily, Fleming's eyes unsteady. "Tell me whether he is the man you saw brandishing a machine gun."

Fleming's eyes flickered. Marza continued to look at Fleming. There was no threat in Marza's gaze, only cold composure. Fleming's eyes darted to a young couple, the parents of the deceased young girl. They tightened their hand hold and watched Fleming, their faces showing terrible strain.

Fleming looked back at the DA, his eyes imploring the DA not to press him further. The DA folded his arms, and his lips pursed.

Fleming was apologetic, "I just can't be sure now."

The DA fired back, "Mr. Fleming, you're under oath!"

Fleming swallowed. "I know."

"Look at the accused, Mr. Fleming. How far is he away?"

Fleming hesitated, then said, uncertainly, "Twenty-five feet?"

The DA was exasperated. "Yes, Mr. Fleming! Yes! As close to you as the man you saw fire the gun!"

Fleming blurted, "But I was very badly shaken that night. I could be mistaken. I just can't be certain. You can understand."

Marza's defense counsel rose to his feet, holding both of his hands in the air and shaking his head. "Your honor, I have been patient. I have given the DA generous latitude. But I must now vigorously object. He is cross examining, even badgering, *his own witness*. At a point of critical testimony!"

Judge Fellows nodded looking at the DA. He had crossed an inviolable line. Sheer desperation had driven him there.

Judge Fellows leaned toward Mr. Fleming. "Would it help if I gave you a few minutes to compose yourself?"

Fleming replied, "No thank you, your Honor. I identified who I thought *might* be the man. I assumed there would be other evidence that might point the same way, or to correct me if I was wrong. Now that I see him actually in person...."

Judge Fellows sat back in his seat with an air of significant concern.

Fleming blurted, "It was dark. Very dark. And the police... shoved picture after picture at me. I felt pressured..."

Judge Fellows took a long breath and looked grimly at the DA. "Counsel, there will be a short recess. Please come to my chambers."

In the Judge's chambers, the DA exploded in the defense attorney's face. "Marza got to him! Didn't he?"

The defence attorney held up his hand as if this was nonsense. "Witnesses can be fickle. You know that. They don't have to be in thumbscrews to correct their testimony."

"Knock it off!" The DA hit his fist on a table. "Marza touched him, dammit!"

Marza's attorney yelled back, "How could he? He was in jail! His organization was under lock-down surveillance the whole damn time! Fleming was under extreme police pressure to nail somebody that night! A little girl dead. There was blood in the air! We've seen it again and again!"

In the courtroom, the murmuring spectators went silent when the DA and Marza's attorney returned. Marza's attorney leaned back in his seat and took, what seemed to the spectators, a satisfying deep breath.

Judge Fellows entered and climbed the two steps to the bench and took his seat. He leaned forward and his gaze swept slowly across the courtroom. It stopped at Marza. Without hurry, Fellows opened the hardbound notebook in which he made trial notes. He removed the top from his fountain pen. He pressed the notebook open. He wrote for a few moments. Then he carefully replaced the top of his fountain pen and gently closed the notebook.

He looked again at Marza, then spoke, very quietly. "Mr. Marza, this case is dismissed. You are free to go."

Marza stood up, a smug smile on his face. He shook hands with his lawyer. He turned and pushed by two stolid policemen who did not make easy way for him.

The young mother began to weep. Tears came to the young father as he tried to make his way along the bench row to the aisle to meet Marza before he passed. He almost made it. He leaned over the last two people in the row, trying to stretch to the aisle as Marza passed. With a barely controlled sob and a voice that trembled helplessly, he said, "Our daughter... our daughter."

Marza didn't acknowledge that he had heard anything, his smile still ripe. He pushed open the courtroom doors.

Outside, at the bottom of the courthouse steps, Marza roughly shoved through reporters and jumped into a waiting car, driven by one of Marza's lieutenants. They were alone in the car.

As they sped off, the lieutenant said, "Isn't the law terrific?"

"Very smooth," said Marza. "How much did it cost me?"

"Three hundred. Cash."

"I thought it was half a million?"

The lieutenant smiled. "Three hundred. The Watcher says he hopes you're happy."

"Happy? I'll fucking say. I would've paid the half mil and still been over the fucking moon! Fleming wouldn't have recognized his own mother if it wasn't convenient for me."

Marza eased back into the thick leather seat and watched the crowds scurrying along the sidewalks in the shopping district. "Take me to the best steak dinner in this city. And I want a couple of girls to go with it."

The lieutenant smiled at the request, nodding. Then he said, mulling, "The Watcher does one hell of a job, uh? I wonder who he is."

Marza held up his hands. "Well that's the fucking genius of it, isn't it? Nobody knows. If we could know, then the cops could know."

<hr>

Lawrence heard a sudden knock at his office door. "Come in!" he called.

His assistant, Cummings, opened the door, an angry look on his face. "I just heard Lorenzo Marza walked. The key witness, Fleming, wouldn't identify him."

A weight seemed suddenly added to Lawrence's frame. He took off his reading glasses and set them on the desk. He turned in his deep chair and looked out the window. He spoke quietly. "We were watching Marza's men."

"Around the clock!" Cummings confirmed. "Those animals haven't been out of their cages!"

"And Fleming was getting police protection."

"He was! Every minute!" Cummings began to pace. "But somehow... *somehow* Marza got to him. I don't know how he could have. It's a damn travesty! If I were that little girl's father, I'd want to kill the slippery..."

Lawrence held up his hand. "Bring me the file, will you? Everything."

CHAPTER THIRTY-EIGHT

Three wide sun umbrellas shaded Cavaco and Nix from the late afternoon sun. They were alone, celebrating on Cavaco's sculpted granite patio near the water's edge.

Cavaco was jubilant as he poured the last of the Chablis into his glass. He held the empty bottle in the air to telegraph to the attendant up by the house that he wanted another bottle.

Two hours earlier they had received the news - Marza had walked from the courthouse a free man. Cavaco now raised his glass to Nix. "To you, my friend! What a coup! Well done!"

He grabbed another skewer of barbecued lamb and peppers from the silver platter. "But", he paused, more subdued, "in my joy, I must not be forgetful of vigilance. Where are we with our friend Lawrence?"

It had been a week and a half since they had put a tail on Lawrence and Nix had never given a report. Nix began, "He doesn't have contact with anybody outside of the office. No visitors at his home. No meetings. He's very solitary. He has a cottage an hour and something north of here on an isolated lake. No phone. No neighbors. One long private lane in and out. He has been followed there on two occasions. He's working on some project - a wheelchair ramp and boardwalk kind of thing. I'm told he digs holes, puts in sono tubes, saws boards. A busy beaver. But always alone. They watch his road. Nobody but him goes in or out."

The second bottle of Chablis arrived on ice, the attendant quickly uncorking it.

"Who's in a wheelchair?" Cavaco asked as he reached for the bottle.

"Lawrence's sister. Lives in Coatesville with the parents. He was followed there last Sunday."

"We're still getting his home phone records?"

"Yes. Nothing there."

"Maybe his outside help was a one-off thing, although I don't see why it would be. He hasn't solved his leak problems. Let's stay the course for now. I don't want to be blind-sided again."

———•◦•———

It was early evening and Lawrence had just arrived home from work when he got a phone call from his assistant, Cummings.

"Wes," said Cummings, "you know we had Marza's people's phones tapped everywhere but got nothing from it. They were obviously well instructed to stay quiet. But we knew the habits of some of his people. One of his lieutenants frequents a little Portuguese restaurant and always takes one of the tables in a certain corner. Three weeks ago we planted a bug in the wall hoping he might come in. Well, last night he did. He was with a guy who isn't really on the inside about Marza. I'm going to play a part of the tape for you. It picks up with them just arriving. The lieutenant had obviously been drinking. His is the first voice."

Lawrence heard the flecking sounds of a tape playing, then restaurant noises - murmuring conversation, cutlery against dishes. An approaching voice, loud and harsh, noticeably under the influence. "Thanks, Afonso. Is he cooking arroz de pato tonight?"

A servile response, "But, yes. For you, he always has."

"Good, good." The scraping of chairs. The harsh voice was now subdued, conspiratorial, "What you said, ya, about the law watching us." A crackling, wheezy laugh.

A new voice, thin, "Ya...what's so funny about that?"

A rasp sound, twice, like a flint wheel on a cigarette lighter being flicked. A long pause. A metallic snap. The lighter cover closed? The harsh voice of the lieutenant, "The law watching us. Ya, of course."

The thin voice, "Ya, so what's the deal?"

The lieutenant said "They watched us all day. Didn't see nothing. 'Cause there was nothing to see."

A smoker's hacking cough. Another wheezy laugh and the lieutenant's voice continued. "The law watching us. We could play the watcher, too. *And nobody sees nothing.*"

"You talk riddles when you're drinking."

"Ya, that's the way I like it. Enough about all that. You like duck? Ya? Get the arroz de pato. Comes with smoked sausage. The best...the best."

Lawrence heard a click and the tape stopped. Cummings said, "What do you think?"

Lawrence said, "Yes, I see. 'Play the watcher'. You said the other guy's not part of the organization?"

"No. But a good friend of this lieutenant."

Lawrence said, "So... while under the influence, the lieutenant's kind of telling this other guy something...kind of not. But would love to tell him. Being coy is the best he can do."

"That's what I think."

Lawrence mused, "Yes, it's odd phrasing, 'we could play the watcher, too.' He didn't say, 'we could watch them, too,' or something like that. 'Play the watcher' as in 'put the watcher into play.'"

Cummings chimed, "That's what I'm thinking."

Lawrence said, "Certainly possible. It's only conjecture that Marza somehow got to Fleming. But if he did, could he have pulled off an intimidation that good while we had surveillance that tight on his people?"

"Impossible," Cummings declared. "He had to have somebody's help."

"But still, it doesn't get us one inch closer to knowing *who* The Watcher is, if Marza even used him."

"I know. Frustrating."

"Okay. I want to pick up a typed copy of the transcript and think on this over the weekend. Can you have one ready for me? I'll be there in under an hour."

"Will do."

Thirty minutes after Lawrence hung up, he left his house and drove to a pay phone four blocks away. He called Andrew's second line. As per the protocol, the phone was never to be answered. He left a message. "Andrew, we might have a break. Meet me at the cottage tomorrow morning as soon as you can."

He then drove on to the office to pick up the transcript.

———·—

When Lawrence had entered the phone booth, a 1978 white dodge charger had driven past and turned down a side street and parked out of view. The driver penciled the precise time, 7:10 p.m., and the street intersection of the payphone. He got out and walked twenty steps back and saw Lawrence leaving the payphone.

They had seen Lawrence make only one payphone call before, to order Chinese on his way home after work so it would be ready for pick up when he got there. If he wanted fast food tonight, why not order it from home?

The white charger followed Lawrence to his office. Chinese? Do they deliver to the FBI offices?

Twenty minutes after Lawrence entered his office, he was out again, and was followed all the way home. He didn't go anywhere else that night. No visitors. No Chinese.

It was not the driver's job to reach a conclusion about what he observed, just observe. But he pondered nonetheless. Making a call from a payphone, after you've just left your home, where there's a phone. Then drive directly to work. Where there's lots of phones.And it's a Friday night. And it's after work.

Something very suspicious.

CHAPTER THIRTY-NINE

At the cottage the next morning, Andrew and Lawrence were at the kitchen table. Lawrence unzipped a leather portfolio and withdrew a file two inches thick. "Lorenzo Marza," he said. He shoved the file across the table to Andrew. Andrew didn't open it. He looked across at Lawrence.

Lawrence slid a glossy picture across - a close up of a sparkling-eyed, smiling child. Samantha King. Andrew looked at it. Lawrence said, "Innocent bystander. Five years old. Gunned down."

Andrew looked at Lawrence a moment then opened the cover of the file. A large print of Marza's face looked back.

Lawrence said, "We had him in custody, had him nailed, had a trial. But he walked. I am reasonably certain someone got to the key witness, a guy named Fleming. There is no way Marza's people could have done it without outside help. We had them under close watch. And Fleming himself had protection 24/7. His office phone and home phone were tapped. There was nothing there, no threats."

Andrew studied Marza's face. Lawrence continued, "Nevertheless, I have reason to believe The Watcher was involved."

Andrew looked up quickly, expectant, eager. Lawrence produced the written transcription of the relevant section of the bugged Portuguese restaurant conversation and gave it to Andrew. He read it.

Lawrence said, "What do you think?"

Andrew said, "play the watcher. Sounds like somebody wanting to boast about some clever, secret goings on but shouldn't. But a little something made its way out as drink made its way in."

"Yes. That's my take on it. So if Marza used The Watcher, Marza may give us something that can lead us to him."

Andrew mulled, "But we don't know for sure if Fleming *was* actually touched. How about I talk to Fleming? Persuasively. See what he'll cough up."

Lawrence nodded, "Yes. Good." He got up.

An 8½ by 11 glossy picture was still sitting on Lawrence's side of the table, upside down. Andrew's finger pointed, "Is that for me?"

Lawrence glanced down at it. He hesitated a moment, reluctant. "I....held it back from the file. What a 9 mm machine gun does to a little girl...same age as Chris."

They looked at one another a moment. Then Andrew held out his hand. Lawrence slid it across, still upside down.

Andrew turned it over and looked. His eyes closed and his hand balled. He took a slow, deep breath. He opened his eyes and slowly slid the picture into the file. Lawrence saw Andrew's jaw muscles clenching. He looked like a powerful man set to explode.

———————

Fleming had worked late into the evening and had decided to go to a restaurant to have a meal before going home. He lived alone, and tonight he felt like being around people and having a couple of drinks. Lately, since the trial, he had more often felt like being around people and having drinks.

When he got home and entered his bedroom, he was startled to see the window curtain shift slightly in a breeze. He always closed and locked the windows, especially lately. Had he forgotten this morning?

He had just walked through the house, hearing nothing, seeing nothing out of place. He stood stock still, straining to hear any sound. He would have to check the house, in particular the basement, or he would not be sleeping tonight.

He walked cautiously from the bedroom, ears pricked, eyes darting. He moved soundlessly along the hall, through the living room and into the kitchen. A door on one side of the kitchen led down to the basement. He went to the door and held his breath. He gritted his teeth then snapped on the basement light. He listened for a few moments.

He descended the stairs, his knees a little weak. He cautiously checked every corner. Even behind the furnace. *Especially* behind the furnace. Then his breath eased. He must have just left that window open this morning. He clambered back up the basement stairs to the kitchen and closed the door behind him. He turned.

Andrew was wearing a balaclava. "A long day?"

Fleming stiffened in huge surprise as if he had been hit by a brick. He saw a fat pistol protruding from Andrew's waistband.

"Don't k-kill me!" Fleming sputtered.

Andrew led him by the arm to the bedroom. Beads of sweat formed on Fleming's forehead, his skin a distinctly unhealthy pallor.

Andrew pulled the gun from his waistband and forced Fleming to sit at the edge of the bed. Fleming stammered, "I didn't say a word to anyone. You people promised! I did what I was told! You saw that!"

Andrew could hardly believe his luck. He couldn't have asked for a better unsolicited opener. Now he just had to milk it. He shoved Fleming onto his back and held one hand on his throat. "We heard some cop came around snooping. Getting you to talk."

"No! No one came!" Fleming's voice was tremulous. "I swear it! I swear it! I haven't said one word to anyone. Not one word!"

"Not good enough! I've got to know the truth! Or I'm told to end it!"

"Didn't say a word. No one came. No one. I wouldn't say a word."

"And why not?"

"Because the police can't protect me. You guys are too big. You have friends in the police." He was sobbing now, tears smearing his cheeks.

"Right. That's why you wouldn't say a word. Because what would happen if you did?" Andrew gripped the throat tighter.

"I'm more afraid of you guys," Fleming gurgled, "than the cops."

Fleming was struggling to breathe. Andrew lowered his face close to Fleming's. "I've got to be sure!" he threatened, his knee now leaning on Fleming's chest. "Maybe I can believe you. Maybe not. I want to hear you tell it again. What if the cops ask?"

"I wouldn't tell them anything. I promise. Nothing."

Andrew's knee pressed into Fleming's chest and he lowered the gun to Fleming's eyes. "Because what's going to happen if you do?"

Fleming was crying hard. Andrew's eyes narrowed and his jaw clenched, but he only whispered, "I said, what's going to happen if you do?"

Fleming tried looking away from Andrew.

Andrew screamed in Fleming's face. "Tell me!"

Fleming raised an arm as if he were being hit. He stuttered, "I g-g-get it. And my n-n-niece and n-n-nephew, too."

Andrew breathed hard and lowered himself close to Fleming's face again. He whispered, "This was a little memory tune up. And don't forget it. Don't ever give me reason to come back. Now forget I was here."

Andrew walked to the bedroom door. He stopped and turned to look back. Fleming was watching him, terrified, his arm raised to his face. Andrew raised his thumb and first finger to make a gun and pointed it at Fleming. "Pow!"

Andrew walked out the front door. He was furious. He was going to make Marza pay, give up everything he knew about The Watcher. Whatever it took. *Whatever it took! And damn the consequences!*

<hr/>

Nix received a radio message on the Lawrence surveillance. This morning Lawrence had gone to the cottage. The tail watched the lane all day from the highway. Nobody but Lawrence in or out. The tail had checked once near the cottage. Lawrence was just working on the wheelchair ramp affair.

Nix wondered about Lawrence. He certainly prized his solitude. Nix was also getting impatient to hear back from Teresa at AT&T. Who had Lawrence called last night from that payphone booth at 7:10 p.m.?

CHAPTER FORTY

Dawn had just broken when Andrew lifted the Pitt off the grass runway into a pale sky. In twenty minutes he was banking gently at two thousand feet over Sandhurst Woods Golf Club.

The fairways were empty, but he could see greens keepers moving hoses and equipment near the clubhouse preparing for the day's work.

He had reviewed and eliminated all realistic possibilities of getting to Marza, except one. The FBI file detailed Marza's routines, including his beloved golf. There he was methodical, more planned, stroke by stroke, than he was in murder. And more predictable.

Andrew swung sharply to the east, momentarily blinded by the sun's low glare, then dropped to fifteen hundred feet. He slowed and checked his controls. Below him, wide-open fairways slid by, their boundaries delineated only by thin rows of trees. These did not offer him what he would need.

A large, densely treed area appeared to his right. He banked and made a slow circle, holding the plane steeply, bringing the ground below into full view. He studied the terrain, observing the layout of three fairways directly below him, noting generous stretches of woods which bound them.

What had his attention most was a narrow river dropping through a steep gorge near the sixth tee, creating a cascade. Woods encircled the tee area. A squat, bunker-like, white cement building, which he knew to be a washroom, was set back fifty yards from the tee. A narrow walking path led through the thick woods from the tee to the washroom, which was itself surrounded on three sides by heavy woods. On the fourth side was the river spilling noisily through the gorge.

Andrew circled again. This time he held down the button on the cameras' remote, the three cameras each taking four pictures a second. Andrew climbed another 500 feet, and surveyed all of the approaches to the sixth tee.

He flew back over the clubhouse, where he saw the first golfers stretching and practice swinging. He saw the parking lot in relation to the clubhouse and the clubhouse in relation to the winding golf course road to the highway. He photographed the practice range, the north side of which was rough, unusable woods, which dropped to the river. He noted a narrow walking bridge, which looked ancient, but the pathway leading to it on one side and away from it on the other was well-defined, indicating the bridge was still used.

He climbed higher still until the entire course was visible. He wheeled slowly, considering the elements of the plan he was hatching, refining possibilities.

———————

Two mornings later, Andrew sat taking coffee on the patio of the Sandhurst Golf Course clubhouse. He had been there the day before, and had done an entire dry run to confirm Marza's routine, particularly between the fifth and six holes.

From behind aviator sunglasses, he now watched Marza take several practice swings at the first tee. Marza glanced down the fairway once, then addressed the ball. He swung hard. He watched the ball slice badly into the rough. Agitated hands on hips, he stomped once on the ground.

Marza was accompanied by a bodyguard who doubled as a caddie, a hulk of a figure who Andrew knew concealed an automatic pistol that could rip out a twelve bullet clip in two seconds. The bodyguard, standing silently to the side, reached out to accept Marza's club, offered with an angry, unlooking toss. Marza marched aggressively off the tee in the direction of his ball uttering an array of profanities. The bodyguard shouldered the heavy bag and followed.

Andrew looked at his watch and calculated. The group ahead of Marza was a capable twosome. They had a good ten-minute start. They would not hold up Marza's progress. He would be at the 5th tee in forty-five minutes. And behind Marza was a foursome, two women, two men, all in their seventies, with shapes indicating they favored playing the 19th hole. By the 5th tee, that group would be a good fifteen minutes behind, affording Andrew all of the time he would need.

———————

Marza was not having a good day.

It had started first thing with his empty headed girlfriend throwing a deranged tantrum over nothing. Two could play at that game. He had gone nuts on her, knocking her down, slapping her face while he stood on her hair so she couldn't move her head. He had, of course, slapped her around before. But evidently she hadn't learned much by it. So this morning he added a swift kick to the ribs on the pedagogical principle that it would help her to retain the learning. His calibration had been just so, for he had heard a distinct 'crack' in her chest, then a piercing scream. But still, not much of a start to a day.

And now, after only four holes, he was eight fucking over!

He and his bodyguard walked a steep rise on the fifth fairway, Marza muttering curses and slapping the head of his three iron on the ground. The bodyguard ran ahead bearing the golf bag, over the rise to locate the ball and improve its lie before Marza topped the rise.

When Marza got close, the bodyguard, still puffing, pointed to the ball. A hundred and twenty yards to the green. Marza took a practice swing with his eight iron. He glanced at the green and looked down at the ball and concentrated.

The bodyguard took silent steps backward, hoping they went unnoticed, desperately trying to stifle a sneeze. He covered his face and turned, but just as Marza swung, a snort pierced the silence.

Marza didn't look at the bodyguard, only at his ball lofting weakly, landing and dribbling to a stop fifty yards short of the green. He stared for many more moments, his body quaking with anger. He thought of his stupid girlfriend. And now his stupid bodyguard. He turned and walked to the bodyguard. He made a vicious swing with the nine iron burying the club's head in the soft turf squarely between the bodyguard's feet. The bodyguard was frozen. Marza said into his face through gritted teeth, but his voice low, "You cost me the fucking green!"

———•••———

After Marza teed off at the first tee, Andrew did a little practice putting. Then he packed up and left. Shortly after, he parked on a narrow, deserted, side road which ran parallel to the eighth hole. Woods bordered the road. From the trunk, unobserved, he removed a cart and oversized golf bag.

He had hack-sawed an old set of golf clubs a foot from each club head. Fastened and protruding from the golf bag, they gave every appearance of a normal set of clubs. Hidden in the body of the bag were stuffed Kevlar body armor and leggings, an extra large nylon jacket and pants, a wig, a baseball cap, a rifle with silencer, and a very small revolver.

He lifted the bag and cart over a sagging split rail fence, carried it over high grass, then pulled it through a thick stretch of cedars and stubby underbrush which provided good cover. He exited onto the dog-legged eighth fairway clutching an apparently found ball. A teenaged greens' keeper was turning a tight, bumpy circle in the riding mower concentrating on not spilling his coke on himself. He took no heed of Andrew. Pulling the cart, Andrew made his way unseen to the woods by the 6th tee.

He deposited the cart well back into the woods. Crouched and hidden with good vantage of the fifth green and the sixth tee some fifty yards away, Andrew waited until the twosome teed off the sixth. Andrew saw Marza preparing to pitch onto the fifth green from fifty yards.

Andrew quickly donned the body and legging armor, slipped on the bulky nylon pants and jacket over the armor, and fitted the long haired wig and baseball hat. He appeared overweight, slow, and unkempt. He pocketed the short, snub nosed revolver. He walked around to the door side of the bunker-like washroom building and walked fifty feet into the woods to a spot not visible from the washroom door area. There he hid the silenced rifle in tall grass beside a single birch tree.

———•———

Marza habitually used the washroom after the fifth green. The body-guard, always with the golf bag, habitually stayed outside, taking his leak directly over the gorge precipice a hundred feet away into the loud, rushing water. He always waited there until Marza exited the washroom.

The door to the washroom was on the opposite side of the building from the gorge. There were no windows. Inside the men's, there was one urinal, one toilet cubicle, one sink with one tap.

Marza entered the washroom and walked to the urinal. He became aware of someone in the cubicle, apparently finishing up. There was a flush.

Marza finished at the urinal and walked to the sink and turned the tap. The door to the cubicle opened. Marza glanced in the mirror above the sink and saw a bulky, long haired man wearing a baseball cap, his eyes down. Marza looked back to his hands.

Suddenly Marza felt his throat gripped powerfully from behind and his face pushed forcefully into the mirror, his body pinned firmly against the sink.

His face was pressed so squarely into the mirror that his mouth was mashed half shut. "...out..your...ucking mind? Wha...doing?" Marza struggled but realized he was wholly overpowered.

Andrew locked an even better grip on Marza's throat and put the snub nose revolver against the side of Marza's head and said, "Don't yell or you're dead." Andrew slipped the gun into his pocket and his hand quickly went into both of Marza's pockets checking for a gun. There was none. Andrew could see Marza's eyes narrow, full of hatred.

Andrew put his gun back to Marza's head. Marza was looking in the mirror. Andrew wanted Marza to see the little snub nosed gun to make him draw the conclusion that Andrew was not the law. No lawman would ever use that gun. A stupid amateur would.

Andrew surprised Marza, suddenly jerking Marza's head over just past the mirror. He slammed his face hard into the rough concrete wall. He brought Marza's head back and pressed his face into the mirror. Andrew leaned in close to Marza's ear. "I don't want you. I want The Watcher."

Marza's eyes were springing tears. "Who...uck...are you?"

Andrew said into his ear, "I know you touched Fleming. You used The Watcher. Tell me who he is, how I contact him. Nobody will know. And you don't get hurt."

Andrew pressed Marza's face firmly against the mirror. "Wha... alking...about?" Marza attempted to pull his face back from the mirror. "You think... can just..."

Andrew drove Marza's face so hard the mirror cracked. Blood spurted from his nose, smearing red all over the mirror. Andrew forced Marza's unwilling head back in place against the mirror. Andrew said, "Yes, I do. Just like you do."

Andrew pressed the gun hard into Marza's cheek, distorting the face more. Andrew said, "*Tell me!* And make it the truth. Or I won't be this polite next time!"

Marza's eyes were flicking around, trying to contrive something.

Or maybe just stalling, hoping his bodyguard would come in. But what Andrew registered most was that Marza was not making protest that he had touched Fleming or used The Watcher. He would be showing far more surprise, confounded at the mention of a "Watcher" if it were untrue. Instead Andrew saw a guilty mind trying to figure a play.

Andrew pounded Marza's face again into the mirror, the crack widening. Marza groaned in pain. His lip was split, a front tooth now crooked and bleeding.

Andrew gritted his teeth at Marza's ear. "Your goon can't help you! *Tell me!*"

Marza hesitated. Andrew twisted Marza's head ready to smash his face into the concrete beside the mirror.

Marza blurted through a twisted mouth. "I don't oh who is! Reewy!"

Andrew eased off a bit so Marza could speak. Marza was now breathing hard, pain stabbing him. Andrew knew Marza would talk to make this stop, but wasn't certain he would get the truth. And he knew Marza wouldn't let things end there regardless.

In short, pained bursts Marza said, "I don't know... who he is. You put an ad ... New York Times. Old stopwatch parts. He gets in touch. Nobody knows who he is."

Andrew leaned in. "I want to check that. When did you put the ad in?"

"First week...July."

"If it's not there, I will kill you."

"It's there."

It seemed to Andrew likely to be the truth. It would be hard for Marza to be clever and creative at the best of times, let alone when his face was being ground into hamburg and an unpredictable wild man was pressing a gun to his head. But still, the apparent truth had come out too easily to Andrew's mind. And he knew why. Marza had no intention of letting Andrew walk away from this. Divulging the truth to Andrew about how to contact the Watcher was one thing. But Andrew had obtained more - a confession in the intimidation of Fleming and that he had used The Watcher.

He knew Marza would have to act immediately or lose all opportunity as he didn't know who Andrew was. And acting immediately, impetuously, would be Marza's way in any case, enraged as he was.

Marza's eyes watched as Andrew waved the little gun, the apparent sum of Andrew's firepower. "Don't walk out that door for another fifteen seconds or you're dead."

Andrew threw Marza into a corner and ran out of the washroom. He hurried into the woods unobserved by the bodyguard who was walking towards the building from the other side. Andrew grabbed up the hidden rifle and continued deeper into the woods.

As he began to climb a long, thickly treed slope, he heard Marza instructing the bodyguard. It was clear to Marza that Andrew would go in only one direction. And from Andrew's apparent bulk, Marza would assume he could not travel quickly.

The bodyguard raced into the woods in pursuit, a high-powered, ferocious-looking, semi-automatic pistol in his hand. Marza was right behind, clutching a smaller version produced from the golf bag.

For Andrew, this was now a simple case of self-defense. They had drawn weapons. The bodyguard would certainly overtake him. And you don't have to wait for a pursuer to take the first shot when his intentions are clear. And what other intentions could Marza have? A well-behaved citizen's arrest?

Thickly-leaved branches obscured their view. They raced through, their arms wildly swatting at the branches, their footsteps snapping twigs, crunching leaves. They were clumsy pursuers in the wild, more accustomed to paved back alleys in the dark.

Andrew could hear Marza urging the bodyguard's haste. "Don't slow. He's only got a fucking cap gun." They began the scramble up the long wooded slope, the bodyguard's strong legs carrying him quickly. Marza remarkably kept pace, rage being a great accelerator.

The bodyguard's eyes keenly scanned for any sign of Andrew, any movement, ears pricked for the slightest sound, his face like an angry bulldog. But there was no movement and there was no sound.

The bodyguard was in full upward stride when the sun broke free of a cloud and he suddenly saw sunlight reflect off metal. He hesitated a moment.

The thwack of the bullet piercing the bodyguard's forehead was louder than the silenced discharge of Andrew's rifle. The bodyguard's head lifted and he fell back ramrod straight.

Marza stopped startled, his eyes wild, trying to find his aim. And that was his last stupid expression on this earth.

Thwack. Thwack. The first was for Fleming, the witness Andrew had had to rough up, the second, for little Samantha King who was just walking late one night with her mother.

CHAPTER FORTY-ONE

At a public library Andrew scoured the want ads in back editions of The New York Times for the first week of July. In the Wednesday evening edition, he found it. 'Seeking vintage stopwatch parts.' A phone contact was provided.

The next step would be to place an ad and a contact number. But there was the rub. *What* contact number? The Watcher would investigate that number before making contact. Whatever cover Lawrence and Andrew could create would have to be perfectly above suspicion.

From a payphone he called Lawrence at the office. Lawrence considered the problem. "It would be extremely risky to go personally into that contact process, Andrew. I don't know how good Cavaco's eyes and ears are, how far the reach. If he ever got a whiff of us, things would quickly get dangerous as hell. And we wouldn't even know who it is who's coming for us."

Lawrence wanted some time to think of a way through this. "For now, you go home. You've had a tough few days. I'll be in contact."

For the moment, that sounded very good. He was really quite exhausted.

———•——

When he arrived home, Madeleine was at the kitchen sink wearing an apron and peeling carrots. Chopped onions were heaped on a cutting board.

"Hi," she said, still peeling, wanting to finish. He sat at the table, tired.

A loose contraption of wire clothes-hangers hung at the base of the low kitchen window which looked into the back yard.

Andrew said, "What is that?"

"Chris made a new friend from down the street. He's five, too. Came over to play."

"How did it go?"

"Very well. That's a trap they made. When any bad guys try to climb in through the window, those hooks will pull their pants down." Andrew looked at the contraption, noting the twisty, projecting hooks. Madeleine continued, "And then, you see, their *underwear* will be showing." She gave a little laugh.

Andrew said, "And what bad guys are these?"

"Oh, you know, the usual."

Madeleine was finished now, wiping her hands on the apron. She turned and looked at Andrew. Her cheery smile shrank. She said gently, "Bad day at the office?"

Andrew had no intention of ever speaking to her about Marza. He had no need to.

He nodded, "You might say."

Her voice was sympathetic, "Those bad guys just never go away."

Andrew tapped a finger lightly on the table. "Some do...with a little urging."

Madeleine went and sat down across the table "You're far away, Andrew. Why not tell me what's on your mind?

He looked at her, a tired smile. "I'm thinking...how wonderful it would be to feel your skin touching mine."

"Ya?" She folded her arms. "That can be arranged. Now tell me what you're really thinking about."

He sat forward, leaning on the table, folding his hands. "A lot's been going on. But I can't say."

"You really look terrible, you know. You really need a holiday."

He gave a half-hearted nod.

"I'm serious, Andrew, you need a holiday. We need a holiday. You and me. Alone. We haven't gotten away alone in ages."

"A holiday would be nice."

"Good. I'm a bit ahead of you. Nadine already said she could stay here with Chris. She could arrange a few days off. Apparently she's not indispensable to the survival of The Pizza Palace."

Andrew looked at her. "A few days?"

"From Saturday to Tuesday night. Four days." She twinkled her eyes at him. "Canoe camping. Like we used to. Up north. Do a couple of two-day loops. We could leave Friday at supper. For that night, as a start to the holiday, there's a little Inn up that way I've heard is kind of romantic."

"You mean this Friday?"

"Yes. It's only Monday. What do you say? I'm sure Lawrence owes it to you."

He tried to think about it, but he felt so tired.

Madeleine said, "Andrew, you're hitting a wall. You're exhausted. We need this. Let's take a few days together. Just us. You don't think I feel the stress you're under. But I do. I want to give you room for that. But we need this, too. Private time together. It's been a long time."

A hot meal and a hot bath was what he needed at the moment. And then bed. And a holiday did sound nice.

The hooded man snorted as Andrew's father asked, "Where do the bodies go?"

"What bodies? No bodies, no crime." The hooded man snorted, laughing.

Andrew was sweating, chasing the car. He was so close to the trunk. "Dad. Don't go."

From inside the trunk, his father called out, "Where are you, Andrew?"

Andrew kept pace with the car. "I'm here, Dad. I'm coming. I won't let them do it."

His father called out, "Andrew, where do the bodies go?"

Andrew cried, "I don't know. I'm sorry. I just don't know."

His father's voice trembled. "I looked for you there, Andrew. I waited. But I didn't see you. I waited a very long time..."

"Dad, I'm so sorry I didn't find you."

Andrew cried as he watched the car fly up and over a ravine into the dark woods.

The hooded man sat in a tree and turned to Andrew, mocking his father's words, "Where do the bodies go, Andrew?" Behind the hood shook a bitter laugh.

Sweating. A great flash of light.

"Andrew, Andrew." Madeleine's voice. "You're having a nightmare."

Andrew's eyes squinted. She had turned on her reading light.

He felt the sweat on his body under the covers. Madeleine was stroking his forehead. "You were tossing and making sounds again. What was it?" Her voice was soothing.

He looked over, her hair mussed across her face. His heart was still racing.

He slowly eased out of bed. "Can you get the light?" He went to the window. She snapped the light off. He opened the window, sucking in the cool air.

Madeleine said, "That hasn't happened in quite a while."

He looked out at the trees moving gently to a breeze. "I've got to tell you something."

She sat up straight, an anxious look on her face.

He turned to her. "This top secret assignment...I'm investigating my father's killer."

Her hand went to her mouth. "My heavens. Why didn't you tell me?"

"You shouldn't know anything about it."

"But why *you*? Of all people. Your own father..."

"I can't tell you anything more. I wanted to tell you... because it has stirred up things."

He looked at her. He could see her well enough by the light from the street, her distress. "Maybe I shouldn't have told you."

"No, No. I'm glad you told me. That's just ...so strange. Your own father's case. Are you alright with it?"

"It's been a little rough. It has to be done. I have to be the one."

She watched him at the window, needing the air. He said, "They believe the man who took my father has taken several other men. It's the way he operates. They just disappear. Never to be found."

"Do you have any idea who it is?"

"I can't tell you anything more."

"But..."

"Anything."

After a moment, her voice uncertain, she said, "I'm glad you told me, Andrew. Of course. Thank you."

CHAPTER FORTY-TWO

Cavaco was distraught, which took him and Nix to the cellar for dark rumination.

Nix had just informed him that Marza and a bodyguard had been killed the day before by an unknown expert shooter when they were golfing. Marza's face had been beaten up, too.

Cavaco, at first shocked, had become vexed. "First it's Kennedy and Kipling. Now it's Marza. Our clients are getting knocked off. Hire The Watcher and you soon get snuffed. Like some cause and effect thing. Not exactly good for business."

Nix said, "Can't be a connection. Whoever killed Kennedy and Kipling is Lawrence's outside help - the law. That's *not* who killed Marza. The law doesn't go around assassinating criminals."

"Anyone being fingered?"

"Nobody has any idea. Marza could certainly have enemies. He wasn't loved by everyone. But listen, I have some other news. I just learned who Lawrence called from a payphone four nights ago."

"What took so long?"

"Our AT&T insider had an appendix attack. Had it out. We had to wait."

"They'll lose more than a useless organ if they're slow again."

"It's an unlisted number in the name of an Emily Madeleine Nelson. It rings at a home on Morley Street. An upscale neighborhood. I had the title checked out. The home is registered to a cardiologist, Dr. Edward Curran."

Cavaco showed some relief. "That's good. Not FBI anyway. They don't live in upscale neighborhoods. I wonder if Lawrence has heart trouble?"

"Don't know. But if he was calling his doctor, why at home?"

"Maybe he's a friend."

"But why call from a pay phone? Why secretive?"

Cavaco smiled. "Maybe he wasn't calling the doctor. Maybe the Nelson woman is the doctor's wife and maybe Lawrence has another kind of heart trouble. He calls from a payphone so the doctor can't know who was calling."

Nix thought a moment. "No, Lawrence doesn't seem the type. But I'll get answers for us."

Darkness had fallen. Andrew was alone, driving, taking a series of quiet residential streets to avoid some heavier traffic in the downtown area. Rain lightly patted the windshield, the wipers gently sweeping.

He thought back to yesterday. He had expected to get more from Marza. What he did get only showed how exceedingly careful The Watcher was. You didn't go to him, because no one knew who he was. He came to you. It could become impossible to know who he was without exposing yourself first, in which case Andrew and Lawrence would quickly be dead. He was frustrated at this impasse.

He suddenly became aware of where he was. Without any intention of being there, he was now on the same street and in the very block where Macky had been shot, where his father had kneeled low and been told that startling truth, a truth that had killed his father and gutted his life.

On an impulse he pulled over and parked. He shut off the engine and sat for several minutes, the windows up, allowing his mind to settle. No one was on the street. No cars travelled. Rain spit on the windshield. A light wind lifted the leaves in the splendid old trees.

He wondered where exactly the killer's car had parked that night, and where Macky lay.

His mind turned to the big question. Macky was shot about 11:00, right here. The theory was he had stolen a wallet less than thirty minutes earlier from a man in the ballroom. That was less than a ten-minute walk away. Macky had no car. It was determined he had not taxied. Nobody in the neighborhood recognized his picture. The speculation was that he had walked this far and was overtaken. Meaning he would have left the hotel by 10:50 at the latest. What had happened in the fifteen or so minutes between the time the wallet was lifted and the time he left the hotel?

He had left after taking only one wallet. Why? The man had not known his wallet was taken, no hue and cry in the ballroom. Nobody there even recalled seeing Macky. And yet he had left. The best theory was that something compelled him to leave, and fifteen minutes later he was dead. There had to be a connection. Nothing seemed to make sense but that Macky saw danger while in the ballroom. An experienced pickpocket gets rid of the stolen wallet near the scene; he doesn't want it on his person. And yet in this case it was, suggestive of something unusual afoot for Macky.

Was Cavaco there? Andrew had studied the files top to bottom and with the gravest reluctance admitted Cavaco did not appear to be among the guests that night. Lawrence had said, 'The wallet is what led us to the ballroom, but both seem to be red herrings.'

Andrew mulled the point. How could Cavaco have slipped through such thorough vetting by investigators? The possible answers - it wasn't Cavaco in the room who had seen Macky. Or it was Cavaco in the room but he was not a guest and so was not vetted.

The rain had eased. He needed to walk. He would do the reverse of the walk Macky had done that night. He got out of the car and started along the street in the direction of the hotel.

He had gone there before, after Lawrence had first given him the gist of things, just to see the place. He had walked all of its public areas, considering the well-worn speculations, sitting in the empty ballroom breathing in its atmosphere, trying to hear its voices, hoping that something in the experience of actually being there might spark a useful new thought, a new angle. He had only drawn a blank.

He had gone a second time, days later, when he knew there was a large gathering. He had insinuated himself into the crowd as presumably Macky had. He had played out concocted possibilities, considered where else in the hotel Macky might have tried to ply his trade that night, walked the restaurant, the washrooms, the halls, hoping a connection would happen. But again, another blank.

After eight minutes and five blocks, Andrew pushed his way through the front doors, crossed the lobby, and followed the corridors to the ballroom. The doors were open and it was empty.

He took a seat in the silence and contemplated the grand room, its tapestries, its vaulted ceiling. He imagined the gala that night - the music, the pageantry of four hundred elegantly dressed people. And he thought of Pino Macky, weaving invisibly through the crowd.

If only the walls could talk.

At one end of the room a door opened and two people entered. They were talking, intent on each other, and didn't notice him. One appeared to be a prospective customer, the other a hotel representative.

"Who do we coordinate with?"

"The manager or me."

"And the night of the awards, will there be a hotel representative in this room?"

"For something this size, a staff supervisor will be present at all times. And for something this important, the special events manager will be scheduled as well."

The customer looked around admiringly. "A beautiful room."

"This ballroom was the major addition to the original hotel. Finished in the summer of '61. Twenty years now. The original structure was totally overhauled when the current owners bought in '58. They updated the mechanicals and electrical system. Added the lobby as you see it now. Gave everything else a total facelift."

"A lot of money."

"A lot of money."

"Is this part of a chain or something?"

"No. Strictly a private outfit. Private money. But who it is, I couldn't tell you. Foreign though."

"Oil money?"

"No. Swiss, I'm told."

Something suddenly occurred to Andrew that made so much sense, and made sense of so many other things. He got up. The hotel representative noticed him. "Can I help you?"

Andrew was striding from the room. "Just admiring the architecture."

He quickly found a secluded payphone on a quiet street corner and called Lawrence at home. Andrew's voice was excited, hurried. "I just learned tonight the Hotel Continental was bought in '58 by some private Swiss outfit. Now, hear me out. I know it's speculation, even wild speculation. But it would make sense of what happened."

Lawrence said, "Okay, I'm listening, so slow it down."

"Okay, so in '55 Cavaco 'dies'. He disappears for a while, maybe a couple of years, during which time he gets some plastic surgery in some discrete hospital in a renowned place, like Switzerland. His money is in some tax haven, like Switzerland. But he wants to live back here because this is what he knows. He wants to get his money back here, too. But how to do it legitimately? What better way than to buy a property, a big income producing property like a hotel. Not in his own name, of course. But some Swiss company he incorporates. And then, you see, he can pour dirty cash into it from his ongoing criminal operations, effectively laundering his own money. You know the Swiss have tight privacy laws protecting ownership. When the original investigation was done, they would have thought nothing unusual or suspicious in the hotel being owned by a Swiss company. They're nice people. They make chocolate. It would easily evade notice or enquiry. It's only because *we know* about Cavaco that it raises the possibility."

Lawrence readily followed the argument, although he considered it a thin proposition without more supporting evidence. But it had logical direction to it. And Lawrence wanted to be supportive. He said, "Not only could Cavaco then launder his ongoing dirty money, he could siphon profits back to his foreign company in a tax haven. I'm certain no part of that original investigation came close to considering that hotel ownership might play into it."

Andrew was really revved now. "Right, right. But there's more," he said eagerly. "And it offers an explanation for Cavaco being at the gala. The ballroom had just been completed in the summer of '61. In October, the gala would have been one of its first major functions. Cavaco appears to have been living in the area then; I mean, look, he was at my house the very next day. He would have natural reasons for wanting to drop in to the ballroom and watch the operation, without, of course, anybody knowing who he was. A kind of eavesdropper. He's just there. Nobody's taking attendance. I mean, Macky got in. Nobody knows who Cavaco is. Nobody asks questions. Nobody there knew all of the other four hundred people there. They're from a wide cross section of Philadelphia's business community. So when all the guests on the guest list were questioned and vetted and investigated, *Cavaco wasn't even on it!*"

Lawrence felt himself swept into the flow of Andrew's excitement, but he wanted to inject calm and collection for both their sakes. They had both been through enough disappointments. "A good piece of speculation, Andrew. But still a long shot. You *may* be onto something. It *may* stand up. But let's be patient. And careful. Let's see who's registered as the owner of the Hotel. Start by going to the Philadelphia Licenses and Inspections Office. As a hotel, they need various licenses from the City. Then check at the Recorder of Deed's office."

CHAPTER FORTY-THREE

At the long counter at the Philadelphia Licenses and Inspections Office, an efficient, thin-lipped woman in a tight bun and granny glasses silently perused some papers, frowning with regularity as she did. Andrew's fingers drummed on the counter as he watched her and waited.

"Okay," she said finally. Her manner was brisk. "The Hotel Continental is owned by Moniker Inc. It's a Swiss corporation and has given agent authority to a local firm of certified public accountants, Anderson and Anderson." She looked at Andrew as if to say, 'so now you know all you need to know.' She then added a split second smile.

Andrew said, "What does 'agent authority' mean?"

She gave Andrew a quizzical frown as if she doubted he should be allowed to be out alone. She spoke more slowly, "That means Anderson and Anderson manages all license and inspection requirements on Moniker's behalf." Then, as an afterthought, a lightening quick smile, more like a twitch than a sentiment. Perhaps there had been a seminar on a governmental push for friendliness, at least towards those members of the public who were sorely intellectually challenged.

Andrew said, "How would I go about getting more information on Moniker?"

She raised her eyebrows but otherwise kept the drama in check. She said primly, "The Pennsylvania Department of State, Bureau of Corporations and Charitable Organizations."

"That's a mouthful."

"Would you like me to write it down?" Then she added, "On a piece of paper."

Andrew wanted to suggest she write it down on his hand instead because he might lose the piece of paper.

She continued. "You can review the corporate formation documents there, the articles of incorporation."

Before going to the Bureau of Corporations and Charitable Organizations, Andrew looked up Anderson and Anderson. They were indeed a reputable firm of certified public accountants in Philadelphia specializing in managing the affairs of foreign investors who owned real estate holdings in the U.S.

So, so far, nothing unusual.

At the Bureau of Corporations, Andrew learned that Moniker Inc. was incorporated in 1957, and the sole director and officer (president) was Albert Baumgartner of Zurich, Switzerland. The legal address for Moniker was given as 602-10 Heidel Strasse, Zürich, Switzerland. The 'registered agent' of Moniker was an attorney, Lorne Nix, Suite 404- 22 Chelsea Ave, Philadelphia.

Andrew learned that a 'registered agent' was a requirement under U.S. law when a non-resident corporation has no offices in the U.S. but is carrying on business here. It must appoint a registered agent here so there is an actual address in the U.S. for the company and an actual person, an agent, who can be served with legal documents on behalf of the corporation.

As Lawrence had recommended, Andrew then went to the Recorder of Deeds office where ownership of lands is recorded. The vast room was a buzzing hive of mysterious activity. He clearly needed help. At the front desk he was told he could hire a title searcher, if one was available at the moment. The desk person looked around and said, "Oh, Susy might be able to help. She looks free."

Indeed, Susy looked free. A girlish nineteen, she sat absorbed in a Stephen King novel at a long table, blowing bubble gum, her hand at the back of her head twirling her long flowing hair round and round, sometimes actually clutching at it. Maybe a scary part.

When Andrew went and spoke to her, she positively radiated energy and friendliness. "Sure, sure, I can help you," she beamed as she bounced up and laid the paperback upside down, folded open, keeping her page.

From the Hotel Continental's address Susy was able to access the legal description of that property and then produced a hard copy of the current deed from a tall filing cabinet. "I've never checked title on a Hotel before. Thinking you might want to buy it?" she joked and elbowed him, literally. "Just kidding! Just kidding!"

Title was indeed in the name of Moniker Inc. The address given for the company was that of the registered agent, Lorne Nix, who was also indicated as involved in the registration paperwork. The deed had been registered March 22, 1958. She made a photocopy of the deed for Andrew.

"Oh," she said, "and there's a mortgage registered, too. Actually two. They're pretty old. Did you want a copy of those?"

"Yes, thanks."

As she stood at the photocopier copying the mortgages, she blew bubbles bursting each one with a loud 'smack'. Then she showed Andrew the documents, explaining that the first mortgage was registered in 1958, "at the same time Moniker bought the hotel." The second mortgage was registered in 1960. Andrew wondered if the second mortgage was to borrow new money for the Hotel's addition, which included the ballroom.

Susy said, "It's the same lender both times. A numbered company. See?"

Andrew saw, then asked, "Does this mean the money is still owed, even after twenty years?"

"Not necessarily. Maybe some. Maybe none. Sometimes the mortgage gets paid off but the discharge never gets registered here. Well, I shouldn't say never. That would be stupid. But I mean sometimes registering the discharge gets overlooked. Even for years. I see it often."

Andrew decided to go back to the Bureau of Corporations to see if he could find out who the lender actually was, the person or people behind that numbered company. Perhaps they were dirty money and could be a lead to Cavaco.

Although a mortgage would typically be held by a bank, he gathered it wasn't unusual for a foreign owner not to be able to get the usual bank financing and so would have to turn to private lenders. Especially if they didn't have a lot of credit history. It certainly didn't mean anything villainous.

Andrew considered what he figured was the real problem with his own theory - the registering agent, Lorne Nix. Learning that Moniker's agent was a lawyer had taken the wind out of his sails. It strongly suggested that Moniker was legitimate, aboveboard. Because how could

Cavaco ever use a lawyer as his agent without the lawyer latching onto some funny business that Cavaco wouldn't want known? Why would he risk that? Cavaco would use some straw man, not a lawyer.

That recognition was disheartening. A frustration crept in. The whole thing was beginning to add up *not* to Cavaco owning the Hotel, but to a real, legitimate Albert Baumgartner owning the Hotel. Andrew could see him sitting in his tidy Swiss office in Zurich in his Swiss lederhosen reviewing his world holdings while he sipped on Swiss hot chocolate and listened to alpenhorn recordings.

The Watcher had instructed Leader to find out about the Emily Madeleine Nelson woman. Leader had then briefed Kell. 'A phone rings at the home of a Dr. Curran on Morley street and the unlisted number is registered to Nelson. Might be the wife. Might be a girlfriend. Find out all you can about her.'

Kell had first done a drive by and through sheer luck had seen and photographed a very attractive twenty-something woman in the front yard playing catch with a young boy. But on the theory that it's best not to expose yourself until necessary, Kell went to the office of Dr. Curran to see what he could learn before taking any next steps.

Three cardiologists were listed on the outer glass door of a large office. A few innocent enquiries to the young female receptionist revealed that Dr. Curran was off sailing the world for eight months. His office was, in fact, closed. One of the other cardiologists in the office was covering.

This was naturally a surprise to Kell, having just seen a woman at the house. He said to the receptionist, "Sounds fabulous. Did he take the family?"

She said, "No. He's a bachelor." Her face broke into a wry smile. "He just took .... a first mate."

Kell's job was now more difficult. Presumably the woman he had seen was Nelson, although one shouldn't presume. Was she a renter? A relative? He didn't want to push his offhanded enquiries any further with the receptionist. He shouldn't look too curious.

As he was driving away from the doctor's office, he had an idea.

Gloria, the rich divorcee who had thrown the evening garden party and who lived two doors down from Andrew and Madeleine, was feeling a little depressed, a little lonely. She had woken up that way and hadn't shaken it. She had thought some yard work would help. She had weeded the flower beds and trimmed bushes. She had cut the lawn. It didn't much improve her lonely mood. Now, early afternoon, she was sitting on the front porch in a tight, revealing top and skimpy shorts sipping on her third martini.

And who is this? she wondered as she leaned forward. An attractive young man was walking along the street in front of her house carrying a parcel and casting glances back the way he had come. She took a sip as she watched him.

Kell had just been to Dr. Curran's home hoping to find the Nelson woman in. His ruse was that he had a parcel to deliver to Dr. Curran personally. The Nelson woman had not been in. He would have to come back later.

As he passed a house two doors down, he saw a rather 'out there' woman sitting on the front porch sipping a martini and wearing a come hither look. Kell knew an opportunity when he saw one.

He stopped on the street and called, "Hi. She's a hot one today."

Gloria liked what she saw. And she could use a little company. She gave a wide smile. "Are you being bold? Or are you just talking about the weather?"

Kell caught it but played the innocent, wiping his forehead as if he hadn't quite registered her sly humor. "Must be 95 degrees," he said as he walked up her driveway towards the porch. "Would you happen to know when Dr. Curran is likely in, or someone from his family? I'm delivering this package and this is the second time I've been there. Have to deliver it. Personal delivery." Kell was now on the porch steps.

Gloria leaned forward to take a better look at this delivery man. And she liked him even more up close. "Do you have a boat?" she laughed. "He's sailing around the world. He's got a good head start on you."

Kell laughed. "Oh, I see."

"Otherwise," Gloria said, "you can come back in about seven months."

Kell climbed the porch steps. "Is there any family at the house?"

"No. Just renters."

"Oh. Well maybe I could leave it at his office."

"I think he closed it. He took his nurse sailing with him. Didn't ask me."

Gloria felt the third martini doing its work. She was certainly feeling…what was the word? She dangled her bare left leg provocatively over her right knee, her bare foot making slow circles. Kell made sure to be seen noticing her legs and gave her an admiring look. If he fed her obvious need for attention, he might be able to play this out and get the information he wanted.

She saw his appreciative assessment and said, "Would you care for a cold drink?" Her leg activated again and his eyes duly followed, trying to play restrained lust. He thought he may have overplayed it. He re-calibrated.

"That's kind of you. I am thirsty," he said.

She smiled, a Venus fly trap smiling at a fly. "You *do* look a little… *thirsty*."

"Water would be great."

"Are you sure that's all?" she asked. "You're a very handsome delivery man. Whoops, that just popped out."

Kell laughed and she laughed. But a little voice in her head then told her to put the brakes on. She knew she would cross the point of no return at four martinis. She remained seated to try to think this through, though thinking wasn't her strong suit at the moment. She also saw Mrs. Henderson across the street watering her flowers, trying not to be obvious as she watched Gloria's little seduction of the delivery man.

Kell saw the exchange. He knew his time was limited. He said, "Sailing the world. That's the life."

Gloria was suddenly wistful and drained the martini. "Ya. Certainly gets you out of the kitchen."

Kell said, "We can't hold a package for seven months. It has to go back. And it might be a one-of-a- kind purchase. Art or something. That could be very disappointing to the doctor. I wish I knew if he would approve it being left with the renters."

Gloria said, "I think he would approve. He's letting them stay in his house, fully furnished and all. I'm sure he trusts them."

Kell wanted to appear to need to flesh out that reasoning. "Ya, makes sense. But company policy … But… I guess you know the renters. Do you know them?"

"Oh, I know them. Andrew works for the government. A boring analyst job or something. A nice young man, though. Like you." She paused to look at Kell with a passing longing. She looked across to see where Mrs. Henderson was looking now.

Kell said, "Is there a wife or girlfriend? In case only she's there when I come back next time?"

"Yes. Madeleine. The wife. The possessive wife. A real charmer."

The third martini had reached full throttle. Tipsy was the word she was looking for.

"Okay," Kell said, "Andrew and Madeleine. I really appreciate this. Know their last name?" Kell said offhand, expecting to hear 'Nelson'.

"Locke," Gloria said. "With an 'eeee' at the end. Their little boy, Chris, wandered here one day, and said, 'but it's not spelled like a lock on a door. You have to add an 'eeeee' at the end.' He's a nice kid."

Kell said "So, during day hours, I'm likely to get her?"

"Ya. Madeleine."

Kell wanted to be nonchalant. "She doesn't work?"

Gloria shook her head. "She's at home with Chris. When school's on, she does something. I don't know what. I don't see Andrew a lot. He must travel or something. You'll probably have to leave it with her. But I can tell you", and she leaned closer to him and gave him a tipsy wink, "you won't find her as friendly as me."

Gloria knew something was now wrong; she knew it right away. His smile was there but false, his face harder and distant. What had she said?

She looked at her empty martini glass. She suddenly felt foolish and cheap. And infinitely more depressed than when this charade had begun.

CHAPTER FORTY-FOUR

At the Bureau of Corporations, Andrew viewed the details of the numbered company which had made the loans to Moniker Inc. He found it was made up of three local businessmen.

He called Lawrence and filled him in on everything he had learned so far today. "No flags anywhere. Everything seems so normal. And Moniker's registered agent is a *lawyer*."

Lawrence knew Andrew's enthusiasm had greatly waned. And it took a bigger dip when Lawrence said, "I happen to know of one of the three businessmen, Max Hardy, a wealthy Rotarian. He's straight as an arrow. He wouldn't touch anything even slightly shady let alone a Cavaco. At least not knowingly."

Lawrence listened to Andrew's quiet breathing. The disappointment was palpable. Lawrence said, "Andrew, your theory was inspired. Don't even think of crossing it off yet. Cavaco's hand is never going to be obvious. He's too smart for that. So keep digging."

"Thanks, Wes." He meant it sincerely. "I needed a pep talk."

A few moments passed and Andrew said, "I'll follow-up on the lawyer. But something else, how would a Swiss company, Moniker, get financing from private local businessmen here? What's the process?"

"Moniker could contact a private mortgage broker here looking for private money." Lawrence paused, considering where Andrew was going with it. "You're thinking the broker might know more about Moniker?"

"Yes. He might know more than the lenders. You would think he would have to. We could see who came forward from Moniker. And see what Moniker had to show to make the lenders happy with loaning the money."

Lawrence liked it. "That's good, Andrew. I'm going to put a call into someone who will speak to Hardy for me. I'll say I only want to know if

Hardy can recommend a broker, someone he's used over the years. We'll see what we get."

Andrew made his way to the office address of Moniker's registered agent, attorney Lorne Nix. Andrew climbed the four flights of stairs in the four-story professional building in downtown Philadelphia. He walked the corridor until he came to an imposing oak door which read, 'Lorne Nix, Attorney at Law.' He tried the door. It was locked. At 2:20 p.m. That's odd, he thought. Unless the whole office has taken a late lunch. Or they're closed for summer vacation.

He left the building and found a pay phone. In the phone book he found an office number for Lorne Nix, Attorney. He called it. After only two rings an answering machine kicked in. A man's voice said, "This is the office of attorney Lorne Nix. Please leave your name, number, and a brief message. Thank you."

Andrew didn't leave a message. He looked up the office of the Pennsylvania Bar Association. He called and was put through to a woman who confirmed that Lorne Nix was indeed an attorney in good standing. There were no complaints on his file. He appeared to have an impeccable record.

Andrew asked, "What is his area of practice?"

"Corporate law," she answered.

"And how long has he been licensed to practice?"

"Well...", Andrew could hear her flipping pages, "licensed to practice law in Pennsylvania since...'57."

It struck Andrew that Nix had been licensed only a year before he was involved in a hotel acquisition. He said, "Do you mean he is licensed to practice somewhere else?"

"I see he's a member of both the Pennsylvania bar and the New York bar."

"Do you know when he was licensed in New York?"

"No, you would have to check with the New York Bar Association."

Andrew had already looked for a home address for Nix in the telephone book but found none. He asked, "Would you happen to know his home address?"

"That's not information I am free to divulge."

"Okay. Thank you."

Andrew was shortly on the phone to the New York Bar Association and learned that Nix had been licensed since 1953. The warm voiced, chatty woman added, "Had his office from '53 to '57 in Buffalo."

Andrew was momentarily stunned. Hearing 'Buffalo' was a jolt. That's where Cavaco had operated from back then. What was the percentage chance of a lawyer licensed to practice law in New York State practicing in *Buffalo*? One in 50? The woman had continued to talk. All that Andrew grasped was that Nix had attended law school at Suny in Buffalo. And the only office they now had on record was his Philadelphia office which he opened in 1957. Andrew thanked her and found his hand shaking as he hung up the receiver.

He called Lawrence, his excitement barely controlled. "Moniker's attorney went to law school in, get this, *Buffalo*, and practiced there from 1953 to 1957. Then became licensed to practice in Pennsylvania in 1957. Set up an office here in Philadelphia. And the hotel was bought in '58. And he has not maintained an office anywhere in New York state since then. A series of high of coincidences? Or not?"

"That is significant, Andrew," Lawrence chimed. "Very significant."

Andrew said, "I'm going to reconnoiter his office again. If no one's there, I'm going in tonight."

Lawrence was aghast and half shouted. "Andrew, don't commit suicide here!" Then he spoke more calmly. "Don't be so hasty. If you touch a thread in Cavaco's web, this could all be over. That kind of step has to be better prepared. In the meantime, I have something that might move us forward more safely. The mortgage broker who Max Hardy has used forever is John Forsythe of Equity Mortgages and More. It's very likely he was the broker involved in financing the purchase and improvements of the hotel. There may be useful records there. Check out Forsythe's offices first. That's less risky than going straight to Nix. Andrew, you just can't expose yourself to Cavaco even once or you're dead. But Forsythe's office may tell us something. The more we know, the better our chances of surviving this."

A long pause, then Andrew said, "Okay. Tonight it's Forsythe. I'll call you tomorrow. We'll talk about Nix then."

———•———

Lorne Nix listened to Leader's radio message telling all that Kell had learned. And now he studied the photograph of Emily Madeleine

Nelson that Kell had taken. She was beautiful, a warm smiling face, an athletic form. She was in the act of throwing a ball to a young boy wearing a catcher's mitt in the front yard of an upscale home.

Nix mulled what he had learned. She and Andrew Locke were husband and wife. He worked for the government in some unclear job and was often away. They were renting, and had been there less than a month. An unlisted phone number. Why unlisted? Why in her name?

And why would Lawrence have called that number? There were now threatening possibilities. Was Andrew Locke actually an FBI agent, Lawrence's 'outside help'? It figured as a high likelihood. Nix presumed that the wife was not an agent. And if maintaining secrecy or anonymity was paramount, putting the phone in the wife's maiden name would be a reasonable precaution.

What turned over and over in his mind was the name Locke, 'Locke with an 'e''. Of course, prominent in his mind was detective Paul Locke from all those years ago. Locke was, however, a common surname, hundreds in the phone book. Why would there be a connection of any kind?

To satisfy a niggling curiosity, however, Nix went to a drawer and shuffled down through papers to a yellowed collection of old newspaper clippings. He withdrew a few and spread them, looking for one in particular, the lengthy report in the Philadelphia Post of the abduction of Detective Paul Locke twenty years ago. He found it, the article led by a large picture of Paul Locke. Nix's finger drew down the article quickly, then slowed, then stopped. He read carefully.

The little boy's name was Andrew. Curious.

But Andrew was also a common name.

But he would be late twenties now, about the age of the beautiful Emily Madeleine Nelson.

If he were an agent, and he were Lawrence's secret helper, and he were Paul Locke's son, so what? That had to be simply coincidence. There was no special threat to Cavaco and him. The real point was that Nix may now have found Lawrence's helper. That was the whole purpose of the exercise. So mission accomplished. All the rest was merely 'its a small world' thing.

What first had to be determined was whether Andrew Locke was actually an FBI agent. Through insider informants, he could get that information quickly. The fact that Locke and Nelson had been renting only a month or so, meaning he may have been transferred here at that time, certainly fit with the timing on the scene of some unknown outside agent. Things might start to add up nicely. And once again The Watcher would have the upper hand.

But still, the name Andrew Locke was startling.

CHAPTER FORTY-FIVE

After speaking with Lawrence, Andrew went directly home and told Madeline he would be away a few days on surveillance. She had asked if everything was alright. He had said he might have a lead. She had pulled him to her and kissed him.

He had promised he would be back by Friday afternoon to pack for the canoe trip. She had said, "Nadine will be here by 4:00. We want to get away by 5:00." They would have four days together.

He left home and drove directly to Forsythe's office, the mortgage broker that Lawrence suspected Moniker had used. He wanted to case the premises to see what he would need to get in later tonight. On a side street off Manayunk Avenue, he pulled up to what had once been a grand colonial home but now served as Forsythe's offices and had done so for the past 35 years. Andrew wanted just a few minutes inside to get the lay out and see what he could learn.

He parked around back in the small paved lot. He noted a back door entrance probably used by staff. He walked around to the front, observing as he entered the building that there was no alarm system. He didn't bother to check the lock mechanism on the front door because tonight he would go in the back way, far less conspicuous. He also already knew from Lawrence that Forsythe would not be in today, a Tuesday. Forsythe golfed Tuesdays and Thursdays. A couple of young, hungry associates handled most of the business day-to-day anyway.

In the minutes he had to wait before the receptionist got off the phone, he noted a hallway leading to a room which would somehow connect to that back entrance. He watched a secretary in high heels open a drawer in a tall, narrow filing cabinet behind the receptionist. The drawers were alphabetically marked. The secretary ran her polished fingernail along the tops of index cards. He hoped their file card system would be obvious and tell him something of their archiving system.

She withdrew an index card and left the room, reading the card as she went, down the hall and through a doorway into another room. He heard a door squeak from somewhere at the back of those rooms. He heard high heels negotiating down wooden steps.

The receptionist soon hung up the phone and looked to Andrew. "May I help you?"

"Yes, I would like to speak to Mr. Forsythe if he's available."

"He's away today. But Mr. Baker or Ms. Jones would be happy to help."

"I would prefer to see Mr. Forsythe. Can I get an appointment for next week?"

She took his name, Andrew Naismith, and jotted the date and time on a card and handed it to him. He heard the high heels on wooden steps and the same door squeak again. The secretary with the index card appeared, coming down the hall with a fat file. She was peeved, dusting off an arm, checking a broken fingernail.

Just as Andrew was closing the front door behind him, he heard her say to the receptionist, "what a hell hole down there."

He now knew where old files were archived.

———•—•———

Just before 2:00 a.m., Andrew left the Weeping Willows Motel and drove back into Philadelphia. He parked two streets over from Forsythe's office. He walked to the office and went around to the building's unlit back door. It was old and had both a handle lock and a basic dead-bolt. Training his penlight, he worked a slim jim at the deadbolt, then at the handle lock. In four and a half minutes he was in without causing damage to either lock.

He banged into a rolling chair and knocked over a coat rack before his eyes adjusted. The place was like a rabbit warren. He was in a small room that connected to a back hallway and then through another room and then another hallway to the reception area and the filing cabinet with the index cards.

The penlight beam found the front of the filing cabinet. He looked at the alphabet notations. He opened the drawer marked 'K to N'. Flipping through the index cards he slowed at Monahan, Monger, Mongrain.

Then ...there it was! Moniker Inc! It was like magic. He could have gotten down on his knees and thanked the office manager. But then he saw under 'storage date', there was no date entered. Had it been purged?

The door to the basement was ajar and squeaked when he opened it further. He began down the wooden stairs, closing the door behind him. Walking by the building earlier, he had seen that the basement windows had been completely ply wooded from inside for security. So he knew he could use the basement light. He snapped it on.

He could only agree with the secretary - 'what a hell hole.' The basement was low ceilinged with a stone foundation. Two, dangling, weak, bare light bulbs did their level best to penetrate the darkness but mostly failed. Round, vertical cedar posts supported a dangerously sagging ceiling. Every inch of the basement was honeycombed with ancient wooden shelving which bowed under the strain of overflowing banker boxes. Some unknown powder and a greying dust layered every flat surface including the banker boxes. Cobwebs laced the entire ceiling and ventured downward like hammocks. The narrow walking passages appeared to be sized for midgets. He pitied the secretaries.

The year of the filing of every box was announced in magic marker on its side. He found a short row of '1980', a few of '1979', around the corner '1978', and so on. He hoped they would reach back to the 1950's. He soon discovered the pattern in the system, and took himself to where they should be.

He found two banker boxes marked '1958', the year Moniker had borrowed the money to buy the Hotel Continental. The files appeared to be in alphabetical order. He quickly flipped through the file labels looking for 'Moniker'. He found nothing. He tried 'Hotel Continental'. Nothing. He tried just 'Continental'. Nothing.

He knew there had been that further mortgage in 1960, the monies being required for the expansion the hotel underwent that year and the next, which included the ballroom. He worked his way to those boxes and scanned quickly through all the 'M's. He came upon a tattered brown accordion file with a half torn label, 'Moniker Inc.' Eureka! He withdrew it from the banker box. He immediately saw that buried in it was the separate, original file from 1958. Presumably it was placed with this newer file on Moniker for continuity or context.

It would take considerable time to review the file and this was no place to do it. Nobody would miss it. He carried it up the stairs and left by the back door.

He arrived back at the motel at 3:30 a.m. He put on the coffee and began to read. The oldest notes, dated in late 1957, indicated that Forsythe had been approached by a new, local lawyer, Lorne Nix, looking for substantial private money for his client, a Swiss concern, to acquire some significant property in Philadelphia. One note had the words, "possible Hotel Continental" scratched on the side. He found a commercial appraisal of value of the Hotel Continental. It was evident from his notes that Forsythe was in regular communication with Max Hardy to determine his group's level of interest and capacity to fund this proposed loan. And there had been several meetings with Nix.

The theme that emerged from Forsythe's memos to file was that Max Hardy's group had concerns about lending to a foreign owner, even though there would be relative safety in a mortgage on the Hotel. The concerns came about firstly because the proposed borrower, Moniker Inc., could not provide any credit history. That was because there was no credit history; it was a newly incorporated corporation. Secondly, the owner of Moniker Inc., Albert Baumgartner, would not give a personal guarantee in support of the proposed mortgage. And thirdly, Max Hardy did not want to ever have to chase a Swiss company to Switzerland to get paid. The parties appeared to have reached an impasse.

But then Moniker disclosed that it owned an asset in United States, 800 acres of pristine forest in Franklin County in central Pennsylvania, just bordering the Appalachians. Moniker had bought it outright only six months before for its 'resort development potential'. To make the Hotel loan happen, Moniker offered to pledge the 800 acres as collateral security allowing Hardy's group to seize it if Moniker ever defaulted in payments on the Hotel mortgage.

It seemed this broke the impasse, everyone was happy, and it was cigars all around.

Moniker put up 50% of the purchase price of the Hotel in cash and Hardy's group loaned the other 50%. The loan was secured by a mortgage on the Hotel and by a collateral mortgage on the 800 acres. Andrew found a copy of Moniker's deed to the 800 acres and a copy of Hardy's group's collateral mortgage on the 800 acres.

Andrew was fatigued. The sun was just coming up, and apart from a two-hour sleep before midnight, he had not slept. He closed the curtains tightly and stretched out on the bed in his clothes.

His mind cycled the new facts. Nix had become licensed to practice law in Pennsylvania in 1957. Nix had moved his offices to Philadelphia in 1957. Moniker had bought the 800 acres in 1957, using Nix, only months later. Then Moniker had bought the Hotel in 1958, using Nix, of course.

A young lawyer from Buffalo moves to Philadelphia. He may have just preferred to live his life in Philadelphia than in Buffalo. That was certainly plausible. But still, he somehow immediately comes to represent a moneyed Swiss company. Not implausible. But it did raise the natural question - how did he come to represent such a company so quickly? Or was that the order in which things happened? Or did it instead point to a relationship that existed before he moved to Philadelphia? A relationship in Buffalo?

Reading the whole file, Andrew had been struck by something else - the absence of any mention of a meeting with Albert Baumgartner in person. He was Swiss, living in Zurich. Would it be reasonable that he didn't attend any of these meetings? Possibly. He probably visited and inspected the hotel itself without needing to be around later for the financing meetings. He had his lawyer, Nix, there to deal with all that and Baumgartner may have just met with Nix alone later when it came to signing all documents. Or perhaps they were couriered and signed in Switzerland. Andrew just didn't know what was typical.

He considered all he had learned. It would naturally not arise in the mind of Forsythe or any of Hardy's group that there might be something amiss with a Swiss company owning 800 acres of pristine land near the Appalachians for future development. And there might not be. But as Andrew thought on it, if Moniker were in fact Cavaco, Andrew could readily conceive of a highly nefarious purpose. He found himself wondering, with an aching, if he had stumbled on where his father had been taken.

CHAPTER FORTY-SIX

Andrew woke at 10:30 a.m. Immediately he was on the phone to the operator getting connected to the Recorder of Deeds office in Chambersburg, which handled Franklin County, nearby the Appalachians. He obtained a number of a private title searcher, Phyllis, who would be available to help him. He called her. He had a copy of the deed and mortgage to the 800 acres in his hand from the broker file and read her the legal description.

She called him back twenty minutes later. She said, "Moniker doesn't own that property anymore. They sold it in 1962 to the Pleasant Pheasant Hunt Camp."

Andrew's heart sank. It had been a long shot, but he had hoped he might have discovered where Cavaco was dumping bodies. That was, if Moniker was Cavaco. But the land had been sold nineteen years ago.

Andrew asked, "Was attorney Lorne Nix involved?"

"Yes. He acted for Moniker. Another attorney acted for the buyer, the Camp."

It was sounding legitimate. He was more discouraged. He was about to wrap up the call when a thought struck him. The broker's notes had said Moniker had bought the acreage in 1957 for its "resort development potential." But here it was sold only a few years later to a hunt camp, not exactly the highest and best use of 800 acres which had purported development potential.

Andrew asked, "So....did the Hunt Camp sell it to someone else later?"

"No. They still own."

"The whole thing?"

"Yes."

So it had never been developed. Not even a part of it. Might this have been only a paper sale to break the connection between the property and Moniker, and hence between the property and Cavaco, if Moniker were Cavaco? Not many investigators today would think to dig into a private mortgage broker's personal notes from twenty-five years ago and so would never know Moniker owned that property at any time. And so no one today would have any reason to ever be looking at that property with any suspicion.

But, he cautioned himself, this was thin speculation, hinged on hunches, hanging from guesswork.

"Phyllis, I can be there by 1:30. Can I pick up a copy of that deed from Moniker to the Hunt Camp?"

"Sure can."

Andrew wanted to fly over the camp property to see what was there.

———————

The information Nix had been waiting on came in Thursday at noon. There was indeed an FBI agent named Andrew Locke, age 27. And he had been born in Philadelphia. And his father had been a detective but died when Andrew was only a boy.

Small world, Nix thought.

Nix learned further that Andrew had been transferred from the Minneapolis field office a month ago on a highly classified assignment. The location of the assignment was completely confidential. In Minneapolis he had done normal investigative duties as well as flying air surveillance. He was also a SWAT trained sniper. An odd mix of talents.

A lone agent had taken out Kennedy and Kipling. And with a sniper's accuracy. It was as plain as the nose on your face, Nix concluded – Andrew Locke was Lawrence's secret helper.

Nix pondered why Lawrence had selected Locke for this peculiar top-secret assignment. Locke was not that experienced, not that long in the field. The sniper skills had certainly come in handy with Kennedy and Kipling. But wouldn't those skills have been only incidental, not a prerequisite?

Marza and his bodyguard had been killed by what was described as 'an expert shooter'. But nobody, not even the rumor mills, speculated who even *might* be responsible. Could there be a connection? But on what possible grounds? One common nexus was that The Watcher was involved in both those cases. Did Lawrence somehow come to believe The Watcher was connected with Marza's case, and had Locke doing some checking on Marza, and Marza then got killed? But as Nix himself had told Cavaco, the law doesn't go around assassinating ex-convicts. Or was it not assassination?

For now, he would have Locke's house watched to get a photograph of him for reference. But Nix still didn't think there was any special, urgent concern. He would put a tail on him out of caution. If they ever believed that Locke posed any real threat, they would tighten up on him, and he might have to disappear.

Cavaco was away today sailing, but he and Nix were meeting tonight for a late dinner. Cavaco would be delighted to learn that Nix had discovered who Lawrence's secret helper was. Nix wondered how Cavaco would react when he learned it was the very son of Detective Paul Locke from all those years ago.

Just before 1:00 p.m., Andrew touched down at the small municipal airport in Chambersburg, just past famous Gettysburg, 150 miles west of Philadelphia. In brief conversation with an airport staffer, Andrew learned that a thunderstorm system was moving in quickly from the west over the Appalachians. "If you want to get back to Philly, you've got maybe an hour and a half at most to get in the air and out of here. It won't clear again until late tomorrow morning."

Andrew took a taxi to the Recorder of Deeds office where he met Phyllis. She gave him a copy of the deed and pointed out on a large wall map precisely the location of the 800 acres. Andrew jotted a note. The property was north-west of Chambersburg ten minutes flying time. He hoped the weather would hold off.

Phyllis pointed out on the deed that the Hunt Camp's address was "c/o Mike Wilson, PO Box 385, Chambersburg, Penn." He got directions to the post office.

From an obliging postal clerk, he learned that there was no PO box number 385. "Mistake there somewhere. I've been here 32 years. There's never been box numbers higher than 300."

Andrew asked, "Do you receive mail for a Mike Wilson?"

"Yes, for a couple of Mike Wilsons. I know them both. They aren't neither one of them involved in any hunt camp. The one's been in a wheelchair since he was 12 and the other one's the drama teacher at the high school. Wouldn't hurt a fly. Anyway, he's only been here maybe fifteen years. Certainly not since '62."

When Andrew left the post office, he could see dark cloud formations building to the west. His time was getting tight.

He thought, if the property is undeveloped, there would be no mail like utility bills being sent to that PO box address. Except a property tax bill. And if the mailing address for the Hunt Camp was bogus, what about the tax bills?

He got directions to the tax office. He hurried the three blocks, hoping he might be lucky enough to get another mailing address for the Hunt Camp there. He went in and showed the clerk the deed and said he was Mike Wilson. "I've been having trouble with the mail lately. Was afraid I might have missed getting a tax bill."

The woman looked up the records for the property. Still reading the record she said, "You appear to be all paid up." She was reading something else now, a note stapled on the file. Still reading it she said, "You call in twice a year and get the amount owing and mail us cash."

"Right," Andrew said. Damn, that would make sense if you wanted to avoid being traceable. "But... I was in the area. And you can never be too careful paying your taxes."

She sort of smiled and read further. And frowned. "The bills we send always come back." She looked at him, eyebrows pinched, then glanced back to the record. "PO Box 385, here in town. A problem there? Can you give us another address?"

So no corrected address had ever been provided. He answered casually, "No, I'll speak to the post office about it."

"I definitely would," she said.

From the runway at the Chambersburg airport, Andrew saw to the west a brilliant flash of lightening and black clouds building in intensity. He would outrun the approaching storm. But he wouldn't be able to come back and fly over the camp property until the weather system cleared tomorrow late morning. He increased the throttle and the Pitt raced along the tarmac and he lifted off. Reluctantly he pointed east, in the direction of home.

Late that afternoon, Andrew again scouted Nix's office. Still no one was there.

He called Lawrence. He wasn't at the office. He got him at home. He filled him in on what he had learned from Forsythe's files, that Moniker had bought 800 acres in 1957 near the Appalachians. "That acreage really intrigues me. What would a Swiss company want with that?"

Lawrence said, "You said the file described it as resort potential. Doesn't seem unusual that Swiss money would invest in that kind of thing."

"Yes, but Moniker sold it only a few years later. And not for resort development. It's a hunt camp, the Pleasant Pheasant Hunt Camp. And the thing is the camp still owns it. So it was never developed, any part of it. It's just birds, not condominiums."

"Moniker might have stretched the truth about the property's development potential to get the Hotel loan. Businessmen have been known to exaggerate."

"But why buy it in the first place? And something else smells. The address for the hunt camp is a PO box that doesn't exist. If I wanted to continue to have a property available to me for whatever uses, but didn't want anyone to know I owned it or had any connection with it, I could paper sell it to someone who isn't real. I maintain control without anyone knowing who in reality owns it. As far as the world is concerned, the property is owned by some hunt camp, but care of some bogus Mike Wilson with a bogus address."

Lawrence said, "Was there a separate lawyer for that Mike Wilson?"

"Yes."

Lawrence seemed unimpressed. "It's much harder to manage a fake transfer of ownership with two separate lawyers. Lots of high flying speculation there, Andrew. And mailing addresses get screwed up all the time. But more, if it was important to Moniker to only paper sell the property to hide from ownership all those years ago, why didn't Moniker do the same thing with the Hotel? Moniker still owns *it*."

That hadn't occurred to Andrew. Damn, he needed more sleep. "Well...," and a notion came to him, "there's a distinction. The Hotel carries on legitimate business. Nobody but you and I have any reason to suspect it. But the acreage, well, if a body turned up there, the police are going to go to the registered owner."

"But you're suggesting there is no new owner. That's the point. And the police would find that out too. So Moniker wouldn't duck the heat anyway."

"I suppose," he admitted. "But it would take the police some time. Give Cavaco more time to dodge the bullet if that ever happened."

"Maybe." Lawrence wasn't on board. Andrew knew it.

Andrew said, "I'm going to do a flyover of the property tomorrow. As for now, I'm going into Nix's office tonight. It's the next natural step. I don't know what else to do."

Lawrence didn't know either. He had hoped Forsythe's files would have disclosed more specifics about Moniker, more actual contacts than just the local lawyer agent. He knew that if Nix was in fact connected to Cavaco, things could get suddenly very dangerous with Andrew going into Nix's office. But Andrew was determined, and really, what better next step was there? It was still less dangerous than trying to contact The Watcher directly through The New York Times.

"Okay," Lawrence said with reluctance. "Watch yourself."

CHAPTER FORTY-SEVEN

"That little kid?" Cavaco was staggered and his voice boomed. Cavaco had just arrived at Nix's penthouse for a late dinner and Nix had briefed him, telling him that Lawrence's secret helper was none other than detective Paul Locke's boy, now an FBI agent.

"That little kid?", Cavaco repeated, still astonished by the news. He ignored Nix's invitation to take a seat and stood stock still, eyes darting about as he struggled to comprehend. "Something's rotten here."

Nix tried to soothe. "It's a surprise, yes. But I really don't think his being here is more than coincidence, small world."

"Small world? It's fucking *claustrophobic*."

Nix poured and Cavaco drank. Nix explained at length why he didn't see any likely threat to them in Andrew Locke's being here. He finished by saying, "And remember, he's from Philadelphia. Knows the area. It's not so strange that the Bureau put him here."

The wine finally had a calming effect on Cavaco. He took a seat. He said, "We want to watch this *very* closely."

Nix nodded. "Of course." He then handed Cavaco the picture of Madeleine. "That's the wife, the one with the unlisted number."

Cavaco took his time. "Nice looker. Got a picture of Andrew?"

"No. He hasn't been around home for a couple of days it seems. Day or night."

Cavaco said, "Well let's get one *very* soon." He slowly rotated the wine in his glass, watching it as he spoke slowly, "We killed his father. The kid...is now FBI... a killer agent. Highly secret mission here. Reports only to our old friend Lawrence."

He looked at Nix. "I have survived because I trust hunches. And I'm having hunches right now. Doesn't it look like more than a small world thing to you?"

Nix shook his head. "They don't know a thing. After all this time, twenty years, how could they?"

Nix smiled heartily, trying to bring some cheer to the room. He walked over to Cavaco and held him by the shoulders. "Relax, will you? Let's enjoy dinner. I have everything in hand."

At 1:30 a.m. Andrew slipped on thin gloves and picked the lock on Nix's office door. He let himself in and closed the door behind him. From the slit of street light, he could see the curtains were closed. He switched on the lights.

He was in a single room with plush carpet and a secretarial desk and two waiting chairs. A door to an inner office was closed. On the secretarial desk sat an electric typewriter, a phone, business card holder with cards, and standard secretarial paraphernalia. He went to the desk. The drawers were unlocked. They revealed nothing personal to the secretary, just standard office needs. Things seemed exceedingly tidy for a working secretary's desk. He had expected to find personal items - maybe some women's shoes tucked under the desk or a sweater hanging on a rack like at Forsythe's office. There was none of that. There was no personal address/telephone book. There was no client file index. How did they keep track of clients? The garbage-can was empty, too.

There was only one filing cabinet in this outer office. Locked. On the top, a small sheaf of twenty-dollar bills lay open, fully visible. Before tackling the cabinet, he wanted to see the inner office. The door to it was locked. Strange, he thought.

But it wasn't a difficult pick. He was in quickly. He flicked on the lights. There was more plush carpet, a large desk with a phone, a wall of recessed shelving filled with legal textbooks. Expensive Persian carpets hung on two walls. On another, the mounted, stuffed heads of two snarling tigers looked at Andrew. Wow. Odd in a law office.

By a window was radio equipment and a microphone and two reel to reel tape recorders. Maybe a hobbyist? He expected to see paper littering Nix's desk. But there was just a commercial lease document and a small stack of invoices - for rent and utilities and sundries.

The desk drawers were locked. He picked them. They, too, revealed no personal address/phone book or client lists. Whoever worked here was careful not to leave anything confidential about.

The place didn't give the appearance of a busy law office at all, unless they had thoroughly tidied up and cleaned and put everything away for the holidays, if that was even the explanation for them being away lately.

There were two filing cabinets in the inner office, again both locked. Andrew cracked the locks. A quick search of the drawers seemed to suggest that Nix had only a few clients – mostly international corporations. They seemed to have interests in a lot of places. It was clear Nix was the quarterback for a lot of their activity. There was voluminous correspondence with accountants both here in Philadelphia and abroad. But there was too much dry reading for Andrew to accomplish much for the moment.

What Andrew had really hoped to ferret out was correspondence with Moniker. He couldn't find any at all. His impression was that the office was, in the end, sterile, probably devoid of anything useful to him.

He locked everything back up again and left. He had a few obvious options. Start watching the office next week and keep it up until someone, hopefully Nix, showed eventually, then follow him home. Then do his home. As for checking out Cavaco, fly to Zurich, find Baumgartner, and compare him to Cavaco's portrait. As for tomorrow, fly to Chambersburg and have a look at the acreage.

As he drove to the motel, he kept wondering where *exactly* the truth was in all this. But he couldn't focus, just kept yawning. Another middle of the night outing.

———————

The next morning Nix went to his office at 8:30 to pick up a file so he could work from home as he most often did. When he entered the inner office, he bent absently to a small key pad just above the baseboard to enter a 4-digit code. He almost missed noticing the extremely tiny flashing red light because his mind was habituated to no longer noticing the light, it having been only a dull red glow for years and years.

If the correct code was not entered within fifteen seconds, the light on the pad flashed instead of simply glowing. He had never wanted an alarm, per se, as his goal wasn't to scare an intruder away, but more importantly, to know *who* it was.

He caught himself and looked at the light carefully. It was flashing!

He was jolted. Damn! Someone had broken in!

It wasn't that he kept anything incriminating here. Or had valuables here. It was more, *why* was someone here? Was someone on to something?

He saw nothing disturbed anywhere. The twenty dollar bills he always left in sight for this purpose were still there. So theft wasn't the motive; so that was bad news. What was the motive? He couldn't know that yet.

But as to *who* it was, he would soon have the answer. He reached up and removed one of the mounted tiger heads from the wall. He unhooked a wire running to a camera inside the head. The wire fed back behind the drywall down to the keypad at the baseboard, and activated the camera to take pictures at five second intervals if the code weren't entered correctly or at all. The camera's lens, hidden at the back of the mouth, had excellent vantage to anyone in the room. Nix tested the set up once a year.

He took the roll of film out of the camera and left the office. At the photo shop he paid for the one hour developing. In less than an hour he was handed a thick package of pictures. He hurried back to his car and ripped open the package.

A man, late twenties, handsome, his face somewhat familiar. Why was that face somewhat familiar? Nix felt his heart racing. Naturally, because of all the talk last night, he thought of Andrew Locke. Nix was frustrated. He had no picture of Locke, just the damn wife. He hoped it wasn't Locke, just some nosy snoop. But the pictures, more than sixty, showed whomever looking *carefully* through the desk and the file cabinets, far more attentive than a simple snoop.

But *why* was the face familiar? As he drove, it finally came to him. A chill shot through and he physically shook.

He pulled over at a payphone booth and called Cavaco. "My office was broken into. Meet me at my place right away."

Back in the car he drove distracted and fast, his face angry, his fist repeatedly slamming the steering wheel, other cars blaring at his erratic driving.

That picture. That picture of Detective Paul Locke in the newspaper clipping he had looked at yesterday. That was it. The kid looked *exactly* like his father.

What the hell was going on?

CHAPTER FORTY-EIGHT

When Nix told Cavaco it was Andrew Locke, Cavaco was surprisingly calm. "I think they call this a seismic shift," he said evenly. It was as if Cavaco knew who it was before Nix told him.

He stood at the wide wall of window in Nix's penthouse staring out at the Philadelphia skyline, smoking a cigarette, quietly thinking.

Nix didn't interfere. He had been complacent. He had been wrong. He was deferring.

Cavaco said, "The first question is how did he get onto you? And secondly, what's an FBI agent doing investigating his own father's disappearance? Surely that's against Bureau protocol. It tells me it's completely off the record."

Nix was startled at Cavaco's sudden leap. "Why do you think he's investigating Locke's disappearance from twenty years ago, and not Bloom's murder?"

"A hunch. No one could connect you to Bloom. We've been too careful. But twenty years ago... things were messy there. Something we don't know about has come up. And Andrew Locke is now here...and on an extraordinarily secretive assignment reporting only to our old friend Lawrence. And Locke finds you. Too many planets aligning. Tic tac toe."

Nix wasn't going to question Cavaco's hunches anymore anytime soon. He would let Cavaco take the lead from here on this one.

Cavaco continued, "But what case Locke's investigating doesn't change what we have to do anyway. He's investigating *you* and that's all we need to know. It's not for dodging taxes. We have to go with worst case scenario - he wants you, and maybe me, for murder. Plural. So we stop him dead in his tracks."

Unhurried, thinking, Cavaco stubbed the cigarette in the ashtray, lit another one, and again stared out the window. "I think something else is happening here the possibility of which hasn't occurred to you. There are just too many coincidences, too many unusual strings that don't tie together. Let me toss out a thought. When we took Detective Locke, we asked him if he had told anyone what he knew. He said 'no.' We beat him. He still said 'no'. So I believed him."

Cavaco now took a seat on the couch and a long drag on the cigarette. He continued, slowly, "Lawrence was the FBI's liaison person to the Philadelphia Police Department back then, wasn't he? What if detective Locke had lied to us? What if he had talked, told Lawrence what that pickpocket said but Lawrence didn't say anything to anybody because of that dead girl's body."

He stubbed the cigarette as he gazed toward the window. "Detective Locke's disappearance, Macky's murder, never get solved. But Lawrence carries a burden.... for a long time. He wants to unburden. Find me, find us, and kill us. But he can't do it alone. He sees a possibility. Brings in the kid, who is highly motivated. Enough to sidestep FBI protocol."

Cavaco turned to look at Nix and half smiled. "Sound crazy?"

Nix shrugged a little. "Maybe a few holes. But Locke's onto me somehow. And Lawrence knows whatever Locke knows. That's what we face."

Cavaco nodded. "You know what's beautiful here? All this secrecy they've got going is perfect for us. Not a peep of this investigation anywhere in his office. I think nobody knows what's going on but those two. They're tighter than a vacuum pack. A tidy package for us. We don't take on the whole FBI. We just make those two disappear and the law won't even know what happened."

Nix said, "Andrew Locke's a very dangerous man when he wants to be. And we don't know where he is right now. It seems he's not staying at home."

"There's a way to find him. And make him helpless. And make him sing like a bird." He picked up the picture of Madeleine and eyed it carefully. Then he looked over at Nix.

Nix nodded. "That could work."

"You and I will drive by Locke's house now and have a look. It's only morning. We devise a plan. And we move on it tonight."

"I'll alert the cell."

Andrew slept until 8:30 and he felt refreshed for the first time in days. The storm system was clearing and he quickly got out to the aerodrome and took off in the Pitt at 10:30 heading for Chambersburg.

An hour and a half later in a baby blue sky he flew past Chambersburg. Then on another ten minutes, then slowed and dropped his altitude to 1000' as he swept over the 800-acre, Hunt Club property.

The acreage was mixed – some mature forest, but mostly low scrub, dwarf trees, wild grasses. But what struck Andrew were the large expanses of marsh, swamp and bog. Those would surely prohibit any real resort development. Pheasant, yes. Vacationer, no.

He saw some low buildings and banked slowly, leveling off low at 500' to get a closer look. A cabin was set a quarter mile back from a neglected gravel municipal road. A long, winding, grass lane connected the cabin to the road. A run-down, two story barn stood about 100 feet from the cabin. There was no sign of life. But it also wasn't pheasant season, if that counted for anything.

It looked like ten acres around the cabin and barn may have once grudgingly supported mixed farming but was now wild grass and spare trees. The ten acres were still demarcated with an old post and wire fence.

A kind of gatehouse stood beside the grass lane near the road at the front, but was not visible from the road because of woods. Newer, tall fencing made of wire with steel rod posts ran the length of the front of the property at the road side. There was also a sturdy gate across the lane at the entrance to the road. Clearly they didn't want trespassers.

Andrew circled again, pressing the cameras' remote, taking dozens of pictures of the cabin and barn and immediate surroundings. He really wanted to get into that cabin. There might be something there telling him something about who used it. But there was nowhere to land the Pitt anywhere nearby. And his time and fuel were limited. He would have to come back, but not today.

As he banked and turned away from the buildings, he almost missed seeing a faint trail working its way back from the once farmed area into the woods and grassland, meandering past considerable marsh and swamp and bog deep into the rear of the property. The trail ended a hundred yards short of a little-used dirt road that the acreage backed onto. Andrew guessed that to casual observation from that back road, the 800 acres would look impenetrable.

Andrew thought, if I needed to dispose of bodies over years, what better place than a remote, no-snoopy-neighbor-for-miles tract of 800 private acres of your very own. Particularly acreage with extensive swamp and bog where organic matter decomposes in swift order, where bared bones sink in ooze to unknown bottoms. Nobody around to witness you dispose of it. No corpses floating to the surface in some public lake. No shallow grave uncovered by animals and discovered by hikers. And no cementing required. And a place where you could hide out yourself if you had to. Who would ever think to look for you here?

When he was refueling at Chambersburg, he asked about a landing spot closer to the area of the 800 acres without actually identifying it, just giving mileage and direction. One of the older fellows who flew a Tiger Moth told him there was a disused section of old highway, 'about a half mile west of Rona's Corners. The new highway by-passed it years ago. I've landed on it a few times. Some weeds coming through the asphalt but it's level and firm. And your Pitt can handle that better than my old bird.'

Andrew had seen Rona's Corners on the map. By Andrew's reckoning, it would be walkable from there to the acreage, maybe two miles, three at most. He certainly had no time today.

When he landed back at his home aerodrome, he called Lawrence from a payphone. Again Lawrence was not at the office. Andrew got him on the phone at home. "I flew over Moniker's 800-acre property near Chambersburg. It's half swamp and bog. Some of it's good. But it was never resort potential."

Lawrence sounded tired. "But it does sound like bird hunting terrain."

Andrew said, "Yes, for sure, but then why would Moniker have ever bought it in the first place?"

Lawrence's voice was weak. "If Moniker is for real, then they just made a bad investment and got out of it."

Andrew figured the Swiss just aren't that stupid. But he didn't say anything.

Lawrence continued. "And if Moniker is Cavaco, then it was to launder some of Cavaco's offshore money early on. And then he sold it. Didn't need it anymore because he had the Hotel."

That made more sense, but Andrew still didn't buy it completely. But he wasn't going to argue. He said, "Just a reminder that Maddy and I are away canoeing for four days, starting tonight. I'll call you when I'm back."

Lawrence rallied a bit, "Yes, I remember. Enjoy yourselves. You've been working hard."

He wondered why Lawrence was so tired. "You sound down, Wes. Are you okay?"

"Not sleeping well. Things...are catching up with me a bit."

Andrew thought of depression. And of drugs. And of what Lawrence was preparing to face if Andrew found Cavaco. Was he cracking?

Andrew said. "Are you going to get to the cottage on the weekend?"

"Maybe. I'll see."

As Andrew drove home, the more he felt a sense of urgency, a growing obsession about getting into that cabin. Why had Moniker ever bought that land when it was clear that it had no resort potential? If Moniker was Cavaco, and it was just to launder money as Lawrence suggested, why that land, way the heck out there? Why not something with real growth potential? That land was, as the expression goes, for the birds. Or was it for bodies?

There was that, and there was the post office address that didn't exist and had never been corrected by the hunt camp owner.

Would he find something in that cabin that would lead him to one real person? Just one real person. And from there, to some real answers?

He arrived home at 4:30. Madeleine was in the garage with her younger sister, Nadine. It was easy to see they were sisters, almost like twins, the same attractive features and physique, the same long chestnut hair. Andrew gave Nadine a big hug and thanked her for babysitting Chris for the next four days.

Nadine was so enthused. "Oh, I'm *really* looking forward to it! Chris and I are going to have a blast!"

Madeleine's excitement was also obvious. "Everything's packed and ready to be loaded in, Andrew. The food. The tent. Sleeping bags. Air mattresses. The cooking gear. Your clothes. Your hatchet. Yada yada. Test me if you want."

"Matches," Andrew said.

"Oh shoot!" she laughed, putting her hand to her mouth. Then she gushed, "*Just kidding.*" She tapped her jean's pocket. "Right in here smarty pants."

CHAPTER FORTY-NINE

They were spending the first night, Friday night, at The Lakeside Inn. It was completely charming, their room romantic, white linen on each table at the elegant restaurant, candles glowing softly, the food divine.

But Madeleine was sad. Although Andrew had tried - had held her hand, had smiled at her - she knew he was preoccupied. His mind just couldn't settle and she knew it. She desperately wanted them to have fun together, just them, not them *and* this investigation that was sucking the life from her husband.

They were sitting beside the lake on a dock, alone in the dark, quiet, looking at the stars. They hadn't spoken for three whole minutes. She knew his mind was turning something over and over. She looked from the stars down to the dark water. "Andrew," she gently said, "you've been somewhere else since we started this holiday. Is there anything I can do?"

After a few moments he said, "I'm sorry, Maddy. I'm not much company, am I?"

She didn't say anything.

Andrew said, "I wish I could explain it all. I want it to be over so badly."

She took his hand. Her voice was caring. "I know I don't understand what you're going through, really. I just hoped we could have some time."

He looked down at the water, like black glass. "I know. I know and I'm sorry. There's a piece in the puzzle I had hoped to get to today, before our holiday. I thought...I could then let things go for a few days. But I didn't manage to get to it. I'm sorry about this."

She wanted to do anything to salvage the holiday. She perked a bit. "Do you mean if you had time tomorrow, that would do it?"

He was surprised at the offer. "Maddy, I'm really sorry. I don't want to spoil our time."

She pressed. "No, listen. If that would make the difference for you, let's do it. I'll just take a walk and shop a bit around here. You could be back by…when?"

Andrew raced through some time calculations. Get to the aerodrome. Fly to the property. Check out the cabin. Fly back… "By three, say. If I get away early."

She said, "That would be fine."

Andrew said, "So we would canoe for three days, not four?"

"Yes," she said. "If we can get to the canoe outfitters and then to the launch site by four, we could put in and do a three-day loop."

The original plan was to do a two-day loop, Saturday and Sunday, returning to the launch site Sunday late afternoon to call Nadine from the payphone there to check on things at home. Then do another two-day loop.

Madeleine said, "We'll call Nadine tomorrow instead, just before we launch. Let her know our change of plans."

Andrew nodded.

Madeleine said, "So, you do what you have to tomorrow. And then we give it another try. Just us. Do we have a deal?"

Andrew looked at her and smiled. He kissed her warmly. "Deal."

———————

Earlier that evening at 8:00 p.m., Leader reported that there was only one car, the wife's, in the driveway at Locke's house. He reported also that the wife and young son were sitting on the front porch eating ice cream.

The report was exactly what Cavaco hoped for. He gave the cell the green light to continue as planned.

At 10:30 p.m., as a precaution to ensuring Andrew wasn't home, Leader made a phone call to the house from a payphone a few blocks away.

The Friday night movie, a horror flick, was on television. Nadine was glued to it, curled on the couch. The ring of the phone jolted her. She jumped up and grabbed at the phone. "Hello?"

"Hi, would Andrew be in?"

"No, he isn't. I'm sorry", Nadine said, stretching the telephone cord around the corner to see the television and catch the dialogue.

Leader said, "Any idea when he will be in?"

"He's away. Who's calling?"

"Joe Decker. A friend of Andrew's."

Darn. She was missing a really good part. "Oh. Well he and Madeleine are away canoeing."

Leader was momentarily stunned. *He wasn't talking to Madeleine?* But the woman he had seen? "Oh. You are...?"

"I'm Madeleine's sister."

Leader urgently needed new instructions. "Oh. Okay. I'll get back to him later then. Sorry to bother you."

From the car, Leader radioed Nix on a direct frequency and left a message detailing everything he had just learned. Nix and Cavaco, who were at Nix's penthouse, got the message immediately.

After a few minutes' deliberation, Cavaco said, "We've got momentum. I don't want to lose time or control here. We take the boy. The sister stays put. We use her to inform Andrew."

Nix radioed the details to Leader.

One of the things Madeleine loved about the house was the treed backyard backing onto a large green belt. The moon was weak tonight, but it gave enough light to cause the trees to cast long shadows.

At 11:20, new shadows appeared, moving stealthily toward the back of the house. A ladder was run silently up to a second floor bedroom window. Steve cut the bug screen along the bottom and both sides of the window with a thick box cutter. As he passed his leg through the full opening, his pant cuff hooked on something as he brought his leg down in the room. He brought the other leg in. He saw he had caught on some wire clothes hanger contraption. He unhooked it and slid it to the side.

He listened carefully and heard only the television downstairs – bloodcurdling screams from a woman, chilling sound effects.

He leaned over Chris who was breathing evenly and very deeply. He slipped a loose black hood over Chris' head. If he half woke, he wouldn't see he was in the arms of a stranger. He lifted Chris and walked gently to the window and passed the limp body smoothly through to Smithy who was standing at the top of the ladder, arms in wait. A silent descent. Then Steve passed back out through the window.

In moments the moving shadows disappeared into the green belt.

Three minutes later, the phone rang again in the house.

CHAPTER FIFTY

Andrew was up at 5:30 Saturday morning. He was gone before 6:00, Madeleine sleeping soundly.

His aerodrome was just over an hour from the Inn. He topped-up the Pitt's fuel tank and filled the supplementary tank.

Although the night had been cloudy, with periods of rain particularly to the west, the morning sky was clearing nicely. He was in the air at 7:30.

Just after 9:00, he flew over Rona's Corners, nothing more than an intersection of two roads, each of the four corners boasting commerce – a general store, a gas station, a lumber store, a bakery.

He flew on past and in half a mile saw the disused stretch of the old highway, bypassed by the new highway and running at an angle to it. At least three hundred yards of it ran straight and level. He circled it once to satisfy himself that a safe landing could be made. As had been described, there was some cracking in the asphalt, but no gaps or lifting, and no tall trees on the approach. Rather than land yet, though, he decided to take an extra five minutes in the air to fly to the Hunt Club acreage and back to determine his best route on foot.

He quickly saw the property coming up and estimated that the walking distance, with a detour to miss a fenced sand pit, would be about two miles. That would put him at the rear of the 800 acres on the dirt road. From there he could access the long trail he had seen which meandered its way deep through the property to the cabin.

He began a slow bank to turn around, allowing himself to go out just wide enough in the turn to let him see the cabin appear in the distance.

But he glimpsed something more. Was it a *car*?

He quickly altered his course and flew toward the cabin, maintaining altitude at 1500 feet. Soon he could see clearly that it was a car. It wasn't pheasant season. It wasn't any bird hunting time. But it was Saturday. Perhaps it was only some innocent weekend goings-on.

But perhaps not. He could not risk exposing himself. He could not go marching up to the cabin now. He had no weapon with him, and that had been an oversight. He had not even considered the possibility of people being there today. But still, it might have been too risky regardless.

He dropped to 1,000 feet. As he got closer, he could see it was a later model Ford LTD, brown. It was parked by the barn on a small rise. It would help immensely to know whose car that was.

The license plate. That's what he needed. A good, clear picture. He could phone it into Lawrence and he could run it and track the plate owner.

———————

They are two big men.
I told them I want to go home
They told me to stop crying.
They are bad guys.
I told them I want my Mom.
They told me to stop crying.
It is a little room with boards on the floor.
They told me to lay on the towel.
I was afraid to go to the bathroom.
They told me to stop crying.
One took me to the outhouse.
He was mad.
He uses bad language.
He wanted the other one to do it.
He doesn't like me.
He said I was walking too slow.
It was because I was crying.
He pushed me to go faster.
It just looked like a puddle.
But it wasn't.
I fell into it.
The water covered my hair.

My pajama top got soaked.
He said I just slipped.
To the other man.
They told me to stop crying.
I have just a towel.
I get cold.
They don't like me.
I don't want to die.

———————————

The two men playing cards at a table in the cabin looked at each other when they heard the plane. One moved quickly towards the door.

The second one said, "Stay inside."

So the first one only looked out the window. He said, "He's not flying regular. He's twisting around kind of. Some stunt guy. Now he's fucking upside down."

The second one got up to have a look. They were together at the same window, necks craning. The engine was loud as the plane passed.

The second one said, "Yeah. Sure as hell isn't the law anyway. They don't do that shit. That's a barnstormer type plane. Will you look at that? Loop the loop."

The first one said, "Ya, you'd have to be loopy to do that stuff. Could get yourself killed."

The second one said, "Ya, you couldn't pay me enough to get up in one of those. I'm not living to die young."

The first one said, "Look. He's coming back. Swooping down real low now. Gonna barnstorm the barn. That's what he's doing here. Woooooeeeeee."

The bawling of the engine swept in like a wave, then swept away, the engine note whining as the plane snap-rolled in its ascent and flew off.

And now, because the plane was gone and it was silent again, they could hear the whimpering in the back room. The second one said, "Go tell that fucking kid to shut up. I'm not going to sit here for another two days and listen to that shit."

———————————

Andrew flew directly back to Chambersburg, refueled, and then flew back to his own aerodrome.

He had done a virtual air show near that cabin, partly to deflect suspicion, partly to orient the Pitt for a low photographing angle, and partly to draw faces out of the cabin. But there were no takers, no one coming out to give a friendly wave, and that was unusual, because everyone wants to see a crazy flyer. So either no one was in there at the time, or they had reason to stay hidden. If someone had actually come out and watched him innocently and waved, Andrew would have been much less happy than he was.

He drove to the commercial photo shop. He gave them the rolls of film he took both today and yesterday. But he was naturally most keen to see if the license plate showed clearly.

In an hour he had the photos. He flipped through them until he came to the series he had taken with the slow swooping pass. The rear of the LTD had been tilted up slightly as it was parked on a short rise. Andrew had had a clear, low shot at it as he passed.

But the plate numbers were too small. The plate was clearly Pennsylvania, but the numbers were indiscernible. He had the shop do an enlargement of the best three pictures.

The results were better. '3V90' were the first four characters. That was four out of six. There would be a limited number of possible letter\ number combinations for the last two, given the first four. And the possibilities would be narrowed even further because he had a picture of the car. Its make, model, year, and color would allow Lawrence to eliminate other cars and make a match.

He phoned Lawrence at home. There was no answer. Lawrence had said he might go to the cottage this weekend. Andrew left all of the details on Lawrence's answering machine anyway and said he would call back later in the afternoon from the canoe launch site.

He was greatly heartened. The license plate, this one further piece of evidence, just might prise open the lid.

CHAPTER FIFTY-ONE

At 4:00 in the afternoon, Andrew and Madeleine pulled into the launch parking lot, the canoe strapped to the top of their car. The lot was graveled and big enough for thirty cars. The single dock was fifty yards from the parking lot down a long, gentle slope.

The day was sparkling and they were in excited, sunny moods. Andrew had told her he had made progress and was happy with it. He just wanted to make a quick call to Lawrence, but then he could wait for a few days to follow things up. He told her he was relishing the quiet beauty of these lakes with her. Just them. Some campfires, some starry nights.

About a dozen cars were parked, but there were no people around other than one couple who were getting close to launch, the husband and their canoe already down at the dock. The wife was getting the final few things from their car.

Madeleine said, "Okay, Andrew, why don't you make your call while I unstrap the canoe and get the packs out. And I want to re-pack some of my stuff. I'll just need a few minutes. You might as well call Nadine, too. When you get her, just give me a shout."

The phone booth was on the opposite side of the parking lot and a short way into a picnic area. Andrew called Lawrence. Still no answer. He was very probably at the cottage, and that was a good sign in its own way. The license tracing could wait until he was back home and got Andrew's message.

He looked over and saw Madeleine in busy conversation with the other wife, leaning together over a map spread out on the other couple's car trunk. Madeleine seemed to be giving some helpful directions, maybe where portages were.

Nadine was not expecting their call today and Andrew wondered if she would be in. He dialed and waited. He heard Madeleine and the other wife laughing. She was in such good spirits. He was so thankful things were working out.

The phone rang several times before it was picked up. He expected the quick, cheery, energetic 'Hello' from Nadine. He heard her voice, certainly *her* voice, but barely. "Hello." Nervous, sniffling, afraid, drained.

"Nadine. It's Andrew. Are you alright?"

A long pause. Andrew realized she was choked up. Sobbing. "Nadine. It's Andrew. What's going on?" Andrew's only thought was that Chris had been hurt. Nadine was sobbing, swallowing, couldn't seem to speak. "Nadine....please."

"Andrew...I... Chris...someone...kidnapped Chris."

The words were incomprehensible abstractions. They repeated in Andrew's head, falling one at a time like blocks of stone. 'SOMEONE KIDNAPPED CHRIS'.

Then Andrew jolted, his brain racing, the meaning penetrating. "When?"

"Last night. Late. I got a phone call." Her crying lessened as she fought to gain control of herself to help Andrew understand. "I didn't see them. They used a ladder... to get into his bedroom."

"Did they say who they are?"

"No."

His mind saw Cavaco. But how? How could Cavaco know? Andrew had the slimmest hope it was not Cavaco. Someone just random. For money. It was a rich looking neighborhood.

"Did you see anybody?"

"No. Just the telephone. Not to speak to police, or won't ever see Chris again. They said you, Andrew...you must come forward."

The terrifying explanation, the one he feared the most, the one he hoped just couldn't be. It was Cavaco. Where had he made a mistake? Chris, innocent Chris. His heart ached.

They wanted him in exchange for Chris. Of course he would do that. Chris... my son.

Andrew said, "Did you speak to anyone about this?"

"No. They're going to call again. I'm to tell them if we've talked. And where you are."

Andrew knew that Nadine wasn't expecting his and Madeleine's call until tomorrow.

"Nadine, what exactly did you tell them?"

"That you and Madeleine were wilderness camping for a few days, out of contact. That you would be calling here tomorrow afternoon to check in with me. They want to know where you are."

"Nadine, we haven't talked. *We haven't talked, alright?* I need some time. What did you tell them? Did you tell them where we are?"

"No, I couldn't actually remember. I couldn't find Madeleine's note. They told me I better remember. I finally found the note. What do I do?"

"So you haven't yet told them where we are?"

"No."

Andrew's mind raced. He saw one chance in this.

"You tell them where we are. And that we parked at the launch lot. Tell them! So they know you're cooperating."

"Andrew…they …I had to tell them what your car is. Olds 88, blue."

"That's ok, Nadine. That's ok. They will come here and check it for themselves. They'll know you're cooperating. *Just don't tell them we talked.*"

Nadine was crying again. "Andrew…" Her voice was so weak. "I'm so sorry…Andrew. I keep thinking maybe I could have…"

"Nadine, there's *nothing* you could have done. *Nothing.* Please calm. We need your help now."

"I don't know that I can hang on."

"You've got to hang on! For Chris, Nadine. Be strong for Chris."

"I'm trying."

"I will call you back sometime. *But we didn't talk just now!*"

"Okay. I understand."

He hung up the phone. He could feel his body convulsing with pain and fear and hate, every muscle taut, his mind wild. He fought to check his base instincts, to go to that place in his mind where he could seal himself from this emotional onslaught, where he was not a cornered animal of simple, brute, enraged fear.

His back had been turned to the parking lot. He glanced and saw Madeleine still talking. He picked up the phone again and put it to his ear to appear he was still talking while he considered what to do. He opened his chest to breathe deeply, slowly, sucking in the air, holding it in, then releasing it slowly, the sniper's exercise. His hands were balled into tight fists, and he forced himself to uncurl them.

His mind raced. How had Cavaco found out? The break-in at Nix's office?

Chris was all that mattered now. Andrew's heart felt like it would burst. *They had one day before Cavaco expected Andrew to learn of the abduction.*

Lawrence was probably at the cottage because he hadn't answered Andrew's call earlier or just now. He had no phone at the cottage. Andrew had to get to Lawrence there.

But… was Lawrence also found out? What did Cavaco know?

Andrew put that out of his mind. Until he knew otherwise, he had to assume that Lawrence was still in the clear and could help.

Cavaco would soon send men here to check that Andrew's car was still here, to know that Andrew hadn't talked with Nadine. And they would then wait for Andrew's expected return here tomorrow, Sunday.

But if he did it right, he would have one day. One day to find Chris.

He glanced down towards the dock. The husband had fully loaded the canoe and was sitting in it, ready to shove off, just waiting for the wife.

He needed to get to Lawrence right away. The fastest course would be to get to his plane and fly to the cottage. Lawrence could pick up some trusted agents directly from their homes and fabricate a story. That way they avoided any leak. And they would devise some strategy so things were already in place before Andrew supposedly learned of the abduction.

He was suddenly aware of gravel crunching. He turned. Madeleine was coming, only ten yards away. "Yes, okay," he said casually into the dead phone and hung up.

"Hey, what are doing?" She looked perplexed and a little put out. "You were talking to Nadine. I heard you say her name. Why'd you hang up?"

"She had to get something on the stove. Chris is at his friend's. Wasn't expecting the call from us today."

"Ya, but she could move the pot or whatever off the stove and talk to me. Gee, Andrew." Her tone suggested he was a dunce. "I want to call her back."

"She said give her fifteen minutes."

"Oh, okay. Sorry. Okay, so we can get the gear loaded into the canoe first and then I'll call."

"Ya."

She studied Andrew. She looked disappointed. "You seem a little tense. We have a deal, remember?"

She took his hand and brought her face close to his. She smiled playfully. "Hey, handsome, shake it lose, will ya? We both deserve to have a *nice* break."

He took her hand and they walked to the car. She said "The canoe's all unstrapped. You can take it off."

Andrew made a quick survey of all the other cars in the parking area. He saw the woman looking toward her husband hoping to get his attention. She walked halfway to the launch and called to him. "Greg." She dangled a set of car keys in her hand, then pointed to the car. He signaled her to come to him.

City people don't appreciate how well their voices travel in wilderness areas. Especially when they've just listened to the car radio for three hours turned up loud against the highway din. The husband reached into a vest pocket. He lowered his voice to what he thought was now private conversation. "Lock up with this set. Leave your set in the car, in the Kleenex box in the back seat."

Madeleine was digging out packs and other bags from the trunk and setting them on the gravel. Andrew spent two minutes wasting time in the front seat. Then he got out and said to Madeleine, "Did you tell that woman we're going north?"

"Ya."

"Okay." Andrew hoisted the canoe onto his shoulders and carried it down to the launch. The other couple was now shoved off, paddling fifty feet from shore. Andrew returned their wave. The woman called back, "Have a nice time."

The couple was heading south to the first portage, about half a mile away across the lake. So that worked with his plan. His immediate concern was someone else pulling into the parking area in the next five minutes.

Madeleine turned and saw Andrew just standing there at the dock. She didn't say anything, figuring he was enjoying the views, the quiet, finally beginning to relax. She watched a few moments, happy, and went back to checking the pack pockets.

Andrew waited a full three minutes until it was safe, until the other couple wouldn't see anything. Then he carried the canoe into the woods forty steps and placed it well out of sight.

Madeleine saw him coming out of the woods. She called out, flabbergasted, raising her arms high. "What did you do with the canoe?"

He didn't answer, just strode quickly up from the dock. He had already spotted the large rock he needed. He walked to it and grabbed it up in both hands. He walked to the other couple's car, two cars over from where Madeleine stood. Madeleine's eyes followed. The look on his face made her extremely nervous. Something was seriously wrong here.

"Andrew?" She swallowed hard and stared. He stood by the driver's door a moment, testing the heft of the rock in his right hand. Then he leaned back and heaved it against the window. The window gave, shattering through. Madeleine dropped the pack she was holding and put both hands to her mouth.

Andrew reached through the broken window and lifted the lock button. He opened the door and got in. He reached into the back seat. He grabbed the Kleenex box and retrieved the keys. He turned on the ignition, then got out, leaving the engine running.

He finally looked at Madeleine. His look was now diamond hard. She knew Andrew well. Nothing she could say was going to change whatever was going on. Not one iota. She was terrified. She couldn't speak.

"Madeleine," he said calmly. "We need to load our stuff into this car and get out of here. *Now.*"

"Andrew... please..." Her voice was a weak pleading. And she kept wondering, why this other car and not their own?

Andrew grabbed up three packs at once. "Get in the car."

CHAPTER FIFTY-TWO

They drove from the parking lot, out the dusty narrow gravel road, heavily treed on both sides. Madeleine stayed quiet, watching his face. Andrew just said, "I need to find a place hidden to pull over."

In a minute he passed a short lane that took a jog out of sight. He stopped, backed up, and drove in. He shut off the engine.

Madeleine was sitting sideways in the seat staring at him, her face warring with anxiety, fright, tinged with anger.

He said, "It's Chris."

Her eyes widened. She grabbed at him. *"What? Tell me!"*

"He's been kidnaped."

Her mouth opened but nothing came out. Her eyes darted back and forth across his face, unbelieving.

"The man who took my father. I got too close to him."

Madeline screamed, *"What have you done?"* Her body convulsed with rage. She hit at him. He let her swing, but blocked her. *"What have you done?"*

Andrew had to let her get it out. She would be unable to listen or understand yet.

"My baby! Where is he?" She screamed into Andrew's face. She tried to strike him again but he grasped her hands. She was bare rage and strength.

Andrew said, "They will *not* harm Chris, Madeleine. They will *not* harm Chris." But he didn't know that for sure with Cavaco.

Then she was overtaken, an emotional tidal wave crashing. She wailed loudly. "No! No! No!" She hit at the dashboard with her fist.

Her flailing weakened. All the outside power was now turning inward, wreaking havoc. She cried uncontrollably.

After a minute, it slowed. She said, "Where is he?"

"I don't know."

"What do they want?"

"They want me. Only me, in exchange."

She looked at him, her breathing erratic. But he knew she was registering things now. Survival instincts kicking in. Have to think clearly.

He continued, "There is a chance here. They don't know I know about Chris. Nadine told them we weren't calling in until tomorrow afternoon. They think we won't know anything for another day. It's a chance to organize something."

Madeleine stumbled the words, "We need the police."

"No, we can't. They said that if anyone goes to the police, we never see Chris again. They have insiders, informants. I know they do. They would find out. We can't go to anybody. Except Lawrence. He can pick some trusted agents, pick them up directly from their homes without telling them what it's all about. We have *one day*. We have to get to Lawrence quickly."

Andrew pulled back out onto the road and shortly they were on the highway. Madeline was working it through, her body squeezed tight into a rolled knot, her arms gripping her legs to her chest, swaying in pain. "What did Nadine say?" she moaned.

"She didn't see anyone. They took Chris from the bedroom. Sleeping."

Her eyes closed tightly, her face tortured. She sobbed, "Right from his bed."

"Chris will be okay, Madeleine. I'm going to make that happen for sure."

She stared straight ahead, then suddenly banged the dashboard hard with her fist. She cried out loud once, a piercing wail, like a knife.

He shouted, "*They're not going to hurt him, Madeleine. I know it.*" He said it as much to convince himself, and to blast the world with his anger.

She didn't look at him. After a few moments she said, her voice a whisper, "They're going to hurt you."

He didn't answer. At least she understood.

He kept grilling himself, twisting the knife in his bowels. Where had he made the mistake? Was it Nix's office? Lawrence had warned him of that danger, that exceptional danger, and now ...Chris.

There had been no alarm. Was there a silent alarm? Had he been followed? Is that how they found his home? And got Chris?

Regardless, he had blundered. Fatally. And now he was tied to a stake and couldn't move. And Chris…Chris and Madeleine… would pay.

His insides were dissolving into liquid.

Madeleine said, "You have to tell me everything you know."

"If you know too much… you would have to die, too."

They drove on. Andrew was conscious of the time, conscious of the sun's position for flying.

He pushed words through his head: They came in through the window; Chris sleeping in his bed; a strange man standing over him; 'right from his bed.' Words. But now they came as clear images: cold eyes, callous mouth, strong body, bending and picking Chris up; Chris's thick chestnut hair; his deep breathing angel face; his limp, light limbs; his soft pajamas.

Suddenly Andrew said, "Madeleine! What pajamas was Chris wearing?" There was urgent hope in his voice.

She looked at him quickly. "The yellow ones," she blurted.

"Are you sure?"

"Yes." She reached to touch his arm. Her words ran. "I told him he could wear them while Nadine was there. What is it?"

Andrew hit the brakes and swerved to a sliding stop on the shoulder. He reached into the back seat and grabbed up the knapsack he carried when flying. His hand was shaking. He took out the pictures he had taken today of the Ford LTD, and of the cabin area.

He said, "What kind of yellow?"

Her voice quavered, "Primary…yellow."

Earlier, when he had been looking at the enlarged photos of the area of the Ford LTD to try to read the licence plate, he had noticed something yellow hanging nearby. He remembered thinking it was a rag.

He flipped through the pictures he had taken today. He found one, then two, then three, that captured that tight area. He studied them a moment. What had appeared like just a rag hanging from a cedar fence post beside the car now seemed like possibly something more.

He gave them to Madeleine. Her frantic eyes devoured them, her fingers gripping the edges.

He grabbed in the knapsack for the pictures he had taken yesterday on his first flight over the buildings. He flicked through twenty-five trying to find that same spot along the fence by the barn.

He found two. Nothing seemed to be on the post!

"It's the right color," she said, determined. "I think I see a sleeve. Not just a square cloth. It's a child's size, compared to the diameter of the post."

"It wasn't there yesterday. I took that picture this morning. It had to be put there last night or early this morning."

Madeleine's voice broke. "To dry...." Her face was strained.

"Yes, maybe."

She stared at one of the pictures. She began to cry and her lip trembled.

Andrew said reluctantly, "But...can't be sure ..."

He saw Madeleine's fingers rubbing the picture, tears dripping. He wasn't sure she heard him. She whispered to herself, "yellow...is...sunshine."

------·•·------

From the aerodrome, Andrew tried calling Lawrence at home. No answer. "He must be at the cottage", he told Madeleine. "There's no phone there. We have to fly."

They touched down just after 6:00 on the grass airstrip. They jogged the mile to the cottage. There was no sign of Lawrence. His car wasn't there.

Andrew smashed a side window and climbed in. Madeleine stayed out. Andrew knew that Lawrence sometimes went to a local bar or for groceries or other supplies in the village. They had no way of going to find him there without a vehicle, if he were there at all. He might be on his way back home, or on his way to the cottage from home. If he were coming back here, he would see a note.

Andrew found a pen and wrote on an envelope and put it in plain sight overhanging on the corner of the kitchen table. 'Wes, Saturday, 6:30 PM. *Extremely* urgent. Please go right home and check messages. I will telephone you again later. Andrew.'

As they hurried from the cottage back to the Pitt, Andrew told Madeleine that he needed to fly to Chambersburg while it was still light. "I want to fly over the Hunt Club property before dark and see if that Ford's still at the cabin. If it is, I can land about two miles from the back of that property on a rough strip. There's a phone at Rona's Corners about a mile from the strip. I'm going to coordinate with Lawrence from there. And I can keep an eye on the cabin. When Lawrence and the agents get there, we'll do a takedown before daybreak. The abductors aren't expecting anyone."

"And what if Chris isn't there? Or was never there? What if the guesswork has been wrong?"

"It's a chance we have to take. If Chris is there, we have the advantage of surprise. If he's not, we've haven't risked talking to police and it getting leaked. And we would still have another twelve hours before Cavaco expects me to know anything."

When they got to the Pitt, Andrew stopped and looked at Madeleine. He took her hand. "The truth is, Madeleine, I'm never going to the police. If Lawrence and I and those few agents don't find Chris before the abductor knows I know, then I'm giving myself up to him as if I haven't talked to anybody. I'm not going to risk Chris. The best I can do is bargain it so you and Chris will be safe."

Madeleine looked like death.

He said, "Madeleine, it's all I can do right now. But it's a chance."

They flew back to his aerodrome. He had explained that he had to refuel there and get all of his SWAT gear from his storage compartment. He would then fly on alone to make observations of the cabin both from the air and the ground. And he would coordinate with Lawrence by telephone from Rona's corners.

At his aerodrome, as he refueled, he watched Madeleine walk back and forth across the tarmac, again and again, her head down.

In his storage compartment he checked and cased his sniper rifle and his M-16 assault rifle. He fully loaded them. He took two boxes of rounds. He holstered the semi-automatic Smith and Wessons 459 pistol and three clips. He took night goggles.

He had no working silencer. The threads on the quick detach suppressor had seized and he had had to discard it earlier. A new one was on order. He wished he had something quiet.

His eyes went to the corner of the compartment. There was nothing quieter - his Dad's oak cross bow, the one his dad had hand carved. Beside it was the leather quiver and six handmade bolts. All his father's workmanship.

Seeing it there seemed to bolster him. He picked it up and shouldered it.

When he got back to the Pitt, Madeleine was standing beside it. She said, "I'm coming with you."

"No, Madeleine. It's better we're not together. For Chris....we ...can't both die."

"I can't go home! I can't go anywhere! I *have* to be with you! I have to know what's going on!"

Andrew understood her feelings. But it was foolhardy. "Madeleine, please don't...."

"If you think he may be there, I'm going. *I have to know what's happening!* I'm not staying back! Andrew, nobody will know I'm there. If things look like they might go bad, I can disappear."

Andrew barked, "Yes, if you're lucky enough to have a choice! What if you don't?"

"Listen, if he's not there, then no harm. If he is, *I may be of some help! That's what counts now! Don't argue with me!*"

Andrew looked at her. A mother's love, her fierce resolve, her strength. He loved her so much.

He was supremely guilty for all that was happening. He had succeeded in suppressing his immense guilt so he could just think straight, put one foot in front of the other. But looking into her face now, tears came to him. His innocent wife, his innocent son, paying for his *stupid failure*.

"Madeleine," he grabbed her and held her close. His voice shook with emotion. "I'm so sorry...so sorry I brought this on Chris and you. I will *gladly* give my life for you. *Gladly*. I just hope I have that chance."

Madeleine held him tightly, her cheek against his chest, crying with him. "I know.... I know."

CHAPTER FIFTY-THREE

From Friday afternoon on, Cavaco had known where Lawrence was every minute.

He had been home Friday afternoon, Friday evening, and Friday night. He went nowhere, had no visitors. Saturday, late morning, he made a brief trip to the liquor store. Surveillance described him as disheveled, distracted, unslept. And all the lights in the house had been off now all Saturday evening.

Cavaco had decided to first get everything he could from Lawrence tonight so he would be better informed when he interrogated Andrew after he was seized at the canoe launch parking lot.

Nix had instructed surveillance to cease the watch on Lawrence's house at 10:00 p.m. Now, at 11:00 p.m., Nix worked quietly at the lock on Lawrence's back door. A tall cedar hedge offered him privacy from neighbors as he did.

Shortly, upstairs in a dark bedroom, Lawrence woke to the feeling of being molested. Hands were pulling at his legs; hands were fingering his head. Eyes in a black hood.

Was it real, or a dream, or heroin made phantasmagoria? He knew he was wired last night and sometime today, had had lots of wine, his senses disoriented.

A deep voice, "Get up Lawrence."

When he finally got his eyes to work, he saw clearly a man in a black hood, two holes for the eyes. Another man pointed a long-barreled, silenced pistol.

Cavaco. Lawrence's mind grasped it dully. How had Cavaco discovered? Did he know anything about Andrew?

They dragged him out of bed and into the bathroom. The tall, solid man with the pistol shoved his head under the bathtub tap and ran cold water. Nix?

They forced him downstairs into the livingroom and shoved him into a captain's chair. Nix bound his feet, then lashed his hands behind him into the chair's back. Then Nix strapped his neck tightly to the chair with a leather belt.

Cavaco sat in a chair opposite. He slowly removed the black hood. Lawrence didn't recognize him precisely, although he presented a familiarity to the latest, age-progressed portrait.

Cavaco said, "Do you know who I am?"

"No."

Looking disappointed, Cavaco said, "No? Actually, I think you do. I don't want this meeting to be difficult between us." Cavaco got up and put one hand into Lawrence's hair and yanked. Lawrence's body and the chair lurched forward.

Cavaco continued, "No one will ever know what happened here. Your body will never be found. No body, no evidence of crime. Right, officer? A little tactic you're personally familiar with, that poor girl. Does that help your memory?"

Lawrence looked squarely at him. "I don't know what you're talking about."

Cavaco studied Lawrence a moment. "Some answers, please. You know who I am. How did you know I was alive?"

Lawrence said, "Who are you? What are you doing here?"

"Oh, I see how it's going to be. Okay. Let's start with FBI agent Andrew Locke. He has to go too, of course. A clever snoop."

An almost imperceptible flick in Lawrence's eyes.

Cavaco said, "I saw that. You're a little slower than you think...in your current state. So, Andrew has to go. The real question is who else has to go? That's what it's come down to. And you're going to be the one who decides."

Cavaco took a picture from his pocket and showed it to Lawrence. "Recognize little Chris?" Cavaco tapped the picture. "He's crying. See the burly man with the gun? Chris doesn't like his new babysitter."

Lawrence looked down, his face dark with understanding.

Cavaco said, "So now you see. But not *everybody* has to die. Only you and Andrew. That's if you give me complete answers. But if you don't, little Chris and his attractive mother, Madeleine, have to go. And, of course, you remember I know about your sister and mother and father in their little house in Coatesville."

Cavaco sat down opposite Lawrence. "So…how did you know I was alive?"

Lawrence was quiet. "Paul Locke told me that Pino Macky whispered that you were alive."

Cavaco, momentarily unbelieving, glanced to Nix. Then a smile. He looked back to Lawrence. His voice showed his amazement, "You knew for the last twenty years?"

Lawrence nodded.

"But were afraid for yourself if you spoke up? Or *did* you speak up?"

Lawrence shook his head, "No."

Cavaco said, "Except …to Andrew?"

Lawrence was crushed, his voice slow in coming. "Except to Andrew. His wife doesn't know. I told him everything I had done, everything I knew. But I didn't know who you were. And even now, I don't know your assumed name, or anything more about you."

"Andrew is the only one who knows anything at all?"

"Yes."

"Nobody else at the office? No other confidante?"

"No."

"So I only have to remove you and Andrew and I'm safe again. Is that correct? No lurking exceptions?"

Lawrence was very quiet. "I involved no one else."

————◦—◦————

Two hours earlier, at 9:30, Andrew and Madeleine had reached Rona's Corners in a quickly darkening sky with barely enough light to make a safe landing on the dim stretch of disused highway that Andrew had this morning flown over. They were too late to fly on to reconnointre the Hunt Camp to see if the Ford LTD was still there.

They had made a call to Lawrence's home from the pay phone in front of the little lumber store in Rona's Corners.

There was still no answer at Lawrence's home.

Andrew had considered there might be something wrong on Lawrence's end, that Cavaco might have learned that Lawrence was connected to Andrew. He had to factor in that possibility now.

So he had been careful. In his telephone message, he said only that he would call again at 11:30 and gave the number from where he was calling. He gave no other details, nothing about the abduction, and not where he was. He knew that with the phone number, Lawrence could quickly learn from AT&T exactly where Andrew was calling from.

After making that call, Andrew and Madeleine had walked to the cabin and observed, at 10:30, the Ford LTD was still there. There was no activity, no lights on in the cabin. But Andrew didn't want to risk making any move on his own. That would be reckless at that point, not knowing who was in there.

It was now 11:20 p.m. and Andrew and Madeleine were walking quickly, almost back to the phone booth in the dark, deserted, single intersection of Rona's Corners. They were desparate to find Lawrence in.

Andrew had decided that if Lawrence didn't answer, hopefully only because he was just out late, Andrew would now risk laying out the full situation. Time was far more pressing. If Cavaco *had* actually gotten to Lawrence and Lawrence was taken or dead, there would be no harm in leaving the full message on the machine. On balance, he decided he should take the risk and leave a detailed message in the hope that Lawrence hadn't been found out and *would* get it, and could act on it. He could only hope.

In Lawrence's livingroom, Cavaco looked to Nix. Nix nodded. They were both satisfied that Lawrence was telling the truth, that only he and Andrew knew anything, so only he and Andrew would have to be extinguished.

Cavaco drew a long, hypodermic needle from a pocket. He said to Lawrence, "You know me. I don't like to contaminate the scene. No shooting you here. No shooting you anywhere, if you want to know. Guns are just for show. So, this will put you to sleep. Of course…you won't be waking up."

The phone rang. Cavaco and Nix looked to one another. As it continued to ring, Nix glanced at his watch. 11:30. He also now noticed a tiny, red light flashing on the answering machine. There had been some earlier message. They waited in silence.

After six rings, the call went to the answering machine. But the caller leaving the message could be heard openly. The sound of air came over the speaker, then an urgent voice. "Wes, it's Andrew. It's 11:30 p.m., like I said. I left you the number here earlier. Chris...Chris was abducted, last night from our house."

Nix glanced to Cavaco, startled. Cavaco's jaws clenched visibly.

Andrew continued. "Madeleine's sister was babysitting at our house. It's Cavaco. They don't know I know. They're not expecting me to call home until tomorrow late afternoon."

Cavaco's eyes flashed with anger.

"Wes, I may know where they have him. That 800-acre hunt camp I told you about near Chambersburg."

Nix and Cavaco made anxious eye contact.

Andrew kept speaking, "I saw some things in a flyover today. Madeleine is with me. They said if I went to the police, Chris is dead. I need you. Grab three or four agents right from their homes. Don't tell them anything. Get to Rona's Corners before daylight. Go to the phone booth in front of the lumber store. I've drawn a map on page 100 of the telephone directory. It will tell you where to meet us near the property. You've got to get here. Got to do the takedown before first light. I need you, Wes."

Lawrence's head fell. All was lost. He had brought Andrew, a brave, decent young man into this dangerous enterprise, and now Andrew would pay the price. And Madeleine, too, who knew too much. And little Chris...

The phone clicked off and the answering machine beeped once and stopped. Cavaco lifted his finger to Nix to indicate he was thinking. He quickly said, "I want him to think Lawrence got the message. I know the place he's calling from. Retrieve that earlier message and get that phone number."

Lawrence guessed what Cavaco was thinking. Even though his neck and hands were strapped in the chair and his legs were bound, he struggled mightily, falling over in the chair towards Nix, trying to kick at him as Nix worked feverishly at the answering machine.

Cavaco hit Lawrence hard on the head with the gun, knocking him out. Nix quickly got the machine working and they heard the quick, earlier message and quickly jotted the number.

Cavaco said, "Wait another full minute, then phone the number and let it ring just three times. Then hang up. Then take the phone off the hook."

———————

Andrew and Madeleine had walked almost two hundred yards from the phone booth down the dark, empty, four corners road. Madeleine was lightly crying, "What do we do if he doesn't show?"

"We don't know for sure if Chris is even there. Only that someone's there."

"But if Chris is there…"

Andrew didn't answer. He just kept thinking, feeling more anxious.

Two hundred yards behind them came a sudden tiny ringing in the darkness.

The phone! Andrew turned and raced. It rang only a few times and stopped. Andrew got there fifteen seconds after it stopped. He grabbed up the phone. There was just the dial tone, no one there.

He fumbled for four quarters in his pocket. Madeleine now reached the booth, breathing hard, her face expectant.

Andrew frantically inserted the coins. He dialed Lawrence's number.

Agonizing moments passed. Then… a busy signal. Madeleine, too, could hear it.

Andrew said quickly, breathless, "He was hoping we might still be here. Just missed the call. Must have been listening to the full message just now."

"But the line is busy."

"He's on the phone making calls. Thinks were gone. Doesn't want to waste any time. Finding what agents are available."

After a minute, pacing, Andrew called again. The line was still busy.

"He's connecting with people. It'll take awhile. He'll pick them up and then get on the road. It'll take probably five hours for him to get them all rounded up, all geared, and drive here."

She wanted to get back to be near Chris, if he was there. She said, "Best thing we can do now is watch the cabin."

After another two minutes, Andrew phoned again. It was still busy.

"At least he's there and has our message," he said. "Getting help."

Madeleine could see his confidence again.

They dragged Lawrence's drugged, unconscious body out through the back door.

Cavaco said, "This is going to wrap up more nicely than I thought. Locke and the wife, and the boy, too. All together. And no one the wiser. We'll deal with Madeleine's sister tomorrow."

Nix walked half way around the block and retrieved their car. He drove it backwards into Lawrence's driveway and parked at the dark end by the hedge. They lifted Lawrence into the trunk and quietly closed the lid.

"He'll be dead soon," Cavaco said.

They got in and slowly drove away. Quiet neighborhood, nobody about, nobody watching. It was a stolen car anyway, taken that morning from owners who were away at a cottage, this their second car sitting ripe in their driveway. There would not be any stolen report for days.

Cavaco said, "Locke was so close. I can't figure how he learned so much. It'll be a pleasure to ask him."

Nix said, "We have the two guards at the cabin. I'll contact Leader to get some of the enforcement cell members together to get going to the cabin right away. They should get there before daylight. We won't get there until then either."

Cavaco said, "That's okay. Locke's going to sit tight, expecting Lawrence to bring the cavalry. He won't make any move on his own before daylight. That'll give us lots of time."

CHAPTER FIFTY-FOUR

There was a three-quarter moon and stars. And it was warm.

Andrew and Madeleine had again walked the dark country road the two miles from Rona's Corners to the neglected dirt road that ran at the back of the Hunt Club's 800 acres. From that road they had followed a narrow pathway another half mile across the rear section of the property.

Just after 1:00 a.m. they arrived and took up a position with a good view a hundred yards to the rear of the cabin and barn.

The Ford LTD was still there. But no light came from inside the cabin and there was no sound. No sign of life inside or out.

Was Chris there? Was anyone there?

When they had come the first time, Andrew had manoevered to get a good look at the cedar post to see if that yellow something, possibly Chris' pajama top, still hung there. It did not, which Andrew took to be a good sign.

But really nothing was certain. All they could do now was wait for Lawrence and the others.

The night was long, one heart beat at a time.

At one point, Andrew had become impatient and edgy. He considered rushing the inside of the cabin himself, with Madeleine staying outside with the 9mm handgun. But he knew, ultimately, that would be foolhardy. He had no idea who was in there, how many were in there, what the configuration of the rooms was, whether he risked Chris too much. A rescue works when sufficient numbers, well armed, well trained, instantly overwhelm resistance. Andrew alone was not overwhelming. And help was coming anyway.

He had to remain patient, and clear headed.

Madeleine was emotionally and physically exhausted. She lay beside him. He had heard her quietly crying. He had stroked her hair. She had drifted into a fitful sleep about 2:30, curled, her knees tucked up.

Now, at 4:45, he began to hear a faint sound, a car far off, somewhere out on the front road. The sound grew louder, getting closer. He put on the night finder goggles. He brought the M16 into his hands.

Shortly he saw dimmed headlights slowly approaching on the long lane in from the front road. Madeleine awoke, startled that she had drifted. She put on goggles. They watched.

The car stopped near the cabin and the engine was turned off. Three men got out, one with a flashlight on, each with a rifle.

One knocked at the door and whispered loudly, "It's me, Leader." The other two stood looking out around the property, eyes searching into the darkness, cautious, as if they thought something might be out there.

After a few moments, the door opened an inch, then quickly opened wider. The three men went inside and the door closed.

Andrew expected to see light come on inside, a lantern maybe. But the windows stayed black, except for some dim shafts from the flashlight, the beam bouncing off a wall.

The name, 'Leader' was remarkably strange. And those weren't shotguns for bird hunting, but rifles.

Andrew was now certain that he was right. Chris was here. *Or had been here.*

After three minutes, the front door opened and two men stepped out. One was the same as before, 'Leader'; one was not. They looked cautiously about again and made their way to the car with the flashlight. Andrew focused on the guns they carried. They were clearly both automatic rifles.

They entered the car and did a slow U-turn in the yard and rolled away out the lane, the lights kept dimmed the whole time.

Still no light came on in the cabin. Only a flashlight showed every so often. Andrew knew they were being extremely cautious. It made it impossible for anyone on the outside to get any view inside, to get any sense of numbers, positions. And to rush a building with not a single light on inside would be suicide. They knew what they were doing.

Andrew considered that this was not just a changing of the guard, although an additional man was there now. It must also have been information passing. Andrew had noted earlier there were no telephone lines to the cabin. They had had to come in person.

Why at this hour? Something very time sensitive, obviously important to be out here at 4:50 a.m.

Things were much worse now. And he knew Madeleine knew it, too. But she only whispered, "It's almost 5:00. I'll go now and wait for Lawrence." She crawled away and then stood up behind some trees. She put on the goggles to make her way along the meandering half mile path which stopped just short of the narrow dirt road at the back. That was the location Andrew had designated on the map at the phone booth for Lawrence and the agents to meet them. Madeleine would wave them down.

It would take her fifteen minutes, picking her way carefully. She would guide Lawrence and the others back here.

She set off and shortly Andrew could hear nothing of her.

He kept wondering about the arrival of that car, and the cautious looks cast out into the darkness around the property. Were they expecting someone? Could they possibly know he was here? But how?

He kept pondering. He thought it would be impossible for them to know. But anything was possible, and you had to think that way to survive.

That car...at this strange hour.

Something came back to him, now pressing, prodding, opening a door in his mind. He had felt such disappointment that he didn't actually get to speak to Lawrence when Lawrence had called back at the phone booth last night. But at the same time, he was so overwhelmed with relief that Lawrence had called at all. But... why had Lawrence let the phone ring only a few times? That's not a lot of rings knowing Andrew wasn't likely standing right beside it, but might be still within hearing range. Wouldn't Lawrence want to give it a full minute, not just a few rings, given the importance of that contact? Lawrence would feel the urgency, of course, would be impatient to get making calls to agents at home, not want to waste time in useless waiting, believing Andrew wasn't near the phone anymore. But still... just a few rings...

Andrew's mind accelerated. What if it weren't Lawrence who had phoned back last night to the phone booth? If Cavaco had gotten to Lawrence, it was certainly possible Cavaco could have Andrew's full message. If Cavaco somehow did know, what would flow from that? He would want to inform and reinforce his people in the cabin. Cavaco would expect Andrew to wait for Lawrence because of the phone call back to the phone booth.

Had he been tricked?

His mind went to the map he had drawn in the telephone directory. It showed where Lawrence was to meet them, at the road at the rear of the property where Madeleine was going now.

Cavaco would know.

The car...was it possible?

Madeleine was almost at the end of the path. She thought she heard something beyond the trees by the roadside. Yes, quiet voices! Lawrence and the agents were already there! She felt a wave of relief.

She hurried. Now she could make out the shape of a car parked to the side, its lights and engine off. Right where it should be!

The overhead light was on inside. She wasn't careful now, pushing her way through the overgrowth. "Hey, hey. Lawrence!" she called, still coming through some brush, not yet visible.

She burst out from the woods onto the roadside.

She was surprised and disappointed there were only two men. She had expected at least four or five. And neither looked anywhere near the age of fifty that Andrew said Lawrence was. One said, "Madeleine?"

It hit her like a slap. She recognized them! What? She had just seen them at the cabin!

They each had a rifle in hand.

She turned and ran. She got sixty feet back into the bush before Leader overtook her and pulled her to the ground. He dropped his rifle and grabbed her up with both his arms. He dragged her. She kicked. She punched. She cried out. He slapped her face hard, his own face angry. "Shut the fuck up or I'll kill you right now!"

But Madeleine was fierce. She fought like a lion. He punched her in the stomach and she grunted, but she fought on. She grabbed at his hair, she bit at his nose, she kicked to the groin. He punched her in the face, stunning her.

Leader had her almost to the car, the other man fifteen feet away, holding his rifle. But Madeleine again kicked and punched and cried out. Leader slapped her across the face. Still Madeleine battled, knees trying to slam his groin, her fists, elbows, swinging at his face.

'Thhhwick'. The cross bow bolt pierced the rifleman's chest to the feathers. His throat made strangled noises, his eyes wide. His hands clutched at the bolt. His gun clattered to the ground.

Leader punched viciously at Madeleine to shake himself from her clinging, pulling grasp. He dragged her. He got close, close to the dying man's rifle, reaching his hand with Madeleine still tearing him back.

Andrew made the tackle, knocking Leader away from the rifle. He pulled him away further from the gun's reach and drove three solid punches. Madeleine was quick to grab the rifle and get it away. She stepped several yards back and held it in her hands, her body shaking.

Andrew and Leader were exchanging punches.

Madeleine raised the gun and pointed it at Leader, her face livid.

Andrew yelled, "Don't pull the trigger! They'll hear it!"

The sound of a rifle shot would carry to the cabin.

Leader got in two solid hits and maneuvered himself to get closer to Madeleine to get at the gun, risking she would hesitate or couldn't shoot him at close range.

Andrew made a grab at him with one hand. With the other, he pulled his knife from its sheath and lunged and thrust it with a fierce grunt into Leader's side, eight inches to the hilt.

He had wanted to beat the man down, then get some answers, not kill him yet. But he had no choice.

Leader fell to the road, writhing, moaning. Andrew kneeled to him, breathing hard. His voice was firm, but not loud. "Is my son at the cabin? Tell me!"

Although it was clear to Andrew that Chris had likely been in the cabin, he might not be now. He could have been moved, and this was all an ambush.

Andrew had to know. He shouted, "Tell me!"

Leader's eyes were closing with the pain, his face grimacing. Andrew said, "You're dying. You're going to die here. Do one good thing before you do. For an innocent boy...Tell me!"

Leader was in extreme agony, moaning terribly. His eyes, wild, looked at Andrew then passed to Madeleine who was now leaning over, too, her face alive with grief. Leader tried to fight the pain, his hands clenching.

Madeleine took one of his hands in hers, opened it, held it in both of hers, squeezed it. His eyes looked at her face close to his. His body was now in throes. He strained, his eyes concentrated on hers, seeing her looking into his.

His head nodded once, and his mouth whispered, "yes."

His eyes passed to Andrew, then were drawn slowly back to Madeleine's, pain flickering. Then his body relaxed, but his eyes held hers.

After a moment, they were lifeless.

CHAPTER FIFTY-FIVE

It was 5:40 and the eastern sky was now gray with light. Crouched a hundred yards back from the cabin and barn, Andrew and Madeleine surveyed it urgently with the benefit of the growing light. They knew they had no time now.

He said, "They won't be expecting anyone to come from the rear here. That's our only hope. I don't know how many are in there."

But he still hadn't settled on a plan.

The light was now enough to clearly see trees, shrubs, the cabin, the barn, the outhouse.

They heard a door open. A man, Kell, carrying a rifle, walked out from the cabin and began down the grass lane towards the front road. Andrew knew from seeing it from the air that there was a small building at the front of the property beside the lane just before the road, a kind of gatehouse. Using the binoculars, he saw the man also carried what looked like a walkie-talkie.

Soon he was out of sight. Andrew had estimated from his flyover that the gatehouse was at least four hundred yards, almost a quarter of a mile.

He said, "I've got to get to the barn. They won't expect me there."

Andrew gave Madeleine the 9mm pistol. He showed her the safety. "Don't put your finger on the trigger until you are ready to fire." Madeleine nodded. "Don't give yourself away by shooting. Don't use it until you have to. Then use it as best you can."

Andrew looked at her for several moments. He squeezed her hand.

All was quiet. He crawled forward flat on his stomach, out from behind the scattering of trees and shrubs. He had slung the crossbow and quiver on his back. He gripped the M16 in his hand.

Not even the tall grass swayed as he wormed through it, hidden.

Madeleine remained in concealment, crouched in the wooded area.

She saw the grasses move just once in an open stretch at the rear of the barn. He had arrived and was out of the line of vision from anyone in the cabin. He stood and looked back to her position. He turned and began to edge west along the rear of the barn.

She heard a door creak and saw another man emerge from the side of the cabin, a rifle in his hand. He gave his limbs a morning stretch and looked around. He lit the morning cigarette.

Madeleine could hardly contain her fear. She knew Andrew could not see him. She looked anxiously towards Andrew hoping he would turn to look back at her so she could signal. Unaware, Andrew stepped around the corner of the barn and disappeared into an open doorway on its west side.

She heard the creak again. The cabin door pushed slowly open all the way.

Out stepped Chris.

Shocked, Madeleine started, then stifled her cry. But a small sound carried. She ducked to conceal herself. The man had heard it and looked, quickly raising his rifle, pointing it in Madeleine's direction, his eyes closely searching. He spit out the cigarette.

Chris had not seen or heard anything and walked to the outhouse, about twenty yards back from the cabin, diagonally in Madeleine's direction. Chris entered the outhouse and closed the door.

Madeleine was overwrought. She saw the man looking intensely in her direction. She pressed herself lower.

The man whistled, signaling. Another man quickly came out in answer. He saw the first man standing stock still, peering into the woods, rifle raised. The first man whispered, "We may have company."

The second man peered at the woods then took a step back and, without taking his eyes from the woods, reached through the open cabin window and drew his rifle out.

The first man whispered back as he moved a step forward, "Tell Kell to come back." He began to creep cautiously toward Madeleine's position.

The second man watched a moment, scanning the woods, then backed up and went just around the corner of the cabin to be out of any line of fire from the rear. He pulled the walkie-talkie from his belt. He pressed himself tight against the cabin wall to avoid being in any sight line. He was facing the barn. He pressed the button and whispered, "Kell. Kell."

A sudden bolt drove through his chest, the shaft burying inches into the cabin wall. He was pinned like an insect on a display board. The rifle and walkie-talkie dropped from his hands. His head slumped.

The first man heard only the clumsy clattering of the gun fall. He glanced back. From his vantage, however, he could not see the second man.

Kell's voice broke in loudly on the radio. "What is it?"

The first man heard Kell's voice but heard no reply. He dropped to one knee, anxious, gun swiveling.

Kell's voice again came on the walkie-talkie. "Answer me!"

As in answer, the weight of the second man's body finally snapped the arrow and his body fell full length forward.

The first man spun at the sound and saw the last of the second man's fall. Startled, the first man dropped flat to the ground for cover, uncertain where the enemy was. He heard Kell's voice over the walkie-talkie, "I'm coming in."

Through an open barn window, Andrew saw the first man crawling slowly back through the grass towards the outhouse. Chris was still in there. But it was a poor angle for the crossbow, and he didn't want to use his gun, which would inform Kell.

Andrew quickly climbed a stairway to a loft. He glanced out. He could see the man crawling back getting close to the outhouse. Andrew took aim with the crossbow.

A barn pigeon flapped violently out of the next window. The man glanced up and quickly rolled as he saw Andrew. The bolt missed, thudding the ground beside him. The man fired two rapid shots at the window, bullets ripping into wood near Andrew's head. Andrew jerked his head in and grabbed for his rifle.

Jumping up, the man continued to fire at the window as he scrambled to the outhouse. He yanked on the door. Chris had locked it. The man turned and fired again at the barn window, then jumped to the rear of the outhouse. He concealed himself behind it knowing that the shooter wouldn't try to fire through it with Chris in there.

The man yelled through the outhouse wall to Chris. "Chris, get out, quick. Come around behind here. Someone's trying to kill you."

The outhouse door opened only partway. Chris poked his head out, looking around, frightened. The man's hand and forearm snaked around the outhouse corner trying to grab at Chris. Chris, scared, stared at it flailing.

Whack! A bullet ripped through the man's hand. He shrieked and whipped his hand and arm behind the outhouse.

Andrew called "Chris! Chris!"

Chris saw him. He threw the door open and began to run towards the barn. Andrew trained his rifle on the side of the outhouse and fired twice more as Chris ran.

Andrew yelled, "Run to Mom," pointing in Madeleine's direction. Madeleine stood fully up and began to run forward, fully exposed. She and Chris were two hundred feet apart, running towards each other, Madeleine's arms outstretched.

The man was crawling away from the outhouse so he could see Madeleine's position while still having the outhouse shielding him from Andrew's view. He kept crawling, moving out, improving his position, until he saw her. He stopped and poked his head barely above the grass. Although his hand was crippled and bleeding, he steadied the gun on his forearm and drew a bead on the running Madeleine.

He pulled the trigger. The shot missed.

Madeleine kept running, her face determined, her eyes fixed on Chris.

In his urgency to improve his angle on the fast running Madeleine, the man shoved himself quickly forward another foot across the grass. His finger almost found the trigger again.

Whack! The man's head whipped sideways, then flopped forward to the ground, a crimson hole gaping.

Madeleine reached Chris and dragged him to the ground. She began to crawl him back to cover.

Kell, who had been running back from the guard house out front, had heard all the rifle fire and knew someone was in the barn.

Andrew bounded down the loft stairs and leaped out through a narrow door. Two bullets splintered the door as he did. He ditched onto the grass and rolled. He glanced and saw Kell running, eighty yards away.

Kell chanced two more rapid shots before he disappeared behind a thick tree beside the grass laneway. Andrew had been unable to get off a shot, but had seen Kell take cover. Andrew lay flat, spread-eagled, and prepared his aim. Drawing a bead on the very edge of the tree, he relaxed his breathing.

The width of the tree was two feet, giving Kell little room to either side. He would have to make a move. Training had taught Andrew to note how a shooter held his rifle. He had seen Kell shoot right handed. So all else being equal, the odds were he would either shoot from the right side of the tree, or run to the right. Andrew saw a spec of fabric descend. Kell was either readying to run, or squatting to make himself smaller before taking a quick shot. Andrew moved his aim twelve inches to Kell's right of the tree. His finger resting lightly on the trigger.

Several seconds passed. Sudden color. His finger pulled.

Kell took it in the shoulder and he tumbled at the edge of the lane. He grasped for his fallen gun.

Andrew stood and steadied his aim. Just as Kell swung the rifle to aim, Andrew fired again. A jerk in the jacket fabric at Kell's chest. Andrew fired again. Kell's head snapped backwards.

Andrew crouched now, and waited and watched. No movement from Kell for twenty seconds. Andrew got up and made his way cautiously forward.

Kell was stone dead.

CHAPTER FIFTY-SIX

Hidden in the front woods at a distance, Cavaco and Nix watched Andrew walk away from Kell, still carrying his rifle. They also saw Madeleine and Chris bent low at the edge of the woods at the rear. She and Chris were too distant from Nix and Cavaco for them to do anything yet.

Nix whispered, "He's very good with that thing. Let's wait for the opportunity."

They had arrived ten minutes earlier but had at first stayed outside the property. They knew they had arrived much later than the others. They didn't know if anything had transpired so had parked off the road and proceeded onto the property on foot with caution in case anything had. Also, they didn't know what Andrew's map in the payphone booth said about where he would meet Lawrence. Nix had directed Leader to pick it up on his way to the property to know where to ambush Andrew. Was Leader still there now?

As they had made their way through the thicker forest at the front, a hundred yards to one side of the lane, and moving roughly in the direction of the cabin, they had heard the eruption of gunfire. They had crept in the utmost concealment to gain a position where they could make observation, sorting out the players, see who was winning. And, unhappily, who was losing.

Nix carried an automatic rifle, Cavaco a long barreled, semi-automatic pistol. But neither had any particular skill, and from very recent observation knew far better than to attempt any long range gun fight with Andrew. They knew with a dreadful certainty that if they announced their presence with an attempted shot at this long distance, and missed, they would be in for a very bad morning.

They watched Andrew walk to Madeleine and Chris. They watched

Andrew hug Chris. They watched Madeleine hug Andrew. They watched them all hug each other. They watched them talk a few moments. Then Andrew walked to the cabin, Madeleine and Chris staying back.

But he still carried that rifle.

Nix whispered, "He doesn't want the kid seeing the bodies."

Andrew was in the cabin only a moment, then came out and examined the dead man with the bolt through his chest. He set his rifle down in the grass and turned the body over flat.

Chris was now jumping with unrestrained excitement at being freed and safe with his parents. He ran in a circle around Madeleine. He couldn't contain himself. He began to run towards Andrew. "Dad!"

Madeleine called out, "Chris!"

Andrew saw Chris coming. He got up to intercept Chris, walking towards the other dead man who lay in the grass by the outhouse.

Andrew hadn't picked up the rifle. It lay in the grass.

Nix and Cavaco tensed.

Andrew scooped Chris up in his arms and walked toward Madeleine.

Andrew was perhaps seventy yards from Madeleine.

Nix whispered, "We both run straight towards his rifle. But we don't shoot until we're close. They may not see us for a few seconds."

Cavaco said, "Let me shoot first. We don't want him dead yet."

When Andrew was fifty yards from his rifle and twenty yards from Madeleine, Nix and Cavaco broke cover in a dead run.

In a moment Madeleine saw them. "Andrew!" she screamed, pointing.

Andrew turned. He dropped Chris. He ran for the rifle.

It was a foot race, but Nix and Cavaco didn't have to get there first. Only get to maybe thirty yards from the rifle before Andrew got to the rifle, because at that distance, between Nix and Cavaco, they couldn't miss.

Andrew was twenty yards from the rifle when Cavaco fired, the bullet catching Andrew's thigh. He lost balance and tumbled. Nix was ahead of Cavaco and got to the rifle and grabbed it up. Andrew struggled on the ground, clutching at his leg.

Cavaco stopped ten feet from Andrew, fearing he may have some other weapon. He trained his gun on Andrew. "Don't move. Keep your hands out."

Cavaco glanced to where Madeleine and Chris had been. They had run into the woods and weren't visible, although snapping twigs told him they were running away.

Nix checked Andrew for more weapons. There were none. Nix grabbed up Andrew's rifle and carried it to the well thirty yards away, watching Andrew as he did. He reached out and dropped the rifle down the well. "That thing's caused enough havoc today," he said as he walked back.

Cavaco said, "This is good. I'll stay and watch him while you get the wife and kid. I know you want to be here when we have our chat with Andrew."

Nix looked at Andrew, "Yes. Don't bleed to death yet. I'm looking forward to learning a few things from you. I would like you to see your family once more, to put you in a fully cooperative mood."

Andrew tried to make a lunge, but it was futile. His leg immobilized him, couldn't take any weight. Cavaco stepped back quickly, very agile, very confident.

Nix looked calmly towards the woods and said, "How fast can you really run dragging a five-year old in this swamp filled property? And I know the area. No place to hide, unless you want to flap around in the ooze for a while and hope I won't notice." He looked back to Andrew a moment to make eye contact. "Won't be long." Then he took off at a loping jogger's pace carrying his rifle.

———————

Madeleine had heard the shot and had seen Andrew fall.

Then she and Chris had run. She didn't know how far behind the men were now. She ran ahead of Chris to pace him, to show him the path, to force him to go faster like her.

She didn't have the pistol Andrew had given her in the night. She had left it on the ground when she had gotten up and run for Chris when he had come to her from the outhouse. After that they had been hiding, and then it seemed it was all over, and she had forgotten it. And then when the men were running towards Andrew's rifle, she had panicked, and couldn't quickly find the pistol in the grass.

She had been careless. And it could mean everything....

She had to get to the car on that back road. Would the keys be in one of the dead men's pockets? Or in the car?

She didn't want to leave Andrew behind. But what could she do? She could only save Chris and herself *if they were lucky*. Why had she been so careless about the pistol? The difference possibly between saving Chris, saving Andrew. And not. I'm so sorry, Andrew.... I should have had the pistol...you counted on me...

They were nearing an open stretch where swamp lay on both sides narrowing the trail to almost nothing for a hundred yards. They would be hopelessly exposed from behind. She glanced back but saw nothing, heard nothing. Yet.

"Hard, Chris, hard."

They crossed the hundred yards and now Madeleine was sure she heard something far behind, a snapping. Someone calling.

The growth ahead was dwarf trees and bush, sparse for as far as she could see. No place to hide anywhere, even if you wanted to try. She looked back. Chris's legs were just too short to keep up. His face was red and dripping sweat. She slowed and reached her hand back, outstretched, grasping his hand, pulling him along as fast as possible without lifting him off the ground.

She was too fast. He fell and rolled, his leg hitting a jutting rock. He opened his mouth to cry.

"No!", Madeleine censured. But she quickly picked him up and carried him on the run for a full minute until she couldn't maintain any pace. "You've got to run now. For dad."

He cried. She began to tear. She looked around - wide and far, impassable swamp. Nowhere to run but this trail. No other way out. He could follow so easily. She looked back to check for Nix.

Chris was crying harder.

She looked like a trapped, terrified, animal.

CHAPTER FIFTY-SEVEN

Cavaco said to Andrew, "Your friend, Lawrence, is in my car trunk. He needs to be disposed of quickly. It's getting hot out here."

Cavaco was walking slowly, back and forth. "Yes, in the trunk, like your father was. We have come full circle, you, me, your father." He paused and looked around him, then back to Andrew. "You should know something. I should be telling you this. When I took your father, I told him to tell me if he had told anyone what he knew, what Pino Macky had told him. I told him that if he lied to me, held anything back, I would kill his son."

Andrew looked closely at Cavaco. Cavaco continued, "Your father said he had told no one. I guess he didn't believe I would do it. All this time I believed he told me the truth. But I know now that he told Lawrence, that very day, before I took your father. And now I'm killing his son. Odd how things work out. Keeping my promise."

Andrew closed his eyes and turned his head. Cavaco crouched down to be more on the same level, and came a little closer. He continued, "I don't know what you thought of Lawrence, but I think it's interesting. Lawrence saved your life by not turning himself in and exposing me to the police about the murder of Pino and your father. Because then I would have learned that your father talked. And I would have been some upset, I can tell you. I would have said to myself, 'He shouldn't have lied to me. I promised him. Now I have to do his son. We had a deal.'"

Cavaco stood up, scanning the woods a moment, then sounded philosophical, "But then Lawrence dragged you into this thing anyway. I guess you can't thank him for that. Funny how life is."

Madeleine and Chris were slowing, exhausted.

Still she saw no one behind yet. And heard nothing more.

"You can do it, Chris," she panted, her legs like lead now. "Be strong, Chris."

They were almost through the wide expanse of dwarf trees when it happened. A rifle crack. Simultaneously she heard a tree trunk thwack near her.

Chris cried out.

Another rifle crack.

She glanced back and saw Nix, a distant figure. He was further back than she thought he would be. Maybe a couple of minutes, maybe more. But he was jogging steadily, looking strong, the rifle held well up.

They crossed the final stretch of scrub and there would now be some cover, the forest thickening. He would not be able to see them well. And it also meant the road was near. "Hurry, Chris!"

They plunged on through the ever thickening stand of trees. She just had to get to the car. Get it started. If they were lucky.

Lucky ...... leaving Andrew behind....

The trees multiplied, were bigger, closer together. The road was very near. The brush and grasses grabbed at her legs, the way it had last night.

And then she remembered.

———————

Nix was certain he was gaining on them now. He had stopped twice to take careful aim and fire, only to scare, to get them to stop running, to get them to give up. But she seemed a determined woman. She had kept a pace with the boy he hadn't expected of them.

He entered the thickly forested area. He knew that the road would be close, just beyond the end of this trail. If they got out on the road, they would be easily visible. But would they cross into the next woods? He sped up.

Shortly he heard a car door. He was getting close to the road. He heard a car engine start. Dammit! He would have to shoot them now if they pulled away. He knew the road was level and straight for a half mile.

He ran faster. He quickly saw the roadside coming up through the trees. He could hear the engine running, but sensed the car wasn't moving yet.

He broke headlong out from the trees and rushed towards the car not twenty feet away, his rifle aimed. But she wasn't in the driver's seat. Ducked down? He ran to the car. No one there.

He looked up and saw Chris up the road, just disappearing into the woods on the other side. Then why the engine running?

Madeleine stepped out silently from behind a thick tree trunk ten feet behind Nix. In her hands, pointed at his back, was the automatic rifle that Leader had been carrying when he had taken her to the ground back in the bush off the roadside. It had been left there. Andrew hadn't known it was there so hadn't taken it. He had taken the other man's but she didn't know what he had done with it. She had remembered it all of a sudden as she got close to where it had all happened. She had found the keys, started the car, told Chris to run and stay hidden in those woods on the other side unless it was she calling for him.

As a decoy, the car had done its job. Nix was a stand-still target.

She squeezed the trigger. The gun jumped alive, the sound deafening. Nix was thrown forward against the side of the car, his body punched twenty times, a full two second burst. She didn't know that the rifle would do that and, stunned at the clamor, she kept the trigger squeezed. Nix was almost in shreds before she finally let her finger go. Her ears were ringing.

Quickly she thought, how many bullets are left? She had no way of knowing. Are there *any* bullets left? She didn't know. She didn't know if she had stopped pulling the trigger or the gun had just emptied.

She shoved Nix's torn and bloody body off of his gun and looked at it. His gun looked *exactly* the same as the one she had just fired. But he had fired only two single shots. How do you do that? But it would have many more bullets left.

She quickly examined the two guns more closely. Each had the same, small, metal lever on the side with two options, a '1' and an 'A'. She saw that on Nix's, the lever pointed to the '1'. On the gun she had just used, it pointed to the 'A'. Is that why it shot so many bullets at once? Was 'A' automatic?

She pushed the lever on Nix's gun to 'A'. She held the gun firmly and pointed back at the woods, gritting. She pulled the trigger a split second. A short burst erupted, the gun jumping.

Andrew and Cavaco had heard Nix's single rifle cracks. And they had heard a long burst of automatic fire, quiet in the distance. And a short time later a short burst. Andrew kept looking in that direction, his face fearful.

Now all was now still. He looked at Cavaco with burning hatred, and struggled to make a lunge at him. Cavaco stepped quickly back. "I'll shoot!"

Andrew screamed, "*Go ahead!*" His fists pounded the ground in rage.

Cavaco said, "Don't fret, Andrew. Nix is just scaring them out of hiding. You heard him; he wants you to see them again. He's just being... enthusiastic."

Andrew closed his eyes and tears came. His precious son. His precious wife. What had he done? What had happened to Madeleine, to Chris?

Andrew shouted, "Unless I see them, you get *nothing* from me. *Nothing.*"

"In good time. Be patient. I need you to tell me some things."

Andrew felt he would explode. He closed his eyes. If he looked at Cavaco any longer, he would lose control over himself completely. He would then accomplish nothing but his own futile suicide. He realized he had to know what happened in that gunfire. Stay alive at least until he knew that. If there was any hope for them.

Minutes passed like hours. Cavaco had been sitting fifteen feet from Andrew. But now Cavaco was up, pacing again, casting looks towards the woods.

"Your boy has no doubt slowed them down on the way back."

Andrew avoided looking at Cavaco. He looked at the woods, listening with every fiber. After a minute, he rolled slightly to take some pressure off his wounded leg, blood gently seeping through the jean fabric. As he did, and turned his head away from the woods, his eye caught sudden movement. In the grasses almost a hundred yards out behind and to the side of Cavaco. The wind? There wasn't any wind. A discrete set of grasses was moving.

He glanced towards Cavaco and saw his eyes were considering the woods. Andrew glanced to the grasses again. He tensed.

In SWAT training they had learned to crawl. Crawl through everything. Flat on your belly. Invisible. He had watched grass fields hundreds of yards away through binoculars, observing closely, seeing who could snake through the field without disturbance, and who couldn't. Who would get shot, who wouldn't.

The movement he saw now had the signature of someone crawling, someone without the benefit of any training.

Andrew suddenly said, "Where did you put my father?"

Cavaco was startled. "So urgent a tone. Well…you have already figured that out. So why do you ask?"

"But exactly where?"

"Is that so much a concern for you now?"

"I want to know."

"Back there in a bog, of course. Do you think I'm going to stroll you out there? For a …quiet moment?"

Andrew looked an angry moment towards the distant bogs. He knew Cavaco was watching him. He avoided Cavaco's look.

He glanced again a moment to the grasses. The movement was getting closer, now about eighty yards.

Andrew pressed, "Tell me exactly."

Cavaco was impatient. "Let's wait for Nix. He'll find your curiosity amusing."

Andrew's heart leaped! A swatch of chestnut hair bobbed a moment over the top of the long grass. Then the hair progressed further sideways, moving to get more directly behind Cavaco.

Andrew said, "I'm not afraid of death, Cavaco. In fact, I'm going to die happy knowing you've been beaten."

"I've been beaten? Oddly, it doesn't strike me that way."

"So Lawrence didn't tell you everything, then?"

Cavaco laughed. "Tricks, Andrew. I don't fall for tricks. Keep your ingenuity so Nix can watch, too. He'll be along soon."

The grass stopped moving. She was now sixty yards out.

Andrew said, "Did you ever wonder what you did to me that day twenty years ago? Do others matter to you in your world? Do you have a heart? Or is it just a pump?"

Cavaco looked at Andrew dismissively and peered towards the woods.

Andrew again rolled lightly, squeezing at his leg to slow blood flow, his hand bloody, trying to manage Cavaco's attention.

Cavaco said, "I do sincerely hope you're not bleeding to death."

Shortly the moving grasses were only forty yards out. Andrew began to calculate. What weapon did she have? The pistol? Or a rifle? His heart was hammering like a drum. When she fires, do I stay down or try to make a lunge, however feeble, for his gun? If single shot, I go for his gun. If the automatic ...stay flat, very, very flat.

Thirty-five yards out and directly behind Cavaco, the grasses stopped moving. Andrew looked at Cavaco but really saw a barrel now ease up from the grass. She had a rifle! He hoped she wasn't going to shoot from there. Thirty-five yards was still too far for her aim. She would probably miss with a single shot; then Cavaco would shoot her. If it's on automatic, the recoil kick would spray her fire everywhere and possibly not even hit Cavaco. And again, he would shoot her.

But at thirty-five yards she would be able to hear conversation.

Andrew's tone became angry, taunting. "Do you ever *think and feel and see*, Cavaco, other than as a grasping, greedy fool?"

Cavaco looked at him. "Trying to redeem me? Rescue me from myself? Here and now?"

Andrew knew she was rising to a crouch now, aiming.

Cavaco was bemused with Andrew but cast his look again towards the woods. Andrew caught her eye just a moment, then looked at Cavaco. He began to shake his head unmistakeably and said with resignation, "No. You're too far ...from redemption yet."

Madeleine hesitated, watching Andrew, sensing his meaning. She rose slightly and eased forward, one slow step at a time.

She was now thirty yards away. Still too risky, Andrew thought, if it's a single shot. She needed just another few seconds, another five or ten yards.

Andrew rocked his body, grasping at his wounded leg as if the pain sharpened, wincing. Cavaco watched him. Andrew hoped Madeleine had gained another few yards, but he dared not glance.

Andrew suddenly cocked his head towards the woods, as if startled. "I think someone's calling you *now.*"

But Cavaco had sensed an oddness. He turned his head and saw Madeleine twenty yards away, down, braced on one knee, the rifle aiming.

His pistol arm jerked towards her.

Her gunfire exploded in a roar.

Andrew rolled. Cavaco's body danced, bullets whacking, his pistol arm flailing.

A one second burst. A very long time when you know the shooter doesn't know how to aim and you're right beside the target.

Resounding echo and reverberation. Pain in the ears.

Then silence.

Cavaco lay flat, dead as wood, two feet from Andrew.

"Andrew, Andrew." She fell to him, clutching him.

He grabbed her. "Is Chris okay?"

"Yes. Yes. He's hiding. Oh Andrew, Andrew." She was crying.

"And Nix?"

"He's dead, too."

Andrew hugged her, his tears flooding, delirious in his relief. He said, "Maddy, Maddy," squeezing her tightly, "I heard all that shooting before...I thought...you and Chris...."

"I know, I know," she sobbed, "I didn't know how to use it right."

"Use it right?" His eyes were running with tears. "Maddy..." he held her tightly, "you did *very* well. *Very, very,* well."

CHAPTER FIFTY-EIGHT

The late afternoon sky had become a mass of heavy grey in Philadelphia, adding to the solemnity as the bells tolled at the Cathedral Basilica of Saints Peter and Paul. Hundreds of silent mourners spilled from the Cathedral's front doors, down its front steps and out along its sidewalks. Lawrence's casket was lowered by pallbearers to the rear of the regal hearse.

Andrew, Madeleine, and Chris watched as the casket was eased into position, Andrew leaning lightly on a wooden crutch.

Lawrence's father and mother and sister, all in solemn black, watched, too, crying, holding each other.

As Andrew watched, he thought on the fact that Lawrence's silence all those years had probably saved Andrew's life. But Lawrence had died not knowing that. Worse, he died believing he was responsible for the imminent deaths of Andrew and Madeleine, and maybe even Chris. Andrew couldn't imagine what his final moments must have been like.

Lawrence had also saved another part of Andrew's life. He had closed off the past; it could never haunt him again.

His thoughts went to his meeting yesterday with Lawrence's parents and sister. Andrew had told them, "I got to know Wes only recently. But I feel I came to know him well. I can tell you with certainty, he died doing what he needed to do. He was dealing with ruthless men. He knew he was putting his life on the line. He made that decision. And I can tell you he would be so happy with how things turned out. He would tell you that. Keep that in your heart."

Lawrence's father had nodded, tears in his eyes, very proud of his son. His father had said, "I think Wes feared something like this might happen. Do you know what he did? A little over a month ago, he changed the ownership of his cottage to Marilyn. Didn't say a word to anyone."

The mourners stood quietly in wait and observance as the hearse pulled slowly from the curb. Madeleine held hands with Chris. When the hearse was half a block away, the crowd began to disperse.

Andrew felt a tap on his arm. "Andrew Locke?"

Andrew turned. A gray haired man with a smile offered his hand. "Jack Morgan, Washington HQ. We spoke briefly on the phone."

"Yes, "Andrew said, shaking his hand.

"I haven't had the chance to congratulate you in person, Andrew, and thank you for the extraordinary job you did here. Just extraordinary."

"I couldn't have done it without Wes, Sir," Andrew said solemnly. "Not at all. And he knew the risks."

Morgan was more somber. "Yes," he nodded. "We'll miss him greatly."

Andrew said, "This is my wife, Madeleine. I wouldn't be here if it wasn't for her."

"Yes, I've heard the whole story," he said, shaking Madeleine's free hand. "A pleasure to meet you, Madeleine. Extraordinary action and courage. Extraordinary. The Bureau extends a very big thank you."

Madeleine gave a brief smile and a slight nod, a polite acknowledgement of well intended words. But she said nothing, a tear suddenly appearing in her eye. She looked down and squeezed Chris's hand a little more.